DUNGEON HUNTER
ACT I

LAZARUS JAMES

CONTENT WARNINGS

There are numerous sensitive topics covered in this story.
Details are available on the last printed page of this book,
as well as my author's website.

DEDICATION

I didn't start this book thinking I'd finish it. I began it with the aspiration to enjoy writing something I would like to read. Unfortunately, my interests when combined together have woven a story that is so niche, perhaps only I would ever have read it in the first place.

In fact, if this tale resonates with you, please get into contact with me; I think perhaps we may be soul mates.

That aside, and I know it's cliché, but I'd like to thank several people in my life: my father, my mother, my sister, my close group of friends who I'd foisted this upon long before it became complete, all the internet people who commented along the way, and also you for picking up this book.

I love you.

I

ACTIVATION

"HAVE YOU SEEN THIS ONE, L-man?" Axel asked me, pushing his iPhone into my face.

He played the video, and I watched as a man inched toward one of the black holes, tentatively reached up to touch it, and then vanished. Here one moment, gone the next. In a single frame. I wondered if the man had a family or friends. Hoping his loved ones would see the video so they may have closure, I shook my head.

"No, but that's kinda messed up. Why didn't the person filming stop him?"

Axel shrugged and continued scrolling. Sitting across from him, I tried to find the good of his parents in him. There was nothing of their warmth there. Not anymore, at least.

In a marvel of genetics, Axel took after his father in almost everything physical, and thus had been graced with innate athleticism, especially in sprints. Like something of a newer model of Uncle Seb, Axel Masson was a blond man with an undercut nearing his thirties, with deep bags under blue eyes that were blessed with thick lashes, his full lips currently pressed together in idle thought.

I had heard in passing people compliment his looks, with girls in high school even swooning over him, comparing him to the Greek god

Apollo. He used to get outdoors a lot more when we'd been younger, granting him a golden tan that had since mostly faded.

I had stopped comparing myself to him years ago. As far as I knew, Axel didn't even exercise but still managed to have the kind of build men spent hours at the gym to achieve. It did, however, give me some semblance of mental peace that, despite all that, the blond had never fully settled into his height, having sprouted up during puberty to compete against skyscrapers. Even now, to compensate, he hunched over his phone. Part of me thought it might be a confidence thing.

Not wanting to suffer something else from his social media feed, I left him at the dining table and moved to the lounge. I'd gotten these armchairs secondhand at the dump much to Axel's chagrin. As I sank into one, I tried not to think about what these black holes meant. Unfortunately, avoiding the idea just sent me right back to it.

Was it aliens? Demons? Alternate dimensions? There were so many conspiracy theories floating around online with no official explanations from any government or authoritative sources that it would've been easier to figure out time travel at this point than to find out what was actually happening.

Lost in my thoughts, I only vaguely heard the audio from another video play off Axel's phone. The sound of several people screaming slingshotted me back into reality. Turning around in my chair to face him, I shot him a worried look.

I'd known Axel all my life. We weren't so much friends as the second generation of friends. Our parents had been super close, and as a result, Axel was like a sibling that I didn't really understand. Simply due to circumstance, we now shared a flat in the city. Sometimes life is like that. You get tied to someone for life because of things outside of your control.

Most people assumed since we'd been together for so long that we were a couple or a terminal situationship. It didn't help that when family and family friends saw us heckle each other they often joked about what a married couple we were. Axel hated it and was always first to correct it, but it had played in my favour for a long time, especially since I didn't know how to break it to my parents that I was ace. That was a conversation I'd been avoiding since I'd realised there was a label for the way I'd felt way back when I was twelve. A decade-and-a-half long con to avoid an awkward exchange with my mother and father.

Omission wasn't lying, was it?

Again, Axel shrugged in reaction to my expression, jutting his chin at his phone. In explanation, or perhaps defence, he said, "Same man disappearing, different person who filmed it."

"How about stop?" I suggested, a pit of tar sinking in my stomach, as I looked away from the uncaring form of my flatmate.

The appearance of the black holes around the world had initially seemed like a stunt meant for virality, but the way that people appeared to no longer exist after touching them had gone beyond the uncanny reach of special effects. There were too many angles, too many reactions. I had laughed the first time I'd seen one, but now I was beginning to feel sick. There was something seriously wrong. This wasn't just some media blitz or social experiment.

~System Loaded. Dungeons Active~

For a moment, I wasn't sure what had happened. I had definitely heard someone say those words, but I had actually not heard them say it. There was no audio in the exterior world, nothing had entered my eardrums. But I'd heard it crystal clear all the same. As if someone was speaking directly into my head.

Was I going crazy? Had the anxiety from the black holes caused me to start hallucinating? Perhaps the videos Axel had been showing me were affecting me more seriously than I'd thought. Wondering if I should ask him if he'd heard the voice too, another mental sound played, interrupting the thought. A long high-pitched beep. I tasted static.

Blue flashed in front of my face, blinding me.

My eyes stung as I blinked away the fading light, taking in what I was seeing. It was a notification, like a push notification on a phone. It floated in front of my face, maybe one metre away. Instinctively, I tried to wave it away, but my hand just phased right through it. Oh, so I was going crazy.

The notification read:

Player Lee Bastion Castillo registered.

Title: None.

Class, traits, and abilities generating...

I pinched at the bridge of my nose and closed my eyes. Taking a deep breath, I opened them again and was still met with the same screen. Had I been exceeding the healthy amount of screentime on games lately? Something similar had happened when I played *Skyrim* too much when I was a kid. When I'd walked around, I would think about all the different plants and insects I could harvest and even hallucinated the E-prompt button when close to a bush or shrub.

However, I hadn't played anything recently. I'd been too busy fretting over how to break it to Axel that I wanted to move out by myself. I'd finally saved up enough to afford a deposit for my own place and was actively checking out apartments for rent in different suburbs.

Before the Doomsday tag had started trending, I'd been practising in the mirror again and again, but it had done nothing to relieve my nerves. I had planned on breaking the news to him tonight come hell or high water.

My thoughts returned to the apparition of the blue window before me. If it was talking about class and traits... Was it imitating a game, like an RPG or something?

"Lee."

My heart skipped a beat, as Axel's voice sounded in my ear. He was standing right behind me. Somehow, he'd closed the distance between us without me noticing. He was not a quiet person by nature and, honestly, not the most graceful. Yet he'd managed to get right behind me without so much as a creak on the wood-veneer floor.

I moved to turn around and face him, but he stilled me, his hand on my shoulder. Like an iron weight. It was weird that he was touching me. Like most guys, after primary school he'd stopped being fond of physical displays of affection. I likely knew its cause. Since then, a lot had changed about me too.

That's when it hit me. Axel had called me "Lee." He hadn't called me Lee our entire lives, as an age-old in-joke that had long since worn out its charm. Specifically, when we were three, he'd thrown a tantrum about me stealing his mother's name.

I hadn't contested the thought since my parents had explained my name was based on both Axel's parents. When I said our parents had been close, I hadn't been joking. I was Lee Bastion after Li Hua and Sebastian; Axel's mother was first generation Australian, like my father. It was part of why they'd always gotten along so well.

I had never known if Axel knew my parents were his namesake, but with him being Axel Zeke for Alessandra and Ezekiel, it would've been obvious to anyone else. But often when it came to me, it was as though he didn't care to care.

Unable to ignore it, I said, "You never call me Lee."

Axel laughed. It was bitter. Bitter? That made no sense. He was the one who decided to use any name under the sun other than my birth name. Well, I guess I'd never understood him before, and that wasn't about to change.

"I've just been wanting to say it for a while."

"You're welcome to, you know. It's literally my name."

The warmth of his hand slid from my shoulder, the strangely charged moment past, and so I turned to look at him. There was a smile I'd never seen before on his face. Or rather, maybe I'd seen it once but on a much younger version of him. But for this moment in time, the expression in his eyes was nonsense.

On anyone else, I would've believed it was grief, but what did Axel have to feel mournful about? There were very few people on Earth that

Axel held in high regard, and even fewer that would cause such emotion in him.

My heart jumped into my mouth, thinking the worst. "Are our parents okay?"

He blinked, and, just like that, the sorrow was gone, replaced by his usual noncommittal gaze. "For now, at least."

The shift in his expression was like a weight off my shoulders, a physical relief that calmed me and allowed my lungs to expand properly, to breathe. There was something about the look in his eyes that said things I didn't understand, far more than the usual detached Axel. Trying to make light of the situation, I said, "You're being kind of weird, dude."

"I know, I just… heard this voice in my head. Something about Dungeons…"

Everything odd that Axel had done was immediately forgotten as I stood to face him. "You heard it too? I'm not losing my mind! And this blue notification menu, you see it too, right?"

I pointed in front of me where the ellipsis at the end of the sentence continued to type in and disappear, like a loading bar. Axel shook his head, and for a brief moment, I felt despair well inside me. But then he gestured in front of himself. "I see a blue screen here."

So, we had our own screens. I guess that made just as much sense as anything else. My screen had my name. So, Axel's probably had his too, then.

Was everyone around the world getting these same notifications? I pulled my phone from my pocket and tried searching online but realised the Wi-Fi was dead, and I wasn't getting any reception. When I mentioned it to Axel, he just nodded in acceptance and mumbled something about server overload. If anyone would know, it would be him—he was something of an IT guru. I wasn't familiar with the exact details of his day job, but I decided to take his response at face value.

He asked, "Do you have a title?"

"Mine says, 'None.' You?"

I watched as the muscle in Axel's jaw twitched, and he said, "No. No title either."

We were both quiet. I knew Axel's tell. He knew I knew. I used to make fun of him about it when we were kids.

Why would he lie about his title?

If I was right about this screen imitating games, then titles were usually assigned because of events completed, feats achieved, or evident qualities of the character being played. Maybe his title was something embarrassing? Racking my brain, I tried to imagine anything that would cause his reaction.

If his prior grumbling had been anything to go by, he'd recently been doing a solo-run on *Divinity: Original Sin II*, so…

Could his title be something like "Lone Wolf"? Getting assigned that by this random all-knowing screen would be the kind of secondhand cringe that would make anyone hurt. The idea of anyone considering Axel a lone wolf almost made me laugh, but I quickly smothered it. The truth was Axel was a social butterfly. Actually, that kind of title might be more humiliating for him.

Maybe it was the current state of events, and how they didn't align with the reality I'd known my whole life, but in my head, I imagined rainbow wings sprouting out of his back, and him gracefully soaring through the air. Before I could contain it, laughter snorted out of my nose.

Axel raised a single messy blond brow at me. Coughing a few times, I thumped a fist at my chest. "Allergies."

"Sure."

"How long do you think the—"

~Class and traits loaded~

The blue menu transitioned like a PowerPoint slide into a new larger screen. I instantly recognized the information provided. Indicators for a game character. Health, stamina, experience, mana, abilities, traits. I paused and did a double take. Mana? Did that mean there was magic?

The absolute absurdity of the situation dawned on me.

It felt like a whip in the face. There were black holes appearing around the world, my lifetime acquaintance for the first time had randomly called me by my real name, a random blue box knew said name, and now, there was a very high possibility that magic existed.

I wondered when my mind had broken and what had caused it. Was it from the stress of telling Axel I wanted to move out? Maybe I was sitting somewhere in a padded cell with my arms straitjacketed to my body. That made more sense. Obviously, I was having a psychotic break. Somewhere nearby, there was probably a repeating message urging me to come back to the real world.

I closed my eyes and imagined waking up.

"You're not crazy."

I looked over to Axel. "What?"

"You're not crazy. This is real. This is happening."

His unshakeable gaze met mine.

Taking the armchair opposite mine, Axel asked, "What are your stats?"

"Uh, I…" I looked at my status bar. It was minimal, really. Like barebones. The game devs probably would've gotten bad reviews if they released even a beta like this. "20 HP, 20 mana, 20 stamina. No traits, but one ability: Channel."

Even though I'd only skimmed the data before, when I said it aloud, it seemed like a fairly bad character sheet. This was like a throwaway. If I had rolled this poorly, I would've restarted the game.

This hallucination was an incredibly depressing one.

My mouth started going dry.

I didn't know why, but some part of me knew if I played a game like this, I probably would've died a few times in just the tutorial level.

Axel swore creatively under his breath, something about time. "And your class?"

Having ignored the largest piece of information on the floating screen before me, I flicked my gaze back up to the very top where my class was situated.

"All-Rounder?"

Well, that'd account for the low mana, low health, and low stamina. Not great at anything but middling at all. I hoped that meant it was a middle of the grid kind of class with the chance to move in any direction. Normally, character upgrade trees for blank slates like this were usually for pro players who knew what they were proccing into.

Or that was what I was desperately praying was true. Because if that wasn't the case, and I literally could never really focus into anything, that'd mean my stats would remain under average all round. Which, with the sudden changing of the world, felt like a very dangerous thing to realise.

I could feel the hyperventilation start in the swelling of my lungs, but I tried to slow my breathing. I swallowed back my concerns. There was no point thinking too far ahead right now.

"What about you?"

"70 HP, 25 mana, 55 stamina, one trait of Swift Footed, and three abilities: Ground Smash, Intimidation, and Thick Hide. My class is Combatant."

Combatant. That sounded like a frontline damage type. Again, the muscle in Axel's jaw twitched. Was he lying to make me feel better? Were my stats literally so awful that even with all the info he just shared, which by the way completely dwarfed mine, he was still trying to be humble to spare my feelings?

"It looks like I'm strong," Axel said.

I didn't want his pity, but I smiled nonetheless.

~Dungeon 5 entered for the first time. Player Sung Jin-woo rewarded title of First Contact~

We let silence settle in between us for a moment, trying to absorb the full repercussion of the most recent mentally projected notification.

"First Contact"? That referred to aliens, didn't it? And then there was that word again. Dungeon. It was like everything was connected to it. Within my chest, I felt something sprout. A foreign desire taking root, so clearly removed from my own that I could almost identify exactly where it began inside me.

I voiced this newfound feeling.

"I guess we're supposed to go into these Dungeons? Like dungeon diving?"

"Yeah. I guess."

Neither of us moved.

~Dungeon 13 entered for the first time. Player Kim Dokja rewarded title of Dreamer~

Briefly, I wondered why both the first players to enter a Dungeon were Korean but quickly ignored the thought. It was probably just coincidence. I wondered what about Dungeon 13 qualified the first player entering to receive the title of Dreamer. Were the Dungeons different? Were the Dungeons more like game dungeons or like real dungeons? Would there be loot? Boss fights?

In the silence that fell between us, Axel asked, "Do you think the Dungeons are the black holes?"

I pulled my mind from the current train of thought it was on and replied, "They appeared just before all this started happening. That can't just be a coincidence. There were at least a dozen reported, right?"

~Dungeon 10 entered for the first time. Player Fahd bin Khan rewarded title of Trendsetter~

~Dungeon 1 entered for the first time. Player Kerstin Berg rewarded title of Hotspot~

~Dungeon 6 entered for the first time. Player Jibari Kimachu rewarded title of Alter Ego~

~Dungeon 9 entered for the first time. Player Riku Nakamura rewarded title of Eagle Eye~

It was unnerving hearing all these notifications almost

simultaneously. It was like worldwide everyone was coming to the same conclusion. Everyone was thinking the same thing. The Dungeons. Clear as day, I could taste the invading compulsion blossoming in my chest.

We needed to enter the Dungeons. I didn't doubt a single other person the world over wasn't feeling the same thing. A hand grasping my heart, slowly starting to squeeze.

"Where's the closest Dungeon?"

"When I was scrolling through the tag, the closest one was in central Brisbane. There's no way we'll get to it first. Neither of us has a car." I hated driving and had never gotten my learner's, and Axel was a notorious passenger princess.

I chewed on the inside of my cheek. "Well, we don't need to be one of the first to enter, do we?"

"Those title notifications sound important."

I didn't want to bring up that he had a title and lied to me about it, and instead just said, "Well, if this is anything like a normal game, we'll probably just be able to buy titles or be rewarded them. Besides, it's not like they ever have that much bearing on anything. Like max, they usually end up being an unlockable cosmetic skin. Shouldn't we try to figure out what the Dungeons are all about first?"

Immediately, he laughed. For a second, I felt my ears grow hot with embarrassment. I had gotten used to Axel being brutally honest with me—it was part of who he was—but he rarely outright mocked my ideas. He must've caught my expression, because he stopped laughing.

"No, think about it, man. If titles weren't important, why would it be one of the first things to appear after your own name when the Dungeons 'activated'?"

The embarrassment faded away, but the anger remained, a sting in my cheeks. "Why didn't you just say that first?"

"I... Yeah, you're right. I'm sorry."

Yeah, that pretty much cinched it. Surely the world was truly ending.

Axel apologising? Axel admitting he was wrong? He'd die before doing either of those things. I regarded him in suspicion. His eyes were closed in thought, and his face was pressed into his hands.

Oddly, though, he was sitting up straight. The permanent stoop he existed with since he'd shot up to telephone pole height was missing. It was strange to be forced to look up at him, even slightly. I swallowed back my doubts, though it was getting harder and harder to ignore all the subtle differences I was noticing.

There was something fundamentally wrong with Axel.

And I didn't know what it was.

Maybe he'd seen something on Twitter that had shocked him to his core? I mean, it was Axel sitting there, that was unmistakable, but if you put a gun to my head and demanded to know what was sat opposite me, I couldn't tell you with full confidence that it was the same Axel I'd grown to know.

He was hiding something. And it wasn't something small either. Did it have to do with the title he wouldn't share with me? Or his stats? What wasn't he telling me? Why wasn't he telling me? I stared at him a while longer, trying to weigh up the pros and cons of confronting him.

There was something in his current stature that made me hesitate. Besides, this was Axel I was talking about. Dude could be as stubborn as a mule when he was forced to do something.

He'd share his mind with me when he was ready.

~Dungeon 11 entered for the first time. Player Adrien Galbraith rewarded title of Boy Wonder~

Clearing my throat, I said, "It's all good, man. So, what? You're saying we should… find another Dungeon that hasn't been found yet? They stand out a lot, so I don't think that's gonna be possible."

~Dungeon 8 entered for the first time. Player Bonnie O' Brolchain rewarded title of Scorned~

Axel removed his hands from his face. "When I was scrolling, it looked like there were around thirteen of the black holes globally. But there was nothing from China on there, so let's hazard a guess for one more from them. So, fourteen. That's not a lot for a population of eight billion people, is it?"

I rubbed at my chin in thought. "If being the first person to enter a Dungeon is really as important as just you think it is, then the rarity of a Dungeon should be pretty high. You can't just be handing out titles like you're Oprah. But with only fourteen for the entirety of humanity… That's— I can't even do the maths." Plugging the numbers into the calculator app on my phone, my eyes widened at the results. "That's a probability of receiving a first entering title less than 0.000000002%."

"Right, so astronomically low odds. Those titles are special, for sure, but they can't possibly be *that* rare. That'd be kind of unfair. So…"

Understanding formed in my mind. "You think there's gonna be more Dungeons. We need to wait for new ones?"

"Pretty much. But we can't just stay here like this. People are gonna be going into those Dungeons, regardless of titles. You can feel it too, right? It's like an itch…" I nodded. "Since all the info we've gotten so far has been like a game, the Dungeons have gotta be some sort of boss fight or a challenge. And what do you do before a boss fight?" Axel asked.

He played more MMORPGs than me, but I knew what he was suggesting.

"Gather a party?"

Axel laughed again, and this time I knew he wasn't mocking me. I had no clue what he found so hilarious, but I just smiled back. I'd never understood Axel, and despite whatever he'd gone through today, that wasn't about to change. That was comforting. But…

~Dungeon 4 entered for the first time. Player Althea Santos rewarded title of Infinite~

It was weird, actually. What was happening was absolutely insane. Black holes didn't just appear out of nowhere. Weird gamelike notifications didn't just materialise into our individual minds. This was not normal. So, why did I feel so calm? Was it simply because I wasn't alone in this? That Axel was here with me?

I should've been losing my goddamn mind. But I wasn't. Then again, I wasn't entirely sure I hadn't already. Focusing on the present, I ran through my priorities.

"Should we call our parents first?" I asked.

He shook his head. "All telecommunications are down right now. I'm thinking government mandated to control chaos or maybe interference from the formation of the Gates."

The worry in my gut intensified.

"But they'll be okay, right? If they don't enter the Dungeons, nothing bad should happen to them?"

For university, we'd both moved to the state capital from a rural country town. The population was probably in the hundreds. Our parents owned hectares of land, mostly empty bush, that they occasionally allowed cattle to graze on from neighbouring properties. I made it a point to go to my hometown at least once a year to catch up with them in person. Other than one or two friends, they really were the only other people in the world who I constantly worried about.

"Yeah, there's no Gates so far into the bush. My parents and yours should weather this storm perfectly fine. I doubt anyone so far out would even be affected."

With his words, my body felt lighter. My fears allayed, I frowned, catching onto something he'd said. "Gates?"

"Gates," he said matter-of-factly.

Seeing the clear obliviousness on my face, he followed up with: "Since we can't see where they lead, the Dungeons have got to exist somewhere else. The notifications say 'entered.' So, people are going inside them, but you've seen the black holes; they're something less than 2D but more than 3D. I think the black holes are just doorways." I listened carefully as he continued, "Kind of like an older game when you enter a house or a castle. The new room has to load, and you're taken to a completely new zone that previously didn't exist. Plus, the people who touched them simply disappeared. They must've gone somewhere." He paused. And then concluded, "So, yeah. Gates."

I mean… The logic checked out. What didn't was how he'd come to this conclusion so quickly. Whatever. Axel had been taking this entire situation better than I had been. So maybe he was more well equipped to think about things like this. I was still trying to play catch up.

I shrugged. "Sounds better than black holes in any case."

"Circling back to making a party. Who do we know who we can recruit?"

Not even a cricket chirping could've properly punctuated the silence that fell between us. Since high school, I'd been pretty introverted. I had made two close friends during university, but they'd moved away, one rural and the other international. We kept in touch online with weekly gaming sessions, but that was it. It wasn't like we could ask them to meet us here in Brisbane. I probably wouldn't have wanted to pressure them into it, even if I could've asked them.

As for coworkers, I didn't really have any that I'd considered anything more than acquaintances.

~Dungeon 2 entered for the first time. Player Yī nuò Huang rewarded title of Lighter Than Air~

Axel held a finger up in thought, his blond brows furrowed, and he opened his mouth, but then closed it again. To be honest, I wasn't surprised Axel didn't have anyone that came to mind either. Though he was the party life incarnate, none of the groups he hung out with were particularly reliable. Sure, some social circles were better than others, and I'd seen them all during the time we'd lived together, but I didn't think any of his friends could be counted on.

"Don't look at me like that," he growled.

"Like what?"

"I don't need your pity." He poked a finger into my shoulder. "I have friends. I have tonnes of friends. You wouldn't even know!"

"Well, I do know, man. I see them all the time, you have a party like every other week here."

"Exactly. I got friends, capiche?"

Axel only became Al Pacino when he was genuinely angry. What an absolutely unhinged thing to be mad about. I threw my hands up in defeat. "All right, all right. You've got friends. Thousands, even."

He smirked. "That's right. Thousands."

Resisting the urge to roll my eyes, I inched an eyebrow up. "So, how many of them would want to join our party?"

Axel's face scrunched up in thought.

Yep, go ahead and think on that.

I could see the numbers and figures flying around in his head. If he did the maths right, he'd come to the same conclusion as me. The total number of his friends who could be counted on equalled nil, zip, zero, zilch, nada.

His face went blank. Ah, there it was.

"So?" I asked, feeling a sick amount of pleasure beginning to build from Axel's incoming realisation.

A flicker of disgust ran over his features. His shoulders sagged, and gravity increased threefold over his body. He let out a pained groan. "I know one person, but they probably don't remember me. You haven't met them before." Under his breath, he sighed, "God, I fucking hate Jye. Their takes are so bad."

Disappointment settled over me. Sifting through my emotions, I found I was sad that Axel didn't have to apologise again. That was almost definitely probably messed up. Well, when in Rome.

~Dungeon 12 entered for the first time. Player Mila Bachmann rewarded title of Unsanctimonious~

It didn't escape my notice Axel had referred to this Jye person with they/them pronouns. Though I wouldn't say it aloud, Axel suffered from internalised prejudice, despite being openly gay. He'd once said to me that there were men and there were women, so that he'd associated with someone who might be outside of the gender binary was not a small surprise.

Half-an-hour-ago-Axel probably would've accidentally deadnamed them. Now-Axel used they/them like it was second nature. Half-an-hour-ago-Axel would never have asked me to join his party. Now-Axel referred to the party as "our party."

I was slowly coming to grips with the fact that this wasn't just some simple shock from a Reddit post. This was something deeper. But that was future me's problem.

"All right, well, where can we find them?"

"What am I, their keeper?" Axel spat.

Okay, no, scratch that, it was the same old Axel. Pinching the bridge of my nose, I asked, "Where do you think they'd be then?"

"At 5:30, they're midway through their HIIT session at the gym which is when they take a smoke break out back."

The word "stalker" sat on my tongue, posed ready to leap out. I stared at him. He stared back, like he was daring me to say it. I could see the deranged chaos in the cogs grinding in his mind. No, I wouldn't let myself be baited into this.

For some reason, he wanted this. Denying him this was better in the long run. Besides, answers would be forthcoming whether I asked them or not since I'd be meeting said friend soon.

Instead, I said, "Which gym?"

"It's about a block from here." Casually, he added, "I know a shortcut."

Yeah, you would know that, wouldn't you, you stalker.

"What was that?" Axel asked.

"I didn't say nothing."

His eyes narrowed, and he let out a long, loud sigh.

Then he walked off to his room. The sounds of him rummaging through hangers in his closet made their way to me, and I patiently waited for an explanation. There was no point in doing anything until he told me what it was I was meant to be doing, because despite the fact I was taking this situation rather calmly, I still didn't understand what was actually happening. Luckily Axel's grasp on everything was so much clearer.

So, for now I'd wait and listen to him.

~Dungeon 15 entered for the first time. Player Igor Stepanov rewarded title of Magic Itself~

Oh, Axel had been wrong. There were fifteen Dungeons. Maybe more?

Axel stuck his head out through his doorway. "I'm grabbing some stuff. You should too. Use that backpack Auntie Sandra gave you for paintball. Pack anything you think you'll need for the next week. I don't think we should count on being able to come back here anytime soon."

I didn't even remember I'd gotten a backpack from my mum. How did Axel? Shaking my head, I stood up and proceeded to follow his instructions. While it was completely within character for Axel to be bossy like this, him specifically taking me into consideration was rather new.

⌐⌐

"**I**T FEELS WEIRD LOCKING THIS DOOR knowing this might be our final goodbye to it."

"Glad we didn't get a cat now, aren't you?" Axel dryly commented.

Murmuring a defeated agreement, I turned the key. The lock clicked. Our apartment was secured. The sound echoed in my mind, and a deep unsettling curled inside my stomach. It was like a snake coiling around in my intestines. My chest felt tight, and I could hear the hammering of my heart thrumming within me.

Seeing that closed door, that locked door, was so final.

Absolute.

Inside, all this was stuff that wasn't happening to me. But now… Now I was where everything was happening. And that meant everything was real.

~Dungeon 7 entered for the first time. Player Gael Viegas rewarded title of Timekeeper~

Fuck, those people who disappeared before the Gates activated… Despite what Axel said, I was sure they were dead. We'd all seen it. They just stopped existing when they touched the Gates. Jesus Christ, would we die? Were we going to our death? Would our parents die?

Breathing became difficult, lead in my lungs, and I gasped for air. This was fucked. This was fucked up. The world began to spin, the edges of my vision going hazy.

"Yo, slowbro, hurry up, man."

The gates of panic didn't so much as slam shut as rage suckerpunched it aside to wrangle control. "I'm having a panic attack over here, asshole!"

"I know."

He wasn't looking at me, but in the hand he held out to me was a single Warhead. It was black; the most tongue staining of flavours. My gaze flicked between it and him, and I took the lolly wordlessly. He didn't say anything and started walking. I followed mindlessly, eyes glued on the sour candy cradled in my hands.

~Dungeon 3 entered for the first time. Player Rohit Dibik rewarded title of Insatiable~

Just the sight of the lolly was enough to begin calming me.

The pounding of my heart began to even into normal rhythm.

The heat in my veins cooled.

The world settled.

DUNGEON
HUNTER

II

TWO'S A PARTY

I HAD ALWAYS THOUGHT AXEL didn't know about the Warheads and my panic attacks. I'd done my best to hide it from everyone except the childhood therapist I'd seen when they'd started. I guess my dependence on the lollies originally stemmed from Axel, though I never remembered telling him about it. Maybe he was more observant than I thought. We had known each other all our lives, after all.

Pocketing the Warhead for later, just in case, I spoke to Axel's back. Without him hunching, it seemed wider than it'd ever been. "I never told my parents, you know."

"Never told them what?" he said, looking back with a toothy smile.

I scoffed. "That you have a shit eating grin."

"And that's why you love me."

"You're confusing love and loathe."

Axel started singing a song so off pitch that I didn't recognise it, and I said as much.

He looked stricken. "You don't vibe with Pink?"

"Not with your tone deafness I don't."

He snorted. "Like you can sing any better. I've heard you in the shower."

"You need better hobbies."

Though our conversation flowed casually, it felt out of odds with the current swing of our relationship. Axel didn't talk with me like this at his own behest. These kinds of exchanges were usually just his way of passing time. In fact, I couldn't remember the last time we'd just shot the shit like this outside of our apartment.

Regardless, we naturally fell into step and continued on in amicable silence.

The world around us was anything but.

Security alarms were screaming, sirens were wailing down streets in ambulances, police, and fire trucks, and the farther we went along, the more it became clear that nearly every other window on ground floor had been smashed in.

As though it mattered, Axel and I walked down the footpath, like we were clinging to the vestiges of human etiquette, even as people sprinted past us faster than should be physically possible, screaming and shouting, items falling from their hands. Looters were amok, and smoke rose into the skies of the setting sun in several locations. I'm certain at one point I saw someone materialise inside a storefront next to a dapperly dressed mannequin.

Somewhere a child was crying, but it sounded like it was coming from all different directions. Part of me wanted to go looking, unable to dismiss the noise, but the other half of me suspected it was bait. Still the guilt formed inside me. What if it was a lost child in the middle of all this chaos?

For that's what it was.

Absolute bedlam.

In the span of an hour from the first Dungeon announcement, Brisbane had fallen to lawlessness. With no way of communicating with law enforcement, I guessed perhaps even radio was getting interference, and no method of getting news to each other, it was everyone out for themselves. Maybe that was a more sane reaction than what we were doing.

"We're here. Come on, the back is accessible through this gate."

It was a nondistinct gym, clearly not a franchise, with large glass windows so you could see the people exercising within. Why pay for advertisement when your clientele would do it for free? There were three people on exercise machines, all looking incredibly toned. How could they continue like normal after all those announcements? Sweat glistened on their skin, their AirPods probably blaring some sort of pop as they worked.

I glanced down at myself. I'd never been the type of person to hit the gym. Hell, I was probably considered unfit. I preferred just kind of existing rather than forcing myself onto reality.

I hoped that our stats weren't actually a reflection of our real-life bodies. 'Cause that would be a blow to the ego more than I could take. Below average in all stats…

~Dungeon 14 entered for the first time. Player Fati Okeke rewarded title of Jester~

Axel met my gaze. If he'd been tallying them up like I had been, that was the last one, unless there were more than fifteen. I held my breath. Surely something would happen now that all Dungeons had been entered.

~All current Dungeon initiations completed. Sponsorships now available~

I frowned. "Sponsorships… Like advertisements?"

He opened the gate for me, and I walked through. Closing it behind him, he said, "Does that mean people are watching us?"

Pulling my phone from my pocket, I checked for reception. Still zero bars, and my battery was now at 53 percent. "Nothing's up. It'd be impossible for anyone to watch anything right now. And if people were watching, how would they be doing that? It's not like there's a camera on everyone on Earth." I paused, rethinking my words, having just put away a personal camera that I technically carried everywhere. Still not *everyone* had a smartphone. Some people had to be rocking those minimal T9 physical-button Nokia bricks somewhere in Japan.

Axel continued, "Lee, we're hearing voices in our heads."

It was still weird for him to call me that.

"A single voice," I corrected him.

"We're hearing a voice in our heads," he said. "We're seeing personal AR-like stat windows. We're feeling driven to enter the Dungeons. We just walked through several active crime scenes on the way here. I think I saw someone bleeding out down an alley."

It was only a brief recap of what events had taken place, but when he put it so simply like that… "I get what you're saying. Somehow having something like invisible cameras filming everyone on Earth isn't that farfetched in comparison, huh?"

"Maybe not even cameras. You remember the first Dungeon title. First Contact, right?"

I laughed. "You're not saying aliens are watching us."

"Is that really so hard to even consider?"

Sighing, I shrugged. "I guess anything's on the table. Aliens, mythical monsters, gods, entropy incarnate. You name it, it could be it."

We turned the corner to approach the cloud of cigarette smoke wisping from the dark under the stairs. Only the very red glowing, ember end was visible, a slight breeze stealing the smoke away. An exasperated groan wafted from the shadows. So, this was Jye? They didn't sound overly enthused at our arrival. Though with everything going on, that wasn't entirely surprising.

"Jesus, can't I get a fucking break?" said a deep voice.

"We're not clients," Axel replied. In the same breath, he slapped the cigarette from their lips. "Smoking is a disgusting habit, and it'll kill you. Now join our party."

From the shadows loomed Jye, all muscle, and at least a head taller than Axel. I'd bet they could rip apart a coconut with their bare hands. Or someone's head. With red hair in a mop framing their face, green eyes, and freckles, they appeared every inch a lumberjack sans axe.

Their square jaw and deep-set eyes really sold the look despite the fact they currently wore black sports tights and a loose long-sleeved shirt.

Eyes wide, I waited and watched, hoping Axel had some sort of plan after harassing this goliath. Maybe a way to cash in a life debt? Blackmail? Extortion?

"Yo, Jye, old pal. You know me, it's Axel! We go way back. To that party in the Bahamas! You know the one where you were trying to hook up with the DJ. Jye, this is Lee, Lee, Jye. Now we all know each other, let's form a party."

The muscle in Axel's jaw twitched, and I desperately tried to hide my reaction, covering it with a cough. Thankfully, Jye didn't seem to notice. Inside, I was reeling. Why the hell would he lie about where he knew Jye from? Was Jye even his friend? Hell, did he even know Jye at all? Spiralling, I was frozen as the redhead cocked their head at an angle, somewhat akin to a dog.

Their thick red eyebrows furrowed together. The world fell away, and Jye appeared to increase further in size. In the back of my head, I heard static. Then they leaned down, pressing their nose into Axel's and growled, "The Bahamas, you say? I don't remember seeing you there. And I have a great goddamn memory."

Was this how we died? In the back of a gym lot?

I guess there were worse ways to go. Chrissie crossed my mind. She was always there somewhere.

Axel scoffed. "You told me to take some classes with you here since we lived in the same neighbourhood after we discussed the best *Hunter x Hunter* arcs. Greed Island is mid as fuck, but I do concede it was a foundational moment in Gon and Killua's friendship."

Jye roared directly into Axel's face, "God, you're so wrong! Greed Island was the *only* time that Gon and Killua were able to have fun without worrying about the world or family. It's the purest arc, and it shows how much they truly care about each other!" They actually and genuinely growled, like an upset husky. "You're probably a Chimera

Ant arc nerd, aren't you?"

Axel rolled his eyes and slid a little farther from Jye who was now all but frothing at the mouth. "Personally, the strongest arc, in my opinion, is the Yorknew City arc."

Whoosh.

Jye's roundhouse was aimed perfectly at Axel, on the square of his jaw. I was half expecting his head to explode from impact like one of those slo-mo watermelon videos. Instead, the redhead's attack flew through empty air.

Axel stood two steps to the left of where he had previously been.

What the fuck? Had he teleported? I tried to recall his abilities and his traits but couldn't remember what he'd said. The long forgotten rational part of my brain was screaming about the impossibility of being able to use gamelike abilities to move faster than sight, but the present portion of my mind was simply scrambling to keep up with what I was witnessing.

Looking unimpressed, Jye chuckled. "Oh, you got tricks? Well, so do I. Can't read them, though."

They couldn't read their tricks? What did that mean? Was that their abilities? My brain leaped ahead. Was Axel's potential recruit illiterate? A non-English native? But they spoke so fluently... Before I could think another thought, I heard the static hiss again.

Jye took a step. He was closing in on Axel. And now it was Axel's turn to frown. He glanced quickly down in blatant confusion, then continued to stand there. What the hell was he doing? Couldn't he do that... Was it [Swift Footed] thing again?

With a grunt, Axel pulled at his feet. They wouldn't move. It was as if they were glued to the floor. Something was pushing or pulling them with so much force they literally wouldn't budge.

He was stuck.

Jye had to be using an ability on him. But what was it? Some sort of immobilisation? I wanted to give Axel the benefit of the doubt. It's not like he would've taunted them without having some way of dealing with them…

Right?

"So, that's what that does," Jye said with a grin.

A panicked expression began to bloom over Axel's face. Oh. He had no idea how to get out of this situation. Typical. When we'd been kids, it had always been me cleaning up after his messes. I guess, the more things change the more they stay the same.

I steeled myself, mentally mumbling self-affirmations.

Okay. You got this.

Jye probably won't kill you.

I slipped in between the two of them. Not because Axel didn't deserve a thorough thrashing. This was just my way of paying him back for that time in high school when he'd stopped my bully from continuously pelting into me. Though he only interfered because he thought his parents would get mad at him for not doing anything. Still, I owed him for that.

"Jye, actually Axel made me watch *Hunter x Hunter* with him, and I agree with you about the Greed Island arc." The giant's eyes focused on me. "Gon and Killua's friendship was the core of that storyline, and it really showed that Gon needed Killua as much as Killua needed him."

"You…" Jye's finger dug deep into my collarbone.

Oh, shit, this was it. I was a dead man.

Then suddenly Jye's arm was around my shoulder, and they were squeezing me tightly. "You get it. You're one of the good ones. Lee, was it? You're one of us."

The breath I didn't realise I'd been holding sighed out of me. I wasn't quite sure who Jye was including when they said "us," but I was glad the situation had been diffused. Perhaps we'd get out of this without any sort of physical altercation. After all, we all were supposed to work together going forward. Or at least, that was the plan.

Wiping the nervous sweat from my forehead, I opened my mouth to speak as Axel slapped a hand onto Jye's back. "Good to hear that, now we can—"

THUNK.

Quick as a flash, Axel's head was smacked deep into the concrete ground. I grimaced in secondhand pain knowing firsthand how much that had to hurt.

"Not you," Jye said. "You're still on my shit list. Fucking Yorknew City arc…" They continued under their breath, and I caught a few choice swears I didn't care to repeat. Clearly, they cared deeply for the anime. I couldn't say I didn't relate, though truthfully my heart lay in Western animation. I probably wouldn't ever mention as much to Jye, though.

Ignoring Axel as he struggled to fight against whatever was forcing his face into the floor, I tried to placate them, "Okay, so honestly, fair reaction. Axel is hard to like, but hear me out. He's not wrong. We need to form a party for future Dungeons. You've got to be feeling the pull as well."

In slow motion, the inner workings of Jye's mind flickered over their features. Oh no. The pure confusion on the redhead's face would've been comical if it didn't fill me with dread. This was not going to be good. Their follow up question did nothing to reassure me either.

"Dungeons?"

Leave it to Axel to ask for help from the one person who wasn't in on the whole mess. Though if their abilities were anything to go by, they were better than having no one. And they also looked incredibly strong. Hopefully their stats would match up.

I gestured to the smoking buildings in the distance, hoping it would expand on the whole thing. "Didn't people, like, sprint out of the gym? No, don't worry about that. You have been hearing a voice in your head, right?"

Stoically, Jye said, "All my life. It's called a conscience." With that, and another static hiss, they glared down at Axel and his face pressed deeper into the concrete. "Something a Yorknew City arc sympathiser probably wouldn't be familiar with."

I wondered if Axel could breathe. Ah, well, Jye was just a buff nerd. Not a killer. They wouldn't let Axel die from suffocation.

Would they?

Axel's voice was muffled and strained as he asked, "Nothing new lately?"

The giant ran a hand through their hair and pulled at a knot, then they said, "Well, yeah, now that you mention it. There's been this like… speaker feedback. I thought it was just tinnitus." Smiling guiltily, they added, "I listen to music pretty loudly."

"So, no actual words?"

They shook their head, red hair swaying with the movement. Again, I was reminded of a puppy. Actually, more like Clifford the Big Red Dog.

The resemblance did nothing to quell the pinpricks of panic beginning to swell in my chest. Doubts began to form again. Maybe I *was* hallucinating.

I had just simply accepted the world was essentially ending due to the cataclysmic appearance of black holes that turned reality into some sort of weird game. Wasn't it easier to believe I was crazy? I had just gone along with Axel on this whole thing. And Axel wasn't even being normal either! The differences with him were definitely something I could have dreamt up.

God, was I really just in a coma?

Nonplussed by his new station in life, Axel inquired further, "What about the status window?"

"Oh, the little blue screen? Is that what it is? That I got. But can't read shit. The fonts all messed up. I can barely make out the headings. Stuff like abilities, traits, titles."

My mind went back to their words when they'd begun using their ability. They really didn't know what their abilities did. It had all just been a gamble?

Needing clarification, I asked, "So, you can't read your stats or abilities?"

"Nope."

What the actual fuck. This couldn't be right. It had to be some sort of error, a glitch. Could we do bug reports? Was there a reality altering game dev on support right now? How did we submit an IT ticket to someone I wasn't sure existed? God, would it be to someone or something? I was stopped from going too deep into that rabbit hole as Jye's hand on my shoulder pulled me back.

"I'm not gonna lie to you 'cause you seem like a good bloke, but that smoke this fucker flicked out of my lips? Not the nicotine kind." They threw their hands up into the air. "I just thought it was kicking in fast, all right. Like the screen was part of the trip. The abilities too."

"There's no one who wished that were true more than me," Axel dryly commented.

There was a crunch and a hiss, and his face was then pushed so far into the concrete that I was genuinely worried his nose had been broken. His face was flat like a pancake across the floor. No longer convinced that Jye wouldn't just kill him, I found myself pinching the bridge of my nose.

"Please, can you let him up?"

Jye sighed. "I just wanted him to learn a lesson."

I waited for them to elaborate.

"Start shit, get hit," they explained.

"I think he's learned that. Haven't you, Axel?"

He spoke, but no words he said were discernible; only the sound of his voice muffled by the floor. Jye didn't look convinced. They had folded their massive guns over their chest and had a blank expression on their face.

Taking creative licence, I feigned sadness. "Look, Jye, he even said sorry."

The giant thought for a moment, rolled their eyes, and then turned to start walking away. Thank God for that. In the same moment, Axel gasped for air so loudly and quickly, like a balloon exploding in reverse, that it startled me. Smoothly, he pushed himself up from the floor, and, in a blink, closed the distance between Jye and himself. He still seemed winded, thankfully. It gave me enough time to intercept, my back to Jye and theirs to mine.

I mouthed to him, "Don't you dare."

Axel's eyebrows shot up, and his lips parted to object.

I slammed my pointing finger against my own, the international sign of shutting the fuck up.

His lips pressed together, almost pouting, and he backed off. I nodded appreciatively at him. Jesus Christ. It was like trying to wrangle a cat. The creatures just do whatever they want, but occasionally yours and their desires align. And that's when you could cooperate with them.

Jye had walked to the gym's back entry and was holding it open. "I got some XXXX in the staff fridge, if you guys are keen. Axel, you gotta pay for yours."

The crash of another window storefront smashing nearby was all it took to convince me to follow them inside. Axel trailed me in, dour expression and all. We passed through the hallways connecting the different rooms to the staff kitchen; a dingy closet-sized shoebox with a bar fridge, microwave, sink, and a single table and chair. Axel proceeded to take the only available seat, and Jye cracked open the fridge to retrieve the promised alcohol.

"To be honest, I really don't understand what you're talking about when you say Dungeons and joining a party. Like, my high is definitely dead, but those words mean pretty much nothing to me."

With my eyes, I tried to communicate with Axel to explain, but he avoided my gaze.

This fucking guy.

I took a deep breath and then attempted to lay out the broader points of what had happened, as well as our plan, which when I said it aloud really didn't amount to much more than make a group and go look for something. After a solid fifteen minutes, I had thoroughly explained everything I knew so far. Jye took in the entire thing in silence, sucking on their lower lip, a solemn expression on their face.

They blew a raspberry. "So, the gist of it is, the modern world is over, life's a game, and you want me to help you guys win it?"

"That's pretty much it. You in?" Axel asked.

"Man, if you had just led with that, this would've gone so much faster. Of course I'm in. Fuck capitalism. I'm sick of the grind. If you're telling me I never have to work a day in this sweaty ass gym again, I'm in. Where do I sign?"

III

QUESTIONS & ANSWERS

L ETTING OUT A GUTTURAL SOUND, Jye groaned in extreme pain.

"So, we have to stay in this gym?"

The place in question wasn't so sad. All the exercise machines within were relatively new, though the decoration was sparse. Nowadays, I expected at least one pot plant to clash against the commercial beige of the walls, but there was no such thing. Just the machines and bland dark gray carpet. Who knew how many litres of sweat were stored within their fibres? At the very least, Jye had kicked the remaining clients out, and now it was just the three of us.

"This place is perfect for us to figure stuff out."

"I hate to agree with Axel, but generally we all know our roles before trying to fight a boss. I'm an all-rounder, so my start is gonna be pretty weak before I can start looking at specialising into something." I hoped, at least. "Do you have any idea what your class is?"

Jye folded their arms, irritation clear in their stance. "I told you, I can't read it. That I was able to use my ability was me grasping at straws. But you saw what it did. Pinned him right to the floor. Maybe I'm a support class?"

"No, I think that skill is more suited to backline damage," Axel said, rubbing his chin.

What a stupid idea. I said, "That's a stupid idea. It's clearly some sort of immobilisation skill. How're they meant to do damage with that?"

He pointed aggressively at the scrapes over his cheeks. "The scars-to-be marring my face say it's possible."

I scoffed. "All right, please share with the rest of the class how they're meant to do damage from the back."

Out of all the things I was expecting Axel to say next, it wasn't: "You ball, right?"

"At this height, if you don't, people make fun of you."

He raised an eyebrow. "You any good?"

They shrugged modestly. "I can dunk."

"Your aim must be decent too, then."

"It's okay."

"Then you can do backline damage."

"Uh, can I interrupt here for a second?" I was lost as to where this conversation was going. What did basketball have to do with backline damage? Was he implying that Jye could apply a real-life skill to the new game ones? It made sense to an extent. At least in regards to Axel. He'd always been a fast sprinter. Had the trait [Swift Footed] stemmed from that?

"No interruptions," Axel said.

Oh, okay then. It had been a long time since I thought about how much I fucking hated Axel. But it was good of him to remind me.

"Don't be rude to your partner, man."

Axel scowled. "We're just friends. Purely platonic. Just because two dudes are close doesn't mean they're dating. That's very close-minded of you."

Seemingly genuinely chastised, their big green eyes widened and they said, "My bad. You guys just have that married-bordering-on-divorce vibe about you."

Appeased by the apology, Axel began to continue his thoughts, but Jye then said, "Still though, that's a shit way to treat a friend."

Though barely able to do so, I repressed my sigh. A sinking feeling in my stomach began to form. Since it wasn't clear when new Gates would appear, anxiety was building inside me. The pressure of an unknown deadline made it feel like we were running out of time. Not to mention that Axel was acting like we had all the time in the world—when there wasn't even a world in the way we knew!

"He doesn't care. Besides, it's for his own good."

I couldn't stop myself from reacting, and my eyebrows shot up. "My own good"? Axel being a dick was for my own good? Had he always thought that? Maybe that was why he had stopped talking to me for so long after primary school. And how was him being awful something for my own good?

Unable to properly process his words, I let them pass. I'd store them away and look at them again later. Though that particular partition of my mind was rapidly being filled. It was only a matter of time before I couldn't stuff anything further into it.

"That's messed up," Jye commented.

That was definitely one way of putting it.

Flat out ignoring them, Axel clapped his hands together, a smile on his face. "Having lived through your ability, I can assure you that it's better for backline damage. Combine that with your hand-eye coordination, and it's the perfect match. In fact, we can test it out right now."

"You wanna eat dirt again that bad?"

The enthusiasm in Axel markedly dropped, and he gave Jye an empty stare. "If you ever use that ability on me again, I can't promise what will happen."

"Fair enough. So, what do you want me to do then?"

"Just a sec."

First, whinging all the way, Axel dragged the scale at the back of the gym to a spot about two metres in front of Jye. Then he grabbed one of the two-kilogram dumbbells by the wall and placed it onto the scale. As would be expected, the arrow on the scale jumped up to the two-kilogram mark. Axel then flourished at the scale.

What the fuck.

The giant watched him wordlessly. There was nothing to say. Because nothing Axel had done made any sense. Again, Axel flourished at the dumbbell on the scale, this time with increased frustration, his fingers locked in claws.

"You can use your words, you know," I said.

Jye mused, "You want... me to use my ability on the weight?"

Axel gave them two thumbs up and an excessively toothy grin. Again, I stored away this lunatic behaviour into the "think about later" section of my brain. These thoughts were beginning to overflow into other parts of my memories, though.

Words of my childhood therapist ran through my mind. "Compartmentalising these thoughts isn't healthy, Lee. If you don't deal with them, bad stuff can happen." Well, shows how much Mrs. Brown knew. Nothing bad had happened so far. And I'd been doing it for twenty-eight years.

Jye bent down and touched the weight. So, their ability only applied to things that they'd made contact with, then? As they did so, the sound of static buzzed in my ears. Yep, the coincidence was too big. I could hear when someone activated an ability. Could others? Should I ask Axel and Jye if they could too? Before I could voice my thoughts, the arrow on the scale shot up, flickered for a moment, and then settled just above four kilograms. Jye's eyes widened.

Still smiling in a way most people would describe as deranged, while walking backward, Axel pulled the scale toward the other side of the gym. All three pairs of our eyes remained on the arrow, as it grew farther and farther away. Soon, Axel had almost entirely crossed the gym, and I could only just make out the weight marked.

He took one step. Two steps. On his third step, he reached the back wall of the gym.

Axel was at least thirty metres away. He could go no farther.

"Your ability has no range after it's been applied."

Jye took this in quietly. Being able to stay such a large distance away from their target was definitely something that supported Axel's backline theory. But nothing about damage.

"This really still feels like a support skill," I said. "I don't see what you're trying to—"

Jye pelted a new two-kilogram dumbbell into the air. Their muscles rippled as it left their hand, raising up through the air, clearing at least fifteen metres as it reached the climax of its arc. Then I heard static bursts multiply in loudness, like someone overlaying the same sound again and again.

I blinked and missed the weight's descent.

CRACK.

Directly at Axel's feet, the carpet had exploded apart from the force of the plummeting dumbbell, and it had punctured the fabric to further pierce through the wooden floorboard beneath. The weight had disappeared into the foundation of the building. Smoke steamed off the edges of the singed floor hole. The words were still frozen in my mouth.

Axel coughed and waved away the fumes. Stepping carefully around the damage, he made his way back to us.

"Backline damage," Jye said.

"Backline damage," Axel confirmed.

With a sigh, I conceded, "Backline damage."

I HAD TAKEN SOME INSTANT NOODLES from home, and planning on using the gym's kettle, we unpacked them in silence. Axel complained that they were tasteless, as the flavour packets were missing. Last week, I had bought them on special, but I hadn't read the markdown description. Eating noodles in hot water was probably about as enjoyable as eating raw dough.

"So, what can you do?" Jye asked, sipping at the noodle water like it was hot cocoa.

The small kettle in the breakroom hadn't been large enough to fill three instant noodle cups, so I was waiting for it to boil. As a cheap electrical device, it was taking ages. It probably didn't help that I was watching it. I could hear the saying from my mum in the back of my head.

Frowning, I realised I hadn't actually read the description of my ability. "Well, I can Channel. Uh…" I thought about the menu screen, and it opened in front of me. Focusing on the abilities, the [Channel] ability expanded to show more detail. Not having interacted with the menu screen since it first appeared, it unnerved me that it reacted as if reading my thoughts.

[Channel] Use a consenting party member's skills.

"I can use someone else's abilities?" I said.

Jye whistled. "That actually sounds pretty good. How does it work?"

The kettle clicked to announce the completion of its cycle. I poured the boiling water into my noodles and pressed the plastic lip back down to keep the heat in.

Jye wasn't wrong. It seemed like a decent skill that suited my class. Depending on whoever's ability I used, it could even be overpowered. Though I guess it would have to be someone who consented to it. In the corner of my eye, Axel mindlessly chewed on his instant noodles. I picked up my own and peeled the lid back to check if it was ready to eat.

"Can I use some of your abilities?" I asked.

"If I say no?" he smirked.

It was like the straw that broke the camel's back. My patience had finally reached its limit with Axel's antics the past day. That was it. I slammed my cup noodles down onto the table so hard the liquid shot back up. It splashed over the edge. Snatching my hand back from the instant sting of the boiling water, I hissed and wiped the liquid away on the hem of my shirt. The skin had already begun to redden. Shit. First degree burns were exactly what I needed right now. From the open menu screen, I heard a short pip.

Eyes wide, Jye blew at their cup noodle and then carefully sipped it.

"Your hand good?" Axel asked, more as a courtesy than genuine concern.

My menu screen, which had remained open, showed I had taken 1 HP damage. I had 19 remaining. Holy shit. That's all it took? If spilling boiling water on my hand resulted in a whole health point in damage… Didn't that mean I was ridiculously weak? Did I have any health regen? How did you restore health? I thought I had a decent chance of being useful in our party, but if my health was this bad…

"How much damage did you take from Jye's abilities?" I asked Axel.

"Only a few points, but I had Thick Hide activated. It reduces damage taken."

I grumpily ate the bland, searing noodles, shoving the now too soggy carbs into my mouth, ignoring the minor pain. Of course he'd get an ability that's so useful in fighting. He was a combatant class after all. And of course he wouldn't let me use it. This fucking guy. God.

Before I knew it, the noodles were gone. Jye was staring at me in abject horror.

"You got a problem?" I asked, my lips stinging.

"*I* don't," they said and then slurped up the last of their warm noodle water.

Axel cleared his throat. "It was just a joke. You can use Channel on me."

I scowled. "Don't wanna anymore."

"Then use it on me," Jye said.

In the corner of my eye, I saw Axel frown but focused on Jye. "But I don't know what your abilities are? Don't you think I'd need to know what the names of them are?"

They shrugged. "You might as well try, especially since you don't have any other abilities."

Jye wasn't wrong. If I couldn't use [Channel], I was merely deadweight. As I thought about the ability, there was a rush of heat in my core. It built, and built, and the warmth spread over my body, flowing down my limbs and tingling in my fingertips. It was a completely foreign experience. Strength was within me, but it had nowhere to go.

Turning my attention to Jye, my menu window popped up.

Bzzt.

The buzzer sound of the wrong answer in a game show. Accompanying this was a red written error: **Player not in party.**

Oh, there was an official party mechanic in this system. With my focus lost, the warmth dissipated, and I felt lightheaded. Only vaguely aware of it, I could sense, like a phantom limb, I must've used some mana, maybe all of it.

It was different from physical exhaustion. The closest I could come to comparing it with was pulling an all-nighter studying for an exam the next day. My brain felt tight in my skull. So, when I failed to use a skill, there was a cost associated with even trying. At least that was good to know.

"It only works on party members."

"Then I'll join your party. Just send an invite."

"Uh, invite Jye to party?" My confidence downgraded the request into a question.

Jye swore loudly, their hands snapping up to clamp around their ears. Groaning, they said, "What the fuck, dude. A little warning next time. This speaker feedback is earsplitting." From under the hood of their eyelids, they looked up at what I assumed was their screen. "I got two unreadable options. Left or right?"

Unprompted, Axel sighed for an extended amount of time.

"That's really a UX question. I'm more backend. But to answer you, it actually depends on the intent of the designer."

Both Jye and I were silent. It seemed like the type of thing that someone would elaborate on regardless of further inquiry. Plus, it was Axel. Given the chance, he loved showing off his knowledge. I'd listened to his rants about how inefficient the workflow was at his company as well as his proposed solutions which he never submitted. Get him going and it was like witnessing a group conversation with only one speaker.

"If we assume that parties are the preferred playing status, we'd have reason to believe 'Accept' would be first as we read, so on the left."

Jye nodded. "Left, got it, just a—"

"But," Axel continued, "if we assumed that the system would rather have us players solo, then 'Reject' would be read first."

The redhead's brows furrowed. "Okay, so…The one on the right, then?"

Hit with a sudden idea, I interrupted, "But what if the system takes into account the preferences of the player? Like, people in any number of those other countries with Gates surely don't speak English. Which means their notifications must be written and spoken in their own languages. The system has to consider a player's preference in some way."

"So, you're saying that depending on the player 'Accept' might be on the right or the left?" Axel asked.

Both our eyes swung over to Jye. "Would you say you're an extrovert or an introvert?"

"Uh, neither?" Jye said.

"Well, that doesn't help. Oh, what about… Axel you invite me, and then Jye you invite Axel."

"Like some sort of party invitation orgy?" Jye asked.

I blinked. "I wouldn't have phrased it like that, but sure."

There was a brief exchange of invites, and then a little screen pinged up in my peripheral vision. It reminded me of the friend invite notifications you got on apps. For a second, I thought about the friends I couldn't contact online. I hoped they were doing okay. Well, one of them had moved outback, so they'd probably be fine. The other had moved to America...

The notification read: **Party invite received from Axel.**

Underneath the invite were the two options of **Accept** and **Reject.**

I pointed to my screen. "Accept's on the left for me."

Axel said, "I think mine's on the left?"

"You think?" I asked.

"It's— Uhhh... Really hard to make out. Probably something with Jye's issues."

Jye made a face. "My bad."

Letting out a painful groan, I said, "Invite Axel to party."

"For yours, it's on the left too."

Unimpressed, Jye said, "Okay, so on the left. I'm glad we spent the last ten minutes figuring this out."

I rolled my eyes. "It's better to find out this stuff before we go into a Gate. 'Cause now you know with a yes and no prompt the affirmative response will be on the left. So, there's that."

"Do I accept your invite now then?"

Pondering for a moment, I replied, "No, actually can you invite me, Jye? I want to see what your notifications look like."

They sent the invite, and this time the notification ping was the screech of metal scratching metal combined with nails on a chalkboard. I involuntarily shuddered and checked the written notification. Oh, Axel hadn't been joking. This was near impossible to make out.

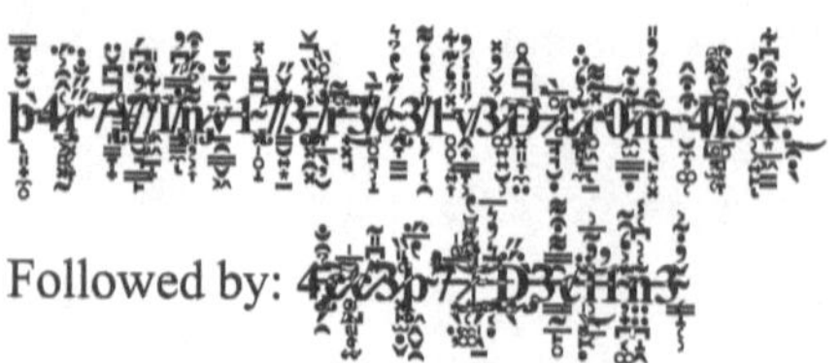

Followed by:

If I squinted hard, I could barely read what appeared to be leetspeak but glitched over. However, it was still legible to me and had been to Axel as well. Damn, I didn't want to know what Jye's actual notification writing looked like if they couldn't read it at all.

"Now can I accept the damn invite? And also, can I have another cup noodle?"

"Yes."

Jye's eyes sparkled. "Yes to…?"

"Yes to both."

Another teeth-gritting sound, courtesy of Jye's fantastic error-ridden status, and I received the following confirmation notification: **Jye has joined your party.**

Register party name?

A party name? How quaint. A million options ran through my mind, ranging from absolutely cringe to the name of friend chat groups that only a select few would understand the inside jokes of. Ah, well, I'm sure we could change it in the future anyway, like most game systems. I'd just go with whatever. As I looked over the rest of my party, an idea formed in my head.

Party name registered.

"Axel, accept my invite too."

A high-pitched ping alerted me to his acceptance. The confirmation read: **Axel has joined your party.** The thrill of pissing Axel off was building, and I eagerly awaited his response to the party name. He was silent for a long time, and then he was right in front of me. His fucking [Swift Footed] trait. I didn't have time to react as he grabbed me by the scruff of my shirt.

"Are you kidding me?"

"What are you talking about?" I asked, eyes innocently wide.

"You registered our party as Just Friends?"

Jye, in the midst of making their next cup noodle, commented, "Jesus Christ, you guys have problems. I'm okay with the name, FYI."

Laughing, even though I was choking a little, I pulled at Axel's hands. "Come on, let go." I echoed his previous words. "It's just a joke."

I'd been expecting him to get annoyed about the name, especially since it was digging at a long-term joke, but nothing like this. His grip on the collar of my shirt tightened, knuckles whitening. I added this to the list of weirdness about Axel, which was growing longer and longer by the minute. My feet began to lift from the ground, and I glanced down in concern. He was literally raising me off the floor.

"Damn, I'll change it if you hate it that much."

Like a switch had been flicked, he dropped his hands. My shoes made full contact with the floor again. Through clenched teeth, he said, "You're so predictable," and then stepped back. Which was good because I hadn't even realised how close he had been.

"Look, I'm changing it now."

I focused on the party, and a new screen appeared.

Just Friends Party | LVL 3

Lee | LVL 1 | All-Rounder (Party Leader)

Axel | LVL 1 | Combatant

[illegible] | LVL 1 | [illegible]

It was nice to see that the party function worked correctly and even more useful that it tracked our classes and levels. Probably to make sure that we were aware of our separate levels. The level next to the party name was a little weird, though. I'd never really seen that in a game before. Was that the sum of our levels? Not to mention that Jye's class was completely unreadable. Putting those thoughts into the "think about later" box, whose lid wouldn't shut now, I thought about changing the name of the party.

Bzzt.

"Well, what are you waiting for?" Axel said, glaring at me.

"I— Uh…" I closed my eyes to concentrate, desperately pleading for the party name to change.

Bzzt. This time it was followed by a notification: **Party names**

registered by party leader are permanent.

Smiling in what I hoped was an apologetic manner, I said, "I can't change it."

Jye finished their second instant noodle cup. "I'm good with the name, by the way. Just thought I'd reiterate that for clarification. Actually, I like the name. It's cute. Like a sign outside a treehouse saying 'Friends Only.'"

"So, we're stuck as 'Just Friends'?" Axel asked, simmering.

"It could be worse. I nearly called us JALbait. You're lucky you dodged that bullet."

Both Jye and Axel groaned. A new sound beeped, similar to a vital signs monitor, from my menu window. Oh. My missing health point had regenerated. Curious, I glanced at my scalded hand and found the flesh unmarred though it tingled weirdly.

Well, at least that answered that.

DUNGEON
HUNTER

IV

GROCERIES

THE NEXT FEW DAYS we spent familiarising ourselves with our abilities and figuring out what kind of teamwork would be best with our current composition. Though we had all agreed that Jye was better at backline damage, the only projectiles we found at the gym were smaller weights, but we'd talked about hitting up a Kmart and pocketing bags of knives.

Though it was accidental, we figured out that Axel's [Ground Smash] did a decent amount of damage while also stunning people. Jye had ended up in bed for half a day recuperating 12 HP, and while tending to them, we'd watched in horror as their broken foot creaked and cracked to correct itself. They'd been in intense pain too, screaming and writhing upon the gym mat we'd laid on the floor. Perhaps it was witnessing that that made me confident this wasn't just some delusion. What kind of coma patient imagined healing hurting?

On the third day, electricity flickered out. Axel had thought ahead and had filled up the beer bottles with water, so we still had a couple litres left. We started soaking our cup noodles. Honestly, it changed very little about the experience other than having to chew a little more.

I'd finally been able to use [Channel] without a system error. Unfortunately, with my current mana and stamina pool, I could only use

Axel's [Ground Smash] without major detriment. It turned out that I had to use whatever stat was required for the channelled abilities. Though we still couldn't determine the true name of Jye's first ability, we discovered that as long as they had enough mana and stamina, they could increase the effect of it without limit. Given that it seemed to increase the weight of an object, we took to calling it Dropping A Load. The first time we ended up in stitches, but it just stuck. But we called it Load for short.

Suffice to say, after multiplying the effect ten times, the dumbbell had sunk through the floor, past the concrete foundation, and into a deep dark hole. After that we didn't test out Jye's Load to its fullest capacity since the ramifications of sinking a weight into the Earth's core probably wouldn't be good.

Eventually, we came to the party pattern of Axel closing the gap between the target with his [Swift Footed] trait, then using [Ground Smash] to stun them, then backing off, and then Jye would pelt projectiles and layer on their Load on their down arcs. Since I could only use [Ground Smash] with my [Channel], I was delegated to protecting Jye and locking down anyone who approached. If the projectiles didn't finish the target off, Axel would dash back in, and we'd repeat the process.

On the fifth day, we ran out of cup noodles.

It was probably for the better.

"SO, WOOLIES AND KMART?" I asked, closing the gym door behind the three of us.

Axel led the way. "Yeah, though all the groceries are probably gone. We'll pick up what we can. Kmart, we all need to grab weapons. I'm thinking a bat for me. Knives for Jye. What would work for you?"

I thought for a moment. "I might get a broomstick? Staffs seem cool."

"Staves," Axel said.

"That's what I said, I want a staff."

"No, you said staffs. The plural of staff is staves."

I glared at him. "You're really hard to get along with, you know that, right?"

"I know that only too well."

Despite food being the more pressing matter, Kmart had simply been easier to get to. Woolies was another block, and none of us wanted to risk the trek without being able to properly defend ourselves. While our training allowed us to work together, I don't think any of us were truly ready to fight anything or anyone. Jye's brush with the "healing" foot also made us want to err on the side of caution.

Regenerating health points was far worse than losing them.

It was weird, but the streets were eerily quiet. Even the sirens and alarms had long since faded down. The looting had lulled too. Cars were abandoned on roads, doors left ajar is if people had just up and left. People had seemingly withdrawn into hideouts or perhaps they had been driven to the Dungeons. I hoped they had left for the bush, to escape all the shit happening around here, though I knew that was unlikely.

When we arrived, the Kmart store's front doors had been smashed through, with bricks sitting inside. Avoiding the jagged edges, we squeezed in and weren't surprised to find a lot of the merchandise had been taken. Large electronics were the most noticeably missing, which was the sad reality of life. Too bad they wouldn't be able to use them anymore, not with power down. We all went our separate ways to the different sections in Kmart. Axel went to sporting goods, Jye headed to the kitchenware, and me to the cleaning supplies.

Luckily not many people had use for broomsticks during the end of the world. There was a plethora of options to choose from, ranging from cheap plastic to name brand wood. To test them out, I gave them a thwack against the floor. The plastic was too slippery in my grip, so I ended up picking a wooden one. It was surprisingly sturdy and fit nicely in my hand. I guess ergonomics mattered a lot when it was something someone was going to be using on the regular.

"Guys?" I called, wondering if they'd finished their selections too.

Walking through the clothing department, I picked up a few exercise clothes in my size and shoved them into the backpack my mother had bought me for paintball back when I'd been attending uni. The bag had several different compartments, all specifically designed to store various types of ammo or paintball supplies. Honestly, it'd been extremely helpful. I was glad that Axel had remembered it.

I made my way to the electronics, hoping to find the only other items I thought would be necessary in this post-electricity world: batteries. It wasn't surprising to find the shelves empty of the better lithium brands with only a few spare home brand AA and AAA left. A couple of Ds too. Better than nothing. I packed them into one of the smaller compartments of my backpack, hoping they wouldn't be damaged by anything.

Taking one more quick scan of the electronics section, I looked for anything else that would be useful to us. On the smaller knickknack shelves were several thin watches, more closely resembling bracelets than timepieces. Without phones, it would be hard to keep track of time… I grabbed the lot of them and headed back to the entrance. Hopefully Axel and Jye would be there soon enough.

"How's your staff?" Jye asked, approaching me with an armful of glinting knives.

I gave it an experimental twirl but fumbled and it slipped out of my fingers. It clacked against the ground. "Ah, fuck. Well, let's pray I get better at that." I stepped forward to pick it up, but my toe caught the edge of it, kicking the cylindrical wood into a roll. Ears now hot, I shuffled after the broom handle before plucking it from the floor. This time I held it firmly in my grasp.

"You sure you're gonna be okay with that?" said a familiar grating voice.

Fucking Axel.

"I'm sure it's just a steep learning curve."

"Keep telling yourself that."

Axel too had apparently taken the time to check out the clothing section and had changed. He was now wearing black jeans that had hanging chains and a white tee with metallic fangs in the centre accompanied by the words "BITE ME." The shirt was probably two sizes too small and clung to his chest and midsection in a way I'm sure was appealing to others. Aesthetically, it was the type of thing I expected a teenage K-pop wannabe to wear, to be honest. It was also ridiculously impractical. I was about to make a comment and joke with Jye, but the slight blush and their inability to meet Axel's eyes made me rethink my words.

Despite the hatred Jye harboured for him, I guess it was difficult for others to forgo their attraction to Axel. For a moment, I wondered if the name of our party would end up being a lie. Maybe Jye and Axel would hook up. Maybe hatefuck? Though I wasn't sure if Jye was Axel's type. Historically, Axel tended to prefer men shorter than him with soft eyes and easy smiles. Most of the party-goers that came and went from his room were like that.

That wasn't to say Jye didn't have a shot. With the differences Axel had gone through, I wasn't confident with my knowledge of him anymore.

In the blond's left hand, he held a metal baseball bat. "You sure you don't want one of these too?"

Statistically, left-handed people die earlier than right-handers. I wondered if that was a promise. In response to his question, I shook my head. "I'm not melee enough to be comfortable that close range. I'll stick with my stick, thanks."

He shrugged, and the small shirt rode up to reveal part of his abdomen. Jye physically jerked away to walk to the entrance. I could imagine the expression on their face. I'd seen it on many a passersby's features before. Judgmentally, I frowned at the six-pack that was now peeking out.

Noticing my silent words, Axel tugged his shirt back down. "Suit yourself."

Axel and I followed Jye to the exit. Just before we stepped outside, I remembered the watches. "Oh, yeah, I got these for us too."

Already wearing mine, I handed out one each to Jye and Axel. The blond ran his thumb over the cheap metal accessory, deeply examining it. Then his gaze flicked up with a mocking smile. "Matching bracelets? How very kindergarten of you."

Again, I resisted the sigh and said, "They're practical. Just wear yours."

Jye had already wordlessly slipped theirs onto their right wrist. It was the first time I noticed the whole tattoo sleeve they sported on that arm. The small glimpse of it I'd seen was hard to make out, but I was very sure I saw at least one snake. From what I knew about Jye, it was probably some sort of fandom reference. Axel clipped the watch on their left wrist.

In the broken windows of Kmart, I saw our reflection. With the matching watches we genuinely looked like a team. It was weirdly pleasant. The last time I could remember feeling like this, like I belonged to something, was probably when Chrissie was still alive.

I cleared my throat. "To Woolies with our weapons?"

Axel pointed to the east. "To Woolies!"

⌐┴⌐

THE PLACE WAS ABSOLUTELY RANSACKED. If Kmart had been robbed, Woolworths had been completely trashed. Any fresh food that hadn't been taken was beginning to rot on the shelves, filling the entire building with the stench of decay. Jye, who apparently didn't have a functioning nose, didn't seem to care and walked in without a thought.

Breathing through my mouth, I trailed in after them along with Axel.

Entire aisles had been tipped on their sides, resulting in a barely navigable area. The place was practically bare. The only things left were health foods that needed extra processing or preparation. I watched in horror as Jye shoved several protein containers into their gym bag. Maintaining eye contact with me, Jye bent their arm in front of them, tensing their bicep into a sizeable lump before kissing it. My own lips curled down in disgust. Jye was the kind of buff that scared me. If I met them in a dark alley, I'd run away in fear.

We got maybe two aisles in before I saw it. In one section, three of the shelving units had dominoed upon one another, creating a triangular tepee that was sealed off from the outside. It was probably our best bet to discovering untouched food. Just ahead of me, Jye kneeled to pick up a discarded can of anchovies. Let me correct that. Our best bet to find food that I found palatable.

I leaned my staff against a nearby wall and tried to recall best heavy lifting protocols from when I worked part time in a warehouse. Knees, not back. Knees, not back. Bending at the knees, I squatted by one of the fallen aisle's shelving units and began to lift. Both my legs and my arms shook as I struggled to stand. I could barely imagine what kind of activity had knocked them over in the first place. The place must have been violently rioted.

Noticing my actions, Axel took a position to my right. We breathed in, and then, as we exhaled, we heaved. With the two of us, the unit began to slowly raise. It was exhilarating seeing it lifting those few millimetres.

Before the appearance of the Gates, I don't think this would've been possible with just the two of us. It further confirmed that our bodies had been changed beyond just accelerated healing. And were there more stats that were hidden? Health, mana, and stamina weren't actually stats. Those were just indicators.

"Leave me alone!" said a small voice muffled by the shelves.

Startled, my hands instinctively released their grip. Unable to handle the sudden extra load, Axel fell forward, and the unit slid back down with a thud. He glared daggers at me, flicking his fingers to wave away pain.

I shot him a sorry-for-that smile. "You heard that too, right?"

He nodded. And was uncharacteristically silent. Was this something else I needed to consider later? No, we'd let that one pass.

"Go away!" the voice repeated.

Attracted by the commotion, and with their bag bursting at the seams with food I almost wouldn't acknowledge as such, Jye returned. In between licks of a lollipop they had found somewhere, they said, "You got yourselves a bona fide kid in there."

What the fuck was a child doing in Woolies by themselves? Were they trapped? Had they gotten separated from their guardians?

I pinched the bridge of my nose in thought. We couldn't just leave a kid alone in an abandoned grocery store. But what if their caretakers were looking for them? For a moment, I remembered Chrissie but immediately shoved that thought so deep into beneath my thoughts that it was swallowed up in my concerns about Axel's behaviour.

Said flatmate gestured at the shelves, eyebrows raised, inviting me to take control of the situation. Ah, his silence this time figured. He was shit with kids. Didn't have any patience or empathy for that matter. And children were good at sussing out people who were faking anything. Who knows what they'd pick up from Axel.

"Hello?" I ventured. "We're just looking for some food."

"I have none!" yelled the child.

Weirdly enough, I swore I recognised their voice. Maybe they lived in the neighbourhood and I'd seen them around? I circled the shelf tepee, searching for any entrances and discovered two hazel eyes peering out from a slight gap about knee height. "Are you okay in there?"

"Yes, and I'm staying in here."

"Okay, okay." I sat down near the gap and crossed my legs. "I'm Lee. What's your name?"

There was no response. A different tactic then?

"The three of us are stocking up food before we go into one of those black holes. You've seen those, right?"

The kid said something so quiet that I wasn't sure they had spoken.

"What?" I asked.

"You shouldn't go into them."

The hazel eyes were watery, and I could just barely make out the drying tracks of tears trailing down their cheeks. Oh, yikes. That explained where their caretakers were.

"We have to. Well. I think we do. But we're waiting for new ones to appear. My friend Axel thinks those titles we're told about are important. He's the blond one."

Their gaze flicked behind me to where Axel stood. He struck a pose. No doubt the kid was considering the sanity of our group. Somehow Axel had also managed to find a chain to wrap around the upper section of his baseball bat and had attached it to his jeans, so now it swung by his hips like a sword in makeshift scabbard.

"Who's the other one?"

"They're Jye. They're my friend too, I guess?" We'd just spent the past workweek together, training and preparing for the Dungeons. If we weren't friends, maybe companion was closer?

Jye shot me a thumbs up with a lazy smile. Okay, nice. We were friends. That was actually nice to know.

"Why go into the black holes? They... they're dangerous," the kid said, pressing their face closer to the gap.

They looked around ten or so. Of course they had to be the same age as Chrissie. Their mouse brown hair was cut short in a pixie style. Under hazel almond eyes, their cherry nose was only just visible. At least mercifully they didn't look the same.

"You don't feel it?" I was genuinely curious. Maybe children didn't have the same draw to the Gates, the strange compulsion that was growing stronger the longer we waited out. It had begun as a vague desire, but was now niggling into my thoughts when I let them wander.

They didn't reply, but they sank farther from the gap, the shadows swallowing their face.

"Well, nice knowing you, kid," Axel said and turned to walk away. I caught his eye, but he winked. That wink had set many a person giggling in its time, it was so practised. Wondering what he was playing at, I stood and began following. If he thought he knew how to handle this, I'd let him give it a try.

"Oh, we're just gonna leave them here?" Jye asked, only vaguely concerned. They crunched down on the lollipop, decimating the sweet.

Trying to play it cool, I shrugged, and the three of us began to walk.

"Wait!" yelled the kid.

Looking back, I could see their face pressed up to the gap, eyes wide. "You're definitely going into those black holes? What about the one in the CBD?"

"Maybe eventually," Axel said, wobbling his hand in that semi yes-no motion.

There was a beat.

"Can I come?"

I wasn't able to fight the smile. "Of course."

A kerfuffle followed from behind the shelving unit, and beneath a carefully displaced box, the kid emerged. Sporting pink overalls over a plain white shirt and black Converses dirtied by probably a few days of wear, she approached our group carefully. If it weren't for how dishevelled she was, she would've been the picture of a picket fence kid. On her back was a small backpack in the shape of a Pikachu. Well, her and Jye would get along just fine.

The girl's thin brows were furrowed in concern. "I'm only coming with you for now. Okay?"

"That's fine with me," I said.

"Same," said Jye. This time they weren't eating anything. For once.

"Well, I'm not okay with it, but majority rules, I guess," Axel grumbled.

It suddenly occurred to me that perhaps Axel had truly intended to just leave the girl here when he had originally started to walk away. The dude was so cold. How could he be like that when he had known Chrissie too? Swallowing back anger, I waited for the girl to catch up. The speed of our party noticeably slowed as we kept pace with her. Well, it was what it was.

After walking in silence for a short time, she said, "I'm Wren."

"Oh, like those little birds?" Jye asked.

Axel shook his head. "You're thinking of sparrows."

Holding their hands out in front of them, they gestured a very small spherical shape and said, "No, they're like puffy and brown. You know, friend shaped."

"Mmm, that sounds like a finch," I replied.

Axel scoffed. "No, now they're describing a dunnock."

"What in the fuck is a dunnock?" asked Jye.

"Language!" I exclaimed in outrage. Glancing down at Wren, I hoped we hadn't scarred her.

Instead, she chuckled. It was good to see her smiling. Who knows what she had been through in the past couple of days? And if she didn't feel the same need to enter the Gates, why had she been so interested in them? The other curious thing was that she appeared a little too calm. Then again, I didn't know too many kids these days. One of my uni friends had them, but it's not like I'd ever needed to speak to their children.

She said, "Wrens *are* small brown puffy birds."

"See?!" Jye shouted. "I'm a bird savant!"

"That title is all yours," Axel flatly said.

I asked, "Speaking of titles, Wren, do you have any, or traits, or abilities?" I thought for a second and then added, "Oh, and what's your class?"

The smile faded from her face. Oh, I'd stepped on some sort of emotional land mine. Several different responses ran through my mind, but I settled on remaining silent. Sometimes it was better to let others fill the quiet than ask questions. It's how I managed to get through most of my therapy sessions with Mrs. Brown.

Jye, unable to read the room, confidently said, "I can't read anything on my menu screen, so as long as you can read yours, they can't be all that bad."

Swearing under his breath, Axel whispered to Jye, "Ixnay on the itchglay."

Jye frowned and then replied in full volume, "I don't speak French, man."

"You can't read your menu screen?" Wren asked, voice surprisingly timid.

Ignoring Axel to my pleasure, I answered for Jye. "Not a bit of it." And hoping to assuage her of any concerns continued with, "And it doesn't really matter to us that much. We're pretty open to anything. But only if you want to work with us."

She thought for a second and then nodded. "My class is Scourge. I can use Imperil and Death Mark."

[Scourge]? That really wasn't a class I was familiar with. I think I remember it being in one of the *Final Fantasy* games? Based on the name of her abilities, it seemed like a support class that focused on debuffs. I didn't want to admit it, but having someone else in the backlines was just further unbalancing our party composition. It was already too heavily reliant on range with only Axel in the front. What we really needed was either a tank or someone who was frontline critical damage, like an assassin or rogue.

The disappointment must've been written on my face because Axel, of all people, nudged me with his shoulder and then shot me a pointed look. Wren's face was downcast. God, I was a shit person. The poor kid had shared information with us that she felt should be secret, and here I was thinking about how useless it was.

Trying to correct the failing trajectory of our conversation, I asked, "Do you want to join our party?"

Axel's glare bore a hole into my forehead, and Jye's curious gaze was on my back, but I didn't meet either of them. I probably should've asked them first… But what was done was done. We could talk about it later. Or rather Axel would talk at me about it later.

Wren clearly hesitated in responding.

"You can always leave it. I think. Wait a second, let me just make sure that's true."

I focused on the party menu screen, and it popped up. Thinking about leaving the party, a small confirmation window appeared.

Do you wish to leave party Just Friends? Accept | Reject

Selecting Reject, I smiled at Wren. "Yep, you can leave whenever you want."

She nodded. "Okay, I'll join."

A few moments after officially inviting Wren, I heard the confirmation of her acceptance.

Wren has joined your party.

The information updated, adding her name to our list of members. It confirmed her class and level. Well, at least she wasn't lying. That was a relief. After a brief discussion with the others, we agreed to give her one of the smallest knives from Kmart, so she could defend herself if the situation called for it.

Now she was safely in our fold, it was time to get into the nitty gritty.

"You don't need to answer if you don't want to, but where are your parents?"

"I don't know."

"Did they go into the Gate, the black hole in the CBD?"

"No."

"Why do you want to go into the CBD Gate?"

She didn't answer that question at all. God, some shit must've happened to her. All right. It was time to back off. Pivot topic. Let her cool down. She probably didn't trust us yet. I mean, if I was a kid and a bunch of randos asked me to join them I probably would have run off screaming. So, at the very least, Wren had spunk.

"Me and Axel's parents live in rural. You know where Charleville is?"

She shook her head. Yeah, figures. A handful of people probably knew of Charleville but not where it was. I'd seen a satirical TikTok espousing Charleville as this luxury destination with at least six different biomes including snowy mountains, lush forest, and sandy beaches. Truth be told, Charleville was just another rural town with more than the average amount of derros.

"I thought you said you're friends?" she asked.

I frowned. "What?"

"You said yours and Axel's parents. You guys don't look related."

Axel and I exchanged a look before exploding into laughter. It was the kind of belly laugh that wouldn't stop. My eyes were watering as I tried to calm myself. Every time I went to correct her, the idea of being Axel's brother was so ridiculous that I devolved into another fit of laughter. Axel too seemed to be laughing uproariously.

While we were preoccupied, Jye answered, "Nah, they're just friends."

"Oh, like our party name?"

Axel's laughter stopped immediately, and he cleared his throat. The tiniest iota of guilt riled around in my gut. For some reason, the name had really hurt him. And now I was going to have to live that for however long this game lasted. That's life, I guess. You make choices and sometimes they're wrong.

Flatly, Axel stated, "Our parents are best friends. So, we kinda grew up together."

I smiled, reminiscing. "Yeah, in fact, this guy used to have stupidly curly hair when he was your age, Wren. Almost like an afro. I kind of miss it."

"Shut up, Lee," Axel growled. He'd hated the hair when he was young. One day he'd come to school with it completely shaved off. His mother had told me he had tried to cut it himself, and they couldn't save any of it, so they'd decided to go with a clean buzz cut.

I'll never know what inspired him to do it. Having dead straight hair except when I slept on it funny, I'd always thought curly hair was really cool. During the later stages of puberty, Axel's hair had permanently become straight. The style he sported now—an undercut with a fringe to his brows—suited him, but part of me would always mourn his curls.

"Both my parents are retired now, thankfully. They deserve some peace and quiet." I nodded at Axel. "Yours still freelance sometimes, don't they?"

He scowled. "Yeah. I've told them to stop, but they keep on saying they don't know what else to do with their spare time."

"That's capitalism for you," Jye commented soberly. "Boomers suffering from zoochosis."

As if in agreement, we all ignored Jye's words. "At least there's no way for them to do remote work now," I said.

"Yeah, I guess that's true."

I smiled at the redheaded giant. "What about your parents, Jye?"

They shrugged. "I'm no contact with them."

Yikes. I regretted asking. So, half of the party had parents they wanted to talk about and half of them didn't. I think I'd probably avoid the topic in the future since it had killed the conversation. We walked in solemn silence.

I hoped my parents were okay. The closest Gate was the one in this city, so even if they felt the compulsion, it would be difficult for them to get here.

Tsss.

It was the same static sound I'd recognised whenever someone used their abilities. As I glanced around, it didn't look like anyone in our party had done anything. I stopped on the spot, worried about someone ambushing us. It's not something I had been expecting, but it was never far from my mind. Now we basically all had superpowers, there was bound to be people using them to their advantage.

"Guys, wait, I can hear—"

With a comically loud pop, a Gate appeared in front of us.

~Dungeon 9 cleared for the first time by Kimi Kishimoto. New Dungeons Active~

Oh.

V

SURPRISE

CLEARED?

Did Kimi defeat the boss in the Dungeon? That was insane. It'd only been six days since they first activated. Not to mention that name was different to the one who received the title for Dungeon 9. I guess they didn't end up clearing the Dungeon. Did that mean… Did they die in the Dungeon? Ever since the disappearance of that man in the video, in the back of my mind it had always been a possibility. Dying in the Dungeons. Never seeing my parents again.

But there was that pull that made me want to step into the Gate anyway. Without it, would we still have such a dismissive attitude toward our own lives? I doubted it, but then again, there were a select number of people who were carefree with everything they possessed.

When the Gate had formed, it was instantaneous. Nothing, and then Gate.

"Well, that's pretty serendipitous," Jye said.

It was unnerving standing in front of one in real life. The videos and photos really hadn't done them justice. The edges of the Gate blurred completely with reality, a distortion of our plane in whirling tendrils. In the centre it was not just black but a lack of existence. And something in my head was screaming at me to stick my hand right in.

"Are we ready to go in? Wren just joined our party. We haven't practised with her yet."

Axel shook his head. "We're not prepared, but this might be our only chance to get titles."

"I'm good to go," Wren said, jutting her jaw forward.

Well, that made one of us. I was suddenly getting cold feet about this whole thing, even with my body slowly stepping toward the Gate despite my aversion. Jye made a considering sturgeon face and added, "I mean, what would go wrong?"

I stared at them. "There's the obvious."

The rest of the party gazed at me blankly.

Throwing my hands up, I elaborated, "We could all die?"

"Yeah, but what's there to really live for?" Jye replied, laughing a little too much for my comfort.

We really didn't have the time to unpack that, but I left a mental memo to have a sit down with them later. It did make me reflect on how little I knew about Jye. In fact, I could probably list the number of actual facts I could recall about them on one hand.

Again, turning away from the Gate played in my mind. We could *not* go in. It was an option. And it was looking more and more like the preferred one. Especially with Wren to consider as well.

If the original Dungeon 9 title receiver had died in their Dungeon, what chance did a ten-year-old girl stand? No, that cinched it. We weren't going in. This was a terrible idea. Maybe instead we could form some sort of shelter for those who were still resisting the effects of the Dungeon compulsion. We could make a type of found community. Perhaps we could build a new world from the ashes of the old and just forget the Gates altogether.

"You probably won't forgive me for this," Axel said.

Barely paying attention, I snorted. "There's a lot I don't forgive you for. What could possibly top the—"

Axel's shoulder rammed into my stomach. It stole the rest of the words out of my mouth, and only an embarrassing *heugh* came out instead. What little remaining breath I had in my lungs was squeezed out as we crashed to the floor, and I took the brunt of Axel's weight. Pinned under him, I gasped for air and inhaled a lungful of dust that our movements had kicked up.

It took a moment for me to process what had happened.

Axel had tackled me through the direct centre of the Gate.

We were in the Dungeon.

Unable to see anything from under the blond's body, I pushed him off me and floundered to get to my feet. "What the fuck, Axel!"

~Gate 16 entered for the first time. Party Just Friends rewarded title of Student~

As I glanced around, trying to take in my surroundings and comprehend what was happening, I realised Wren and Jye were here too, coughing into the kicked-up dust. My mind was struggling to catch up.

Had they stepped in after Axel's attack? But how? It had literally just happened. And where was the dust coming from? Before coming through the Gate, we'd been standing on a cement driveway. Now it looked like we were… in some sort of ancient cabin? And our entire party had received the title. Student was the title for this dungeon?

Oh, God.

We were in the Dungeon. We were all here. We could all die. Axel, Jye, Wren, Chrissie, me.

Dead.

My throat began to close up, chest tight and collapsing into itself. Blood thrummed in my ears, through my veins, singeing my heart. It was itchy, and hot, and I couldn't… I couldn't do this! Fuck, not now. Not now! I'd gone for almost a week.

The world started spinning. I struggled to fill my lungs with air.

Breathe, goddamnit!

I couldn't. Air creaked through me. Too many things were

happening at once.

Out of my control, my knees buckled, and I sank to the ground. The Warhead. It would help, I just had to… Hands shaking, I reached for my pocket, but as I wheezed to breathe, my jaw clenched and locked. I couldn't focus, couldn't see, couldn't align my fingers to get inside my pocket.

I was so fucking useless. Defeated, I let my hands fall to the ground.

This was the best I could do?

Darkness was beginning to form in my peripheral vision, vignetting my sight. God, a black out? It'd been a long time since I'd fainted from one of these attacks.

The dust began to settle to reveal a frowning Jye. "What's wrong with Lee?"

"Fuck."

I was vaguely aware of Axel fumbling for something in his own pocket. In a flash, he was by my side and had dropped to his knees next to me. His movement awakened a new cloud of dust, swirling wildly about us.

"Here."

Axel's hand approached my face, and, mustering every ounce of my willpower, I managed to look at it. Pinched between his forefinger and thumb was the familiar sight of a Warhead. I couldn't take it, my body not listening to me, limbs weighed down and chest constricted, the world beginning to fade, tears of frustration and panic hot down my cheeks. Axel grabbed my chin with his other hand. He squeezed.

My jaw opened in reflex.

The sourness of the lolly exploded over my tongue, shocking me from the grips of the panic attack. As the tartness spread through my mouth, tendrils of control sprouted throughout my body, grounding my mind. It began to pull all my senses back to my head. The world started to regain saturation, the blackness retreating like a tide. The muscles in my torso loosened, my lungs fully expanding with air. Tasting only sour,

I found I could finally breathe.

"Look, I know you hate the green ones. Green apples are already sour, so what's the point in having them as a sour lolly. I know. But beggars can't be choosers, all right?"

I barely registered Axel's words, but his voice and the flavour of the Warhead centred me.

"You're lucky I kept those on me, you know? I'm an amazing friend. The best kind."

Slowly, ever so slowly, my body became my own again. I wiped away the wetness from my cheeks. God, I forgot how awful the panic attacks were. I'd gone for so long without them before the Gates that I thought I was "cured" of them. Guess I'd just managed to bury them away.

A few moments passed as my party sat in silence. My breathing evened out, and my heartbeat regulated. Everything was… It was all right.

"Are you okay?" Wren asked, her eyes wide.

I delivered what smile I could and deposited the lolly into my left cheek. "I'll live."

"So, like, is that a normal thing for you?" Jye asked.

Sighing, I tested my balance for a moment, then stood and dusted off my clothes. "Kinda?"

"Noted."

Sometime between giving me the Warhead and me regaining myself, Axel had left the three of us alone and had started patrolling the room we'd arrived in. It was a large mostly empty cabin with rotting furniture and dilapidated walls. Spiderwebs decorated the rooftop, spiders concerningly absent. Everything about it screamed "forgotten." Dust lined each surface, and simply moving brushed up the allergens.

Had we been taken to a haunted house?

"The title's pretty good," the blond said as he neared us again.

It was very Axel of him to ignore what had happened. It was also very Axel of him to not take the blame for it. Well, I guess no one was really to blame for the root of my anxiety attacks. Just bad luck. Taking a page out of Axel's book, I decided to brush past everything that had just occurred as well. Yeah, yeah, yeah, who cares about compartmentalising being bad for your mental health, Mrs. Brown.

I checked out the new title we'd received.

[Student] Boosts all experience gain.

Holy shit, Axel wasn't joking. This title was insane. The benefits of a permanent experience increase meant we had to do less to level up. As I thought about the levelling system, my menu screen loaded in and then expanded to reveal further information. Jesus Christ, why didn't it just tell us everything from the beginning? Though, I guessed info dumping was frowned upon in most games. Especially those without tutorials that you had to learn by doing.

On the new screen, underneath my current level was a progress bar with a few words below.

[____]

0% completion toward next level

So, nothing we had done had given us any experience. None of our training in the gym had counted even though we were using abilities. Not even entering the Dungeon had done anything. This system was really stingy with rewards. If practising didn't give us experience it seemed like there was only defeating opponents. My stomach became a pit of tar. That meant we would have to… kill something? Or someone?

"Yeah, what an amazing title," Jye said, sarcasm oozing.

Wren patted them on the back. "We get better experience gain."

"My words stand."

"Okay, it's really good, yeah, but can we rewind for a second. How did you guys get here?"

I replayed the events in my head as I had seen them. The Gate appeared. I was thinking about entering but then changed my mind. Axel volunteered us as tributes. At that moment, we had to have been at least a metre away from Wren and Jye. Axel wouldn't have been able to drag them along too, unless he was lying about more than just his stats. But it couldn't have been an ability because I would've heard the static. That meant something else had interfered.

"We went through the Gate..." Wren said, her brows pushed together in confusion.

Glad someone else was questioning this, I said, "Yeah, how did that happen?"

Jye scratched their jaw. "The second Axel tackled you through, a tentacle osmosised from the Gate and lunged toward us. Then we were here."

"Must be a safeguard to ensure party members remain together," Axel commented.

Then he poked the tip of his shoe through the crumbling remains of a wooden chair. His top lip curled in disgust. He was always a bit of a clean freak. "Looks like this place is empty and hasn't been touched in a while."

Despite me wanting to let go of what he'd just made happen, his reaction and calm behaviour rankled at me. I'd had a panic attack, and he'd come out of it scot-free?

Pointing a justifiably angry finger at him, I said, "You... You stop talking. I'm angry at you."

He looked like a cashier who was finishing up his shift only to realise a Karen was coming through with receipts in her hand. Was I just something he had to deal with? If I reflected on our relationship during the time we'd known each other, it made sense.

He didn't interact with me more than necessary unless I was in the path of some harm. Was me being in his party just an extension of that same thing? I guess maybe I felt that way toward him as well. Like a responsibility to remain his friend because of our parents.

Had our entire relationship been built on simply *dealing* with each other? God, that was too depressing to dwell on. My longest relationship was just two people bearing each other. How sad. Were we even friends? I guess I hadn't really considered him one for a while now. We'd become something more like coexisting entities that had shared a space.

Jye cleared their throat. "I hate to interrupt whatever… this is, but shouldn't we be doing something? Like, what if someone else enters the Gate?"

The giant had a point. We had only been notified of the first people to enter each Gate, but since it hadn't been the same person who'd cleared Dungeon 9 but Kimi instead, it meant that anyone could follow in after. But what were we meant to do in a dusty-ass cabin? And better yet, how were we meant to get out?

"Something touched my leg!" Wren screeched.

She slapped at her calves in panic. All our gazes sank to her feet, hoping to catch sight of whatever it was. There was nothing there. Her head whipped back and forth as she checked around her vicinity, eyes wide and watery. The poor girl. She must've been imagining things. Man, this must be so scary for a ten-year-old. She spoke so maturely that I had started forgetting that she was only a kid.

Shaking her head, Wren said, "I swear. I swear there was something here."

"Maybe it was some dust. Despite when he proves otherwise, Axel *can* be reliable. If he said the place is empty, it's empty."

He opened his mouth to reply, but I held a finger up. "Still not talking to you."

Axel sighed. Yeah, now we were dealing with each other like we always did.

"What the fuck?!"

It was Jye this time. They'd squealed in a pitch I didn't know they were capable of hitting. I spun around in time to see a shadow dash behind the broken-down vestiges of a bookshelf. Oh, shit. There *was* something else here.

I cast Axel an accusatory glare.

"I thought you weren't talking to me," he said.

Rolling my eyes, I gestured to the party to back off from the bookshelf. If the thing behind it was dangerous, it would be better for all of us to be farther in range. Especially since Axel was the only frontline class we had right now. Without a word, they followed my silent command, stepping toward the opposite wall of the cabin.

Axel crept to the forefront of our group. This was similar to what we had practised in the gym. If he used [Ground Smash], we'd been able to stun whatever it was and maybe rush it. Damn, was shit about to get real?

The static of an ability zapped in my ears.

The floor did not shatter, to my disappointment. Which meant Axel had either activated [Intimidation] or [Thick Hide]. Annnd it also meant he'd immediately gone off plan. That'd figure.

Another *tsss*. He was using both of them? With the 10 mana cap of [Thick Hide], he'd only have 15 mana left, which drastically dropped the amount of [Ground Smashes] he could use. To my left, Jye had drawn their knives. Though now that Axel was writing his own script, they had no idea how to act. Standing behind them, Wren watched, her legs visibly quivering.

"Come out!" Axel shouted.

Was he trying to taunt it to reveal itself? It'd be safer than going in blind. But what if it didn't understand English? What if it wasn't intelligent enough to even comprehend communication?

My thoughts evaporated as the soft falls of footsteps sounded. From the shadows, a figure slowly emerged. My heart was in my throat. Though it was hard to make out, it looked like… No, that'd be stupid. There's no way what I was seeing was real.

Hiss!

A cat. There was a cat here. It looked like a common calico house cat. Its hackles were raised, and its bright green eyes were wide in alarm. What the fuck was a cat doing in a Dungeon? Was it part of the experience? Were we meant to kill it? What kind of sick person would design this?

As it approached, I realised it was missing its tail. No. It had one, it was just shorter. It was a bobtail. They had been her favourite.

"Don't go near it!" Axel shouted as he pulled the bat from his hip.

"Calm down. It's just a cat."

The cat came closer. Axel raised his weapon. Wren clenched her eyes shut, and Jye turned his cheek. What the fuck was wrong with everyone? Were they just going to…

"Stop!"

Axel ignored me, and the cat stopped moving. Its back was arched in alarm, ears drawn back in fear, hackles standing even further on end.

"Axel," I said in warning.

His grip on the bat tightened.

Fuck this.

It happened faster than we had practised in the gym. In an instant, [Channel] filled me with that river of limitless potential; like flame running through my veins. And then I borrowed from Axel. He'd never rescinded his consent.

Focusing my attention, I pushed the power lower in me as I lifted my right foot. I kicked down. [Ground Smash] torpedoed through the movement, bursting into the floor of the cabin. Through the explosion, I heard multiple bursts of static. Wooden shrapnel went flying, and the shock waves knocked the rest of the party around. The dormant dust kicked up, blurring the room, masking everyone from my sight.

In the commotion, the cat fled with a yowl.

Axel fell to his knees, the bat tumbling out of his hand. Jye and Wren who'd been in range had to have been caught in the blast too. Through the dust, I couldn't make out if they'd been hurt badly. I hoped the damage was minimal. The dullness of mana usage throbbed in my brain.

My head felt like it was partially stuffed with wool, and as the dust settled, a heaviness dragged down my limbs. My stamina was worryingly low.

"Lee…" Axel began as he pulled himself up.

Just Friends earned 5 XP.

Oh, I guessed we didn't have to kill things? I mean, technically our opponent had fled. So… we'd won this round of combat by default? My experience progression bar filled in slightly.

[|___________________________________]

2% completion toward next level

I did the mentals maths. So, it was 250 XP for me to get to LVL 2. That was good to know.

Jye let out a groan of pain. Oh, fuck.

I turned around to check their status. Jye was lying on the ground, their arms wrapped protectively around Wren. They were both covered in the planks of the floor that [Ground Smash] had sent flying. I rushed over and brushed the debris from their bodies. They didn't appear to have any major injuries. In fact, they looked mostly unscathed. I stared at them in disbelief. Wren slipped out of Jye's arms and helped them stand.

"How are you okay?" I asked.

Jye grinned. "Fool me once, shame on you. Fool me twice…"

They bent down and picked up a sizeable piece of plank debris from the floor. From the size of it, it should've weighed close to fifty kilos. But Jye lifted it like it was lighter than a feather. As understanding dawned on me, my mouth dropped open. I'd heard an ability be used during my attack, but this was not what I had been expecting.

"You can make things lighter too?" I asked, the relief causing me to laugh.

"Panic will make you try some weird shit," Jye said back.

"Yeah, and, dude, I'm sorry for the friendly fire. I just couldn't…" The words weren't coming out. Somehow saying it was harder than doing what I'd just done. I took a deep breath. "My sister loved cats."

"Chrissie would've done the same thing," Axel admitted.

His face was covered in scratches from the [Ground Smash], and he was standing hunched over, gripping his side. Red had begun to form underneath his hand.

I stared.

No.

No, no, no, no, no!

What had I done?

Axel wasn't meant to get hurt. He had [Swift Footed]! He could've gotten away from the attack. There was no way he should've taken any damage. Sick roiled in my stomach, sliding up my throat as bile. I was at his side before I knew what I was doing, and I pulled his free arm over my shoulder. Jye and Wren weren't far behind me.

"Why didn't you just dodge?" I yelled at him.

"I'm glad you think I'm that good."

Together, we helped Axel to the wall, and he leaned against it with a groan. My brain didn't know how to react. My hands shook. I'd done this. I'd hurt Axel. This was worse than being uselessly low specced. God, I'd hurt my friend.

"I only took 10 damage from the [Ground Smash], but it's this…" he gestured to the growing red spot on his side. "I think something pierced me. I'm losing HP by the second."

Hands trembling, I lifted the punctured, bloodied shirt. Beneath was a stake-like piece of floorboard, poking out of his abdomen. Red, blood, it was blood, trickled down his stomach. I could taste vomit on the back of my tongue, but I swallowed it back down grimly.

"What… what do we do?" I asked.

No one said anything. The only sound was Axel's laboured breathing.

"Axel, what do we do?" I repeated, panicked.

He laughed again, and the stake piercing him jumped with the movement. Blood spurted out. "Now you want to listen to me, huh?"

The world started becoming blurry. "Stop fucking around! You're gonna bleed out. Tell us. What do we do?" Oh, I was crying. My nose was running, and I had started to blubber. This was embarrassing. I wiped at the tears, trying to clear my sight.

"...pull the stake out," Axel said.

In half a panic, I grabbed the edge of it, struggling to take a firm hold of the slickened wood, and then yanked. Immediately, the blood previously held back began to flow at a quickened rate, gushing out across his body. Axel screamed in pain, and he grabbed at my bloodied hands.

"I said *don't* pull the stake out, you idiot!" Axel sunk to the floor. "Oh, shit."

Party member Axel at critical health.

I could see that! He was bleeding out right in front of me. I tried to recall anything I could remember from movies or shows about how to treat a stabbing, but nothing came to mind. The only thing was... pressure? Apply pressure?

Lunging forward, I slapped one hand over the other and pushed down on Axel's wound. He didn't have enough energy to scream even though I knew it was impossible for what I'd just done to be painless.

"This is beginning to feel a little cruel," he said with a croak.

"Stop talking," I instructed, and it was suddenly more than real that my best friend was dying.

I hadn't called him that since we were just kids. Hell, I hadn't thought of him as my best friend since then. But that didn't make it not true. For a second, as I kneeled there with my hands slick with blood, us as twelve-year-olds played in my mind. Just hanging in the local park, taking turns pushing each other on the swing. Chrissie had tagged along, as she always had. Axel pouting because I was paying more attention to her. He'd always been the jealous type.

We'd been inseparable until we were thirteen. But then Chrissie... And I wasn't the same after it. Axel had been too young to properly comfort a grieving friend. Anybody would've been. It's never obvious how to act when your best friend loses their sister. He'd made one sincere attempt, but it hadn't been enough. After that he pulled away entirely. It was not the right thing to do. But I guess he never really left, not fully. If he had, he wouldn't be here dying.

I couldn't do this.

I couldn't be the reason why someone I loved was dead.

Not again.

So, I held down firmly on Axel's wound and hoped and hoped and hoped. I wasn't religious, praying would mean nothing, so I begged whatever forces of unpredictability that reigned in the universe to turn the odds in our favour. Maybe that's all religion was. Putting a face on chance.

"I'm down to 5 HP. The bleeding isn't stopping."

I focused on Axel's face. His eyes were watery. The usually healthy golden skin he had was pale, ghostly, and his lips were tinged blue; they twitched into an attempted smile. It was wrong. Axel wasn't meant to look like this. He was meant to be stirring me up, ignoring me, giving me a shit-eating grin. Not this. Anything but this.

He said, "You gotta make sure you survive this thing, okay?"

"The Dungeon?" I asked, my voice barely making its way out of my mouth.

"This whole thing. You gotta win. Promise me. No matter what, you're going to win."

I scoffed through my tears. "Only you would have the audacity to think you could win against an apocalypse."

His weak grip found my arm, and he squeezed it. "Promise me."

"I…"

If I finished that sentence, it would be goodbye, I knew. He was barely holding on. If I promised him, he would let go. But he was stubborn, too stubborn to give in before he heard my words. If I could keep him here for even a moment longer, he would never hear those words from my lips.

"2 HP," he said, and his hand on my arm slipped off.

"I'll make you a promise."

I met his fading gaze.

"I promise you'll be here with me when we win."

His eyes shot wide open for a second, and his laugh turned into a sputter. "That's new."

Breathing now weakened, his chest rose and fell almost imperceptibly. Axel's eyes began to close. I could no longer see through my tears.

"God fucking damnit, absolutely fuck this shit, this is the most fucked up thing, after I swore I wouldn't... Fuck me."

Both me and Axel's focus shifted to the sailor's language coming out of the ten-year-old girl's mouth. She had approached us both and was standing by our sides. Axel clearly wanted to make some sort of comment but lacked the bodily control to do so. It might've been for the better.

"I didn't want to do this. I don't even trust you. But I can't watch two grown men cry. It's fucking embarrassing. Goddamnit, and this was meant to be a hidden ace," Wren continued, muttering under her breath.

I heard the static of an ability being used. What was she doing? As a [Scourge], she should only work with debuffs. It didn't make any sense. Then again, she'd never explained how she'd ended up alone in Woolies. I had assumed she would in time, but maybe this was the reason why.

A soft green glow emanated from her and then focused into her right hand. What the hell was happening? There was no way an ability called [Imperil] or [Death Mark] looked like this. She glared at me.

"Move your hands."

I stared at her incredulously. "This is the only thing stopping him from dying right this second."

"Yeah, but I gotta touch the wound for this to work. He's gonna die in the next couple of moments anyway. Your choice, buckaroo."

Axel's eyes finally shut. He was directly on the brink. Jye, who'd been quiet the entire time, chimed in, "She's got a point."

"Why don't you stick to the whole mute act, man?" I spat back, already feeling bad about it as I said it.

They held their hands up and stepped away.

Wren's eyes were on me. Jesus Christ. What should I do? Did Wren have the ability to save Axel? My hands were covered with Axel's blood. Figuratively and literally. Maybe this was the universe's answer to my pleadings.

Please let that be the case.

I retracted my hands and watched as the blood flow immediately increased, no longer impeded. Wren's glowing right hand went down. A bright, warm light encompassed the skin beneath her hand, so vivid that I couldn't stare directly at it, but I forced myself to not look away. If this was Axel's last moments alive, I would be there to witness them. He deserved so much more, but this was the least I could do.

Time passed, but I lost all sense of it.

Finally, the light faded.

Wren's face was drenched in sweat, and a distant look was in her eyes. She had the kind of eye bags that resulted from days without sleep. When Wren spoke, her voice was dry, cracking. "I think the wound's been closed, but I can't use Healing Hand anymore. I'm completely out of mana. You better take care of this body. Fuckers."

And then she fell into an unconscious heap next to Axel.

VI

APPROACH

I N AN AWKWARD SILENCE, Jye had helped me as we set up a makeshift med bay for Axel and Wren. We'd barely spoken since I'd lashed out at them during the chaos. It burdened my conscience, but as we worked, I couldn't find the words to apologise or explain my reaction. It had been ugly directionless anger that had turned Jye into collateral. I'd have to address it later, unfortunately. I simply didn't have the mental bandwidth to get into it now.

When I'd examined Axel's wound, it had healed over. The scarring was ugly; jagged and raised but definitely closed. I was worried about any internal damage that he had suffered, but there'd be no way to check that. Hopefully whatever passive healing we had would fix him.

It was worrying how much empty faith I was putting in things lately.

Wren slept well. Jye and I took turns in guarding the resting part of the group. Though I doubt either of us got much sleep. The events of the past day seemed to replay in my mind without pause. Axel had almost died. I'd almost killed him. Just to save a fucking cat. Chrissie shouldn't affect me so much anymore.

Why was I so weak?

Trying to distract myself from my thoughts, I summoned the status window and poured over the different menus we could access. It seemed like every time something new happened another screen would appear. But it also appeared as though the windows reacted to our understanding of events. Maybe if I spent time studying them and thinking about everything any way I could, I'd be able to learn more. It was better than dwelling on my guilt, at the very least.

While doing this, I noticed Wren's class had changed.

She was no longer listed as a [Scourge] in our party list, but was instead a [Synergist]. It explained her ability to heal. But how had she swapped classes? Did she have some sort of trait that let her lie to the system about her class? An ability? If she did have that ability, what good would it do?

Unless… Perhaps she was anticipating future opponents who would read one's status windows? It wasn't too far-fetched, especially in RPGs. Was Wren truly thinking that far ahead? It wouldn't have been surprising from Axel, since he seemed so switched on, but from a young girl… She had to be hiding more than just her ability to supposedly change classes. Especially with the sudden change in her vernacular.

The system we all were supposedly in seemed less than perfect. Jye's stats were bugged, and Wren might have access to two classes. If this was just two out of the four of us, that meant it was possible 50 percent of humanity on Earth had just as messed-up statuses. I could imagine the Steam reviews now. *Overwhelming negative. "One of my friends loaded in and couldn't read their own status screen!" "Completely unbalanced character creation randomizer." "No tutorial. No explanation for how to even win the game." "0/10."* IGN would probably still have given it four stars.

"Your sister is gone, huh?" Jye said.

The voice startled me since I'd thought they'd been asleep. It was my turn on watch, to check on Wren and Axel as they recovered. But sleeping right now felt impossible for me, and it must've been the case for Jye too. We were in a strange place with strange people doing strange things. There was no way sleep would easily come.

"Yeah. Her name was Chris." I smiled, remembering her cute scowl. "She hated that it was so boyish. Demanded we call her Chrissie."

They rolled to their side, propping their head up on a bent arm. "Did she… pass away when the Gates appeared?"

I shook my head. "No, it was ages ago now. She was about the same age as Wren, actually." I paused, ready to defend myself against an attack on my lapse of judgement, but it seemed none was forthcoming. Still feeling a need to justify my actions, I said, "It's not the only reason I asked Wren to join our party, but it's a big one."

Jye was silent as they took it in. Usually, Jye was pretty easy to read, wearing their heart on their sleeve even if they didn't speak that much. Had I met them in my day-to-day life, I probably would've classified them as the golden retriever type. Head empty but positive vibes and energy. That's if you weren't Axel, at least.

"I had five siblings. Three brothers, two sisters. About a year difference between each one of us," they said, green eyes unfocused.

"Had?"

"Like I said, I'm no contact with my family. I have no idea what they're doing, and they have no idea what I'm doing. It's better that way." They sighed, deep and long. Their expression was complicated, too many different emotions layered onto each other. "If for a moment I thought any one of them cared about me the same way you do about your sister, I probably would've stayed. Even despite everything."

This was more I'd heard from Jye talk about themself the entire time I'd known them. It helped me stop thinking about Axel's shallow breathing and Wren's unconscious body, both of which were my fault. "You moved out pretty young then?"

Jye's top lip curled. "Wasn't really a choice. My parents didn't really understand who I was. Were scared about what I was. But that's life, you know? Sometimes you win, and sometimes you lose."

I was silent for a moment, letting the thoughts settle. In this day and age, how did people have kids and then treat them so poorly? It shocked and appalled me.

"They kicked you out?"

They sat up, and pulled their knees in close, hugging them to their chest. Jye's voice was muffled through their legs. "Sometimes they pretended I wasn't there at all. Sometimes everything bad was my fault, and I'd get punished. I could deal with all that, but I think the worst was when they acted like I was a stranger, like I'd killed their kid and replaced them."

Jesus Christ. Jesus fucking Christ. The worst I was expecting was their parents abandoning them. But this... This was just child endangerment. Child abuse. Call it what you want, it was wrong. Why hadn't anyone reported their parents? When Axel had come out, our parents had thrown him a party, where unbeknownst to them Axel had lost his V plates. The stark contrast between the parenting styles was enough to give me whiplash.

"I'm sorry. No one deserves to be treated like that."

"I know. Well, I know that now. It took a while to get there, but I know who I am, and I know there's nothing wrong with that." They hesitated and closed their eyes. "But sometimes I think about them, you know?"

"Your parents?"

"My siblings. We were close once. When I was forced out, they avoided me, played monkey see, monkey do with my parents." They breathed in and opened their eyes, staring into my soul. "Do you think they cared about me at all? Because I left them all there, and I never looked back."

How did someone answer a question like this? What was I doing in a Dungeon with a person I'd met less than a week ago baring their soul to me? And why me of all people?

Still, I considered their words, trying to find what I wanted to say. Like me, Jye had lost loved ones, even though the situation was completely different. A part of me had been stuck there, always, wondering if I'd done anything differently if things would've changed. If things would be different now. If Chrissie would be alive.

"Jye… That you're asking me this means you have looked back." Their mouth opened, like they wanted to interrupt, but I waved them away. "In fact, what you actually want to ask isn't if they cared about you, is it?"

They snorted. "Look at you, acting like some sort of therapist."

I ignored their provocation.

"You want to ask if it's okay for you to still love them. Despite everything."

A long silence fell between us.

I wondered if they had decided to stop talking to me.

Jye's voice was small, so small compared to how large they'd trained to be. "Is it?"

"You can't stop yourself from caring about someone," I said. I'd spent enough time trying to move on myself. "Your love for them does fade with time and distance, but it's still always there somewhere."

Jye loosened their grip on their legs and leaned back to hear what I said next.

"Your brothers and sisters didn't protect you, didn't support you, didn't help you. There's no denying that." For a second, I thought about Axel but refocused. "But you were kids. I'm sure, as much as they could, they worried about you too. So, you've every right to care about them. Your parents, though…"

"Nah, fuck my parents. I'll never forgive them. I hope they died when the Gates appeared, but I'm not that lucky."

That Jye was back to the usual self made me feel a little better. When they didn't ask another question, I turned to check on them but saw their eyes were closed, and their breathing had slowed. Probably emotional exhaustion. Or just plain exhaustion. The past day had been stressful, and that was putting it lightly.

"You look like hell," said a smug voice to my right.

"You should see the other guy."

"Got a mirror I could borrow for that?" Axel said, grimacing to sit up.

Using just a minor bit of force, I pushed down onto his shoulder. He struggled for a second before thumping limply back onto the bedroll beneath him. Axel was scowling at my hand. I gave him a look that said, "Don't be an idiot."

Out loud, I asked, "How's your HP?"

"About half way back now. You can probably let me sit up."

I pressed down harder on his shoulder. That was good. It meant he was regenerating at a reasonable rate, similar to when Jye had broken their leg during the party's gym practice. A huge weight lifted from my shoulders. Knowing that Axel would be okay, that I wouldn't be the reason he'd died. Suddenly I could breathe freely.

Axel's tone was neutral. "Did you mean that promise?"

With a scoff, I replied, "Pretty sure I'd have said anything."

"Anything, huh?" He sounded hurt.

Clearing my throat, I lessened the force with which I was pinning him down. "But I did. Mean it, that is. I think."

Axel's eyes grew wide. It was one of the first times that I'd seen him look surprised since the Gates had activated. The expression was comical on him. His mouth was slightly ajar, blond brows high. It gave me a thrill to know that even after all this time I could still shock him. Especially with how he had called me predictable. This would show him.

"If this is the end of the world, all I have left is family and friends. Out of everyone, I guess you're practically both. What'd be the point of winning without you?"

I was surprised by his reaction. He started laughing, low and quiet at first, but then it built into full body shaking, tears forming in the corners of his eyes. Oh, yeah, that wasn't concerning at all. I filed the response into the "Worrisome Axel Behaviour" slot in my mind and let him continue until he tired himself out again. The laughter died down into gentle snoring.

Sooner or later, we'd have to talk about why he was acting so crazy. He'd been hiding something since our classes had been granted. And lying every now and again. Axel was deeply affected by something, so much that it was causing these insane mood swings and completely unjustifiable behaviour.

Before the Gates, he would have never even considered hurting a cat. They were his and Chrissie's favourite animal, even once taking home a stray that had still lived with Axel's parents until several years ago. My sister had named him Scribble, after how he'd been scratching and playing in the dirt like he was doodling.

Meow.

It was like I could hear Scribble now. The vets had called him the healthiest tom they'd ever seen. It wasn't a surprise he lived for so long. He'd passed at the guessed age of eighteen, close to the longest the animals could healthily achieve. I always thought he lived that long for Chrissie, living out his whole life for her. It was a silly thought, but whenever I'd visit Charleville and see Scribble it made it more bearable.

"Meow."

There was Scribble again. Wait. Scribble didn't meow. His mewling was closer to a squawk. As he'd lived on the street for the first few years, he hadn't learned how to meow for humans. Slowly, Uncle Seb and Auntie Li had taught him through mimicry, but even then, it was never a proper meow. This sound I was hearing…

In the corner of my eye, I saw the movement of the calico bobtail. It was back! That it had returned when everyone else was asleep was fortuitous, especially with how trigger happy they'd been before. I was not about to try and fight the party to keep the cat safe again, not with how everything had turned out last time. With as little sound as possible, I stood from the wall I was leaning against and approached the cat.

Leaning down, I turned my back to the feline. It was Cat Behaviour

101. Don't face it, because that would be seen as aggression. Presenting your back showed you weren't trying to dominate it. Out of the three of us, I was the only one who'd needed to learn these tactics. The felines had been naturally drawn to Axel and Chrissie.

"Are you lost, little guy? How'd you end up in the Dungeon?"

The paws stepped closer until the cat was right behind me. I tried to peek at it from my peripheral vision but only caught a glimpse. Then I felt the soft fur brush up against me, the warmth of its small body. I had always wanted to get a cat for Axel's and my apartment. My parents had been allergic to cat dander, so I wasn't allowed one as a kid.

Lifting a hand, I tried to pet it, but it darted away, strutting in front of me.

"Don't like pats?" I asked.

It flopped onto its back and trilled at me. What a sweet little kitten! But the stomach presentation was one 100 percent a trap. If I tried to touch the tempting belly, it would rabbit kick my hands to shreds and tear into my skin with its claws and fangs. I'd fallen for the trick too many times to count. But the behaviour was definitely basic cat. There was nothing off about it, except maybe its willingness to reapproach us after what happened.

It was probably just desperate.

Grabbing some of the protein+ plain jerky from my backpack, I shredded it and put some out for the cat. It was too salty for normal cat food, but, as a rare snack, it would be fine. No sooner did I put it down did the cat snatch it up. Without even chewing it, she gobbled it down. The poor thing was starving.

I rummaged further through our inventory, searching in Wren's bag too since she had quite the stock from Woolies, and found some spam. Again, it was high in sodium, but since cats got most of their hydration from food, it would be better for her.

I peeled open the can and scooped out some onto the removed lid. She wolfed it down.

"Damn, you can eat, huh? Well, that's all I can give you right now. I can feed you at this time each sleep, but you gotta make sure the others don't see you. They think you're a danger to us. But you're just a cat, aren't you?"

She didn't respond, just licked the can lid, green eyes pleading for another serving.

"No more. Now scram before they wake up."

I reached out to pet her, but she ran, this time disappearing into the shadows. Well, this was going to be a problem for future me. I had almost killed my best friend to save a cat and was now secretly feeding it behind everyone's back. Was this a type of betrayal? Did this make a bad person?

My brain hurt.

DUNGEON
HUNTER

VII

WHAT NEXT?

THE REST OF MY WATCH passed without comment, and I woke Jye for their turn. As soon as I closed my eyes, I was unconscious. That slumber was exhausting and filled with dreams of people I loved dying without me being able to do anything. Again and again, I watched as my beloveds breathed their last breaths while I sat by their side, simply witnessing it, eyes blank and empty.

When Jye shook me awake, I felt more tired than I had before sleeping, but it looked like my stamina had regenned to almost full. That was good at least. It seemed to restore faster with rest. That made sense. Axel's injuries recovered faster when sleeping as well. Now we just needed to master the act of actually falling asleep. It was something I was bad at even before all the Gates appeared.

Wren was already awake and was chewing idly on some jerky.

"So. I guess I should explain," she began as everyone gathered around.

She passed the packet to me, and I took a handful before giving it to Jye.

"That would be nice," Axel oozed.

Rolling her eyes, she said, "By now you guys have guessed that I'm not just a Scourge."

We all nodded. She had healed Axel, which definitely wasn't a debuff.

"And that I'm also a Synergist."

Again, we nodded. This much we all knew from the party information accessible via the status window. I'd mentioned it to Jye and Axel in passing while Wren had still been unconscious. Axel hadn't seemed surprised. Jye had seemed delighted that there was another glitch character like them.

Wren cleared her throat. "All right, well. How to explain... I can swap between the two classes. I was originally a Synergist, but..." Her hazel eyes darkened.

"But?" I prompted, intrigued.

"But everything was so confusing when it started. I felt such a strong need to enter the CBD Gate. I didn't even think about it. I crawled out of my bed and rushed into it. There were a bunch of people in it already that I ran into. Maybe seven of us?"

I guess I hadn't been wrong when I thought she'd been through the gauntlet. However, this was far more complex than I'd been imagining. I thought maybe she'd gotten separated from her parents in the Gate and then gotten lost. This was so much worse. Jye's eyes were wide as they listened, but Axel had crossed his arms over his chest. There was a sceptic tone to his stance. Axel didn't believe her? Why? What would she gain from lying to us?

Wren shivered. "It was like the arctic in that Dungeon, and none of us were prepared. But it wasn't like this one. The entrance was still there, the same Gate but inside the Dungeon. We could've all left. We could've all lived."

"What do you mean?" Axel asked sharply.

Her eyes shot over to him, lips quivering. "No one wanted to leave except me. They..." She took a deep breath, "They demanded to know my class and abilities and threatened to hurt me. I didn't know what else to do."

Understanding of the situation was beginning to dawn on me.

"They made you join their party?"

She nodded softly, and her voice broke as she continued, "I told them everything I could see on my screen. We went farther into the Dungeon. Eventually, we got into a fight with some sort of monster. It was big and furry, with sharp teeth. People got hurt. They screamed at me to help them. When I couldn't heal them quick enough, they…"

It didn't need to be said.

"Then what?" Jye asked, laying a comforting hand on her shoulder.

"The remaining party members blamed me. Said I was the reason everyone had died. I did my best!" She was crying now, sobbing. Snot trickled out of her nose over her blubbering mouth.

Jye pulled her into a hug, letting her tears absorb into their shoulder.

In between gasps of air, she continued, "They left me there. In the middle of the Dungeon, as they went farther in. They kicked me out of the party. I tried to track my way back to the Gate, but it was all white, the sky was white, the floor was white. My footsteps in the snow disappeared as I moved forward. And it was cold."

She was shaking now in Jye's embrace. "I couldn't feel my fingers, and I knew that was bad. So I tried to use Healing Hand on myself. But I was low on mana. It drained me, like it did when I used it on Axel. I blacked out."

All of us remained silent, waiting for her to finish.

"When I woke up, I was outside the Woolworths you found me in, and my class had switched to Scourge. I have a trait that appeared then. It's called Mercurial. It lets me switch between the classes."

That meant someone had to have helped her. But it sounded like her party had abandoned her. Maybe another person had come across her, but hadn't wanted to take on the responsibility of her proper, and yet still couldn't leave a child to die. It wasn't beyond the scope of reasonability. I mean, we had picked her up, and she hadn't even been in that dire of a circumstance. The possibility of other Samaritans wasn't that low. Although I guess leaving her alone without protection while she was still unconscious downgraded them to something closer to an antihero than a do-gooder. Still, I silently thanked them for helping her, whoever they were.

Axel pursed his lips in thought. "That's why you wanted to know if we were going into the CBD Gate?"

"I was trying to think of a way to stop you going in."

He didn't look convinced, but Axel was like that. Despite his social butterfly tendencies, he still believed the worst of everyone. Maybe it was because of them, actually. He knew a lot of different people and lived between rumour and gossip. But a child was not the same as the type of people he hung out with. Besides, what did a ten-year-old girl gain from lying to us about herself? Even if she wasn't telling us the full truth, stepping up to take care of a kid is what any decent adult should do.

"You could've told us," Jye said, pulling back from her.

"You might've been just like them," she said.

"You're right." The words I wish someone had told me when I was young suddenly found themselves pouring from my mouth. "You were right to distrust us." The words would've protected Chrissie. "Sometimes adults can't be trusted." God, I wish someone had sat me down properly and set me straight. "Sometimes adults are bad." I smiled at her, as kindly as I could. "But thank you for telling us now. And thank you for saving Axel. You didn't have to."

Axel cleared his throat. Not meeting her eyes, he said, "Yeah, thanks for that."

She laughed through her tears. "You're the first ones to thank me for using my abilities."

"It won't be the last time we'll be thanking you either," Axel replied.

He wasn't wrong. A healer in our party was crazy beneficial, especially when we still didn't have a tank to take on damage. I reflected on the current party composition. It was still incredibly unbalanced in regards to ranged positions. Axel did frontline damage and had some crowd control, Jye did backline damage, Wren's abilities varied from buffs on contact to debuffs at a distance, and I could only barely use anyone else's skills without levelling up.

"Your old party was shit and that's not on you," Jye said.

"Right. You did what you could. And I'm sorry I forced you into a situation where you had to reveal your second class," I continued, the guilt of Axel's injury still incredibly fresh in my mind.

"It just sped up the sharing," Wren admitted. "I was going to wait until we got out of this Dungeon, and if nothing had happened like the CBD Dungeon, I was going to tell you all."

I nodded. It was a smart plan, though incredibly optimistic. Sussing us out, making sure we could be trusted. Good instincts for such a young kid. Chrissie had always been too trusting because there had been no need for caution in our small hometown of Charleville. Stupid. I'd been so stupid.

"Not to sound like an ass and change the direction of this heartwarming moment full of thank-yous and sorrys, but we all got experience from that fight, right?" Axel said.

There was a murmur of agreement from the rest of the group.

Thinking of it brought the screen up. "The notification said our whole party got 5 XP."

Jye's brows furrowed. "Oh, we got XP?"

"Yeah… I need to hit 250 to reach my next level."

"That seems a little steep," they replied, probably thinking about their own levelling requirements.

I shrugged. "I don't make the rules. I honestly don't really know who does."

Wren, her eyes now dried of tears, was frowning in very clear confusion. I shot her an inquiring look, and she clamped her mouth closed, lips forming a thin straight line. Right, that wasn't normal.

"What's wrong?"

She hesitated before confessing, "I don't think I got any experience from the fight."

"But the notification said our whole party got some," Axel said, suspicion colouring his tone once again.

God, why did he think this little girl was lying to us so much? I knew he expected the worst of others, but this was too much. Repressing my desire to berate him, I instead pulled up the party screen. Wren was still part of the group, listed below Jye's mess of a status. Her [Synergist] class hadn't changed since she'd gained consciousness, which meant that her [Mercurial] trait was something she had to activate.

"Wait, you swapped to Synergist after we received the notification, right?" I asked.

She nodded once, the earnest expression on her young face oddly comical. The others all seemed interested in my next words, even Axel who rarely believed others knew more than him.

I lifted my pointing finger in the air. "Maybe your experience went to your Scourge class."

The repercussions of what I suggested rippled over her face. Her expression went from consideration to dismay, which was a fair reaction. It would be a crippling disadvantage if I was right. If Wren could only level up as per the current class she had active, it meant she'd essentially grow at half the speed of everyone on our team, should she continue to switch back and forth. Well, that was assuming Jye levelled up normally. At least with Wren we could prove this theory.

"Can you switch back to Scourge to check?" Axel asked.

Looking upset, she shook her head. "There's a cooldown."

"For how long?"

Her eyes focused on what I assumed was her personal window.

"It's a twenty-four-hour cooldown, so I've got another sixteen hours until I can change back."

I sighed. "Well, I guess there's nothing we can do until then. What about you, Jye? Can you make anything out on your screen?"

They chuckled and then flatly said, "No."

That figured.

I pinched the bridge of my nose and took a deep breath.

"Well, if everyone's rested, should we just... head out? I like this haunted cabin as much as the next person, but if we want to complete the Dungeon, we should probably get started."

"I guess?" Jye said, a lack of conviction in both the tone of their voice and the way they idly poked at a piece of wood debris.

Axel rolled his eyes. "It's not like we really have any other option."

"I'm ready!" Wren said, pumping a fist into the air.

Kids could really bounce back from anything. I was worried we'd stirred up some traumatic memories for her, but she didn't seem that badly affected. That said, I think I'd keep an eye on her. When Chrissie had... After Chrissie, I'd probably seemed fine within the year. But I had definitely not been. I still wasn't, if I was being honest. Though Wren seemed more emotionally mature than I had been back then. Maybe she was just built different.

Jye ran their fingers through their hair, which I realised they did when they were nervous. I'd only known them for a week, so I still wasn't super sure how to comfort them. Even after our heart-to-heart about siblings.

I decided to change the subject. "Actually, can you use your ability on all our bags?"

Axel scoffed. "You want to add weight training to our Dungeon quest?"

"No, Jye figured out they can lighten the weight of things too."

"Huh, no shit," Axel replied.

"Yes, shit," Jye said back and strode over to the packs.

After several static hisses, they turned back around with a thumbs-up. "All done."

Jye experimentally pulled on the strap of one of the bags and watching it lift was uncanny. It reminded me of poor animation where the weight of items hadn't been drawn in properly, with characters picking up nothing but air. It was like poor CGI augmented into a live action film. It was just wrong.

In silence, we all went over and grabbed our remaining backpacks. It truly did feel lighter than a feather, and I could barely sense its presence when I pulled it over my shoulders, and it added little to no pressure to my back. If I wasn't careful, I would probably forget I was wearing it and get snagged on something.

Axel let out a huff as he struggled to lift his bag. He cast an accusing glare at Jye.

A wide grin distorted the lumberjack's face. "Oh, did I accidentally make yours heavier? Silly me."

I'd forgotten the level of animosity that Jye held toward Axel. Clearly, his first impression had left quite a mark on the gym junkie. The blond's constant suspicion toward Wren was also not painting him in the best light for Jye either.

I couldn't resist smiling as, with a grunt, Axel heaved the backpack over his shoulders, and it let out a solid thud upon making impact with his back. He said nothing and began walking to the front door. I guess he was taking his lumps this time. Unusual for Axel to suffer in silence. Ah, well. Another thing to add to the "Axel Weirdness" mind prison.

It occurred to me as we approached the cabin's front door that we'd been in the Dungeon for quite a while now, but no one else had appeared, except for the cat, which probably didn't count. Did that mean no one other than us had entered this Dungeon? It seemed unlikely considering the Dungeon compulsion. So, it either meant that the Dungeon wasn't letting anyone else in, their entry points were different to ours, or there were different instances of the Dungeon.

It'd be nice if it were the first, though somehow the last seemed more likely. If the point of this game was for people to enter the Dungeons, then limiting the amount of people who could enter would be a stupid move. Then again, who knew by what logic this system truly operated by? Some part of me was always trying to find reason behind it, when possibly there wasn't any to be found.

Axel's hand curled over the door's handle. "Are we ready?"

Jye sighed. "Ready as I'll ever be."

"Good to go," Wren said.

Axel's gaze lingered over me, and an entirely different emotion flickered over his face for a moment. I wondered if I was seeing things. For just a second, there was hurt weighing down the blue of his eyes. Again, guilt coiled in my stomach. I thought he'd been fine with what I'd done. That he'd understood. We'd joked about it. But I guess I hadn't apologised…

The expression was gone immediately, replaced with one of his shitty smiles. "You good?"

"Are you?" I asked.

Axel's eyes widened ever so slightly, his thick lashes brushing against his eyelids, and his smile slipped a few millimetres. Oh, that seemed like a clear no. But then he laughed, and the smile was back. Jesus fucking Christ, he had to be some kind of sociopath. I couldn't follow this rollercoaster that was Axel's inner emotional turmoil. At the very least, it didn't seem like this was due to how my actions today had hurt him. This was related to the whole shift of him that he hadn't explained. Surely he knew I'd noticed how unhinged he was being?

"Not that I'm losing my nerve the longer we wait, but are you guys done with whatever this is?" Jye asked.

"Let's go," I said.

Axel's hand twisted the handle, and he pulled the door open.

DUNGEON
HUNTER

VIII

CONFRONTATION

"WELL, THIS ISN'T WHAT I EXPECTED," Jye said.

Leave it to the giant to make such a grand understatement.

Axel had opened the door to reveal endless dunes of golden sand, the heavy rays of sun momentarily blinding me as it filled my gaze. Immediately, the scorching heat of the desert stretching out in front of us caused sweat to begin beading on my skin. It had to be at least forty degrees outside the cabin. On the plus side, it was a dry heat. Mugginess was something that was barely tolerable at the best of times, but at such high temperatures, it could actually boil you alive. At least that's what one documentary I'd watched one time had said.

"We're... in a desert?" Wren asked, her voice small and full of wonder.

"Looks like it."

The door clicked shut behind us. I glanced back at the cabin and then at the desert in front. Neither of the two locations seemed linked. It was almost like someone had plucked a model of a haunted cabin from the Unity marketplace and placed it half-heartedly into a desert biome. Hell, the lighting inside and out didn't even match. Truly not a masterful creation. Whatever or whoever had designed this Dungeon did not have much of an imagination.

Jye threw their hands up in the air. "Where the fuck are we meant to go?"

It was a good question. As far as the eye could see, there wasn't anything on the horizon. Only countless dunes and endless sand. Nothing stood out. In fact, the longer I looked, the more it all blended into one seamless smear of golden yellow. Yikes.

"Maybe the cabin *was* the destination?" I said.

Even I wasn't fully convinced by the words coming out of my mouth. But since it looked like the only thing in the whole map, it seemed like the only reasonable thought. What else was there?

Request received.

Jye swore, their hands slapping around their ears. "Shit, I hate it when it does that."

A new screen popped up, this time not the normal blue but an off-white. Perhaps it was the colour for Dungeon-based notifications.

Spend five nights in the desert without returning to the cabin.
Reward: 1,000 XP
Failure: Death
Accept | Reject

"A thousand?!" I exclaimed.

That'd shoot me past LVL 1, maybe even LVL 2. It'd answer my further questions about what happens when we level up. However, the failure penalty was extreme. I assumed it meant we'd all die. Surely spending five nights in the desert was possible? I'd seen my fair share of *Naked and Afraid*. It wouldn't be a fantastic experience, but we'd be able to do it.

"Reject it," Axel said.

I frowned. "Hey, wait a second, let's talk this out."

Letting out an exasperated groan, Jye pleaded, "Please, for the love of God, someone explain what's happening. What was the notification?" I told them, and they snorted. "Accept it, of course. I used to go extreme camping with my family. Surviving off the wilderness and all that. I can carry you all easily. Hell, we could do ten days if we needed."

"Could Wren?" I asked.

Letting a kid stay in the desert for five nights sounded like the beginnings of a call to child protection services. I glanced over to check Wren's expression. As much as I didn't want Wren to feel like she was keeping our party back, I also wanted her to be aware of her personal limits. She seemed to be deep in thought. That was probably the best kind of reaction I could hope for.

Jye scoffed. "Of course Wren too."

"Even if Wren could take five nights in the desert, we're still rejecting it," Axel commented.

"Five nights does sound kind of doable," I reasoned.

With Jye's skill in survival camping, perhaps we could do it. That's if they weren't lying. I don't think Jye had ever lied yet, so that was promising.

"I think I should be fine," Wren added.

"Reject it," Axel said.

"Why do you keep saying that?"

Axel crossed his arms. "Just think about it, just for a second. This whole thing is shifty. The notification wasn't the normal notification, it was something else. And a thousand experience points is a ridiculous amount. We got *five* from a failed fight that almost killed me."

"To be fair, we were fighting a cat," Jye interjected. "And it fled. And it was Lee who hurt you."

Ignoring them, Axel continued, "And it's the first time we've been given a 'request.' Nothing else has ever been asked of us. Us entering this Dungeon was a planted urge, but it was never a request. Whatever that notification is, I don't think it's from the base system or has anything to do with clearing it. This is something else."

The worst thing about what Axel was saying was that it made sense. How awful.

He raised his eyebrows. "Besides, compare the worst thing that happens if we reject it and the worst thing that happens if we accept it and fail."

Axel would be insufferable in ghost form if he turned out to be right. I just know he'd haunt me, even if I died with him. Not to mention, avoiding potential death when possible was almost always the better option.

"He's got a point," I groaned.

Jye shrugged, their enormous traps bunching up and then loosening. Seemingly still lost in thought, Wren hadn't further added anything to the conversation.

"Wren?" I asked. "This is a full party decision. What do you think?"

Her hazel eyes darkened, and her lips pressed into a thin line. "Dungeons are dangerous. We should be cautious about everything."

"Wise beyond your years," Axel commented with a hint of sarcasm.

She really was. At around her age, I think I had been obsessed with Lego. Muttering under my breath about how he better not lord this over me, I selected the Reject option. As if rubbing salt in a wound, it checked for confirmation, which I promptly selected, and then the pop-up faded away. I mourned the loss of a reasonably easy way to achieve level ups. That had probably been our only chance.

Sourly, I said, "There, are you happy? I rejected it."

Gift received.

This time Jye let out a little cry of pain. They closed their eyes, and they breathed in deeply. There had to be something we could do for Jye later that stopped the notifications from hurting them so much. But it was just another thing to add to the growing list. And, God, there was a lot of stuff on it. Though, really, the top of the list should probably be talking to Axel. But it'd been impossible to get a solid, sane moment alone with him with everything that had happened.

Instead, I tried thinking of the gift. In the default blue screen, a small icon of a gift box with a little bow on top appeared. It flashed and wiggled around a few times in an excited fashion. I was surprised to see that underneath it, there were two options.

Open | Sell

Part of me desperately wanted to try and sell the present to see what that even involved. Was there a player accessible marketplace? What was the currency? What could we buy? Who was selling things? Was it the system? Other players? Rubbing at my temple, I ignored the sell option, especially considering we'd received the gift directly after rejecting a request. Why had we been rewarded for *not* doing something? And who had rewarded us?

"Uh, everyone else get the same notification?"

Jye stared at me blankly.

Wren frowned. "We got a gift."

"See what I'm talking about. You gotta trust me with these things. My choices are always best," Axel said with shit-eating grin.

"I'll just open it, then. Maybe we can sell whatever is inside it."

"We can sell things?" Jye asked, their eyes focusing just in front of themselves. With a defeated sigh, they made a dismissive gesture and returned their attention to me. I doubted their screen had changed. I was momentarily appreciative of my own status window. While my class was relatively plain, at least I could *use* mine. A brief cloud of guilt drifted through me, berating me for celebrating someone else's misfortune.

I announced to the others that I was opening the gift. With a rather delightful animation, the gift icon did a spin before bursting into little orbs of light, revealing an image and text beneath it.

Anonymous says: Smart choice.

The image was rendered in almost lifelike detail, like I could reach into the screen and touch the three-dimensional curves and angles. It was a graphic of a sword, not a traditional one but something straight out of *Dark Souls*, with jagged ridges and edgelord aesthetic. I held back the cringe. The other person in our party who would even find this weapon appropriate was—

"Claimsies!" said Axel, reaching forward.

As his fingers closed, the sword materialised into his hand with a blinding shimmer. Oh, so you could grab them from the screen. I guess it made sense. How else were you meant to receive the gift? The *Hunger Games* drone drop seemed like far more effort when I thought about it.

Though now, of course, I had more questions. Had the weapon been stored somewhere else and then teleported through the system? Was the sword just data and were we right now just zeroes and ones in a game? I repressed a sigh and took in the sight of Axel swinging his new sword around. He seemed rather pleased.

"Does it have stats or bonuses or anything?" I asked.

Axel focused in front of himself and then nodded at me, "Yeah. It increases the dexterity of the wielder."

So we had dexterity stats. I brought up my own menu and tried to think hard about strength, dexterity, and other attributes that I knew were common in RPGs. Nothing new appeared. Either they were locked until they were triggered or players couldn't access them. It just seemed incredibly stupid to not let us see our own stats. How were we meant to level up without knowing what was an appropriate challenge? Oh, well, it wasn't something I needed to worry about right now.

"There was a message from one Anonymous attached to the gift. They said, 'Smart choice,'" I explained to Jye as Axel continued to whip his new sword around. His movements seem oddly practised, but before he'd fallen in with the popular crowd, Axel had briefly been very into backyard cosplaying swordsmen. Given enough time copying someone, and you'd be good at appearing to do the same thing as them.

"A sponsor? Like that message we got when the first Dungeon was cleared?" Wren said.

I shrugged. "I guess."

Jye sighed deeply. "I must've missed that too. So, like Nike or Adidas sent us that sword?"

"I don't think it's got anything to do with humans or human corporations," I said.

"Aliens?" Wren asked, eyes sparkling with interest.

"I'm not ruling it out. This entire thing is clearly out of the technological reach of anything we're capable of as a species, right. So, it's either aliens, us from the future like in *Interstelllar*, or…" I paused because it seemed like the most ridiculous of all possibilities that my agnostic brain could imagine. "Or like super powerful beings beyond our imagination. Something like gods."

Clang. The sword had slipped from Axel's hand and clattered to the wooden floor. Unperturbed, he picked it up with an embarrassed smile. "Gotta practise a little more to get the hang of it." He went right back to it. Part of me wanted to confiscate the weapon, but I ignored that petty side of myself.

"I hope it's aliens," Wren said with a smile. "I think aliens would be really cool."

"With the way capitalism is headed, I wouldn't be surprised if this was us from the future. Just think about it. If you subscribe to the idea that every choice made creates a branching off timeline, then future humans coming back to this singular one and messing stuff up means that nothing changes for them. They use our struggle as entertainment, to stream back to future people, and make profit off it. Hell, they probably bet on us as well."

I stared at Jye in concern. "That's pretty fucked up."

"Everything about this is."

"What do you think, Axel?"

He splayed his hand out, and the sword dematerialised. At this point, I had to just accept that Axel had been dreaming of living in a game for most of his life. How else would he even think to do that? Actually, that reminded me that I had left my wooden staff inside, leaning against the wall. I should probably pick it up before I forget it permanently.

Axel made a noncommittal noise and rubbed at his chin. "What's the point in thinking about it? Will it do us any good? We're stuck inside a Dungeon without knowing what to do, so it'd be a better use of your brains to think about a way to clear this place."

The rest of us must've shared the same disgusted look because Axel then scoffed and said, "Fine then, I'll say I think it's all three. Super powerful aliens from the future. You happy?"

I scowled at him. "That's such a fake out."

"God forbid I do anything," Axel said.

Jye dryly commented, "I wish She would."

Stopping myself from inquiring further into Jye's response, which I'll admit had piqued my interest, I moved toward the door to reenter and grab my wooden staff. As my hand gripped the handle, I heard the distinct static of an ability fizzle in my ears.

I stepped away slowly, trying to ensure that I made no noise. Either noticing my change in behaviour or hearing the ability activation, the others were on alert now too, eyes darting around. Axel summoned his sword, and Jye and Wren each pulled a knife from their backpacks.

I whispered, "None of you used a skill, right?"

I was met with several shakes of heads. Great. That meant someone else was here. It almost meant my idea of separate instances of Dungeons was out the window. And that meant we were in more danger than I thought since anyone else could be in here with us. I just wished I could tell where the ability had been used from.

"What do we do, boss?" Axel quietly mocked, an eyebrow cocked.

Like he'd listen to me anyway. Regardless, I replied, "We stand our ground. If they're inside, they're trapped there. If they're outside, this is a strong defensive position."

You really can just make up anything and make it sound like you're talking sense. For a moment, I wondered if this is how politicians felt. Stringing together words in any order and believing people would accept them as gospel.

"Sounds like bullshit, but okay," Jye said.

Yeah, that checked out.

We all stood there, tense, and stressed, waiting for our potential opponent to reveal themselves but hours passed. The sun didn't seem to move in the sky and shadows did not shift. Still, we remained there, poised, ready to defend ourselves. I began to worry I'd made the wrong call in standing firm. Maybe we should've been proactive. Investigated the cabin again.

We waited a few more hours.

Nothing.

Well, in for a penny in for a pound.

"What now, boss?" Jye asked.

I sighed. "We take shifts. If there's someone here, they can't hide forever. Who wants to take first watch?"

We figured out the shift order, some of us sharing so Wren would not be forced to take a shift alone, and for that "night," we settled into a routine of sleeping, watching, eating, sleeping, watching, eating.

During this time, I learned from Jye that the main subject of their tattoo sleeve was an ouroboros, and that they also didn't know what it meant, just the idea of a snake eating itself was, in their words, "so messed up, I had to get it." They also pointed out several other of their tattoos, a collection of anime-related pieces, ranging from Totoro to Gon's forced adult form midtransformation. I expressed my appreciation of them, and Jye told me they knew a guy if I wanted a decent price. Not wanting to remind them that their tattooist might already be dead, I instead just thanked Jye and said I'd consider it.

These watch shifts also gave me a much needed chance to finally talk to Axel alone. But when it was just him and me, with Wren and Jye snoring softly nearby, I realised I didn't know how to word what I wanted to say. In fact, as the silence stretched out between us, it became more and more difficult to figure it out. Something told me that just starting off with "Hey, man, you're acting really different lately, and could you tell me why you lied to me?" would not end well.

"I'm sorry, you know," Axel said, his voice low to not wake the others.

I blinked. "What?"

"I shouldn't have attacked that cat."

Scoffing, I replied, "This is the second time you've ever apologised to me."

"I've apologised more than twice."

With a confused frown, I ran through every possible memory I had where an apology would be necessary from him, but only found the one right after Dungeons activated, and his words just now. He was trying to outright gaslight me. I turned to face him, my tone flat, "No, this is the second time."

He smiled, that same smile that I didn't understand, and said, "It's not."

A rage filled me, partly fuelled by fear of the unknown that existed in Axel's expression. "Stop that."

"Stop what?"

Frustrated, I breathed out. "You've become someone I don't know and I hate it."

Axel was silent.

I couldn't meet his eyes because I hadn't realised that's how I felt until I said it. The Axel I'd come to know, the flatmate I'd had for several years, it was like he was transformed into something I didn't recognise anymore. What remained of him was not really Axel, not the Axel who'd ditch me when convenient. Perhaps the thing that made me feel even more nauseous was that what I hated wasn't the current Axel, it was that I preferred him. I liked Axel more now. It was like admitting that you liked a changeling over your original child, a clone over the original.

It made me feel sick.

I didn't hate this Axel. I hated myself for betraying the Axel of the past.

"I didn't realise you felt that way."

Fuck. Despite the fact this wasn't the same Axel, I knew that tone in his voice. He was fighting back hurt. What had I done? And still, I couldn't meet his gaze. This wasn't how this conversation was meant to go. I was supposed to casually bring up how he'd been acting different. How I'd like to know what caused it. Not this. I could still save this. Let him know I just wanted him to open up to me about this situation. I could still bring this sinking ship into harbour.

Taking a deep breath to steady myself, I said, "What I mean is that I just wish you'd be honest with me."

This elicited a peal of laughter from Axel that was so unhinged I was worried he'd become possessed by something. When he finally stopped, he wiped aggressively at his face, and I saw the remnants of tears that had tracked down his cheeks. Posed as he was, he could've been the model on a magazine cover, curled in on himself, head slightly askew. I found myself, once again, unable to react.

"You're just going to have to deal with it," he said, voice cracking.

Deep inside my chest, I could feel a throbbing pain, and the sickness in my stomach roiled around. I don't think I could ever bring this topic up again anytime soon. There was no backpedalling on this. What the fuck. Jesus fucking Christ. Maybe I could apologise, explain what I meant. It would not be good to leave this conversation as it was.

"Axel, I just... I want—"

"You don't have any more of that spam, do you?" asked a feminine voice from behind me.

"No, we don't. There's some jerky, but let me finish my thought. Axel, I just want you—"

"Lee."

"Don't interrupt me! I'm trying to say something important here."

Axel's eyes were narrowed. His hands slid from his lap to the sword at his feet. Wait, wait, wait. A feminine voice? Jye's voice was deep, and Wren's was still childlike.

Oh.

I turned to find the glint of a knife greeting me.
Very cool.

IX

CRISIS

"LOOK, I AIN'T ASKING FOR MUCH. Just give me the jerky. It's what Mumma wants."

The edge of the blade was cool against my neck, the hand holding it calloused and rough. My gaze travelled up her arm to her face. A cleft chin, pointed nose, and perfectly manicured eyebrows, the left one with a slit, above dark brown eyes staring into my soul. Her features were handsome rather than beautiful. Long black hair split into braids that cascaded behind her wide shoulders. The way she stood, her square build balanced on bent knees, spoke of some sort of specialist training.

"Tell us who you are," Axel said, sword in hand, as he rose.

His manic behaviour was gone, replaced with a deadly serious glare. If looks could kill…

"Uh-uh, you stay right there, baby." She tapped the blade against my neck. "Unless you wanna see lover boy here take a trip to the land of the dead. Jerky at my feet. In under thirty seconds."

It was crazy that we hadn't noticed her sneak up on us, especially since she was wearing neon orange pants a la *Naruto*, and a crocheted black crop top beneath from which her bra peaked out. Nestled in her bosom was a necklace chunky with charms. Overall, it was giving very Halloween chic.

Axel laughed. "You think I'm going to give you our resources? There's four of us and one of you. Do the maths."

"Oh, honey, I have. And I'm more than sure you place a much higher value on Bambi here. So, if you even so much as step loudly and wake the others, say goodbye." She slid in behind me, and it surprised me that we were of similar height. Her free arm reached around my torso, pulling me closer. I was now squarely between Axel's sword and her. And she had some grip.

Axel's eye twitched.

She said, "Sword down. Twenty seconds now. Mumma ain't playing."

Murder in his eyes, Axel lowered his sword to the floor, and then he took a step toward our bags. Using her grip on me, she turned us to ensure that I was always her meat shield.

I ran through the options in my head. [Ground Smash] would be a repeat of what happened in the cabin, if not worse since Wren and Jye wouldn't be able to react in time. I couldn't use Jye's Load since I'd stupidly never asked for consent once they'd joined the party. Wren hadn't given me permission to use any of her abilities either, but as a [Synergist], they wouldn't be helpful right now. Was there anything from Axel that I could use?

Said blond was putting up a performance of rifling through each one of our bags. He had to be buying me time to act, to do something. But what? [Intimidation] only worked on lower-level targets, and our opponent was almost definitely another "player" and had to be a minimum of LVL 1, so that wouldn't work. I guess there was [Thick Hide]. It'd reduce damage she'd be able to do to me, but who knew what she was capable of? Reducing 50 damage to 40 would still mean I'd be dead in a slip of her blade.

"Ten seconds, babes. No more fucking around."

Her grip on me tightened, and she pressed the blade further into my neck. Okay, even if it didn't get me out of this mess, using [Thick Hide] was just a smart move. Activating [Channel], I felt the energy grow, and then, thinking of Axel's ability, a warmness bloomed over the full expanse of my skin. The vague exhaustion of having my mana permanently halved to maintain the ability settled into the crevices of my mind. That said, I now couldn't sense the weapon directly against me. It was like a layer of clothing or a thin film of plastic sat between the cool metal and my skin. My assailant didn't seem to notice.

I took a deep breath and then cued Axel with, "Am I actually that predictable?"

Her gaze flicked to me, brow wrinkling in confusion.

Taking the hint, in less than a blink, Axel was next to us, a knife from the bags in hand. Its pointy end seemed to be directly aimed at her face. Unlike Axel's ability to move on his feet quickly, granted to him by his trait [Swift Footed], his attack speed was still normal.

This gave her time to react. She pushed her own knife into my neck, and I knew then that she would've killed me if I hadn't borrowed Axel's ability. Her blade slid down my throat upon the slick resistance of [Thick Hide], but still it cut through my skin, like slicing into soft butter. The sharp edge landed on my left clavicle and cleaved straight through to bone. Unable to repress it, a howl of pain tore from my lungs. My HP plummeted to 5. Pissed her accuracy had been put off, she hissed. Axel's blade point was still closing in on her, now just millimetres from her left eye. I saw her gaze harden.

"Fuck," she said, and the knife tore into her eye socket.

But there was no blood. No scream. Just an explosion of black smoke followed by the pitter patter of paws on the wooden floorboards. Through the haze, I saw for a second the shortened tail of a bobcat.

Her first words played in my mind. *You don't have any more of that spam, do you?*

Just Friends earned 50 XP.

Now released, I was bleeding much more than I thought I would, and Axel dropped his knife to wrap his arms around my shoulders. He screamed, "Wren! Jye! We need you now!"

I looked down at my torn skin, at the blood seeping down my shirt. I could feel the pain, understood that it was my body, but at the same time it all seemed like it was happening to another person. This was not good. I was starting to dissociate. Axel's eyes looked red. Did he get hurt somehow? Was he crying?

Static buzzed in my ears. I couldn't tell if that was part of dying or abilities being used. Oh, bleeding was bad. It was not good. I felt my remaining HP begin to tick down.

4 HP now.

I was woozy, like the time I'd come back from a really bad date and had drunken myself into a stupor, like I had been more alcohol than man. My limbs were heavy, but I felt light.

Jye and Wren were by my side, as if teleported. I think I was resting on Axel's lap but wasn't sure. I could see his face hovering over me, concern furrowing his brows. Without hesitation, the ten-year-old laid her hand upon my wound, and the soft green light of [Healing Hand] emanated from her fingers. Everything felt so far away. Even the warmth of party members who huddled around me.

Beep. 3 HP.

Of course the cat I'd saved and then taken pity on had nearly killed me. Could still be the death of me. Axel wrapped his hands around my head, cradling my face. I couldn't tell what expression he had. I wondered if this is how it had felt to him when that piece of wood had nearly done him in. I hoped he wasn't feeling guilty, like I had. He'd done everything he could have to save me.

Beep. That wasn't good. Wren's healing wasn't keeping up with the bleeding.

The green glow slowly took over my vision, the forms of Wren, Jye, and Axel beginning to fade into shapeless blobs. Of course, this is how I'd die. Used as a hostage for food.

How fucking stupid.

Axel's voice was the last thing I heard before blackness took over the green.

"You promised."

Beep.

It's seventh grade, just after second break. An announcement over the school PA system has called Axel and me from class to speak to the admin. Behind the front desk, the receptionist informs us that my parents will be picking us up, and they have some news to tell us. The man's face is blurry. What does he look like? I can't see it clearly.

We wait there, on that bench that was too angular to be comfortable, the coldness of the metal seeping through the cheap polyester of my uniform. I dully realise my sister hasn't been called out of class with us. If mum and dad are pulling us out of school, she should be here too.

It must be a mistake, so I stand to mention it to the admin, and the other people in the office exchange looks and then say they're not allowed to share anything else. Even as a thirteen-year-old, I can connect the dots, sense there's something not quite right.

Something's happened to my sister. I'd seen her this morning. We'd eaten breakfast together. I held her hand until the crossing at the corner store. We'd greeted Mark on the way. I'd left her at the gates talking with friends before the bell. But my stomach is clenching with worry.

"I'm sure it's nothing," Axel says, folding another paper wasp.

I'd normally be distracted by his antics, amused and delighted.

But this isn't right.

"Then where is she?"

He shrugs and pockets the prohibited item. "You want one?"

"No, I want to know where Chrissie is."

She's three years younger than me, and I love her. Being an older brother has been some of the most fun moments of my life, comparable only to the time I spent with Axel. Teaching Chrissie to do things and watching her learn were my favourite things.

To me, it was amazing that I had witnessed a baby become a little girl. My parents had joked that I was more like her second father than a brother. I'd gone absolutely crazy about that and proudly referred to myself as Papa Lee. Chrissie also called me that.

"That's kinda nasty."

I look down and realise I'm subconsciously picking at the skin about my fingernails. Immediately, embarrassed I'd done it in front of Axel, I stop. "Sorry."

Though he probably thinks I don't notice, Axel's head tilts in judgement. "You're so weird sometimes."

I sit there for what feels like forever, and the anxiety echoes through my body.

When my parents finally arrive, I am so tense that I could strain a muscle. As I see them, I rush into their embrace, and their arms clasp about me, hugging me so tightly it's hard to breathe. They finally release me, pulling away to reveal unreadable faces. Their eyes are bloodshot, noses red.

It looks like they have really bad colds. Maybe Chrissie's really sick too and that's what they wanted to say. My heart is in my throat.

Axel and I get into the backseat of the car, and mum angles the rearview mirror so that she can look us in the eyes.

"Lee, baby, I have some bad news." Mum pauses, and dad's started driving now, the engine humming in the silence. She continues, voice hoarse, "Axel, your parents told us it's okay to share this with you too. Do you want to hear it now, or do you want to wait until you get home?"

My mouth tastes like choking. The flavour of air, but it doesn't go down.

"It's Chrissie, isn't it?" I ask. It barely comes out as a crumpled whisper.

"Yes," dad says. I look at him in the reflection. His mouth is a single thin flat line, and his eyes are fighting to stay neutral. It looks like he's been crying. But dad doesn't cry. He's never cried.

I ask, "Is she sick?"

"No, she's not," mum replies, voice shaking.

The words should be relieving, but somehow, they're not. If she's not sick… Does that mean it's worse? In my peripheral vision, I see Axel roll his eyes and begin idly staring out the window. In a dull tone, he says, "Can you just tell us now?"

I take a deep breath to steady myself. "Yeah, I want to know now."

My parents exchange a look. It's silent, and both of them are looking to each other. Sometimes my parents could talk without speaking. They said that if you knew someone for long enough you could do it. They could do it with Axel's parents too.

"Chrissie…" Mum begins and her voice stops coming out.

Dad continues, "You know how sometimes people stop having energy to do things?"

"Like grandma?"

When I was eight, my grandmother passed away—simply due to old age. My parents had explained that when you ran out of energy completely, you stop being able to live. I asked why she didn't just go to sleep to get more energy. But dad said sometimes sleep doesn't help.

Mum nods, her hand on dad's shoulder, and says, "Everyone runs out of energy someday, right? Chrissie—"

Everything shifts into place.

I don't need to hear the rest.

I know.

I knew.

I didn't see her enter the school gates.

Poison tendrils of pain throng through me. It is like someone tearing the heart from my chest, ripping it right through my lungs and out my rib cage. A scream shreds out of my mouth and within seconds, I am heaving with sobs.

Chrissie is dead. I'll never see her again. I'll never get to teach her to spell my favourite words. I'll never read her my favourite books.

She's gone.

My parents are reaching for me through both sides of the car. I didn't realise that we'd pulled over. Axel is… I can't see him, I don't know what he's doing. The four of us sit in the backseat of that sedan, my parents holding me and rocking me as the three of us cry. We are probably only there for an hour. But it feels like forever as I come to terms with the loss of my little sister.

Tired and sore, my tears eventually run dry. The car chugs to life, and slowly we drive home in silence.

My body feels heavy; my limbs not my own. I am staring into nothing. Everything feels fake, unreal. My mind begins to float away from my physical self. Like I'm looking down on my tangible form. I sit there, but I'm not really there. I'm not there in the car in the world where my sister is dead. It's pleasantly empty inside. It feels good to feel nothing.

A sharp sting on my thigh yanks me back into reality.

Incredulously, I shoot a glare at Axel as he pulls the paper wasp from my leg. My skin where he'd managed contact with the projectile is already turning red. The emptiness, the stagnancy, fades as anger takes control.

I can't rein in the words. It's a rush of energy, fuelled by pure rage, of injustice, of unbridled loss.

"I hate you!"

Axel has the decency to look shocked by my yelled announcement, his eyes widening in hurt surprise. He doesn't get a chance to react as I swing my arm around and sock him in the jaw. I've never hit anyone, never even felt like it.

But Axel had interrupted the one thing I could control. And now I was back in my body, and I felt horrible. My fist had made solid contact with his chin, and his head was thrown back from the impact.

It smacks loudly into the car window behind him. The sound is oddly satisfying.

He punches back at me, and soon we're just two boys in the backseat of the car pulling at hair and biting limbs. Scratching, clawing. Flailing. We're even growling at each other. It's an outlet for my emotions because I can't say anything. I don't know what I want to say.

Mum and dad react quickly, pulling us over, and they separate us. They eventually decide to call Axel's parents to pick him up. I don't go to school for a while, and time passes both quickly and slowly. The week afterward is an absolute blur.

⁜

MY VISION SHARPENED.

I was floating in a sea of infinite darkness that started and ended nowhere.

Was I dead?

It was weird, but I'd always imagined dying to be more like sleeping. Awake and then nothing. Alive and then nothing. It's what I hoped happened to Chrissie. But this… I guess this was okay. It was more like a waiting room, a space between spaces, than an afterlife.

Axel's voice echoed in my head.

"You promised."

Yeah, that's right. I had promised him that we'd finish this thing together. What a stupid promise. There was no way I could. I was pretty much useless to my team, to everyone. I'd even hurt my party. I'd gotten taken hostage. I was more of a weight on the team than Wren. Wren who was a ten-year-old child. God, I was why Chrissie was dead.

Maybe it was better to let it all go and just stay here. My parents would miss me, probably. Maybe they were dead already. I hoped not.

But was that all I was really living for? The fact that my parents would be sad?

What had I been living for?

The past fifteen years of my life seemed to have passed me by. I'd done nothing of note during them. After Chrissie, I had completed tasks and achieved output like I was on autopilot. Blankly, without thought. Finish school, get a degree, get a job, try to find someone to share life with. That's what you were meant to do. That's what healthy well-adjusted people did. That's what I did. But I looking back at it, I wasn't really living.

I was just going through the motions in a haze of existence.

Until the Gates.

They were like waking up.

Despite the panic attacks, despite the pain, despite the misunderstandings, when the black holes appeared that's when life had started again. When I'd been forced to start doing things and making choices. Even if they'd been shit, even if they'd ended poorly, even if they'd made things worse, it was *me* who had made them. I'd chosen. I'd chosen to be there confronting Axel before we'd been attacked.

Before the Gates, I'd have done none of that.

Hell, I'd been lying to myself about moving out from our apartment. I wouldn't have. I'd been planning it for months, but I never would've gone through with it. I hadn't been able to. Things I actually wanted were cloaked in a distant fog to me that I had never been able to wade through, never been able to even see through.

But I'd changed. Or maybe now I was finally awake to wanting to change. Is this what had happened to Axel? A sudden understanding delivered by our old world ending?

Was that enough, though? A reason to return? Was something as vague as wanting to change worth living for?

In the corner of my peripheral vision, a dim green glow began to form. Wren. Her ability. A sense of pride rushed through me. I think her and my sister would've been good friends. Chrissie…

Her death had destroyed me in so many different ways.

Would mine hurt them?

I thought about my party members, who were no doubt still sitting around my body.

Wren would feel guilty if she was unable to heal me. Especially given her history with her prior party members. She was strong, but if it happened again, it could traumatise her for the rest of her life. That wasn't a change I wanted for her.

I'd never apologised to Jye for blowing up at them when Axel was injured. Despite our short time with each other, they'd trusted me with their past, their vulnerabilities. Making them lose something again, when they had so little, would be cruel.

And Axel… I guess just him. The new Axel, the old Axel. I owed him something, just like Jye and Wren, but I didn't know what it was. It wasn't the same, it wasn't the hurt I wanted to spare them. Whatever it was, it was both more and less.

Something in my mind finally snapped into place.

This.

Them.

The concept crystallised.

That is what I would live for. The change I wanted. This was my answer. The thought echoed inside me. It filled the darkness, coalesced with the green glow, and rippled about me.

I wouldn't make the same mistake again. I'd protect them, protect them like I hadn't been able to protect Chrissie. Do as much as I could until I could no longer breathe.

It was an odd, being here in nowhere. Since even before the first video of the Gates had appeared, I'd always felt this terminal sense of dread; a fear of dying before I knew what I wanted and never being able to try to achieve it. But here I was, on the precipice between life and death, and it was gone, as if it'd never been.

Dying really had a way of changing your perspective.

Soon a cool, soothing trickle began to seep through my body, washing over my soul, overflowing until the void was me and the energy, and I was nothing but a green liminal space.

THE ROOF OF THE CABIN DECK was a gray aged painted-over wooden rafting.

"I've never been more happy to see those boring brown eyes," said a voice I owed.

"You scared us shitless, dude," said another voice I owed.

"I'm glad you woke up," said the other voice I owed.

Stiff, and with residual pain, I turned to look at them and smiled. "You would not believe the fucking dream I just had."

The three of them laughed, and then Wren collapsed onto my lap, her mana supply dried to the bone. Gently, I laid my hand on top of her head and ran it over her hair. She was such a trooper.

After a moment, Axel gingerly lifted her from me and laid her to rest on her sleeping roll. God, it felt like all we did these days was drain her dry of energy, the poor thing. She spent more time asleep than awake. I would stop that as much as I could.

Jye's thin lips stretched into an evil smile. "You'll never guess what I did."

With a flourish, and not without effort, they lifted a bundle of blanket in front of me, their arm muscles bulging from the strain.

"A present for the boss."

I looked to Axel for explanation, but he just gestured vaguely. Yeah, that was very Axel of him. I don't know what I expected. The same annoyance that generally washed over me didn't happen. Instead, unusually, I felt a brief wave of fondness.

Okay, that was weird.

Ignoring the new reaction to Axel's antics, I unfolded the layers of the blanket, and I discovered at the centre a certain bobtail cat.

Well, well, well.

X

GASP

S HE WAS PRESSED AGAINST THE BOTTOM of the blanket, an invisible source pushing her feline form down so far that it had to be crunching bone. In the back of my mind, I hoped this didn't really count as animal cruelty. Chrissie would never forgive me.

"You used Load to catch her?" I asked in surprise.

"I might not be the brightest crayon in the shed, but I can be quick. As soon as I woke up and saw her fleeing the scene, you with all your blood, I knew I had to do something. I don't even know how many times I used Load on her, to be completely honest. I just knew I needed to stop her. So, yeah."

"Impressive reflexes, honestly," I commented.

"I know, right?"

The cat's eyes were on me, glued to me. I could feel the animosity oozing out of her. If she had just asked nicely, I probably would've given her the jerky. I said as much to the animal before me. She hissed back. I heard static, and her form crumpled forward more. I was surprised she was even alive.

Axel said, "We should kill her while we can. We got 50 XP from winning that battle. Imagine how much we'd be able to get from killing an opponent."

I shifted my attention to him. "Actually, I don't think that's how it works."

Jye's head tilted. "We got 50 XP?"

Ignoring them, I continued, "If my idea is correct, I believe experience is rewarded based on performance. Consider how awfully we did against her originally. The bad teamwork. The way we were in each other's way. But this time, we all worked together. I distracted her, Axel attacked, Wren healed me, and Jye caught her. Like a functional party."

Axel scoffed. "I think you're making a mountain out of an ant hill."

"No, I think he's got it in the bag. It's like what you originally said about UX design. The system preferred response is to accept a party invite. It fits the same roundabout theory," Jye said in one of their rare moments of crystalline insight.

The cat hissed again, and I noticed her lungs seemed to be struggling to inflate under the pressure of Jye's Load. I glanced over to them, and wordlessly Jye rolled their eyes. I heard static. Her lungs looked to breathe almost comfortably again, but it was clear she still couldn't move. We could just leave her like that…

"You nearly killed me for food," I said.

"Exactly why I think we should just let Jye crush her to a pulp," Axel said, grinding his teeth together.

"I'm not exactly against the idea," Jye commented.

I scowled and shook my head. "No. Don't you get it? She nearly killed me."

Understanding hit Axel, and he threw his hands into the air. "Absolutely not. No way. We have no idea what she could do."

"Could either one of you fill me in on your inside conversation?" Jye said.

"This lunatic wants to invite her to join our party."

"I'm no genius, but that doesn't sound great," they replied.

"Hear me out. I nearly died. Our party balance is ridiculously bad.

Our only frontline is Axel, and if he goes down, our entire team is out. We need someone else who can do damage. And she does a lot of damage."

Axel rubbed at his temple. "You're insane. What's to say she doesn't kill us the minute we accept her into the party?"

It was a good question. Especially since she had already betrayed what trust I had built up with her after feeding her. It didn't make any sense, now that I thought about it. I had promised to feed her. I would've easily given her jerky every night. She had to have known I would have, since I had attacked my own party to help her, at least in her cat form. Why had she done that?

Suddenly the puzzle pieces fell into place.

Oh. Of course.

Letting out a long sigh, I said, "You're right. We might have to kill her. There's no way for us to stop her from hurting us. It'd be better for us to get her out of the way."

The cat's green eyes widened at my sudden heel turn. I watched as she struggled to move one paw in front of the other, inching ever so slightly across the blanket away from us. It was a pathetic sight and honestly made me feel a little ill.

"Finally, he speaks sense!" Axel exclaimed.

Swallowing back my nausea, I jutted my jaw at the lumberjack. "Jye, if you'll do the honours."

They threaded their fingers together to crack them, a stoic expression on their face. "If that's how it's gotta be."

Slowly they approached the crumpled form of the cat. I could see the human dread begin to fill her eyes. I heard one static buzz, and her lungs stuttered to inflate. My heart began to beat wildly in my chest. I didn't know if I could let them go through with it. But this was the only way…

Another *tsss,* and she was barely moving, barely a shape at all. Were we going to kill her? Could I make Jye do that? Fuck, I hoped I was right about this.

Jye's brow furrowed, their loyalty unwavering. I don't know what I'd done to earn it. I only hoped I was worth whatever guilt would sow its seed in them when we were done.

One more Load and she'd fold into nothing.

Their gaze met mine.

Please let me be right.

I nodded.

Jye took a breath, and the thought was clear on their face and—

The dull ring of an off-white request notification pinged our status menus up.

Invite Tam to Just Friends party.

Reward: [Collar of Control], 195 XP

Accept | Reject

Jye winced from the notification.

Thank fuck. And that there was no failure clause meant the deal was even better than I was hoping. Jye swore under their breath from the notification. I was elated I'd been right, the zing of endorphins flooding my brain. I don't think I could've let Jye literally crush a helpless animal, despite the fact it was not actually really a cat. Immediately, I selected Accept.

"Stop and undo two Loads."

Confused, Jye followed my instructions, and I could see the minor relief in the loosening of their shoulders. Mentally, I projected a party invite to the cat. The request had called her Tam. I watched as she struggled to accept it.

Tam has joined your party.

Tam at critical health.

Axel let out a long and anguished sigh. "Did that near death experience damage your brain?"

Request complete.

Reward available.

Unlike the gift, the reward simply appeared in a glimmer of sparkles with none of the anticipation. The [Collar of Control] was a neat red leather collar suited for a small animal. Beneath it, its description read: **The owner of this collar may issue one command at a time that the wearer must follow until the command is rescinded. It may only be placed and removed by the owner.**

I clicked my tongue. That was less than I wanted, but more than I was hoping for.

Next to the [Collar of Control] was the listed XP. I selected it and watched the number count down as my XP bar filled up completely, pushing me directly to LVL 2. I wished I could further check out what that meant, but there was no time to contemplate that. I shoved my hand into the menu and pulled out of the [Collar of Control], surprised by the resistance formed as my skin made contact with it.

Wasting no time, I slipped the collar over Tam's neck, and said, "You must never harm anyone in our party, help us when necessary, and never leave our party."

The buckle flew out of my hand and did itself up with a click. I guess my command had been accepted. Tam's cat eyes glared at me in clear distaste. I shrugged at her. What are you gonna do about it?

"You didn't say anything about her following our instructions," Axel commented dully.

"Can someone *please* explain what just happened?" Jye said.

"Well, I figured out why she attacked me. It was a request. Just like the one we got and rejected. Undo your Loads, all of them."

With a sigh, Jye did just that, and it was like a balloon inflating watching Tam gain full height and width again. She hissed at us, and made a move to leave but found her paws would take her no farther. Irritated, she turned to face away from us. Well, at least it looked like the collar worked.

"She kept saying what 'Mumma wants.' I thought she was just talking about herself in third person, but that's when it hit me. She used 'I' when she was talking about herself. Mumma was someone, something else. Mumma wanted her to steal the food."

Axel frowned, "But she failed, and there was no failure condition."

"No, there wasn't. Because she's been officially sponsored."

Jye nodded in understanding and then said, "What the fuck do you mean?"

"Mumma is her sponsor. Mumma wanted to *support* Tam. Stealing the jerky was probably a way for Tam to get XP. Think about it. If I'm right and XP is rewarded based on performance, then her sneaking into our midst and taking food at knifepoint has to be an amazing feat."

"Why didn't Mumma just gift her XP instead then? You said the reward for our rejected request was 1,000 XP," Jye queried.

"That... I don't know. I think there must be something regulating requests. We'd have to see more of the system, more of the way everything works before I can answer that for sure."

I allowed myself to breathe in and out deeply.

No one would have to die today, our party had increased by one and would actually be more balanced now, and I was LVL 2. My health blipped up to 6. Ooof. Now it was time to rest.

We settled on shifts, with someone's eye always on Tam, at least until she became human again and she could corroborate my hypothesis and make her own assurances to the team. When Wren woke up, she'd have a hell of a story to hear from us. As I slipped under the blanket of my bedroll, I allowed myself one moment to reflect on things, though my thoughts ended on Axel's face as I had thought myself dying. What a weird thing to think about.

The second my head hit the pillow I was unconscious.

A SHARP NUDGE TO MY ABDOMEN snatched my mind from its slumber.

"Rise and shine, honey. Your shift's up."

My eyes flew open, and I sat up to come face to face with the unimpressed human features of Tam. She shot a toothy grin my way. "You know you share secrets when you sleep?"

The tips of my ears felt hot. "What? What did I say?"

She looked conspiratorially to the left and right then leaned in toward me, and said, "Well, that's for me to know and you to never find out, sunshine."

A bark of laughter erupted from her as she pulled the blanket from my body, beginning to nudge me from my bedroll. "Now, let me sleep. Your thembo did me some mighty damage. Toddle off."

I stood and went to complain but found her already snug and fast asleep in my bedroll.

Axel met my gaze. "This was your decision."

I pinched the bridge of my nose. Fuck me. Oh, well. At the very least, things would only improve with the inclusion of a party member who was officially sponsored. It'd mean that we'd be one step closer to answering some very important questions, the least of which was exactly who Mumma was.

Wren and Axel were on watch together, which felt like a recipe for disaster, but they seemed to both be sitting in companionable silence.

Axel never got along with kids. As an only child, he didn't really know how to interact with them. He'd technically been friends with Chrissie, but as far as I remembered he was her friend in the same way you were friends with cousins who lived in another country. You acknowledged them when you saw them, played with them when your parents asked, but otherwise didn't really spare them another thought. But there was one time I realised that wasn't quite true, at least in regards to Chrissie.

It was at her funeral.

"Jeez, you could hear a pin fall," I said, taking a seat near them.

Axel rolled his eyes and Wren waved with a single small hand. "You're looking better."

"I'm feeling a lot better. Thanks for the clutch heal. Again."

She smiled. "You're welcome. I'm glad to have helped."

"Oh, I never asked what your other Synergist abilities are."

"I just have one other ability. Whetstone. It increases the critical chance of the target I apply it to."

I considered the ability for a moment. Increased crit chance was a decent buff. But depending on the mana cost, it probably wouldn't be worth it to apply it to all of us. Just the people who were doing damage that could take advantage of it. So not me, Wren, or Axel.

"You're going to be using that one a fair bit with Tam, and Jye," I said, rubbing at my chin in consideration.

Axel didn't say anything. He appeared lost in thought. I guess we really hadn't said anything to each other since I'd nearly died. It'd been weird when he'd nearly died, so maybe he felt the same way I had. In the silence, I remembered that technically I'd levelled up. I guess the whole team had, maybe excluding Tam. I brought up the party menu.

Just Friends Party | LVL 8

Lee | LVL 2 | All-Rounder (Party Leader)

Axel | LVL 2 | Combatant

J▨▨ | LVL 1 | [illegible]

Wren | LVL 1 | Synergist

Tam | LVL 2 | Cutthroat

Repressing a sigh, it didn't escape my attention that Wren and Jye hadn't levelled up. For Wren, it was obvious, since she had split her XP between classes, though she had to be fairly close on her [Synergist] class, maybe around 50 off or so. That was if everyone shared the same requisite XP for levels. For Jye, though… it had to be the glitch. I hoped this was a one-off for them, because otherwise it'd be impossible for them to progress. What did a person do when their levels wouldn't go up?

Tam's class was [Cutthroat], which honestly seemed more like a description of her as a person. Still, it reinforced my assumption she could deal damage. It was a little concerning that our entire team was basically physical damage based, though. Since it was more than apparent that magic existed, didn't that mean there were ranged magical attacks? I guess technically as long as Axel drew their fire and could dodge them, that'd deal with that. That's assuming there weren't homing spells or attacks.

I thought about the level up and the menu changed. Of course. Now I could see my detailed stats. Well, at least some of them. Given the history of the system, it was likely still hiding more that we'd unlock in the future. I hoped sooner or later we'd reach the end of that.

The more I read, the more I despaired at my character sheet. Was I just... designed to be weak? I really hadn't been wrong when I'd seen my stats at the beginning. I really would've just rage quit the game if I rolled this poorly. Even with no one to compare with, I knew instinctively this was not good.

4 STR | 4 CON | 4 DEX | 4 END | 4 WIL | 4 INT

Tam snored loudly as she slept. Ignoring her, I waited for any more information regarding the attributes to load, but nothing was forthcoming. They didn't even bother to provide the whole words for each attribute. At least they were all relatively standard. Strength, Constitution, Dexterity, Endurance, Will or Willpower, and Intelligence.

Jye stirred and groggily turned to Tam's noisy form. They kicked her, which stopped her sounds momentarily. With a satisfied sigh, Jye rolled back over and snuggled back into their bedroll.

If we followed general game attributes, Strength was damage, though that sometimes depended on your class. Constitution almost always directly correlated to health. Dexterity was a little bit of a wildcard. Sometimes it was a damage modifier, sometimes it was more similar to speed and reflexes. Endurance was less standard in games and was usually more or less synonymous with Constitution which meant here it had to mean something else.

Perhaps more like how much a person could endure? Pain tolerance? That seemed a little niche and also a little twisted. Maybe it was more like… damage one could take. So passive defence? Maybe like *D&D* AC, then.

Then we had Will or Willpower. That was on the flip side of physical defence, so mental or magical defence. Intelligence was a no-brainer. In systems with magic, it usually directly affected mana. I never thought I'd be thankful for having played so many different types of RPGs.

Either way, looking at my stats, it wasn't surprising that I only had 20 mana, stamina, and HP. God, I could just imagine Axel's sheet right now. Probably 10s across the board. Lucky bastard. I wondered what Tam's, Wren's, and Jye's looked like. Well, Jye's was probably unreadable.

Which reminded me… Jye had said they had two abilities. As far as I knew, making the weight of something lighter or heavier was one ability. That meant they had another one which was still unknown to us. Could we just get them to think about using it and it'd proc? We'd have to get to the bottom of that sooner or later.

Staring at my stats a little longer, I noticed in the corner of the screen was a new option: **Upgrade.**

I mentally selected the upgrade option and was taken to a new screen that very judgmentally called me broke.

No credit available.

Beneath, it showed my stats and my ability grayed out behind a lock. Okay, well, that was more questions answered. So, we needed credit to upgrade things, but we needed to level up to be able to unlock the upgrades. Other than staggering our upgradability, what was the purpose of levels if they ultimately were nothing but empty numbers? Did it have some other sort of justification?

It all seemed a little bit convoluted, but what did I know about game dev? If I was to hazard a guess, I'd probably say that the marketplace where we could sell things would pay us in credits. Which meant clearing a Dungeon wasn't only about defeating a boss or a set of challenges. It was about collecting items to sell.

As if reading my mind, the status screen changed to another new window.

Go to marketplace? Accept | Reject

Technically Wren and Axel were on watch, so I could probably fiddle about with this for a little while longer. I selected the Accept button and immediately regretted it.

I hadn't for a second considered why it said "go to." Well, the entire thing was a learning experience. I tried to think lightly of it as I lost control over my body, the muscles going limp all at once. As I sunk to the floor, I saw Wren and Axel's horrified expressions.

Before my vision went black, the briefest contact with the floor brushed against the back of my head.

DUNGEON
HUNTER

XI

SHOPPING

THERE HAD TO BE A BETTER WAY OF DOING THIS.

I was beginning to think that whoever designed the system had a deranged sense of humour and derived enjoyment from watching others getting tortured. Despite the instant sense of spite aimed at whoever had orchestrated this whole apocalypse, it did nothing to dull the awe that washed over me when my surroundings finally hit me.

It was nothing like the desert or cabin I'd just come from. In fact, if anything I'd have called it the perfect permutation of a "fantasy marketplace." Little wooden stalls decorated the edges of the cobblestone street, each manned by a different vendor, none of which were human. Species varied from identifiably elven and dwarven but running to nonhumanoid figures I couldn't have dreamt of. A few salespeople called out, sharing their deals, and others were offering samples of their products. To me it sounded like English, but I was sure some of them did not have the necessary mouth parts to create such sounds. Automatic translation? Or was this simply another version of a Dungeon where things were more gamelike?

The tantalising aroma of a freshly baked apple pie with the lightest follow through of cinnamon and vanilla that wafted over to me from a nearby stall smelled so real. Which meant all these people and this place could be real as well. This thought ricocheted around in my mind. I hadn't let the events settle, hadn't reflected.

This was real.

All of this was real.

Axel had nearly died.

I'd nearly died.

I'd nearly killed someone.

Yes, I'd long since accepted that the world was over as I knew it. For about a week now, I'd been willing to be open-minded about what was happening. The abilities, the screens, the Dungeons, the Gates. I had thought I had fully accepted reality for what it had become. That I was okay with it. But I think I was… Fuck. I'd been dissociating almost the entire time.

As the familiar tightening of my chest began, I frantically tapped my pockets for the Warhead but found them empty.

Of course, this probably wasn't even really my body. There'd be no way they'd let us leave a Dungeon like this. Unfortunately, being aware of that did nothing to stop the panic attack. Not as though anything could really stop it anyway.

Without any physical anchor, focusing was impossible.

Panic tore through me, like my spine pulled straight up into my brain.

However, I wasn't the same person I was the last time I had one. I'd basically died. I'd found peace with a new purpose. If this happened, I couldn't protect anyone. I'd never be more than I was. And I wanted to be there for Wren, and Jye and Axel, and fuck, maybe even Tam. They wouldn't die without me, I knew that. But if I could help them, I wanted to.

So, I had to do *something*.

I could feel the attack beginning to sweat through my pores, my muscles trembling, my lungs struggling. No! I had to be better. I wanted to be better. For my party. For Chrissie.

That I was capable of thinking of someone other than myself meant even right now, I was different. Maybe I could actually… change this.

The breathing method my doctor had taught me ages ago when I'd come in about dealing with the stress of university exams came to mind.

Breathe in for six, hold for four, out for six, hold for four, cycle. Think of your calm place.

In for six. Hold for four. Out for six. Hold for four. My happy place.

My chest felt tight, limbs locked.

In for six. My apartment back in Brisbane, watching stuff with Axel, on the sofa he hated, because he had nothing better to do, burning time before his friends came by or he had to go out. *Hold for four.* His expression of disdain as he skipped the Bounto filler arc. *Out for six.* Arguing about the implications of learning the alien language on people's perception of time. *Hold for four.* The laughter we shared at the distorted smear frame of Invincible fighting that we'd accidentally paused on.

The air trickled in through my lungs, thoughts loosening.

Breath in, in, in, in, in, in. Our shock when it turned out to be the Bad Place, though Axel claimed he'd called it. *Hold for four, four, four, four.* When we'd both cried as Natsume said goodbye to another yokai, and Axel swore me to secrecy. *Breathe out, out, out, out, out, out.* Poking fun at the film Axel had torrented being the wrong "Cargo." *Hold for four, four, four, four.* Nodding off, then waking to the dulcet tones of Minako Honda playing over the credits; Axel's snores her backing track.

As I breathed in again, everything began to steady, the world equalling out. My heart still pounded, but I could feel it slowing. A postattack shiver rocked through me, but I felt better. Better than I had before.

I breathed out.

To be honest, it surprised me that what calmed me was TV shows and movies. Actually, was that kind of sad?

I hadn't really ever given this breathing method an honest try before.

My GP was a little on the more holistic side of treatments most times, so whenever she told me to do something that had nothing to do with a prescription or medically backed advice, I'd written her words down and had then promptly tucked them away in one of my dresser drawers. If I ever saw her again, I owed her one. Hell, if I saw anyone else ever again from life before I'd probably give them a long hug out of pure joy they were still alive.

Able to take everything in now, my feet feeling grounded, I approached one of the stalls cautiously.

With a flash, the products loaded in. It seemed like a potions vendor.

"What can I help you with, my friend?" asked the lizard person. Given my unfamiliarity with their species, I couldn't tell what gender they were. There were none of the feminine and masculine presenting traits that I could recognise in humans. Maybe they didn't even have sexes or genders. The colour of wheat fields after harvest, they resembled a bearded dragon more than other lizards I'd seen. Their blue forked tongue flicked between pointed teeth as they spoke. For some reason, I'd been expecting them to speak with a lisp. Shit, was that racist?

I cleared my throat. "Uh, I'm just browsing."

"Please browse away."

They turned their attention to another approaching customer. Curious, I looked at them as well. It was just the silhouette of a human. No discernible details. Like a shadow in three dimensions. Even as I watched, their size and build shifted. Was this identity protection? Did I also look like that? For a moment, the customer turned and I felt their gaze on me. I could've sworn I saw them sigh. Before I could decide how to respond, their faceless figure was swallowed by a throng of other shifting shades.

"Actually, I did have a question," I said.

"Yes, how can I help?"

"Are you... Are you real?"

They chortled. "This must be your first time in Twilight."

"Twilight?" I echoed.

"We call it Twilight, since it's between times. The [REDACTED] call it the marketplace."

I blinked. Was the lizard person being actively censored? Why? Did it have something to do with what was happening to Earth? Did that mean this fantasy trading spot was actually a real place? They'd said it was "between." What did that even mean? Here I had been thinking the marketplace would answer some of my questions. But it just made me ask more. And they were questions that couldn't even be answered because of the moderation that was happening.

"I don't know what you just said."

They hummed in consideration. "You're early here, then. I've no doubt your wallet is empty. Though I'm happy to buy if you've got anything worth selling."

Early? Did that mean their words would eventually become uncensored? Maybe I should come back here later when I could actually ask questions. Though selling something now would be good, just to familiarise myself with how it all worked. I cast my mind back to Axel's sword. No, he was already quite attached to it. It wouldn't break his heart if I sold it, but it would definitely make our relationship that much more messy.

"Do you buy Dungeon-only items?"

"Offer something and we'll see."

What did we have excess of back in the Dungeon? We needed food to survive, our bedrolls for comfort, clothes for hygiene. If anything, the only thing we could really sell off was a few of the Kmart knives since Jye had grabbed far more than they needed. Even if we got rid of five, they'd still have a dozen left. I summoned the image of them in my mind and wasn't surprised they appeared as a digital image hovering above my hand.

"What about these?"

The lizard person's slitted yellow eyes widened, the pupils dilating in the centre. "Yes, we definitely can buy those."

None of the potions in their stall had prices attached, which meant it was difficult for me to gauge the true value of them in the marketplace. Though they were acting like these knives were valuable. Perhaps they were even rare? If I thought about it, they were stainless steel—something that a medieval-esque world wouldn't have access to without furnaces reaching absurd temperatures.

Intending to double whatever they answered, I asked, "How many credits will one of these fetch me?"

Their scaled lips curved into a grin, and they leaned forward. "I'll tell you what. I'll give you a deal. You give me one of those knives and I'll be your personal vendor here. Of course, I'd get a cut of the profit, but you wouldn't have to worry about coming here again."

My brows furrowed in thought. "How could that possibly be in my benefit?"

"Time doesn't work the same here, my friend. Never has. It's always different, every time you come. When you visit Twilight, you pay not only in credits but in time."

My mind boggled. "So, hours could be passing while we talk?"

"Hours, days, months, years." They paused. "Sometimes decades."

A chill ran through me. "What about my body? This one can't be real."

"Your body goes into magic stasis when you project your mental state to Twilight. So long as you have regenerative mana, you'll survive. Of course, someone can always just kill you while you're vulnerable. I hope you left your body in safe hands."

Wren and Axel wouldn't let anything happen to me. They were probably fretting over what to do right now. It was kind of nice knowing they were there to rely on.

Focusing on the lizard person, I hesitated in accepting their deal. If they were telling the truth, it meant that not coming back to Twilight was probably ideal. But it also meant that I'd have to trust them to handle all of my sales and purchases for the future. That was a lot of faith to put on someone I'd met minutes ago. Well, I guess technically it could've been decades ago at this point.

"So, how does you being my vendor work with the system?" I asked, now very aware of the seconds ticking by us, a sand hourglass in the corner of my mind, grains pouring away. What if Axel, Jye, and Wren died waiting for me?

The ridge on the inner edge of their left eye deepened in what I assumed was mimicry of raising an eyebrow. "You're not as simple as some of the early bloomers we get here sometimes."

They cleared their throat. "Well, you sell your items from back in [REDACTED], and I put them on auction. You're guaranteed a better price than selling them straight to a vendor here. I take my cut which is a reasonable 20 percent, and then I send the remaining credit to you. The transaction is instantaneous and through [REDACTED]. Buying works the same way, but you put in a request with me, and I'll try to get it, but there's no promise I can get your desired products. For those, there's a 20 percent buyer's fee too."

Trying to act disinterested, I buffed my nails on my shirt and checked their shine, then said, "Why should I make you my personal vendor? Why not the others?"

They propped a hand on their hip. "You came to my stall first. Is that not a type of fate?"

"You're saying fate led me here?"

It was an amusing idea. I wasn't the type to believe in fate or predestined choices, though. Life was what you made it. Granted, I'd not made a very positive life for myself. Sequestering myself away from others, never having any aspirations. For so long it'd been difficult to figure out what I was meant to be doing.

When Chrissie passed away, it felt like everything tumbled away from me in a domino Sternberg machine of loss. One piece hit another, and soon everything was in shambles. Chrissie was taken, Axel discarded me, the panic attacks controlled my life, my grades dropped, soccer lost its fun, I had no energy to do anything. One by one it all slipped from my grip. And I don't think I ever got it back. I had accepted that life was fine without all those things. I was okay with it all.

It was stupid to think that to get my life together I had to lose it all again. But that meant fate wasn't real. All of these choices had been mine, and they'd led me here.

"Fate or chance. Whichever word you use, it was me who you first sought. I digress, you're welcome to try with the other vendors. But you'll find them far less congenial than I've been. My [REDACTED] didn't so I've a soft spot for [REDACTED], but many of the others did."

This fucking censoring. Hoping he'd be able to reword it so I could understand, I asked, "Your what?"

"You really are quite early, aren't you?" They ran a scaled hand under their spiked chin and then muttered to themself, "There's specific regulations for [REDACTED] to be able to access Twilight. Curious and curiouser."

"Ten percent buyer and seller premium," I offered.

A croaky laugh emanated from them. "You think me a fool? 20 percent is a deal no other vendor would offer as it is."

"Eight precent."

The lizard's eyes narrowed, their second horizontal lid as well. "I'm doing you a favour here."

I took a deep breath and squared my shoulders to stand my ground. "Based on everything you've said, my wares have more value than you're letting on. You don't know a single thing about me, but you're willing to make an exclusive deal with me simply by seeing one item I have access to. This means I have things you know others will want. You're sitting at 5 percent now."

They growled, a low gurgling from their throat. "Early but not an idiot. Fifteen percent."

I shook my head. "It's 5 percent or nothing."

"Ten percent and I'll give you one of my potions. My pick."

Considering their offer, it wasn't bad. When I'd moved in with Axel, I'd still had all the furniture from the uni sharehouse I'd rented while studying. Axel had far nicer stuff than me so we'd agreed to sell my stuff off other than the lounge which he'd admitted was comfier than his. Most of it was flatpack or Ikea furniture, and instead of handling it myself, it was simply easier to drop it all off at an auction house. They'd charged a 25 percent seller's premium and 15 precent buyer's premium, and it was one of the better cuts I'd seen. So, at the very least 10 percent was better than most auction houses back in Brisbane.

"Ten percent, and I get to pick one of your potions," I countered.

The lizard's jaw clenched. The cogs were turning in their mind. They would agree. Ten percent was a decent portion of the profit. And since it was an exclusive deal, it meant that they'd get everything I'd be putting up for sale. It also didn't stop them from selling or buying from other players. So really the only person who was limited was me.

"All right. Ten percent and your pick of potions," they finally said, a smile gaping their scaled mouth. "Your name?"

"Lee. And yours?"

"Xanthe is as close as you'll get."

As they spoke, a screen popped up in front of me. This time it was gray, not off-white like the request we'd gotten, and not the normal blue system window. At the very least, I was learning more and more about the underpinnings of the world we currently lived in. Writing appeared on my screen.

Exclusive Contract: In exchange for exclusive selling rights, Lee will forfeit 10 percent of sale profits to vendor Xanthe. In addition to this, a one-off potion will be provided to Lee from Xanthe's store for no cost and one [KMART 20cm Triple Rivet Chef's Knife] will be provided to Xanthe for no cost.

Accept | Reject

I read and reread the contract, trying to see if Xanthe was attempting to pull something over me, but it all seemed legit. While stress had gotten the better of me when wording Tam's command, I wasn't as panicked this time around.

Before the Gates, I'd been the type of person to read all the Terms and Conditions, clauses, and fine print on everything I signed or accepted. It'd helped me bargain back overtime pay from work for my whole department once. So, with no pressure this time, I was confident this contract was acceptable.

Exclusive Contract signed. Xanthe assigned as main vendor.

The hovering image of the knife I'd shown Xanthe evaporated from my hand and appeared on an empty shelf in Xanthe's store. I wondered momentarily if Xanthe sold anything other than potions. Had my deal been too hasty? Should I have bargained for more?

The lizard jutted their jaw at the potions in their stall. "What'll it be?"

"I'll pick later."

They scoffed, shaking their head with a toothy smile. "A [REDACTED] after my own hearts. You might be a good source of income yet. If time is on your side."

Only vaguely registering the plurality of "heart," I focused on their second sentence. I'd been in the marketplace, no, Twilight, for around fifteen minutes now. If the Jeremy Bearimy of it all even just meant minutes became hours, I'd have been unconscious in the Dungeon for the majority of a day. With Tam being such a wildcard, I had no idea what I'd be returning to if I stayed here any longer. Maybe I'd already been here for too long already.

"How do I leave?" I asked, glancing around.

The words had only barely left my mouth before the blue screen updated.

Return to Dungeon? Accept | Reject

Ask and ye shall receive, I guess. Xanthe nodded sagely and then said, "I expect we'll never meet again. But I hope you do well. I really do. Do better than [REDACTED]. Don't hesitate to contact me about purchases."

I gave them what I hoped was a reassuring look. "Thanks. If you're looking for something specific to sell, let me know and I'll see what I can pick up."

Xanthe's black eyes glinted in surprise, and I waved once before accepting the screen's prompt.

Everything disappeared.

I blinked.

An explosion of pain erupted from the back of my head, the weight of momentum smacking my body into the floor. As my eyes flashed open, I could identify Wren and Axel reaching for my fallen form, their expression almost identical to how they'd looked before I'd left. Oh. I guess Xanthe hadn't been lying. Instead of the time elongating, it had shortened. It looked like only milliseconds had passed, if not nanoseconds, in the Dungeon.

"Ow," I said, reaching to touch the now tender spot.

"What the hell was that?"

As my fingers made contact with my head, a tendril of pain shot through me and I winced. "Do not go to Twilight." I checked my HP and wasn't surprised to see I'd lost 1 HP as a result of my body rag-dolling and smacking my head on the floor.

"What's Twilight?" Wren asked.

I groaned as the two of them helped me stand. Axel held a hand at my waist to steady me, and Wren grabbed one of my hands. The physical sensation of my body felt no different to my mental projection in Twilight, and at the same time it was entirely something else. I could tell this was my real form.

I didn't even know where to begin explaining what had happened, and as my mind settled, I only said, "Not good. The marketplace, Twilight… It's basically a gamble for high rollers."

"I mean, Stephenie Meyer is not a great writer, but she sells. If you have disposable income, and it's your choice of genre, I can't really judge."

"You're meant to be asleep," Axel said pissily.

Jye shrugged. "And you're meant to be not shit, but here we are."

He closed his eyes in exasperation, breathing in slowly. That Axel had not yet permanently maimed Jye was a shock to me. Jye was the type of person that had always rubbed Axel the wrong way. It was the obliviousness he disliked the most. And things just flew over Jye's head.

Luckily Tam was still dead asleep, her snoring barely audible. I couldn't trust her just yet.

Briefly, I summarised what Twilight was and the deal I'd made with Xanthe to the others. They absorbed it in silence with solemn expressions. I'm not sure I did the marketplace justice in my explanation since I saw Axel's eyes glaze over in boredom. When I finished, I said, "Any questions?"

"Did the lizard person wear clothes?" Jye asked.

My incredulity at their question must've shown on my face because Jye pouted.

"I'm asking because there's no point in lizards wearing clothes. They have scales. Their scales are basically like armour and clothes."

"What about if they need to carry extra stuff?" Wren said.

"Oh, I hadn't thought about that. But then maybe they could use bags instead. That's still not clothes."

"What if they want to dress up pretty?"

"It would depend on their culture, but I'd think paints would make more sense for that kind of thing. You know, maybe their kind even employs self-mutilation."

"Jye!" I admonished.

Chastised, they smiled apologetically. "Sorry, sorry. Forgot there were kids around." They cleared their throat. "Let me rephrase that. Maybe they carve patterns into their—"

Axel landed a solid karate chop across Jye's solar plexus, driving the wind out of their diaphragm and stopping them midword. An *ehugh* exhaled from the giant's lungs as they folded, immediately gripping at their abdomen, eyes wide in shock and betrayal more than pain. Axel shot me a look that said, "Can you believe this idiot?"

I repressed my sigh. "No, Xanthe was not wearing clothes. I was taken off guard by the mere fact they were a lizard person. Them being naked did not cross my mind."

"I knew it," Jye exclaimed wheezily, eyes watering, still bent over.

"Do you guys not have any other questions?"

Axel sarcastically raised a hand. "What about when we need to sell stuff?"

I considered his words for a second and then said, "Give it to me and I'll get Xanthe to auction it off instead. I'll just send you credits back."

"Sweet little pea, you're getting a little too big for your britches."

"Does no one care about the watch shifts?" Axel grumbled.

Tam had uncurled from my bedroll and was lazily watching us, her head propped up on a bent arm. "I don't trust you as far as I could throw you. There's no way I'm letting you sell stuff on my behalf. And Mumma would never for a second approve of it."

"You're welcome to risk the time dilation ending poorly for you."

"How do I even know that there's even such a thing without seeing it with mine own two eyes?"

"Well, you're part of the team now, and I'd rather not pointlessly lose a party member to something we could all avoid. You can trust that. Especially after I've saved your life *twice*."

A petulant expression soured her face. "Say this wibbly-wobbly-timey-wimey shit does exist. What if this snake was lying to you about it changing every time and they're taking you for a ride?"

I didn't want to admit it, but she had a point. But, personally, I felt it was too risky to verify that Xanthe had been honest with me. The lizard had struck me as a trustworthy person, but it was impossible to convey that to someone who'd never met them. I knew I should've been more suspicious, but in my gut, I felt that Xanthe was a good person. Just the same way I thought Tam was. Maybe hers was a lot deeper down, though.

I shrugged. "Well, trust has to be earned. If Xanthe doesn't deliver then we won't use them, and try Twilight again. I just won't handle items after that. Someone else can. It was just luck I travelled there first."

The raven-headed woman scowled and folded her arms. "Fine."

Jye, who had now recovered from Axel's attack, sprang forward. "Whoa, whoa, whoa. We've got to circle back. Which Doctor?"

Tam scoffed. "The best, of course."

"Matt Smith?" Jye supplied.

Her top lip curled in disgust. She looked ready to choke out Jye. Her free hand twitched in anticipation. I was trying to think of anything to change the conversation, but my mind was coming up blank. I'd never watched the show. It was only thanks to social media osmosis that I knew what they were talking about.

Wren, thankfully, interrupted with: "I think the Ninth Doctor was my favourite."

The cutthroat's anger fizzled out as she looked over at Wren's smiling face. "He's not too bad either, though Tennant is the right answer."

Axel decided to join the irrelevant conversation. "I'm disappointed we'll never get to see Ncuti Gatwa. I think he would've topped Tennant."

"I don't think I know that actor," Wren said with a slight frown.

Our newest party member regarded Axel sceptically.

"What makes you think he'd have been better?"

The conversation now seemingly had left Twilight far behind. And it appeared like returning to the topic was not likely.

Giving up, I said, "Well, he was great in *Sex Education*."

XII

MOTHER KNOWS BEST

WE SPENT THE REST OF THE HOUR arguing about different actors who could take on the mantle of the Doctor successfully, and had come to the mutual agreement that Tennant could easily take the role on again. Jye, however, had been adamant that the next Doctor should've been their one acting friend from high school who'd apparently made it back to screen tests but hadn't passed. Axel didn't even try to humour them.

Talking with Tam like that so contrasted with the fact she had tried to kill me. Would've succeeded too if it hadn't been for Wren. But she was just another *mostly* normal person. Another human being thrown into this crazy situation. I guess I understood why she'd done it. If I'd been alone without Axel and this had all happened… Maybe I would've done the exact same thing. Still, her condescension wasn't appreciated. And she refused to answer questions about who Mumma was, much to my chagrin.

Apparently, my command tied to the [Collar of Control] didn't count her divulging that information as helping the party. I probably should've thought a little more deeply about the wording I'd used. Well, what was done was done. I couldn't risk undoing my command and letting her run amok even for a second.

Though we'd developed a cordial rapport just now, it did not mean I was willing to let her off the literal and proverbial leash. She might not be allowed to directly harm us but that didn't mean she couldn't put us in danger. And without knowing more about what or who Mumma was, we'd have to keep her at arm's reach.

Eventually we chose to just stay awake for the next shift together and then to reset it from there. Conversation drifted from TV shows to our favourite films and music artists. Wren had surprisingly old taste in music, favouring '80s' love ballads, while Tam liked "electropop bubblegum bass" musicians with names like Diveo. Jye unsurprisingly was into the K-pop scene and confessed of their shrine dedicated to Blackpink in their closet. Axel was just straight up into pop music and whatever was in the top charts at the time. He didn't disclose it to anyone else, but I knew his favourite song was nothing of the sort. But that was his secret to divulge if he wanted to.

When asked, I couldn't supply my preferred genre. I liked a little bit of everything and saw the artistry in most content—so long as the song was pleasant to listen to, I probably liked it.

The rest of the party seemed dissatisfied with my answer. Well, that wasn't my problem.

"Sunshine, what's the plan, by the way?" Tam asked.

Realising she was referring to me, I said, "Well, first we need to figure out how to clear this Dungeon."

She rolled her eyes. "That's child's play. You gotta find a way out."

"What do you mean?" Wren said.

"Well, Mumma told me the domain this Dungeon falls under is [REDACTED], so it's probably something like a puzzle or a labyrinth that we have to solve. She said [REDACTED] loves that sort of stuff."

Jye swore as Tam's words were censored, slapping their hands over their ears. Her eyebrows shot up in surprise. Gesturing at them with her thumb, she whispered, "What's the deal with your local Bigfoot?"

Unsure how much we should reveal about Jye's status, I hesitated in responding. Axel intervened. "They just sometimes do that. PTSD or something."

Aghast at using a serious psychological condition as a cover, I began to explain, "Jye's got this issue where—"

"Where I have these random tics, you know. Clutching my ears and stuff like this," Jye cut me off, smiling through their pain.

It was bad when Axel and Jye agreed on something. Even though the lie didn't sit well with me, it meant they thought it was important to not tell Tam the truth, at least not yet. Maybe that was for the better. It seemed like she was especially close to her sponsor, and if the sponsor had any say about the game maybe they'd report Jye for "cheating." Despite the fact their glitch gave them no advantages, I could see some people arguing that it was unfair.

Given that you could leave your party in this system, it meant it was highly possible Tam still viewed us as competition, especially if she managed to trick me into removing her collar somehow.

"So, you think this is a puzzle or a labyrinth?" I tried redirecting the conversation.

Tam rolled her eyes. "I don't think, darling. Mumma knows."

"Mumma this, Mumma that. If she's so amazing, why'd she nearly let you die?"

The muscles in Tam's square jaw tensed, a vein visibly throbbing, as she glared at Axel. Unfazed, Axel stared back with the same level of animosity. I pinched the bridge of my nose in an attempt to control the exasperation building in me. With any luck, they'd end each other, and I'd be free of both of them.

"It's a puzzle or labyrinth…" Jye murmured, having either not noticed the palpable tension between Axel and Tam or simply deciding they didn't have any skin in the game.

Wren followed suit and commented, "It can't really be a labyrinth."

Maybe the two hotheads would simmer down if we ignored their antics.

"We're thinking it'd be a puzzle, then? Maybe back inside the cabin?"

Wren and Jye nodded.

"None of you cowards have stepped into the desert, have you?" Tam said, voice simmering with loathing.

The rest of our party exchanged a glance.

We actually hadn't approached the sand since we had received that random off-white request. With everything that had happened so far, we'd all decided it was safer and easier to remain upon the porch of the abandoned cabin. Not to mention that the request had implied surviving in the desert was not supposed to be easy. All that combined had kept us far from considering the desert as a viable route.

"No, and we've no intention of doing so," Axel replied.

"The second your feet touch the sand, walls form in all four directions, creating a maze. I assume the cabin is in the centre, which would make the singular correct pathway out lead to our exit."

"Why should we believe you?"

I was concerned that she was being so open about her experiences and knowledge. In the past day that I'd known her, she hadn't seemed the type to willingly give us an advantage. Maybe she was leading us into a trap.

"Why do you think I accepted the request to steal your food? I wouldn't be able to survive long in a maze that has no clear exit in sight without it. I'm not a goddamn idiot."

Well, that seemed like a reasonable explanation. In fact, it was even stronger justification than her simply doing it for the sponsor rewards alone.

Food was essential. But back on Earth, agriculture had ground to a halt—which meant the only renewable food accessible outside of Dungeon in Brisbane was going to be potable or from vegetable gardens in people's yards. Both of which would not last that long either. Ultimately, beyond credits, food would come to be the most important thing to other players. I stored that thought in my mind for when we escaped the Dungeon.

And then I caught myself. For *when* we escaped it? I was jumping the gun. Mentally, I corrected myself. *If* we escaped the Dungeon, we needed to get our hands on more food.

"If you're confident it's a maze, why would you say it could also be a puzzle?"

Today, Axel seemed to be asking incredibly relevant questions. If only he could be like that all the time.

While I lamented the idea, Tam responded, "[REDACTED] is a bit of a wily one. Enjoys making people work mentally for their wins, so Mumma said not to rule out either of them."

"You're saying we should just assume it's a combo?"

Jye hmm'd loudly and then added, "A labyrinth often has puzzle-like aspects. Just like in the *Labyrinth* where Sarah has to go through all those different trials to get her little brother back from the Goblin King."

"Yeah, or like in the *Shadows House* where they have to rescue their counterparts by solving puzzles and using teamwork to achieve success," Axel murmured.

I was only vaguely familiar with *Shadows House* because Axel had mentioned it in passing. He'd watched and read more manga and anime than I knew existed. Jye, who apparently seemed to recognise the name as well, was nodding along in approval. It was hard to read Tam's expression since she always looked like she'd rather not be involved with us at all, but there was a certain glint in her eye that suggested the title was not unknown to her. Was my party full of weebs? There were worse things, I guess.

"Isn't the oldest labyrinth the one with the minotaur?" Wren asked.

Every once in a while, Wren said something that was strangely astute for a ten-year-old girl. Despite the way she had phrased it in a way that a child might say it, the fact she even knew about Greek mythology enough to recall the story of the minotaur was odd. It wasn't often that I was reminded that we knew nothing about Wren apart from how she'd discovered her classes, but whenever it did occur to me I usually just ignored it. In time, I had hoped she would further expand on her past. I guess now the vast majority of my party were people I didn't know much about sans Axel.

"I don't remember there being many puzzles in the classic Greek story," I said.

Jye frowned. "There's not in the original telling, but a lot of YA authors eventually added them. Consider *Mazerunner*, that's gotta be kinda inspired by the same story, and there's definitely puzzles in that. Or at least in the films. Never read the books."

I sighed. Were we really about to base our approach to this Dungeon on our collective knowledge of David Bowie, a strangely poignant dark fantasy manga, and a postapocalyptic film? As the question ran through my mind, it occurred to me that if someone started playing "Lazarus," then all these points technically would've reflected our current position to a T.

Were the events that had unfolded so far not just unsettling but philosophical? It'd been just a week, and I felt like an entirely different person. Was Earth technically not in the death throes of an apocalypse? The world we knew was over. The fact that we could draw such a clear thematic connection to other stories and narratives couldn't be just a coincidence.

There was an arc unravelling as we journeyed…

Jye's words from earlier echoed in my head regarding this all being some sort of *Truman Show* streaming service for future humanity. What if they were right? Maybe not who was doing it, but what it all was. If we combined it with my idea that the better we "performed," the higher XP we received, it all made a weird sort of sense. The moderation and censorship of certain content also tied perfectly into it. Whoever or whatever was orchestrating this thing was wary of letting us know too much too soon and giving us an unfair advantage that could ruin the show.

We were someone's entertainment.

Our suffering, our struggles, was media for consumption.

What kind of heartless audience would get enjoyment from this?

"Let's play it safe and expect puzzles in the labyrinth," I said, scared of speaking my thoughts to the others. "That could extend into traps, as well as problem solving challenges."

If I was right, if I had caught onto what this all truly was, I didn't think I would come out unscathed. At least not so early on. The system liked to grant us new information with no explanation as we progressed. Coming to this understanding so early could be dangerous.

Glancing around the party, I realised that I also didn't want any of them to know either. It wasn't clear how Tam would react, but she could very well know exactly what this whole thing was thanks to her sponsorship with Mumma. Jye would love that I was rolling with their conspiracy, but they definitely wouldn't be able to keep their mouth shut.

On the other hand, I was worried the idea would scare Wren or confuse her too much. She'd taken everything surprisingly well, but to explain to her that this whole situation was for the viewing pleasure of something or someone else might've really been the end of her optimism. Though truthfully, it was Axel's reaction I was most concerned about.

As my roaming gaze finally reached his form, I noticed he was watching me from half-lidded eyes. Wren and him had been awake the longest since our watch shifts had been messed up. He looked tired. I guess under it all, we all were. As his gaze caught mine, the corners of his lips curled into a soft smile that disappeared as soon as it appeared, leaving me to wonder if I'd imagined it.

Yeah, that cinched it. With Axel's mental instability I wouldn't be burdening him with my theory anytime soon.

"So, what's next, boss?" Jye asked seriously.

With far less respect, Axel echoed, "Yeah, boss?"

"We do one more sleep rotation and then try our luck in the desert on full alert."

The party murmured their agreement, and after a brief exchange about whose turn it actually was to stay on watch, we all settled into our individual roles with startling and practised alacrity. Like we'd been a team much longer than we really had. Even Tam rolled into the swing of it.

Maybe that's just how it was going to be now. Connections forged these days had a different kind of weight, a different value, than they had a week ago. Now they would very well mean life or death.

WHEN THE SLEEPING SHIFT AWOKE FROM THEIR REST, we packed up our makeshift camp and rationed out our supplies. It wasn't a far reach to predict we might get split up in the labyrinth somehow, and it'd spell ruin if any one of us weren't carrying any food or water. Granted, we didn't have that much left. If we ate minimal amounts, our party could probably survive another six days in the labyrinth. Hopefully we'd find the exit by then.

I also handed Tam one of the watches I'd picked up from Kmart. It had been a good idea to grab all of them. She ungratefully took it, and instead of wearing it around her wrist, added it to the various charms that dangled from her chunky necklace.

"By the way, how'd you end up in the cabin with us?" I asked as I zipped up my backpack.

"Funny thing, that. Strange as it sounds, darling, I went through the same Gate as you."

I watched her as she stretched, not unlike a cat.

"At the same time as us?"

"No. Your boyfriend gave you a love tap into it, then the child and ranga Terminator were sucked in. Then I leisurely strolled in."

Unable to process anything she said past "boyfriend," I blanched. "Axel isn't— We're just friends, actually. It's a common mistake, though."

She laid a hand on my shoulder and gave me a long, long look. "Oh, honey." Her hand came off, and then she walked to the edge of the cabin porch. "Well, it's none of my business."

Not appreciating the pity in her voice, though I wasn't sure who it was directed at, I mulled over her explanation of the events that had transpired that led her to the same cabin as us. She hadn't entered simultaneously with us. Which meant that maybe it had just been pure chance she had encountered us. If she hadn't, her starving before finding the exit might've been entirely possible. I hoped her luck was contagious.

It also meant that there might be other players appearing soon, or even somewhere else in the maze already. If what Tam said was true, the whole desert was simply a mirage, and there could very well be a dozen other cabins scattered around the Dungeon that we weren't aware of.

"Everyone good to go?"

"Let's go!" Wren shouted, pumping her fist into the sky.

After a little yawn, Jye said, "I'm keen,"

"It's not like we have any other choice," Axel said tartly.

"I was ready yesterday."

"You really weren't," I scoffed. "You didn't have any food."

Tam's lips curled downward in distaste, but she said no more.

I took the front position on the last step, my staff in hand, and glanced back at the cabin. Tam never said we'd be stopped from going back, but I was fairly certain at some distance it would be blocked off or even possibly deleted. Having a safe port of call would be too easy, and there's no way that was entertainment.

Breathing in deeply, I left the cabin porch.

Just as she'd explained, the second my foot touched the sand beneath it, walls sprang up on all sides, rising from below. With a thunder, they ground to a halt once they'd reached about three metres tall. When had Tam triggered the labyrinth, if she had already experienced it before? Perhaps it was when she'd run after I'd nearly accidentally killed Axel.

"At least it's something to look at," he said.

The walls weren't the same yellow sand as what had previously surrounded us, instead formed from a strange fusion of rock and crystal, just opaque enough to not be able to see through but transparent enough to still glimpse obscured shadows. As the sun caught a few jagged edges of the gem wall, it sparkled in a way I could only compare to animated sparkles. The sand itself at our feet had dissolved, leaving only the same stone that made up the walls. The entire formation was ethereally beautiful, and it left something of an ache in the depth of my heart. Nothing like this existed on Earth.

Nothing like this could exist.

"You couldn't dream this shit up," Jye said, following me to the start of the labyrinth.

We took up our positions. Tam, Axel, me, Wren, Jye, in a line. As we moved, it occurred to me that the request we'd received upon arriving would've been unsuccessful. It had asked us to remain in the desert for a certain number of days. There was no desert now. We'd have failed. Our entire party would've been killed.

A chill crawled up my spine and goose bumps formed on my arms despite the beating rays of the sun which was the only remnant of the desert biome. Axel had been the only one who had wanted to refuse the request. If it hadn't been for him, we'd all be dead. He'd been 100 percent right about it not being a system notification, about it being sketchy.

We came to the first left, and per our previously agreed approach, we all kept one hand on the left wall and turned into it.

"How'd you know?" I asked.

"As much as I'd like to claim I can read minds, I can't."

I rolled my eyes. "The request. How'd you know it wasn't any good?"

"Like I said, it just didn't seem right."

"You basically saved our lives. You know that, right?"

"I know."

His back was to me, so I couldn't see his face, but his shoulders were imperceptibly slumped. Part of me wanted to spin him around to check his expression. What face was he making? Was he breaking down again? It frustrated me that I didn't know. Couldn't know. There was something profoundly sad in his posture. It made me itch uncomfortably. I knew he wasn't okay. But what was I meant to do? I'd fucked up last time I wanted him to share.

When it came to Axel, I was always misstepping. Despite our emotional distance as people, though we spent spare time together, living with Axel made me feel like I should be doing more, living life like him, and those thoughts were…

What's the saying when they find people injured beyond survival? Ah, incompatible with life. That's part of why I had wanted to move out. It was a pressure on me. It was like being forced to experience FOMO 24-7, except it wasn't just fear of missing out, but also fear of having to engage, of being forced to confront that I had erased all autonomy.

That felt like so long ago. Building up my courage to tell Axel that I didn't want to live with him. Though I knew deep down I wouldn't have done it, I couldn't fathom sharing that idea with him now. I'd seen the unbalancing his psyche was going through right now. If I ever told him I had wanted to move out, it would probably snap whatever flimsy thread he was hanging by.

I'd never tell him.

I'd take that to the grave. And if there did turn out to be something beyond that, the words would never leave my mouth. I'd sew my lips closed before seeing Axel's expression upon hearing I'd wanted to leave him.

Yeah, he'd once abandoned me in my time of need. It'd cause a divide so deep that I'd tried to stop caring about him because of it. But I couldn't bear to be the person to scar him as he had done me all those years ago. Especially not now, when it felt like somehow… we were friends again, somehow. Or something like it.

He needed me, and I'd be damned if I'd be the one to walk away this time.

I was so preoccupied by thoughts of Axel that I lost sense of my surroundings. There was a sudden difference in temperature and texture under my hand, the cool and rough of the stone becoming warm and soft. I paused in confusion and looked to the crystalline wall.

Axel had stopped, and my hand was lightly resting over his. Before I could blink, he snatched his arm away as if stung. For a few beats he didn't react, holding his hand in front of him. He appeared to be examining it.

Then Axel looked back at me with a shit-eating grin. "Trying to hold hands?"

I scoffed. "Not in this lifetime."

And then he was walking again, as if nothing had happened, and I was walking after him. I checked behind me to ensure that Wren and Jye were still following. Yep. Good. At least the party was still together. That was the bare minimum for the day to be going well. It helped that I generally had low standards.

We continued on like that for a few hours, making idle conversation about our knowledge of rocks and stones, comparing the maze walls to each and every crystal we knew. Eventually we concluded it was probably some type of quartz. It didn't do anything to nullify the strange beauty of it. The unnatural shimmering caused by the unsetting sun still took my breath away.

"I think we might have a trap ahead."

Tam turned around to face us.

I peeked ahead of her, seeing nothing but the same crystalline maze that stretched behind us. Either she had some sort of skill that allowed her to sense traps, or she just simply had better eyesight. Both my parents had needed glasses by their thirties, but I hadn't yet. Maybe the stress of this whole situation was ageing me prematurely.

I hadn't thought about my parents for a while, probably as a sort of defence mechanism. If I allowed myself thoughts of them, my mental stability would probably spiral. With the safety of my party on my shoulders, I couldn't afford that.

Instead, I pushed Tam for more information. "What makes you say that?"

"You got eyes, don't you?"

Jye and Wren came up beside the rest of us, leaning around me to look ahead as well.

"I see fuck all," Jye commented flatly.

"Is it that thing?" Wren asked.

She had raised a hand and was pointing to something I couldn't identify.

"At least the actual baby here is capable of sight," Tam said.

Axel tilted his head, blue eyes narrowing. "The trap is the singular crystal of different colour?"

"Oh, two of you aren't blind. Yes, that's it. This is the only different crystal I've seen the entire time we've been in here."

I squinted, trying to follow the direction of Wren's finger. Briefly, the shimmer of a crystal closer to a blue than the milky white of the rest surrounding it drew my attention. It was smaller than a fingernail and at least ten metres in front of us. I was glad Tam had been leading us because I wouldn't have even noticed it if I'd been standing right before it. That's if it was a trap. But it wasn't like it was worth risking our lives to assume otherwise. It was a distinct and deliberate change to the maze. We had to approach it as if it was dangerous.

Jye held a flat hand above their brow, eyes searching for the same crystal. With a huff, they folded their arms in defeat. Pitying them, I gave them a general description of where the crystal was, and they muttered their appreciation.

Afterward, I suggested, "We turn around then?"

Tam shook her head. "Better to trigger the trap than leave it alone. That way if we need to skedaddle via an escape route, we can always haul on back."

I didn't like that she was anticipating us fleeing something in the future, but at the very least it suggested she was actively looking out for the party. Or she could be trying to get one of us killed off by triggering the trap? God, it would have been so much easier if she hadn't attacked us. Though when I thought about it, I guess Axel had attacked her first in the cabin. Actually, he had been fairly intent on killing her. Fucking Axel.

"Jye, can you throw something and make it around the weight of a person?"

The giant grinned and pulled a small bag of rubbish they'd been collecting, having muttered under their breath about not being a litterbug. "I knew this would come in handy."

I heard the static of an ability, and Jye weighed it carefully in their hand. Then they pulled their arm back in the form of a shot putter and pelted it forward. It flew from their hand, and at its top arc Jye applied several more Loads, and it plummeted to the floor just around the blue embedded crystal, rolling ever so slowly forward. I took a step closer cautiously, trying to get a better look.

Both the team behind me and myself waited with bated breath for some reaction.

Nothing.

Axel snorted. "Well, that was disappointing."

"I guess we turn around then," I said with a sigh.

The heavied bag of rubbish came to a halt about a ruler's length past the blue crystal. There was a small click. The entire party was once again staring down the walled pathway. Then came the ticking, a consistent soft tock like that of a watch hand.

A countdown? Had whatever designed this labyrinth given the potential victim a chance to escape the trap? It would make for more drama, that was for sure. Fit in with the whole streaming theory.

Another click.

We watched on, eyes wide, unsure what would follow.

And then all hell was set loose.

DUNGEON
HUNTER

XIII

WHEN WALLS COME DOWN

T FIRST, IT SEEMED LIKE THE MAZE WALLS just disappeared down the path.

What actually happened made just as much sense. They splintered into tiny little pieces, the shards so infinitesimally small that it all looked like nothing more than a shimmer of air, like the haze in the distance on a hot, humid day. The sound was unlike anything I'd ever heard. A combination of the roar of thunder and a million tiny pings. All in the matter of a millisecond.

Then the shock wave came; an explosion of displaced air carrying with it a cloud of crystal fragments. I had barely enough time to close my eyes as the thunder hit my body, throwing me off my feet, and I crashed to the floor, breath knocked out of my lungs. The crystalline shards whooshed over us, slicing through clothing, glancing across exposed skin and biting into flesh, sending dozens of signals of pain through me.

Death by a thousand cuts.

As air reentered my lungs with a sting, I activated [Channel] to borrow Axel's [Thick Hide]. The warm layer slid effortlessly around me. At the back of my mind, the constant soft pip of my HP going down slowed. I was currently sitting at 15 HP. The initial blast had done the most damage so far. However, three of my party members didn't have the advantage of Axel's defensive ability. And it didn't seem like the aftereffects of the explosion were softening. But it couldn't last forever…

Could it?

A surge of desire to protect my party came over me.

Worried about what the crystals could do to my eyes, I kept my lids squeezed tight. With the wind still whipping wildly around us, accompanied by the glass shards, I reached behind me for my party, hoping I'd taken some of the brunt of the explosion. My hands touched the warmth of someone's torso, and I wriggled toward them, stretching my arms out, to pull them closer. If we all bunched together, it meant less surface area for damage. It also meant I could be a bit of a shield for them. To do as much as I could.

Through the howling wind, it was impossible to say anything, and I didn't imagine opening my mouth right now was a wise move. As ASMR crunchy I imagined the glitter flakes to be, the taste of blood was not something I wanted to revisit.

The party member huddled in next to me, pressing their form tightly against mine. I blindly patted their body down, and I found an arm that led to a hand and grabbed it. Then I army-crawled forward, dragging them with me. After a moment, I felt their presence again by my side. Judging by their physique, it seemed like Axel, which was weird because Tam should've been closer.

Speaking of that cutthroat, I'd definitely let Tam have a piece of my mind afterward since this had been her idea.

Slowly, we pressed ahead, the hurricane of crystal shards still lashing over us, and we came to another body, shaking against the current of wind. By her distinct shape, I could tell it was Tam. Without speaking, Axel split off from me and took to the other side of her. I assumed he'd also activated [Thick Hide]. Shielding her with our bodies, like a tepee of men, I grabbed her hand and dragged. She moved with us. Briefly, I considered my health. I was now at 13 HP.

Still the torrent continued. I was worried about Wren, so small that she was. I hoped she hadn't been thrown beyond where we could find her. Shuffling forward, keeping Tam between us, we eventually came to another party member. As hands connected with flesh, it became obvious it was Jye on their knees, bent forward, rather than clinging to the floor like us. I tried to pull them down, but they wouldn't budge.

Clenching my fists, I battered at Jye's back, provoking them to move, but still nothing. Could they be shielding Wren? She'd been closest to them when the explosion had gone off.

Risking it, I inched open an eye to check and realised it helped little. A smog of sparkling white dust whipped about us. There was no sound. Just a constant bur of roaring wind. Even Jye, who was right before me, was absolutely sheathed in the clouds of shards. I clenched my eye shut almost immediately.

Jye wasn't an idiot, and they cared about the young girl. I weighed up my options. Technically, we'd still not found Wren. It was highly possible that she was what Jye was guarding, unless she'd been blown back farther from the shock wave, which was also somewhat likely.

If I left the party to go search for her, it'd mean Axel would bear the brunt of shielding duties, but it also meant everyone else would still take a fair bit of damage. Add to that, on my own, I'd be unlikely to last long either. I needed Axel to shoulder half. But if Wren was still out there, she would likely die if this crystal tornado continued any longer.

All I wanted to do was protect them. But I couldn't protect them all.

God, this was fucked up. Someone's life was literally in my hands. This wasn't even the first time. Axel had nearly died by my hand. Jye had nearly killed Tam at my request. I'd nearly let myself accept oblivion. It was insane this responsibility kept falling onto my shoulders. But no one in my party had actually been lost yet.

Which meant I had to be doing something right.

[Thick Hide] dropped my standard mana pool to just 10. There wasn't a whole lot I could do. I took a deep breath. Firmly, I told myself that Jye had reacted in time. That beneath them was Wren, safe and sound, and that she wasn't being shredded to bits in the crystal hurricane. She was safe. I repeated it again and again in my head like a mantra.

Now it was my job to keep everyone else alive.

Swearing under my breath, I pulled myself closer to Jye, leaving half of Tam to the elements and opening myself back up to the wind. The gale fought against my movements, buffeting me. The heavy pressure of its current was like hands pummelling me down again and again. Gritting my teeth, I struggled to prop myself up, sweat drenching me under my clothes. My muscles burned, and I managed to make it to my knees.

Reaching back, I grabbed for Tam. I pulled her up and blindly positioned her over Jye's bent form. In a detached thought, I realised this was like posing figurines. This limb goes here, that one there. Eventually, it felt like Tam was huddled over Jye as much as she could. I moved to grab Axel but found my hand patting empty space. Where the fuck had he gone?

I hadn't panicked yet. In fact, I'd been uncharacteristically calm.

But without Axel, this wouldn't work. He needed to be the other half of this. I needed him. The familiar slippery slope of a panic attack began to wind its way through my limbs. My chest, beyond the crystal haze, was tightening, my lungs beginning to fail, body tightening. We'd fail. Everyone would die.

Tam shuddered next to me, clearly fighting back pain.

I froze.

No. Jye and Wren needed protection. Tam needed protection. I couldn't break. Not now. I steeled my mind and gritted my teeth.

Axel was here, somewhere. Definitely.

Breathe in; one, two, three, four, five, six.

My happy place.

Axel was probably just outside my reach. He would be there. Together we could do this. We could keep them safe. Because as much as Axel pissed me off, he was just always there. Even when he didn't want to be. Even after he'd stopped being my friend. He was still there. I could trust that, if there was nothing else.

I breathed out; one, two, three, four.

Then I moved.

I positioned myself adjacent to Tam and Jye, and I wrapped myself over them, trying to cover their bodies as much as I could with my own. Stretching my arms out around them, I squeezed tight to ensure we'd remain together. The relief of having the front of my torso once again away from the stinging bites of the glittery gale was short lived as its absence only intensified the feeling of the shards striking my back. I pressed my head into the nook of Tam's neck to protect my face, and another's fingers threaded between my own.

Reassurance trickled through me. I didn't see it, but I knew. Axel had taken the opposite position of me on the Tam-Jye-Wren huddle pile. The warmth emanating from the rest of my party's bodies was oddly comforting. It allowed me to focus on something other than the painful lashing on my back.

I could keep shielding them for a while since my health was only at 11 HP right now and hadn't dropped much since we'd formed our huddle. With the five of us against the storm, we'd last.

We'd survive.

WE REMAINED LIKE THAT FOR WHAT FELT LIKE DAYS. The gusts eventually let up, though by then my body had since cramped into the position I was holding, my muscles screaming in exhaustion. However, even if I wanted to, I wouldn't have been able let go or move. I was vaguely aware of my health sitting at 3 HP when Axel's fingers finally untwined from mine.

Tam's elbow found my face, smacking me right in the jaw. The pain exploded my mind into wakefulness.

"Get off me!"

Locked into position, I fell back, stiff like a statue. Tam sprung up, her brows furrowed in anger.

"I didn't ask you to do that!" she huffed, brushing shards from her clothes. They made a soft jangle as they scattered over the floor. Speak of ungrateful. My brain was still foggy from the mana cap and exhausted from trying to stay awake so I was unable to make any sort of witty retort.

Jye's torso unfolded following her release to reveal an unconscious Wren's body curled up into a ball before them.

Just like the wind had lifted, so too did the unease inside me. Wren was fine. I'd made the right decision. Control started to tendril back into my body. Everything had gone… well, worse than expected, but better than it could've.

That didn't mean we'd come out unscathed. Everyone looked in pretty bad shape, with scrapes and cuts lining every inch of skin, most no longer bleeding, but in some you could clearly see where the crystal fragments had embedded themselves into the wounds. I probably didn't look too crash hot either. The pip of a single HP returning made me sigh.

"How you doing, boss?" asked Axel.

His back was to me, looking at the remnants of the maze wall ahead. The blond's shirt had been ripped to shreds, and the beginnings of a mottled green-black bruise was starting to bloom beneath the dozens of cuts. I grimaced in secondhand pain.

"Better than you, apparently," I said.

Jye laughed. "Yeah, think again on that, man."

I frowned and angled my head to check my back. It was an almost exact replica of the massacre on Axel's, shreds and bruises and all, but somehow mine seemed redder and angrier, blood slicking down it. Well, duh, I'd obviously taken more damage given my lower health range.

"One of us is gonna have to change," Axel said.

As if seeing them made them real, the pain came back. Whatever had been keeping the ramifications of such damage away from my cerebral system, adrenaline or elsewise, was long gone now, replaced with a weird contentedness and an indescribable pain that exploded from my injuries.

I blacked out.

"Are you feeling better?" Wren asked, the warmth of her hand leaving the small of my back. The soft green glow lighting up the back of my eyelids faded.

Lying face down onto the cold crystal floor, I let out a noncommittal groan. The pain had definitely waned, but unlike when Wren had healed me before, I still felt an ache deep in my bones. I guess her ability had its limits. Though maybe I was just getting old. Wren looked exhausted too, the bags under her eyes even worse than before. I'd told myself we'd stop relying so much on her, but maybe that was impossible.

Still, the guilt about choosing to sacrifice her for the good of the party gnarled talons into my gut. But at least this time I'd made a choice. This time I'd chosen this path. The blame truly was mine.

"Sorry," I said, not meeting her eyes.

"About what?"

Axel scoffed from somewhere to my right. "He thought he left you to die."

"Oh."

Sometimes I wanted to feel the tender flesh of Axel's throat between my hands and to squeeze until he was forever silent. The man had literally zero tact. Though I guess that was part of his charm. Or at least that's what others would have you believe.

"I didn't know for sure Jye had you," I admitted.

She was quiet for a moment. I looked up to check her expression which was in deep thought. Again, I was reminded of how mature she was for her age. Any other kid would've started crying knowing that I'd all but abandoned them.

God, I had abandoned her.

After all my bluster and posturing, after everything I'd promised myself, the second thing's got hard, I'd tossed her aside for someone else to save. What a shit person I was.

"I understand," she finally said with a small sad smile.

That was worse than her breaking down. No kid should feel like they were replaceable. The loss of Chrissie was something that had ruined me. Thinking on it, losing Wren would've destroyed me too. But that was a selfish thought. I should have only been thinking about Wren right now. She must feel utterly distraught. I opened my mouth up to apologise further, to make things right.

"Well, I don't understand," Jye said to my left.

With their words, they slapped me over the top of my head. It was so sudden I barely had time to even comprehend what had happened. As the force snapped my head down, my jaw closed, causing me to bite my tongue. The metallic taste of iron filled my mouth. My HP dropped down by 1 accompanied by a ringing sound in my ears. It was the same pain as hitting your head on a shelf as you stood up, stinging and knowing it'd leave a bump. Hissing in pain, I sat up.

"What the fuck?" I said, clutching at my new injury.

Jye's thick red brows furrowed, and they folded their arms. "Wren's just a kid. She can't stand up for herself. You should know better."

My head smarted, but deep down, I felt I deserved it. Punishment for being a weak person. I had to rely on someone else to protect the people I wanted to keep safe. That acknowledgement was worse than the pain from Jye's hit.

"I trusted you had her."

They stared at me, green eyes narrowed in thought. Then they let out a sigh, long and tired. I didn't think anything could disappoint Jye. They seemed like the type of person that held no expectations in others. But, plain as day, what I saw in their gaze was the same look a parent might give a child who'd broken a glass but brushed the fragments beneath a nearby bed frame. Guilt rippled in me, a vile black inkiness.

"It won't happen again," I said.

And I meant it. There was no point in wanting to protect others if one didn't have the strength to back it up. I'd have to get stronger, have to get smarter. It should be possible. It probably wouldn't have been a week ago. But now… Everything was different. Hell, I was different. Or at least I was trying to be. I needed to think more. To consider other things. There was probably something I had missed that would've assured me of Wren's safety.

Fuck. Of course. The system. If Jye hadn't been protecting her, we would've been alerted when her health reached critical condition. It might not have been enough time to save her, but she also had [Healing Hand], so long as she was conscious, she would've been able to hold out while we had searched for her. There were ways of knowing, I just hadn't been in the right frame of mind to consider them.

"That's what they always say," Jye rolled their eyes.

Axel reached a hand out to me while replying to them, "Come on, as much as I enjoy ribbing Lee, I think that's enough. He already feels like shit. Look at him."

Jye's gaze flicked over to me.

"Oh, yeah, I see it. He looks like shit too."

I sighed. "You guys are really mean, you know."

"If it's any consolation, you don't always look like shit," Axel said with a grin.

Tam, who'd been silent since her upset, cackled to herself. Great, I was the joke of the party. Even Wren seemed to be smiling. At least the mood had lifted.

"I'll take that, I guess," I replied, standing up and brushing myself off.

My body groaned in disapproval. God, I needed another rest, but with our delay because of the trap we'd lost half a day, if not more. It was difficult to tell when the sun didn't move.

The watch on my wrist confirmed that at least five hours had passed. We'd sat in the shard storm for far too long. Filling my lungs with a deep breath, I began to walk toward the now obliterated segment of the labyrinth. The trap was dealt with, so we might as well go forward. Perhaps we'd leave this behind us too.

"I'm fine, you know," Wren said to my back.

I turned to gauge her expression. Shockingly, she did seem okay. I hoped she wasn't disassociating. That was a slippery slope to apathy and depression. Kneeling to her eye level, I replied, "You don't have to be. You're allowed to be angry."

She shrugged. "Life's too short to be angry at mistakes. Especially since it's the end of the world as we know it."

"From the mouth of babes," Axel commented.

"Either way, I am sorry. I'll do better next time."

Tam scoffed. "Men. Can't live with them, can't live with them."

"Preach it, sister," Jye said, snapping their finger in a Z formation.

I repressed a groan. Maybe dying would be better than this.

WHILE THE LABYRINTH WALL had been blown through, with the new edges of the crystalline structure buffed to a beautiful shine from the particle flurry, on the other side still lay more walls, simply just another path. It did not fill me with any reassurance. Because all that meant was this place could be endless, even with any number of traps triggered and walls obliterated.

As a safety precaution, we'd placed Tam in the front position again so her eyes could catch any more errant crystals, and we could avoid another similar trap. Unfortunately, that meant she was standing before me and, every now and again, would glance back with such pure hatred that I could feel it boring a hole into my skull.

Honestly, I was a little afraid to meet her eyes. The animosity in them was feral. I had no idea what I'd done to afford this antagonism, but I was not about to ask either. If anything, it made me thankful I'd added the no-hurting-the-party clause to that collar. Point to me on that.

After continuing walking for a few more hours, mostly in silence, our injuries ticking up with passive regeneration, it became apparent this approach was not working. Or rather that this was working far too slowly.

This place wasn't just a maze. It was a war of attrition. Whoever or whatever was in charge of it had cut off our access to resources and had us locked in fundamentally the same location: in the labyrinth.

I stared forward, my left hand still against the cool gem wall. Up ahead the path split into a T. It was as good a place as any to do this. Tam stopped a few metres down the track at the junction, eyeing the walls with slitted brown eyes.

I said with a clap of my hands, "All right. New plan."

The others paused to hear my next words.

"We cheat."

"Yeah, sure, that's going to go down well. Let's cheat at the game that can teleport us to random third locations and give us superpowers."

I ignored Axel.

"Well, it's not really cheating." I paused. Was it? There hadn't been any rules we'd been given. "There's no knowing how big this maze is. I just want us to get our bearings and check the scope. And just you and Jye alone would clear the wall's height if you stood on each other's shoulders."

Jye held their hands up in immediate rejection. "Not gonna happen."

"Come on, you're both easily the tallest ones in our party."

With a shrug, Axel said, "I'm game."

The giant's eyes narrowed in suspicion.

"Jye…" I said, in a hopefully guilt-inducing tone. "Do it for the party."

An extended groan left their mouth, and then they took a knee. Getting this party to work together was like pulling teeth. Axel grinned in a way that probably more suited a villain, then he clambered intentionally roughly over Jye's legs, stomping his boots into the giant's thigh. The flat, dead look in Jye's eyes told me all I needed to know about how much they were regretting this.

Without warning, the redhead stood with a "hyup," knocking Axel off-balance. They didn't even bother to lift their arms to support him. Was everyone in this party petty? Now half bent over Jye's head, he clung desperately to the giant's clothes, almost definitely swearing under his breath. Teetering slightly, he straightened and, grasping at Jye's head, climbed onto their shoulders.

As he looked out over the wall's tops, he whistled.

"You want the good news or the bad news?"

"Surprise me."

"I can see the cabin. And I think I see other people."

I frowned. "Which of those is the good news?"

He shrugged.

Well, other people were a huge question mark. If they were like Tam had been, they might be given requests to attack us. But they could be like us and simply trying to figure everything out. A big old "fuck you" to our plan of simply looking for the exit.

"We done?" Jye asked.

Axel's gaze met mine, and I stared at him, irritation beginning to grow. As if reading my thoughts, he rolled his eyes, and placed one of his hands across his brows, cutting the sun out of his sight. The rest of us waited for more information.

"They're travelling in a group of three. I can't tell any details. They're headed that way," he said, pointing to the right of the T-junction.

In a bit too much of a calculated manner, Tam inquired, "Far away?"

She certainly did not want to know the answer to wish them well. Axel shook his hand in that middling yes-no gesture. "Not close enough to hear us, I don't think." Axel paused and then cupped his hands around his mouth. "Hey, fuckheads! Can you hear me?"

My heart jumped into my throat, and I shouted, "Axel!"

One day, he'd be the death of us, I swore.

He shook his head in extreme disappointment.

"They didn't even flinch."

I breathed in deep and then exhaled.

"Can you see the exit?"

He swivelled at the waist, looking this way and that. Then, using his heels like stirrups, he nudged Jye to rotate as well. The redhead obliged, albeit with a look that spoke of promised future vengeance. I wondered if in a past life maybe they'd been enemies. It was really the only way I could explain the inherent distaste they had for each other. Surely their first meeting hadn't poisoned their views of each other that much?

"I can't see one. The walls stretch on into the horizon. But there's another building over there," he said, pointing behind us a fair distance rightward. "Looks like a small shrine?"

It was unusual for a labyrinth not to have an exit. But, then again, this place was pretty much magic and sci-fi in one. Still, it begged the question why we were still in range of the cabin. We'd been walking for the better part of a day now. Even with all the twists and turns, we had to have made distance.

"How close is the cabin?" I asked.

"Maybe like a football field away?"

That either meant one of two things. We'd basically walked ourselves in a circle, or the cabin moved. Either were technically possible. It wasn't that much of a stretch to think the starting point might move. If the purpose of this was entertainment, placing all the entertainers in the same starting spot wouldn't have enough building tension. Watching us slowly getting closer, fighting to get the same goal was much more interesting.

The goal had to be the shrine. With no exit, and the only two points of interest being the cabin and shrine… Well, it didn't take a genius to connect the dots.

Though the chance of running into the other group was high if not impossible to avoid if we decided to head toward the shrine. But there were five of us and three of them. If worse came to worse, by numbers we'd be able to hold them off… So long as they weren't stronger than us. With Tam, our composition was a little better balanced.

"Time's up," Jye said, and they shrugged Axel's feet from their shoulders. Static popped.

Axel dropped like a dead weight to the ground, and the air expelled from his lungs from the impact. He just lay there for a moment, not moving, stunned. The rest of us didn't comment. For once, Axel hadn't really deserved this. That wasn't to say that Jye probably had their reasons behind hating him (hopefully just beyond the initial bad "first" impression). But the dude had been giving us pretty useful intel. Feeling a little sorry for him, I reached down to help him up.

He stared at my hand blankly, and for just a moment, I thought I saw his eyes redden, as if beginning to cry. Then he took my hand before using it as leverage to pull himself to a stand. By the time he was completely upright, his expression had returned to normal. At this point, I couldn't even figure out if his reaction had been because of what I'd said at the cabin or if it was a continuation of whatever was messed up with him.

Regardless, since our failed heart-to-heart, I'd sensed Axel had been keeping an emotional distance from me. Which was fair. I'd fumbled hard with my approach. All I had wanted to do was get him to confide in me. But it had come out of me as fear. I wondered if I'd ever find the right time to apologise. To explain that what I had hated then wasn't him but myself.

"Still trying to hold hands?" he asked.

I realised I hadn't let go and snatched my own back, irritated by my train of thought.

"It takes two to tango."

He snorted in response, a bemused expression now resting on his face. I'd forgotten how soft he could look when he wasn't being an arrogant jerk. Probably because it'd been years and years since he wasn't one. At least when he was around other people.

Like a gong struck, a realisation hit me. The changes that Axel had been displaying weren't that he'd become an entirely new person. They *were* Axel. But like the thin veneer of the mask he wore had been melted away, revealing who Axel truly was but only every now and again. That was why I liked him more. He was the Axel I'd... well, the one who'd walked away.

Whatever had happened to him, that he wouldn't share, had done this.

My own words came back to me: "You've become someone I don't know and I hate it." Fuck. *Fuck.* I was so stupid. It was always Axel. I'd just forgotten what he was actually like, under all the shit-eating grins and the cocky facade. This hidden Axel was why I'd never truly given up on him, even after Chrissie.

It was the reason part of me had allowed the fear of failure, of never measuring up to everything he'd become, to influence me so deeply. Because I'd hoped through it all the Axel that I... the Axel that I had been so close to was still there somewhere.

And he was.

And I'd fucked it up.

I was an idiot.

"I love watching baby queers' first steps as much as the next raging dyke, but there's a time and place, boys," Tam said, crossing her arms. "And it's not here or now."

Wren, who'd been silent throughout the entire shoulder-scaling escapade, giggled.

I didn't have the mental bandwidth to deal with Tam's words nor how Wren apparently understood them and found them funny. But Tam wasn't wrong. Whatever apology I owed Axel, now wasn't the appropriate time.

We'd ignore the whole "queers' first steps" thing. Mostly because A: Axel had long since been out of the closet and did not think about me like that, as was evidenced by the twenty-eight years we knew each other, and B: sometimes it felt like being ace didn't even count as being part of the community.

"Point taken," I said.

Axel's mouth opened to say something, but I knew it wouldn't be good, so I cut him off.

"Who's up for a little more semicheating?"

Jye crossed their buff arms over their chest, taking a rather stalwart stance.

"He's not standing on my shoulders again."

"No, trust me, I think you're gonna like this," I said with a grin.

XIV

GIVE THEM AN INCH

JYE'S FACE WAS CRINKLED WITH DELIGHT.

"This isn't what I would've suggested," Axel said as Jye applied two lightening Loads to him and then hefted him up over their shoulder like he was a down-filled pillow. Then, taking far too much pleasure, they grabbed Axel by the scruff of his shirt. Their arm muscles rippled as they yeeted the blond up at the top of the maze wall.

I half expected him to hit an invisible barrier, like an out of bounds stopper in a game, and bounce back. But he landed on top without issue, albeit ungracefully.

Scrambling, Axel grabbed for purchase. He landed on his stomach, his legs and arms dangling on each side of the labyrinth divider. I could hear a few choice words he was calling Jye as he calmed down. The gravity taking hold of him again was clearly perceptible when Jye released their ability from Axel's body. After a breath, he stood, testing out the top of the wall for firmness. Axel stomped his foot down, once, twice, and then three times, then shrugged. He shot me and the others a thumbs up.

"Looks dece."

"Who's next on the block?" Jye asked.

One by one, Jye lightened us and threw us up onto the top of the wall until it was only them standing down on the floor. It was odd being semiweightless for that short time. Like I was wading through water instead of air. Surprisingly, when Axel had been in the sporting goods section of Kmart, he'd picked up some rope. Which had been a stunningly good idea.

As a team, we lowered one end of the rope. Jye applied Load to themself and pulled themself up as we remained anchorage. Yes, we all could've used the rope after Axel got up there, but I didn't want to ruin Jye's fun. You gotta let people get the joy out of the small things, or you run the risk of never wanting to enjoy life again. Not to say I had been there. Well…

Eventually, all of us ended up atop the wall.

From there, I could see that the maze stretched as far as the eye could see, disappearing in hazy lines as the curve of the world hid the true expanse from us. It really simply never ended. That proved that. There was no exit to the labyrinth. Not that I didn't trust Axel's word, but also I didn't trust his word. I guess the shrine was the only option left.

I turned to check the direction Axel had previously said the other people were in. Just vaguely I could see blurry humanoid shapes. It was incredibly difficult to make out anything in more detail, though it appeared one was slightly smaller than the others. Part of me was hoping it wasn't a child. Still, if it was only us and them in here, then our chances were still pretty good with clearing the Dungeon. Axel had to have known the trio was so far away they wouldn't hear us. He'd just acted like that to be an asshole.

Pinching at the bridge of my nose, I scanned for the shrine.

It wasn't difficult to find.

To the side Axel had indicated, in a depressed level of ground, sat a stone shrine glowing faintly blue from the candles lit upon its offering porch. It was reminiscent of a Shinto temple but had none of the red gates. It was also unlabelled, not depicting to whom or what it was dedicated to.

If I were being honest, it looked like a poor asset flip, much like the cabin. Other than the otherworldly gem maze, everything else in this Dungeon lacked imagination and creativity, almost like whoever had designed it had been following a tutorial and had just been fucking around in the developing program.

"This way," I said, and I mentally plotted out our pathway to the shrine.

Being on top of the walls gave us the advantage of seeing more, but it also made it more difficult to get to certain places because of the gaps that turns and splits added to our pathway. That said, it would be easier progress, and we would actually feel like we were advancing toward something rather than wandering aimlessly.

It was amazing what increased morale did for the human spirit.

Wren started playing I Spy and eventually cajoled us all to join. Though initially petulant, Tam also participated, won over by the cheer in Wren's voice. Given the simple environment we were in, the game didn't last long, ending when we looped back to Jye who again chose to spy the pockets on the back of Wren's Pikachu bag. We moved through a gauntlet of other spoken games until we were worn out from speaking. Instead, we walked in silence as the blue shimmer of the shrine's candles grew brighter and brighter on our approach.

"Kinda reminds me of when I went to Nara," Jye mentioned, cupping a hand over their brow.

"Of course you've been to Japan," Axel said, none too dryly.

For once, Axel's reaction was understandable. He'd been talking up a trip to Japan for years now, adding all these visits to his itinerary and scheduling events that he literally kept an Excel spreadsheet of.

Since Axel used his leave almost as soon as he accrued it, he hadn't been able to save enough to cover the length of trip he'd wanted. He usually preferred one- or two-day trips to exotic locations, like when he'd supposedly met Jye. The past few years, he'd been a bit more precious and had almost hit two weeks of paid leave before the Gates. The last tabs I'd seen open on his phone had been airline websites. It had to smart that he'd never be able to live out the vacation of his dreams.

"My parents took me there once," Wren said. "I don't remember much, but the food was really good."

"Don't even get me started on the cuisine, man," Jye sighed, an expression of mourning crossing their face. "Damn, I miss it all so much. Matsuri yakisoba and takoyaki, all-you-can-eat yakiniku and nomihodai, combini onigiri and sandos, the hidden gems of ekibentos, a vending machine around every corner, single stall ramen booths, Mr. Donut's Pon de Rings… Euuuugh, even just the cheapest conveyor belt sushi with complimentary green tea on tap…"

Curious, I asked, "How long did you visit?"

They shook their head. "I worked there for a year. Went more rural where none of the younger people want to stay, but it was a damn dream."

"Where'd you go?"

"Ibaraki."

Axel snorted. "Wasn't that listed as the least attractive prefecture several years in a row?"

"Less tourists, less traffic." They shrugged and then grinned. "Pure cultural immersion."

I checked Axel's expression, and his face was scrunched into bitter jealousy.

"Babes, it's nothing to cry home about," Tam said. "It's just like any other place in the world. Just more difficult to get around if you can't speak a lick of the language."

"You've been too?" Axel inquired, the envy almost greening his face.

She seemed startled for a moment and then crossed her arms, her brows furrowed. "That's nunya."

Clearing my throat, trying to steer Axel away from exploding or having a breakdown, I said, "My dream destination would probably be Antarctica."

This earned a concerned look from each of my party members. Well, it was where I *had* wanted to go. Before the Gates. But I guess if someone asked me that now, my answer would be different. All I really wanted to do was go back to my hometown and see my parents. Back before all this, I hadn't really thought of visiting them for a while now. Typically, I saw them during Christmas and spent a couple days in Charleville. But it was only September. I wouldn't have even thought about scheduling the trip for another month.

"Oh, honey," Tam said, and it was almost like she genuinely pitied me. That said, I didn't know her that well, so it could just as well be scorn. She was hard to read. And something told me she preferred it that way. I wondered where the animosity she'd held toward me had disappeared to. Maybe through the silence, she'd reflected? Or maybe she wasn't one to hold a grudge. Some other people in our group could learn a thing or two from her (hint: it was Jye).

I still didn't know what I'd done to earn her ire. She'd seemed pretty chill before the whole wall explosion. Was it because we'd all be huddled up, and she wasn't fond of physical touch?

Oh, I guess I hadn't told her I asexual. Maybe she thought I was feeling her up the entire time. How did I even clear up that, if it was what she'd been angry at me about? "Sorry for touching you while saving your life"? "I do not find you sexually attractive, so me touching you was not inappropriate"? Well, if she'd forgiven me, or forgotten it, it might just be best I let the whole matter go too.

In response to her comment, with my tone definitely not being defensive at all, I said, "What's wrong with wanting to go to Antarctica?"

"Is there anything… to do there?"

I turned to cast an accusing glare at Wren. "Of course. There's nature tours."

"What nature?" Jye asked.

"Penguins and seals."

"Right."

Candidly, the number one real reason I had wanted to go to Antarctica was because Axel wouldn't be there, and I wouldn't be expected to be a human being. I could just do nothing. I think part of me had always been dreaming about escaping the monotony of life I'd crafted for myself but never had the guts to do it. The others wouldn't hear me say that. "Come on, guys, really, Antarctica is actually cool."

"Like from a distance, yeah," Jye said.

Wren's brow furrowed. "Isn't it night time for half the year there?"

I flung my hand out, aware that now that I was speaking with over exaggerated actions. "That's part of the charm. No risk of sunburn."

Tam snorted, as she tucked an errant braid behind her ear. "You're literally BIPOC. You're telling me you slip slop slap?"

"I— Just because I don't, doesn't mean I'm immune to sunburn."

"Always thought you were more the Arctic kind," Axel said, and through the back-and-forth I realised this was the first time he'd spoken since I'd suggested my "dream destination."

He couldn't possibly know what it meant to me. Axel had stopped trying to understand me ever since Chrissie passed. Once he knew me like I was his reflection, but that'd been when we were kids. Yeah, I'd held him dear when we were children, and it'd been mutual. We'd been practically attached at the hip. Back then, I'd thought… No, I didn't like reflecting too much about the time when our friendship had been at its strongest. The memories just made me feel nauseous. Because in almost all of them Chrissie was there somewhere.

"Same diff," I replied.

Jye blinked in offence. "Excuse-a moi?"

I shrugged. "They're basically mirror reflections, just on opposite sides of the globe."

"The Arctic has cities," Wren said. "People live there."

I stared. "People live in Antarctica too."

Jye folded their arms in judgement. "Like… five people. For a portion of the year. On a research station."

Everyone was now giving me a very worried look. I regretted bringing it up. At the very least, Axel seemed to have forgotten his lost trip to Japan. So, mission success on Operation Stop Axel From Having Another Mental Breakdown. Probably needed to workshop that name.

However, even though I'd pivoted the conversation topic, why didn't I feel very content? Under the weight of everyone's stares, the desire to further redirect the subject of conversation suddenly grew. I didn't need my party to dissect my inner fears like this. That depth of knowing me didn't even come with a lifetime membership.

I cleared my throat, glancing around as we walked.

"I spy with my little eye…"

A collective groan sprung up from the group, especially considering that it looked like the shrine might be one more hour with all the detours we had to take by following the top of the walls.

As I searched, I repeated, "I spy with my little eye…" I frowned, squinting into the distance to our left side. "A fireball?"

The silent ball of fire was jettisoning toward us, closing the distance at an alarming rate. If I hadn't noticed, given how relaxed and vulnerable we'd been, one of us would've been taken off guard and hit for certain. At its trajectory, so long as we avoided where it would go, we'd be fine. Silently, we parted, the party splitting in half with Tam, Axel, and me on the left, and Jye and Wren on the right.

The party's collective gaze watched as the fireball approached the gap we'd left for it to pass through. It sailed right by us, the searing heat warming my arms, the hiss of its flames dancing in the air.

The ball's arc was descending slightly, and Axel held a flat hand to his brow, his eyes narrowed, as he tracked its path long after it had passed any danger to us. The fireball dipped between a pair of walls a few metres away from us, its flight coming to an end out of our sight.

"Well, that was anticlimactic," Jye said.

"Absolutely piss poor performance," Tam agreed.

Wren folded her arms in consternation. "Yeah, it was a bit boring."

It was also the first example of ranged magic we'd seen bar Jye throwing their magicked weapons. And this particular fireball had not been very effective. Part of me was glad none of our party was primarily a ranged damage spellcaster.

I glanced in the direction the fireball must've originated from but saw nothing.

At the very least, the spellcaster had quite an impressive reach. Though with an attack like that, it seemed like a shittier class category. Maybe we should avoid getting a spellcaster in our party. If we looked at it from a performance and entertainment perspective, ranged magic wasn't that interesting either which meant less XP. The only time ranged magic was fun to witness was when there were pyrotechnics and explosions; the whole shebang.

Axel said, "Must've been one of the three other players I spotted."

"Must be. Eyes out for future attacks, everyone."

That answered one of my questions; the other players were not like us. They were more similar to Tam. Ready to kill and attack for whatever they wanted. They'd done a terrible job of it, but incompetence didn't mask their intent. It was clear they were on the offensive. I hadn't been ready to let Jye kill Tam, not fully. But this other party… If it was kill or be killed, I knew what I'd choose if worst came to worst.

We continued on, a speed in our step that hadn't previously been there. The silence between us was anxious, quivering. As pathetic as the attack had been, it had changed the tone. It had sharply brought into relief the fact that this was still dangerous. That was something we had forgotten in our pursuit of the shrine. Influenced by the high of discovering a superior tactic to achieve our goals, we'd lost sight of reality.

We couldn't let that happen again. Despite the human need for highs and lows, and rest and joy, some part of my brain had to remain on alert at all times. There was no skill or shortcut to learning this new thought process. Just pure practice.

I wondered what Mrs. Brown would think of my intentional choice to compartmentalise my actual thoughts.

Well, what did that matter now?

The world was different. Everything was different. Thinking differently was just one part of fitting in now.

As WE WALKED, every now and then I'd glance back in the direction the fireball had originated from, hoping to catch a glimpse of our wannabe attackers. But no luck. They were either incredibly skilled in hiding or, like my previous assumption, their range was out of this world. When I'd seen them before, they'd seemed pretty far away, considering I could only make out their silhouettes.

But that thought would have to wait for later.

We'd finally arrived above the temple.

Its presence as it loomed before us was daunting. A fog clung around the area directly surrounding it, as if warning us that danger lurked within. The candles flickered without wind, their cool blue flames dancing wildly, the melting wax and lit wicks never shortening; a looping animation. The air smelled damp, almost like mildew or mould, but there was no water or moisture visible.

Like the terminator line between day and night, the two biomes of the misty temple and desert sun clashed, blurring together to form something less than the sum of its parts. A dirty mush of atmospheres. Someone needed to get the smudge tool and go ham on their blending.

Our party stood there for a second, closer than we'd ever been to completing the Dungeon, letting the moment sink in.

Fuck. Maybe we could do it. We could clear it. Hell, maybe we'd be more like Kimi who'd cleared their Dungeon than Riku who… could be dead.

The thought gave me pause. We'd heard no announcements about any other Dungeon since we'd entered ours. Were we… cut off from the outside world when we were in here in more ways than I'd originally thought? Did time even pass in the Dungeons? Or were notifications about external events forcibly filtered out to ensure we focused on our own "show"?

Axel looked about ready to say something, his blond brows furrowed in consideration.

"Hello, strangers!"

It was a voice I did not recognize in the slightest, the accent so foreign to my ears I wasn't sure the words were even being spoken in English. And I couldn't pinpoint the origin either. If pressed, I'd have probably said something between Korean and Irish with perhaps a dash of New York in some vowels.

As a unit, we angled our heads, looking straight down from our position atop the wall, interrobangs etched above us.

Gesticulating wildly below us was a short person wearing an overcoat that'd make the biblical Joseph jealous from its flashy design. It was like nothing I had ever seen before, the fabric gradating texture and colour in a way I couldn't comprehend, almost shifting as I watched. I frowned, wondering if I was seeing things.

"Are you coming here?" Again, there was that bizarre accent.

We continued to stare. There was no air of hostility about the stranger, and we were all caught off guard by how harmless and yet completely alien the person appeared.

Built like a barrel, as wide at the shoulders as at the hips, the newcomer held a hand to a brow to cut out the sun. Above that brow was a beauty mark, ala Angela Jolie. And from where we stood, it looked like the stranger's eyes and hair were the same cosplayer silver, the latter of which was cropped close to the head. Perhaps the largest thing of note was a spattering of lighter skin amidst an overall darker hue; vitiligo.

"We *were*," I replied, now wondering if that was a good choice.

"The name is Gigi! It is a pleasure to meet you. Xem— Hmmm. Xir? No. Xe would… That is still not correct. Me would— No, it is I!" Xe punched into the air with a clenched fist to celebrate xir arrival at the correct personal pronoun. "Sorry, your lingua franca is quite complicated. *I* would like to be your friend!"

I'd once considered Jye the golden retriever type, but this person… It was like rocking up to a pedigree contest only to find out that you'd entered a mutt. Jye was barely even a goldendoodle in comparison. In Gigi's expression, there wasn't a hint of malice, no ulterior motive. Xir smile was serene, trusting. Welcoming and without any guile. Like some sort of celestial being from a fucked-up Avant Garde indie film.

"I accidentally entered the Dungeon, and I have been waiting for help," xe continued.

Immediately, Axel was on the offensive. "Yeah, sure, a likely story. Explain how you ended up here, then."

"I walked. The maze was quite large. Should you have further questions to ascertain my trustworthiness, you are very welcome to ask me anything you would like!"

Hit with a seemingly infallible response, Axel froze, not expecting something so unassuming and open. In his hesitation, Tam surged forward to take the interrogator's spotlight. She crossed her arms in front of her, her bosom under the knitted top propped above her forearms. I caught Jye's gaze drop to them for a moment. They seemed to be reappraising their attitude toward Tam as they did so. Though Jye was nonbinary, something told me that Tam, as a self-proclaimed… lesbian, wouldn't so much as bat an eye in their direction. I'd witnessed Axel's cold disregard to those he wasn't interested in enough to recognise the same vibe from others.

Speaking to Gigi, Tam drawled, "Why haven't ya moseyed on into the shrine, huh?"

"I do not believe I would be sufficiently strong enough to succeed in completing the Dungeon."

The honest response, and new information, caused Tam's mouth to pucker up in consideration. It was a reasonable response. Perhaps xe had checked inside and found the challenge to be beyond xem. It was completely understandable. Especially when the alternative might very well be death.

Jye's eyes now back on xem, they tilted their head. "I've only got one question."

"Please ask! I am enjoying this conversation."

"Can I have your coat?"

Xir expression became sorrowful. "You can not. This is my [REDACTED] I have left from [REDACTED]. I could not part with it."

Though the harsh blast of Jye's glitch had to smart, they simply mirrored the same emotion as Gigi, nodding, and then they bowed their head. They brought a closed fist to their chest and tapped it. "Respect."

The only one out of our party to not speak yet was Wren. She was looking on in confusion and interest, one of her mousy brows raised, her head slightly askew. It seemed as though she had at least a dozen questions she wanted to ask and was running through which was most pertinent. I wondered what inquiry would win out.

She landed on: "Are you human?"

I clamped a hand over her mouth, offended on the stranger's behalf. You couldn't just ask if someone was human because of a skin condition. Wait, was vitiligo a condition? Oh God, should I be cancelled?

"[REDACTED]," xe said in answer, then xir brow furrowed. Gigi tried again, xir mouth opening to form words. Xe said, "[REDACTED]." Xe attempted once more: "[REDACTED]."

Ignoring the ramifications of what Gigi's moderation meant in regards to xir humanity, I pinched the bridge of my nose and held up a hand. "Stop, stop, stop. You're not getting anywhere. I don't think we're allowed to hear that yet, whatever it is."

Wren harrumphed in disappointment, clearly annoyed that her question had been wasted. Still, the inability for Gigi to respond answered just as much as any words would have.

Gigi jutted xir jaw in understanding, silver eyes blazing. Were those natural?

"I see! This is an early Dungeon, then. I am most glad to hear that."

I cocked my head. Xanthe had said I'd been quite early to Twilight too. Did that mean… Would there be many other Dungeons?

I knew asking would be useless, since Gigi was likely to be censored from saying anything specific based on previous conversations. I wondered what I should ask. Xe'd been answering all our questions without asking anything in response. Lost in my thoughts, I was dragged back by Gigi waving again.

"May I join your party?" xe asked, a wide grin on xir face.

A beat passed as everyone else's gaze met, then centred on me. I saw the panic in their eyes. As they all each attempted their own silencing technique, clamouring at me, trying to pull me away, slap a hand over my mouth, or tackle me to the floor, I managed to make out my question to Gigi.

"What's your class?"

I struggled against them to hear xir response.

"I am a Vanguard."

It was barely a thought. I would not be looking this gift horse in the mouth. Gigi was going to a veritable fountain of information when we progressed further. Much more than Tam. At least as much as she was willing to divulge, which had been practically nothing. And our party *sorely* needed a tank which the class [Vanguard] absolutely screamed.

Not to mention, I'd technically not made an irreversibly lethal decision yet.

The invite was sent from within the entanglement of limbs that was my teammates.

Gigi has joined your party.

"I am very fond of the party name. What an exclusive group we shall be."

Tam's grip tightened around my neck but stopped before any pressure was too uncomfortable. Thank God for that collar. She let out a frustrated yowl and pulled away. Axel, however, didn't hold back, grabbing me by the scruff of my shirt and shoving his face close to mine. His expression was unreadable but underpinned with exasperation and something else I couldn't comprehend. Yeah, that checked out. Classic Axel.

"Are you genuinely insane?"

I grinned apologetically.

He took a deep breath and then hissed out through clenched teeth, "Every fucking time."

Even Wren appeared unimpressed with my antics.

"You're the party leader, and it's ultimately your decision who joins, but I'll be fucked if this just adds another body to the pile that I have to keep healing," she said.

I shouldn't have been surprised considering her previous outburst when I'd nearly killed Axel, but I was still taken aback. This shift in her vernacular was concerning, but who was to say it wasn't normal for kids these days? Temper apparently ameliorated by her words, Axel released my collar and strode away. If I wasn't getting choked out by Axel, was it really a day ending with Y?

Gigi stared at Wren. "Are you not a child?"

With a sigh, she said, "What does it look like, genius?"

"[REDACTED]."

"I like xem," Jye commented, not reacting with any visible pain.

Huh. I wondered if they were getting used to the glitch sound. The redhead was made out of stronger stuff than I. Recalling the noise myself caused goose bumps to form on my arms and legs.

Well, that was at least one person in my court, even if it was just Jye. That had to count for something.

"Come, come! I am eager to add this Dungeon to my [REDACTED]," Gigi said.

Now what the hell could that even mean?

DUNGEON
HUNTER

XV

DOT DOT DOT

THE MOST ANNOYING THING about it all was that I knew asking would be pointless. I could only form conjecture about Gigi's words. Xe appeared to have foreknowledge of the Dungeons, much like Xanthe, but unlike them, xe was… human? I didn't want to put any stock behind xir moderated response to Wren's question, but it felt like the only real option. Xe looked human enough. If I saw them at Comicon I probably wouldn't have batted an eye. Gigi *could* just be an exceptionally weird person.

We all carefully made our way down from the wall to stand next to the xem. Xe smiled widely at us, flashing pure white teeth more suited to a celebrity who had them blasted with hydrogen peroxide on the weekly. Now closer, I could study Gigi a little more. Xir skin was flawless, nary a wrinkle to be seen. In fact, the only thing that could be said to mar xir dappled complexion was the beauty spot above xir brow. Brows that, in their silver, were so thin and sparse you had to double take to see them.

Judging xir age was impossible. Xe could be anywhere from twenty to fifty, maybe even older. Which would either make xem older than the rest of us or only older than Wren. That was if Tam was actually into her late thirties. I'd never ask her, though. I feel like somehow she'd be able to break the command on her collar and run me navel to nose.

"So, what's in the shrine?" I asked, thinking it a safe question. It wasn't anything about the background or lore of the "game" we were in, so it should be a topic we could breach. There'd be no point in censoring that information since it didn't give us any unfair advantage since Gigi would already know it.

Xe blinked. "I do not know."

"What the fuck," came Tam's understandable response. "Why is everyone so damn chicken shit. This party might as well be called Just No N—" Her gaze slid over Wren for a moment. "—Guts. Even the clown can barely squeak xir nose in the face of the unknown."

The newcomer to our party looked confused. "I am not a clown. I am [REDACTED]."

Jye ran a hand under their chin in consideration, then nodded. "She's just being mean because she can't hurt you anymore."

They weren't wrong. Something in Tam craved violence. Whether it was her sponsorship with Mumma, or an innate quality within the woman, she was ready to throw down and *enjoy* it at any moment. I only hoped that whatever awaited us in the shrine would whet her appetite.

At the very least, she wouldn't be able to come directly at any of us in Just Friends. Somewhere in the deepest vestiges of my brain, something I didn't want to acknowledge, the phantom pain of her blade slicing through my clavicle still fresh in my body, part of me wanted to see her fight someone else and mean it. It would be something worth seeing.

Well, if the shrine held combat, for once our party might stand a chance with its current composition. That's if we could all work together. I cast a glance at the faces of my team and suddenly felt the odds shift dramatically lower.

Tam loathed or maybe pitied me, or had, despised Axel, and thought little of Jye. Jye hated Axel (a lot) in a will-they-or-won't-they kind of way and was a bit on the off-and-off with me but somehow was only judgemental toward Tam. Wren was acting normal, but there was no chance she was *really* okay with what I'd done with the wall explosion. Axel was still his weird self, disliked Jye in general, couldn't tolerate Tam, mostly ignored Wren, and had lowkey been avoiding me.

In fact, the only person in our party who didn't harbour some sort of grudge was the person we'd met not just five minutes ago. And xe looked to be joining us on Tam's shit list, if her disgusted expression was anything to go by.

Oh, what tangled webs we weave.

Trying to put the party's interrelationships on the back burner, I asked, "Gigi, what are your abilities? And, Tam, tell me yours." I paused. "Actually, can you all just give me carte blanche on access to your skills?"

The silver-eyed potentially nonhuman tilted xir head. "I do not understand your usage of French. But my skills are Shield Wall and Focus. I am primarily here to defend."

Cheering my own victory in inviting xem to the party, I said, "You have no idea how relieving that is to hear. My only skill is Channel. I need everyone's consent to use their abilities."

Gigi nodded once curtly. "You have my consent."

Thinking back to the [Collar of Control], I turned to Tam. "This is part of helping the party."

"Jeez, sucks that Mumma says this don't count as 'when necessary.' You should really learn to pick your words better, sunshine." She bared her teeth at me, a smug look in her brown eyes.

I breathed out slowly, not allowing the anger to form. Yeah, that really was on me. But when push came to shove, she'd have to lend a hand. I had to count on that and her own desire for self-preservation. I immediately gave up on even learning her abilities.

For their part, Jye seemed genuinely apologetic. "Oh, damn, sorry, man. Hadn't realised I hadn't given you the go-ahead yet. You can use

Load all you want. Though I really don't know how to explain how to use it." They scratched at their chin. "It's like… summoning the emotion of a grunt." The redheaded giant shrugged. "Yeah, good luck."

"Thanks," I said, and even I wasn't sure I meant it.

Wren smiled. "You're welcome to use mine, Lee."

Returning her expression, I raised a hand and ruffled her short hair. She giggled as she pushed me away. The childish delight made me recall Chrissie, but for once the thought wasn't tinged with regret and sadness and loss. It was just a nice reminder of her laughter.

With a strange surge of affection, I said, "Who knows, maybe I can pay you back sometime. By my count, I think I owe you something like two lives?"

"I mean, you're responsible for everyone. You have to make that four because of Axel and Tam."

A chuckle escaped me. "Did not know you were keeping tabs like that, kid."

Her smile faltered. "Well, a part of me is always thinking about stuff like that. Since the Gates appeared. Lives I've saved and lives I…"

Immediately guilt swamped me. I'd reminded her of the trauma of her past. Real smooth, Lee. Eugh. Kids weren't supposed to carry such weight on their shoulders. She shouldn't be holding on to life and death like this.

"I'll tell you what, let me ease your burden on that. I'll keep tally instead. Sound good?"

Wren's head tilted in consideration, and her lips scrunched together. "You're gonna count us all, right?"

"Does he have to include Tam or Jye?" Axel asked from the side.

I ignored him. "Cross my heart."

She thought for a moment then nodded. "Okay."

Her smile seemed relieved, and I was glad we'd had this moment.

Taking in the expressions of my companions, despite how messy everything was between us all, a warmth filled my chest. I may not be fond of some of them. I may not understand most of them. But was I ever happy to have them.

Without them, I don't think I would be standing where I was. Hell, I was sure I'd probably be dead. Likely would've been killed trying to go into a Gate by myself without any planning, unable to fight the compulsion, and having no clue about any of what was happening. At the very least, with everyone here, slowly learning about the Dungeons, we were progressing.

Surviving.

Granted, Tam had nearly killed me, and I'd nearly killed Axel, so this nice feeling probably wasn't mutual all round.

I jutted my jaw at the empty hall of the walls directly opposite the shrine. "Let's do a rest cycle. After that, we scope out the supposed exit."

"Not to put a hamper on your grand plans, but what about that random fireball? For all we know, that trio is watching in wait for us to be vulnerable. They could get the jump on us like a certain someone while we're recuperating."

I hated when Axel had a point. Tam said nothing, her gaze shifting from side to side. Yeah, like she could pinpoint the others from where we were. We weren't that lucky.

I tried to consider the party's skills, wondering if anything could help us. Maybe I could get Gigi to use… what was it? Shield something? So long as the mana or stamina cost wasn't insane, they could probably maintain it. And maybe even I could use it.

Gigi held up a finger. "Oh, I can use Focus!"

"What's that do?" Wren asked.

It sounded like something an archer or martial artist might use. Intense concentration to ensure that they either hit their target or to ensure they imbued the entirety of their strength into one specific target upon impact.

I wasn't sure what a [Vanguard] could use it for. Possibly, something similar to an archer to ensure they don't let someone through their guard? It might be a little too heavy on the ask for Gigi or me to continue doing that during lookouts.

Xe didn't respond to Wren's question. Maybe xe were trying to think of how to word xir ability? God, I hoped it wouldn't be a repeat of Jye's glitch. Which reminded me, I hadn't checked out the party's status for some time.

We hadn't gotten any experience from the trap triggering, which was quite disappointing, but I guess we'd been entirely obscured from view during it. The crystal wind would've completely blanketed us from curious eyes; the equivalent of watching the static hash on an old analogue TV. If that was that case, perhaps whoever or whatever was observing us wasn't all-seeing. I stored that thought away for future consideration.

As I waited for Gigi to explain xir skill, I popped open the party member menu with a thought.

Just Friends Party | LVL 18

Lee | LVL 2 | All-Rounder (Party Leader)

Axel | LVL 2 | Combatant

J[illegible] | LVL 1 | [illegible]

Wren | LVL 1 | Synergist

Tam | LVL 2 | Cutthroat

Gigi | LVL 10 | Vanguard

I stopped and stared at Gigi's level, then glanced between my screen and xem. LVL FUCKING 10? My mind turned into a mess of thoughts, all of them accelerating into theories before crashing into each other and collapsing into meaningless muck. I had no words. I had nothing to say. Even a question wouldn't come out. After a second, my blue window popped up, revealing something I had never seen before.

Party member Gigi wants to share player data.

Accept | Reject

We could fucking do that?

Giving me an apologetic smile, xe said, "Sorry. It has been some time since I last did this. I forgot how."

I didn't have the time to unpack that statement, and instead, I consented to receiving Gigi's information.

A second screen appeared to the right of mine, in a different hue of blue, something closer to purple. Looking between the two, it became clear that this full menu was Gigi's entire system. It responded to my thoughts as though it was mine, but the information was Gigi's. I scoured xir data with deep interest.

Other Student* Player Gigi | Vanguard | LVL 10

Titles:

[Other] Helping others is the only way the owner of this title earns XP.

[Student] Boosts all experience gain.

100 HP | 10 MANA | 30 STAMINA

Traits:

[Stubborn] One injury per Dungeon that would otherwise result in death results in HP remaining at 1.

Abilities:

[Shield Wall | 5S] Summon a spectral barrier to defend party members.

[Focus | 10Mc] Project an aura that diverts range attacks to the user.

11 STR | 20 CON | 1 DEX | 10 END | 10 WIL | 2 INT

***Title retained while player remains a member of party Just Friends.**

There was so much to take in that I struggled with what to focus on. I hadn't checked my own name since we'd begun, but looking at it now, the title we'd gained upon entering this Dungeon had affixed itself to mine with the same bottom disclaimer. In simple writing, it said:

Student* Player Lee Bastion Castillo.

Thinking back to it, the wording of the announcement had been "Party Just Friends rewarded title of Student." So, the title was attached to the party, not the party members… If anyone joined our party from now on, they would get the temporary title. That was insane. It was like a permanent optional buff. It could even be used as a way to convince people to join our side.

I rescanned Gigi's info. The [Other] title was a weird one. I guess that was why Gigi had been so eager to join our party (and also why xe was so… odd). Xe wouldn't be able to level up without helping others. But at LVL 10 already, did xe even need to level up any further? Could xe level up further? Surely there was a cap.

Though at xir level, their attributes were kind of low. Not like *my* low, but much lower than I imagined someone at LVL 10 to be. As I considered xir stats, I had to agree that the distribution made sense for their class. Xir foundation of focusing Constitution to take damage and then spreading the secondary priority equally into Strength to fend off people, Endurance to survive the damage, and probably Willpower to defend against magic was well thought out. Dexterity and Intelligence being xir dump attributes was understandable; xe was essentially meant to be an immutable wall.

Still, the numbers looked like they belonged to a much lower-level player. If I added them all up, it equalled out to 54. Granted, in totality, mine was only 24, so maybe that *was* a decent sum of attribute points. But it begged the question, how had Gigi gotten credits if xe'd increased their stats? I'd have to ask xem later.

Their trait was interesting too and would be super helpful if things got super dire. With [Stubborn], xe could basically tank past xir death, though not for long. I wonder how it worked for injuries like Axel and I had sustained. Bleeding and lingering DoTs… Did it mean xe'd survive a single hit of either of those status damagers and then die anyway? That'd suck ass.

And, finally, the abilities… [Shield Wall] wasn't half bad. If xe could summon it multiple times, the entire party might very well be incredibly safe. Since I had the stamina required to use it too, we could even double them up. I turned my attention to the ability that Gigi had suggested xe use: [Focus].

It was literally the perfect skill for our party and our current situation. I had been an idiot to think of dismissing it. Or maybe whoever had named it was the idiot. Who calls an aggro skill "Focus"?

But, man, I was a little jealous. Why hadn't my character sheet even slightly looked like this?

"Gigi, damn."

I blinked, realising that I'd been silent for an exceptional amount of time, and everyone was waiting on me to say something more. Briefly, I explained what just happened. In the corner of my eye, I noticed Jye wearing a particularly sour face. That'd figure. They couldn't read their status window at all.

Clearing my throat, I said, "Gigi's ability Focus draws range fire. It'll focus aggression on xem. We'll split watch fifty-fifty between me and Gigi. Pick your poison." I flourished a hand between the two of us.

Tam chose Gigi. I could understand why. She wanted to keep an eye on xem. Jye also chose Gigi. That I understood too. The redheaded giant had taken a liking to xem. Wren and Axel picked me, which secretly made me happy. Maybe Wren had truly forgiven my mishap. I was surprised Axel had gone with me, but he'd been the slowest to react, so he must've ended up with me rather than actually wanting to be on my watch shift.

Ah, well.

In silence, we set up camp, Gigi mixing into the fold as though xe'd been part of us from the get go. I'd given xem one of the watches I'd taken from Kmart, and excitedly they'd added it to their wrist.

I watched xem curl into xir coat, having refused Wren's bedroll on account of being worried xe'd stretch it out. Given the bare ten-centimetre height difference between them, I really don't feel it was a genuine concern but a courtesy extended to her out of politeness (though possibly the width and breadth of Gigi's body might present the issue).

Generally, after a person refused an offer, you were meant to double check, and then they could accept without feeling like they're imposing. But maybe Wren wasn't old enough to pick up on those types of social cues. That or she'd deliberately chosen to ignore the etiquette. It was possible. Out of the whole party, the only person she'd been outright insulting to had been Gigi.

I volunteered my group for first watch, and I activated [Channel] and borrowed [Focus] from Gigi. Much like [Thick Hide], the ability had a mana cap, halving the pool I had access to. In contrast to Axel's skill, which felt like a warm second skin, Gigi's [Focus] was more like someone whispering your name across from you in a crowded hall. You could tell something was there, you knew it, but when you turned to look… Nothing. The ability was an unseeable presence that I could innately tell where it ended. It was like having another sense.

We settled in, cracking open some of the packets of health food we'd scavenged from Woolies. There had still been around four days left, but with Gigi, now we'd be only okay for maybe three. That was assuming xe ate… Yeah. Xe was human, so xe definitely needed sustenance. I wasn't even able to convince myself.

Axel and I divvied out the food between ourselves and Wren, and we passed around one of the beer bottles we'd refilled with water back at the gym. I was surprised that in the desert biome we hadn't been consuming more considering the heat. We'd definitely been sweating more. Well. I had. This fucking temperature. I was essentially a human water fountain, with my pores being bubblers.

I took back what I'd said about dry heat being better than wet heat. Clearly, the narrator of that documentary had never lived through either.

Because both sucked.

After the exploding wall, most of us had had to change, with the material we'd been wearing ripped and shredded beyond usefulness. You could have barely called any of it even rags, to be honest. Not wanting to waste a completely clean set, I'd just changed shirts. My hoodie had been eviscerated through to my tank top underneath. Surprisingly, my tracksuit pants had come out of the gale whole, though they now looked stylishly distressed. Or that was what I was telling myself. In reality, I probably looked like I'd lost my home in Cyclone Tracy.

That was the one good thing about the apocalypse, though. Without the social pressure of having to look decent in public, so long as I wasn't *indecent*, I was fine continuing with the torn legs of my trackies.

However, since we'd been walking for perhaps a solid half day after that, that meant I'd now been wearing them for three days straight. There was no way I didn't *smell* inhuman. I hadn't considered deodorant when I'd packed for leaving our flat. Unlike other people I didn't really have a stay-over kit for infrequent trips to friends and family members' places, so no prepacked toiletry bag ready to go.

I gave myself a whiff test, lifting my arm slightly. The shirt seemed all right, but it was possible I'd just lost my ability to differentiate funkiness from normality because I'd been basking in my own stench for so long. I mean, it wasn't ideal, but what were we supposed to do? Perhaps we could bring baby wipes? Actually, I'd heard sand was a pretty good cleanser. Or we could go Roman and strigil oil off our bodies. Unless there was a potable water source in a Dungeon, traditional modern hygiene was basically impossible.

Along with the baby wipes, maybe I could head back home and pick up the low-profile dry deodorant my mum had once sent in one of her yearly birthday present parcels. I'd never opened it, since my preferred deodorant was roll-on. And while home, I should probably pick out more clothes. Or better yet, why didn't we use our apartment as a base? It wasn't like there was anything stopping us. Other than actually being able to clear the Dungeon.

As much as it felt like I was jumping the gun, thinking about this kind of stuff made the watch pass quickly. I hoped I wasn't jinxing us all by believing we'd clear this Dungeon and even maybe enter more.

Ah, well, better to be pragmatic in my optimism than nihilistic in pessimism. Hope for the best, and prepare for the worst, and all that jazz.

So, was there anything else we should have ready next time, at least human necessity wise?

Wait.

…

It had completely escaped my attention, but I was suddenly hit by an unwelcome realisation. I hadn't had to go to the bathroom since entering the Dungeon. Literally… I'd felt no urge to. No tight bladder or pressure in bowels. Absolutely no signals about relieving those basic human needs had been sent to my brain.

I'd gotten hungry and thirsty, though.

Briefly, I was reminded of a famous wizarding school media franchise. A ridiculous post the author once tweeted; that no one needed to shit because they magicked it out of their colons. No. That'd be ridiculous. That would be stupid.

…

And yet, it was coming up on our fourth day in the Dungeon.

Wren was idly scraping one of the Kmart knives into the crystal floor, etching out stick figure drawings which I'd definitely be asking about later. While she was preoccupied, it was probably the only time I'd ever consider bringing up this topic.

I turned to Axel. "This is probably not the most appropriate thing to ask."

He crunched into a stale vegetable crisp, eyes flat with disinterest. "Hmm?"

"Have you been… regular?"

My lifelong friend blinked slowly at me.

"What?"

"Like… you know. Regular." I vaguely gestured toward my midsection, feeling as awkward as the movement had to look.

His expression upon understanding was a combination of disgust and displeasure, crinkling the bridge of his nose and upturning his top lip. Neither facial change did anything to mar his photogenic features. Yeah, that'd be right. If I so much as smiled wrong, I knew the resulting selfie would be ruined. Eugh. This is what happened when I spent too much time with Axel.

He said, "Look, I know we're on the up-and-up, but we aren't and, being very honest, have never been *that* close."

I'd already dug my grave. "Since we entered the Dungeon. Have you…?"

Axel let out a long, exhausted sigh.

"How much longer is our watch?"

"I'm going to take that as a no."

So, sample size of two meant the Dungeon was… evaporating the human waste from our bodies? I'm pretty sure I would've noticed excrement being teleported out of my internal organs. Whatever. In the grand scheme of things, it wasn't important. Just a really, really, *really* weird perk(?) of being in a Dungeon.

Trying to move past my relatively poor taste of subjects, I noticed in the corner of my eye that Axel's gaze was fixed to around half a metre in front of him. He had to be checking his menu out. Must be nice to have so many skills. And secrets. Actually… maybe I could get to the bottom of Axel's mental instability.

I said, "So, Gigi shared xir player data with me."

"You mentioned it before."

"Yeah." I took a breath to steel myself. "Do you think you could share yours with me?"

Blue eyes met mine. A flash of panic in a millisecond.

"I don't know how to. Maybe later?"

The muscle in his jaw twitched, and he glanced away.

Why was he always lying to me? My stomach clenched in annoyance, and maybe hurt, but I brushed away the reaction. I don't know what I'd been expecting. Axel had said we were on the up-and-up, but it felt like I was just as distant as we'd been since our confrontation on the cabin deck.

"Fair. Maybe I'll ask Gigi about it."

I obviously still needed to work on our relationship. God, whoever thought friendship was supposed to be this hard? Well, apologising for what I'd said back then would be a good start. Since it was basically just him and me again, this was practically the perfect time to.

"By the way, I don't hate you."

His body visibly went rigid. The man I'd known all my life smiled sadly back at me, that look in his eyes that I still didn't understand, the one that was behind his unspoken upset, the source of whatever anguish took over him.

"You never hated me." Then Axel winked, the mournful expression gone like a match snuffed, his sitting position again loose. He preened. "Because I'm simply too perfect."

I decided to let the bipolar dip pass by. Calling it out would just put his guard up again, and we'd be back to square one. Though I often made shit decisions, I wasn't in favour of self-sabotage.

Scoffing, I asked, "Says who?"

"I've a list." He crossed his arms smugly.

"You would."

I shook my head but was unable to fight back the smile. For a moment, as we sat there, sharing the flavourless vegetable chips, it was like we were back in our apartment, watching something on the TV. Normally, after a short time, Axel would get up and leave, to hang out with friends who were more involved in his social life. Or they'd visit and take over the lounge and I'd retreat back into my bedroom. It wasn't like they'd all been bad people. Just not the type that I liked to interact with for any length of time.

It made me wonder why I liked Axel.

Why I even wanted to repair and maintain our friendship.

…

I guess that's just what happens when you know someone for so long. They become a part of you and not having that is like a piece carved from your very being. You're not whole without them. Maybe that's why Axel had never truly left me either.

Hah. Fat chance he was that sentimental.

"Oi, leave some for me," I said, trying to snatch the packet from Axel's hands.

He flipped the bag over, revealing it was now empty.

"Too late," he snickered.

"You can have some of mine."

I looked down to Wren who had finished her floor carving. It looked like six stick figures. As I stared, it registered who they were meant to be. It was Just Friends. All six of us. I couldn't explain it, but tears threatened to prick at my waterline. This etching was like being presented a family drawing to stick on the fridge.

"Who's who?"

She pointed to each of them, naming us off. Eerily, she'd gotten the height disparity quite accurate, and each stick figure had been marked with something distinctive to separate us further, all in almost dynamic poses.

Wren had given Jye jacked arms and traps, and they were dabbing. Tam, with had long braids and a generous bust, was sneaking. Identifiable through xir beauty mark and vitiligo, Gigi was waving. Wren had carved herself smiling and giving two thumbs-up. When I looked at the remaining two, me and Axel, I found we were the only ones she'd chosen to have interacting. Our stick figures were posed in such a way that it was difficult to tell if we were fighting or embracing. I guess her artistic talent could only extend so far.

Still, it was an impressive show of promise for the future.

Huh. Was there a future for artists in the world we lived in now?

"Wren, these are all so amazing! I think my favourite is Tam, actually. You really nailed her."

Even the cutthroat's expression looked quite nefarious. It made me chuckle.

Wren smiled, her cheeks pinking, pleased with the compliment. "I think it's my favourite too."

"What do you think, Axel? Jye's pretty good too."

Said blond's gaze was stuck on our carved interaction. But then he tilted his head, his eyes sliding over the others.

"Obviously the Wren is the best."

I looked back to her carving of herself. It was the one she'd done last, and you could actually visually see the growth over the progress of her etchings. Each one was slightly better proportioned, more confidently carved with straighter and less messy lines. Logically speaking, the Wren was the most practised and skilled drawing.

Leave it to Axel to be so literal.

She considered her response for a moment. "I think it looks the best, but I don't really like it as much." Propping her hands on her hips, she continued, "Maybe because I know what I'm like, and what I made isn't like that."

What a rather philosophical perspective. I didn't even know myself well enough to know what this ten-year-old did about herself. Clearly, we'd lived completely different lives. And she'd lived more in her ten years than I had in my nearly three decades. I crouched down and ran my fingers over the etchings. Part of me wanted to add more to it.

"You mind if I join you?"

She shook her head. "You and Axel can take over. My hands are tired. I'll keep watch instead."

Then, passing me the knife she'd been using, she stood up and headed over closer to the only entrance that led from the labyrinth to the shrine. Kids these days. They had a good head on their shoulders. Or maybe that was just Wren. Certainly, Chrissie hadn't been so assertive and understanding.

"What do you think we're supposed to be doing?" Axel asked, taking a position to my right.

He pulled a knife from his system inventory, as natural as retrieving something from his pocket. Of course we could store regular stuff in the system inventory. For some reason, I'd defaulted into believing we could only input Dungeon items. But if Xanthe could buy our Kmart knives, it should've been obvious to me.

God, why were we even carrying stuff around anymore?

I'd have to address this with the others when everyone was rested.

I focused back on Axel's question. He was talking about the carving of us.

"Obviously, I'm karate chopping your neck."

Axel laughed.

"How'd you know that it's not me hitting you?"

I snorted, and with my palm down flat, I moved it horizontally between our two heads. Even with us crouched like this, where I'd started at my forehead, my hand only came to his lips. His breath was warm against my skin.

"You've got like ten centimetres on me." I withdrew my hand and swapped the knife from my left into it. "High school was even worse since we hit growth spurts at different times." Pointing at the carving, I said, "In Wren's drawing, the shorter one is attacking the taller one." Or hugging them, but I didn't say that out loud. It didn't make sense for Wren to have drawn the latter. She'd never seen us act like that. So, it had to be us fighting.

Axel mumbled something, but I caught none of it.

Instead, I began my own etching, adding some surrounding environment, like grass and trees and flowers. Typical kids' drawing stuff. I added the obligatory black hole in the centre of the tree's trunk too.

Silently, Axel joined me, and we spent the rest of the watch like that.

…

It was nice.

XVI

IT BEGINS

T HAT "NIGHT" I SLEPT AS SOON AS MY HEAD hit the bedroll. It was the quickest I'd fallen unconscious since the whole event of the Gates and Dungeons appearing, unless blacking out counted. My slumber was sound and solid.

I dreamt of nothing, and as the bleariness of waking beckoned me from restful darkness, I became aware of something warm perfectly curled behind me. It further stretched around my waist and was grasped in my own hold; a blanketing that was as comforting as it was foreign. As my mind caught up to the soft exhales tickling against my ear, I dimly came to realise what this all indicated.

Wren had set up her bedroll deeper down the labyrinth entrance hall; she had explained she liked the way the sunlight danced in the shimmer of the crystals, almost like a nightlight. Which meant there could only be one person here lying with me, since Gigi, Jye, and Tam should've been on their watch shift.

Wakefulness didn't so much as shake me as lightning bolted thought into reaction, accompanied with a flush of embarrassment. I rolled out of Axel's embrace, cheeks stinging.

Heart hammering in my chest, I cast a careful glance around to see if anyone had witnessed what had taken place. Jye and Gigi seemed to be chatting amicably while Tam was leant up against one of the maze walls, arms crossed and eyes locked on the one entry.

Thank God for small mercies. Tam, with all her little asides, would never let us live it down, and Jye would definitely react, though I had no idea how they really felt. They appeared to hate Axel but were also attracted to him. Then again, they'd shown similar interest in Tam. Maybe the giant was just an absolute horndog that was attracted to anyone pretty. I didn't know whether to consider it an insult that they'd never displayed an inkling of desire toward me. Maybe they just suspected and respected my identity? Still…

The heat that had been trapped between us was dissipating in the flurry of panic that beset me, my heartbeat now slowing.

Sitting ramrod straight, at least an arm's length away from Axel, I turned to check if he was awake and aware of what comfort the both of us had sought in our sleep. But no. He was still under. I spared a moment then, to scrutinise whether or not he was faking it. I hadn't seen, or bothered to look at, the blond's sleeping face for quite a long time. Though he did appear properly asleep.

I didn't often see him while his defences were down like this.

There was looseness around his closed eyes, a slight flutter in his thick lashes as he dreamt, and the tension held in his jaw was gone. Whatever torment took over him sometimes was nowhere to be seen. He looked younger, more innocent, when asleep. It made me miss the Axel I'd known when we were children. I'd adored that kid. How he'd become the man sleeping here still baffled me to this day.

Though with the addition of the weirdness about him, it was easier to see where that child had gone, hidden away under traits that he'd grown into or adopted. Underneath all that posturing, my best friend was still there. Was still there in the moments between others. It was nice getting that back. I don't think I ever realised how much I'd missed it.

Before, he'd said I never hated him.

He was right

I could never hate him.

"Take a picture, it'll last longer, babes," came Tam's voice, her frame casting a shadow over me as she approached from the wall.

Embarrassed but not knowing why, I said, "Keep your voice down."

The brunette lifted the chunky necklace from her chest to check the watch I'd given her.

"Well, y'all ain't due for your wake-up call for another hour or so." She gave me an appraising look. "But based on your expression, you're not gonna grab any more Zs."

I had to admit I didn't feel tired. My sleep had been restful. In spite of my sleeping arrangements.

She continued, "You caught me headed to do a quick perimeter check." Her arms crossed in front of her chest. "That wasn't so much as a invite, but I'm sure you'll take it that way."

"Yeah, I'll come."

Tam's eyes rolled, and I stood to follow her.

Using [Channel], I activated [Focus] once we got farther away from Gigi so that our abilities wouldn't overlap ranges. Who knew what would happen when there were two people attracting ranged attacks. Would the projectiles be torn between the two and end up taking collateral somewhere in between? I didn't want to find out the hard way.

I waved briefly to Jye and Gigi to acknowledge them, and the two of them nodded back before they started talking again. Considering how bizarre Gigi was, what could they even be discussing?

Tam gave me a sidelong look from under her lashes, the judgement of her brown eyes hard and steely. "You're a strange piece."

"What?"

She raised an eyebrow.

"Even between the ginger Neanderthal and the toy size tank and your broken beau and the child prodigy and me. Out of the whole bunch of us, you're the weirdest of the lot."

There she went again, with the stupid idea that Axel and or I liked one another. It was something she seemed to truly believe. I guess she could join the small group of family members and family friends who thought the same thing. That included my parents who still believed the two of us would end up together as they'd been planning since Axel had come out and I'd never really *not* not come out. I'd just let them think whatever they wanted. I usually did.

I said, "That kind of sounds like an insult."

"It sure as hell ain't a compliment."

"I'd argue I'm the most normal out of all of you."

"Yeah, most would think. But that's what proves you're a bona fide freak, sugar. You've gotta be a whole nother level of messed up to be… well, the way you are."

I frowned.

"That's a little presumptuous."

"No presuming about it. I nearly killed you, sweetheart. And you're walking in step with me like we've been friends for years. You *trust* me for some forsaken reason. It's like your guard is never up."

I considered her words. "I trust the collar."

"And what about Gigi? Xe's got no such leash on."

She had a point, but I wasn't sure what she was trying to say.

"Xe's nice."

Tam swung her full face my way, incredulousness rife in her tone. "'Xe's nice'? That's really your given reasoning? So, you're saying if I had just *nicely* asked for some food, you would've up and given me some?"

I nodded pertly. "Yes."

"Christ, you really are nothing but sunshine and daisies, aren't you?"

I stopped midstride, eyes wide. Is that really what she thought about me? That I was some hippie living in Lalaland? Her mischaracterization churned inside me. She knew *nothing* about me.

The brunette had continued walking ahead, not caring that she was leaving me behind. My anger narrowed into a point.

"The world can be shit, Tam. I know that. I'm going out on a limb every time I do something here. From trusting you to, hell, even taking this next step." I started forward again. "But you know what? It's better than everything I've done for the past two decades. Since my sister died. Since she was killed. You want to know what happened after that?"

Tam turned back to look at me. Was that pity in her eyes? Impossible.

"Nothing, Tam. I couldn't fucking tell you anything important that happened since then. I was a shell of a human. Nothing really mattered. I didn't even know what I wanted to want. Two people. Two. That's the amount of people my entire adult life that bothered to make it through whatever excuse of a person I was. I was barely alive."

Putting everything into words like this was relieving. Being able to say it out loud.

It was true. The day that my sister had been abducted and cruelly and senselessly murdered, I'd shut down. Mrs. Brown had said it was a trauma response. But to me, it was something that just happened. I stopped trying to form connections with others, had stopped allowing myself them, or even wanting them. It wasn't that I suspected other people. It was that I was simply incapable of opening up and trusting.

Up until the Gates, I'd never really given it a second thought.

Maybe it was a problem. Maybe it was unhealthy. But my ability to form relationships really was so compromised, so tenuous, that the only thing I could do was trust complete strangers and hope they met me in kind. Because I didn't know how to do all the things in between. And I knew now I wanted that. I wanted *friends*.

I said, "Not taking the chance to trust others means you're not alive."

The woman's top lip curled up in distaste.

"Puh-lease. That sob story just proves my point. I'm struggling to get a peep of what the others see in you. A sad backstory is a dime in a dozen, sugar pot. We've all got one. It's cliché. As a matter of fact, if my wife were here, she'd—" Tam bit off the rest of her words, eyes widening.

I missed a step.

"Your wife?"

Her sharp brows furrowed, expression flat. "Put that tidbit out of your head."

I immediately glanced down at her left hand, seeking the metal that proved her words, but found the piece of jewellery missing. However, her ring finger still had a telltale pale band between tanner skin.

That one slip up had given me a glimpse into Tam's character. I understood the woman walking beside me in a way I hadn't before. She hadn't been fighting for her life when she'd attacked me. She hadn't been keeping secrets for her own gain. There was a woman somewhere she loved who she was trying to get back to, and everything she did was to ensure she'd find her again.

And everything I did was a risk to their reunion.

I couldn't help but think if this were a story, she would've been the protagonist. Actually, if I considered it, everyone else in the party had equal right to be main character: Axel with his overpowered stats and secret torment. Jye with their glitch and complex personal background. Wren with her two-class system and strangely savant wisdom. Even Gigi and xir foreknowledge and levels.

All of them but me. I wasn't anything special, not really. You're not meant to think that about yourself, but in this case, it really was true. But that just meant it was more crucial for me to try and help them. My party members were all weird as fuck, as Tam had pointed out. And, somehow, I'd managed to finagle myself into the fray with them all. So, maybe the way I protected them was protecting them from themselves. I was already performing that role for Axel.

Perhaps that was my part in this whole thing, to see them through this.

Softly, I inquired, "Where is she? Your wife."

Tam shook her head. "I don't know what you're on about." Then she lengthened her stride and outstepped me so that I was walking behind her in moments.

I repressed a sigh as I pinched at the bridge of my nose. Too much too soon.

"Hey, don't get too out of range. Focus only extends so far," I said to the braids on the back of her head.

Her pace slowed almost imperceptibly.

Well. Gotta celebrate the small victories. Prior to our conversation, she probably would've spat at my feet and deliberately walked farther away.

We'd reached the back of the shrine, following along the walls. On all three sides, the enclosure around the building was closed off. The only opening *was* the one that led to the shrine's entrance. Though Tam had thought it was necessary, I didn't really understand the purpose of a perimeter check. But it had been nice to get up and stretch my legs. It actually wouldn't be a bad idea to extend that to the rest of my body.

Letting out a yawn, the vestiges of sleep still clinging to me, I rolled my shoulders as we began wrapping around the back left corner to finish the full lap. Then, thinking back to the karate lessons I'd taken for a single month since I'd received a voucher from my father, I began to repeat the warm-ups I'd learned; tucking an arm into the bend of the other and pulling it to my chest, folding a knee forward with a slightly widened stance and lunging slowly, rotating at my waist with my arms lifted. Then to finish it up, I turned my head from side to side. Lastly, I tilted it down and up.

Down and—

A movement from above caught my eye.

The arrow was a silent blur through the air. I didn't think. I threw myself to the floor closer to the direction of the party. Its sharp jagged point plunged into the dirt, scattering debris from its impact. At the angle it had been travelling, it passed directly through where I'd just been standing. Of course. [Focus] was redirecting ranged assaults to me.

"Attack!" I yelled, heart in my throat. "We're under attack!"

Like my words had been the signal our ambushers had been waiting for, the snap of a dozen bowstrings echoed from behind the wall. Keeping in mind the mana cap of [Focus], and praying that Gigi was still outside of that ability's range, I borrowed xir [Shield Wall].

Activating it was a very different matter than all other abilities I'd used so far, but I didn't have the privilege of thinking about it. The shield, glowing the same blue as our menus, summoned above my head in a sparkle of light. Just in time to cover me from the volley of arrows that came raining down.

I heard something *thunk* to my feet, but it landed with less force. Looked like just the broken head of an arrow? I glanced back up through the partially transparent shield and watched, gut clenched, as it and the ground around me became buried in fletches, soon resembling the back of an echidna.

The shower of arrows trickled to a stop.

Were they setting up for another shot? How many people were there? The attack had come over like a cloud of projectiles. Was it an ability? I'd heard the bows, but the usual static hiss of a skill being activated hadn't sounded. Nor for that matter had I heard it when I'd summoned the shield. What was happening?

"You good, Lee?" came Axel's voice.

I cast a glance around to see that the rest of the party was peeking out from beside the shrine as a precaution. That must've meant Gigi had turned xir [Focus] off on the group's approach. Thank God.

"Yeah. I'm doing fucking spectacular."

If the volley was an ability, maybe there was only one attacker. If it was one person but they came from the trio we'd seen, then where were the other—

"Keep an eye on your backs!"

I heard the sickening clang of metal against metal as Axel's blade met another's just out of my sight, a few expletives slipping from his lips. The attacker quickstepped back, and a fireball from elsewhere descended. Axel used his [Swift Footed] trait to dodge it. The flame seared into the floor, leaving a black scorch mark.

Fuck, they'd sneaked up on us by using the arrows as a distraction. And had me pinned down.

Still, if there were only three of them, we could do this.

Suddenly, the familiar hiss of abilities activating sounded in my head. I don't know why they'd stopped. It was possible that meant it was unreliable. I'd never followed up on asking the others if they heard the same thing. I had simply assumed they had. Shit. Maybe all along it'd been a glitch like Jye's entire system. It wasn't beyond imagining. But who was activating what now?

I didn't have to wait long for an answer, as I heard the chorus of bowstrings once again.

"Incoming!"

The shield above my head looked half cooked. I didn't know if it could withstand another battering. But burning anymore stamina on one seemed like a waste right now, even though my bar was slowly regenerating. The shrine's roof wouldn't provide any cover even if I managed to sprint the hundred metres or so to it; its overhanging eaves barely extended a handsbreadth. I also had to keep some stamina in reserve, just in case I needed to borrow another skill.

What to do.

If I didn't keep [Focus] up, the arrows would be directed at the party who were dealing with the other attackers. If Gigi activated xir [Focus] while mine was still active, who knows what could happen. We'd have to test it once we made it out of here, but it wasn't a risk I could take, not right now. Shit, shit, shit. I wanted to help everyone… but we all had our roles. Gigi had more health. Xe was meant to tank.

If our newest member took the brunt of this, it would give me more time to think.

"Gigi, sub in for me."

"As you wish!" shouted Gigi.

Three [Shield Walls] formed horizontally in the air, creating a stepping stone of cover between me and Gigi, as the next volley began to fall. The first few arrows bit into my shield, cracks forming where the tips had sunk through the translucent blue material. The shield creaked, groaning against the onslaught. It would not hold much longer. Once it shattered, I could probably take one, maybe two, direct arrows to my body, so long as they didn't hit anything arterial.

More arrows began their descent, arching high in the sky, all tips pointed toward me.

I took a deep breath, thought about praying but didn't, and ran for Gigi's [Shield Wall] coverage, pumping my legs under me as fast as they'd let me go. Momentarily after I left its cover, my old shield exploded in a cascade of light. I would've been roast spitted had I remained there, for sure.

While running, one bastardly arrow glanced against my calf, nicking my skin as it planted itself into the ground. I barely felt the sting of 1 HP loss, attention stolen by the shadow of the main arrow wave closing in.

Springing off the balls of my feet, I dived beneath the closest [Shield Wall] I'd been heading toward. I ate shit, colliding with the dirt floor at full momentum, and all my breath flattened out of my lungs as I skidded to a stop, gasping, just skirting under the safety of the glowing blue shield. Gigi looked to have made xir first one too; a solemn concentration on xir face. Given the wide area of effect, it was a good idea for xem to remain under cover too.

The final arrows plunked against the shield above me. I took a moment to gain my breath and then scrambled up. As I did, the eerie resounding thwack of the bowstrings sounded. Fuck, the next wave already?

I couldn't even think about whatever Axel was doing and how his battle was going. I had no idea what any of the others were doing either, but abilities were activating pretty much constantly, a burr of hissing in the back of my mind.

"Let me know when you can activate Focus."

I wasn't sure about the cooldown since that information wasn't supplied when I used [Channel]. I hoped it was short. I should've fucking checked with Gigi.

"I'm ready now!"

Despite having taken one volley, Gigi's shields were holding stronger than mine. That'd figure. As the next storm of arrows thumped down, no cracks formed in the one guarding me. They were still taking damage, though. It wouldn't make sense to stay here, even with their higher hit points. I just didn't have enough health to tempt fate like that. And neither Gigi nor I had the stamina to keep summoning [Shield Walls] to protect us infinitely.

But at the very least, they would last a while as Gigi took on the archer's focus. Oh. I guess that's where the name of the ability came from. And if xe ended up having no shields left, with xir 100 HP, Gigi was sure to last longer than me against the hail of arrows.

The last few of the current round smacked into the shield above me, followed by silence. No more bowstrings released.

The attacker must've been reloading/regening/on cooldown. It was safer to run now than when the arrows were dropping.

"Go, go, go!" I screamed.

Gigi sprinted forward, and we passed each other, shoulders brushing. Taking that as my cue, I swapped [Focus] for [Thick Hide], trying to take into consideration that I'd be getting closer to a melee battle. I heard a *tsss* and hoped Gigi was activating xir [Focus]. Well, the next volley would let me know.

It'd either target Gigi, or we'd all be fucked.

DUNGEON
HUNTER

XVII

IT ENDS

I TOOK A MOMENT TO GAIN MY BEARINGS.

From around the corner of the shrine, I could just glimpse Axel and another figure engaged in a fight, their weapons sparking as they swung them against each other. Unfortunately, his attacker had the reach on him. It looked as though they were using a polearm, maybe a glaive? Whenever Axel closed in, he was met with a fireball appearing out of nowhere to push him back. I couldn't tell where the magic user was, as the origin point seemed to change each time. I had originally dismissed the idea of a hiding ability in lieu of range, but I'd been wrong. The spellcaster might very well be invisible.

Had they been following us the entire time?

Jye was standing in the backline, waiting for a gap in the melee fighters' movements to fling their knives forward, an arm wound up, tensing, ready for the right moment. Every now and again, they'd flick a blade toward the origin of fireballs, but it would be too slow. Unlike the magic user who seemed to have fairly refined speed and directional control, Jye's attacks were more limited to where and how hard they could throw. They hadn't hurled a single one onto the battlefield, though. The giant was afraid of engaging in friendly fire. Surprising, considering it was Axel out there.

Another hiss of ability. Wren was holding one of her hands out and muttering under her breath. This was probably [Whetstone]. She was buffing someone. Axel? Maybe even Jye. Could she layer on the same buff?

"Hold out here, Gigi," I said.

Xe nodded and then ran to the next [Shield Wall] xe'd previously summoned.

I closed the distance toward Axel's battle, coming up behind Jye and Wren.

The redhead noticed me. Their brows furrowed as they said, "Man, I can't get a knife in edgewise. And I can't pin down the fireballist. I'm hitting empty air 'cause they move too quick after firing."

Axel and his assailant were trading blows, weapons grinding along each other. His opponent seemed to be able to keep up with his speed. Maybe they had a similar trait. It would've been a mostly even battle if not for the fire magic backup on our enemy's side. The same kind of support we couldn't grant without risking hurting our teammate. If Jye or I ran in, we'd be more hindrance than help since our fighting experience was little to none and all I had was a wooden pole. What could we do without getting in Axel's way?

It was then I realised Tam was simply leaning against the side of the shrine, her arms folded. She was watching in faint interest. The brunette could've just as easily been taking a smoko break from a part-time job. That's how engaged she looked.

"Tam. What the fuck?"

Her brown eyes met mine. "I don't got no skin in this game."

"We're your party!"

"If they kill you all, you won't be."

I tried invoking the collar's command. "Helping us right now is necessary."

"Mumma would say that's up for debate."

And here I'd thought we'd had something like a heart-to-heart. Well, if she was being petty, I could meet her at that level.

"What would your wife say?"

Tam's expression became frosty. Target hit. I needed to push harder, though.

"You don't have any right—"

I thought back to the exploding wall trap, why she'd been so angry with me. It'd taken until our prior conversation to realise why she'd been upset. It wasn't that I'd been touching her. It was that she *hated* letting other people help her. She was so derisive toward my attitude toward others because she couldn't even fathom allowing people to assist her.

For some reason, she was afraid of being seen as weak.

"I bet you she'd think you're being a coward. Cowering with your tail between your legs. Letting us do all the dirty work."

Tam's eyes blazed with rage as she pushed off the wall to grab at my shirt.

"Shut your damn mouth! I ain't hiding behind you!"

"Not the way it looks to me, Tam."

She let out an animalistic growl and flung her hands down, her face twitching with fury.

"Tam, I know you hate listening to me, but find the archer." I paused as Axel screamed out, the attacker's blade catching him across the chest, the blood stark red against his white shirt. A fury lit inside me. I met her gaze. "And kill them, if you can."

A blast of smoke exploded in front of my face followed by a yowl at my feet. Tam had transformed into a cat. She rushed off, speeding out of my sight. Behind me, I heard the continuous *thwump* of a line of bowstrings releasing. Gigi was under another hail of arrows. Xe had a few [Shield Wall] worth of stamina left by my count, which meant xe could survive a bit longer. Tam better fucking do her bit.

"I'll give you your chance, Jye, just wait," I said. "Wren, how are you holding up?"

Wren huffed. "I'm good."

"Can you buff me too?"

It was more curiosity than necessity on my part. What did her buff actually do? I felt her response, a zap of her ability being applied to me, like a quick surge of energy. In the corner of my eye, I saw the notification.

15% critical chance increase.

"Thanks." I swallowed and said to Jye, "You'll know when to hit the fireballer."

With a hiss, Axel activated [Ground Smash], directing it through a kick to the ground. But before he made contact, his opponent simply jumped back out of range. The dirt beneath them rippled, breaking, with some of the earthen debris flying up before scattering uselessly to the floor. Had his attacker remained where they were, they would've been damaged and stunned. Instead, grinning, the pole-armist began their reapproach. I could see Axel swear.

Helplessly, I watched from the sidelines running the calculations of what mana and stamina he had left. He'd have enough for two more [Ground Smashes], if I was adding everything up right. But they didn't seem like they'd help him anyway. With his opponent's weapon reach, they would be easily able to stay out of range of the ability.

I could see the slow damage building up on Axel as he struggled to find a way to fight back. He needed some relief, between fending off the fireballs and the glaive. Locking down the polearm-user wouldn't help, since it would just mean the fireballer would be able to defend their teammate easier without both of them darting to and fro; Axel's attacks much more predictable without having to compensate for their party member's. But there had to be something to give Axel a chance, maybe something to close the gap of range.

The thought popped into my head, and I couldn't help but laugh at how ridiculous of a plan it was. But I didn't give myself the privilege of doubt.

Time to fucking go.

Borrowing Load from Jye, which did feel like the emotion of a grunt, I lightened myself, though I had no idea by how much, considering it seemed the strength of other's abilities varied from my use of them, then I began sprinting.

At once, everything felt incredibly wrong. Previously we'd been thrown by Jye while under Load and then they'd released it. But running with it, I much more clearly understood the ability. With each stride, the speed at which I was covering ground was inexplicable. No. This wasn't a drop of my weight. The ability had affected the way in which gravity interrelated with my body.

Jye's ability was some sort of gravity slider?

Tearing me from my thoughts, a fireball singed toward me, flinging in from the right. I darted to avoid it, but with less gravitational force and thus lower frictional force, I didn't manage to calculate the right amount of turn needed.

The flame still caught me as I passed, burning right through my clothes. It seared viciously into the flesh of my side. Thankfully, as I bit into my lip against the fleeting burst of pain, it quickly went numb. But that wasn't actually good. That meant it was a third-degree burn. Good thing I'd had [Thick Hide] on. Without it, I probably would've been flambeed from the outside in. I didn't even want to consider my current HP.

Axel and his opponent just registered my approach as I redirected myself, taking care of the additional effort and torque required with Jye's ability applied. I withdrew the wooden broomstick from my system inventory and, without stopping, barrelled toward them both.

I was next to them in one more step; my staff held horizontally, ready to sweep them off their feet as I bulldozed forward.

To dodge the insane attack, the glaive-user stepped back, irritated by the interruption. Axel's eyes met mine for a moment, clearly asking what the fuck I was doing, but he stepped aside as well. It looked like

I'd just end up running between the two.

Good.

I deactivated Jye's Load, praying to God that I could pull this off. With the weight of my body returning to normal, I planted the end of my staff into the ground to resist against the friction of the floor, turning it into a crude brake.

I skidded for a bit, and, holding on to the staff for dear life, my arm muscles burning from strain, the world smearing by me, I used the momentum I'd built up to swing around it. Taken off guard by the random pattern of my attack, Axel's opponent reacted; assuming I'd be aiming for their open weak points with some sort of hidden ace, they pushed their weapon forward to protect themselves.

Thanking them for their predictability, I flung my hand up as I continued to slide and slapped my open palm over the proffered head of the assailant's glaive. Of course they hadn't been anticipating it. Who would expect someone to touch the pointy end of your weapon midcombat? The attacker's eyes widened in shock, and they snatched it back. But I'd achieved my goal.

I released my staff, letting my body crash away into a tumble, winding myself. My surroundings were a painful blur. I was only able to glimpse the glaive dipping, almost slipping out of the assailant's hold.

I'd applied Load, increasing the gravity applied to the weapon's blade. It would force the centre of the weapon's gravity up, effectively halving their reach with the grip adjustment needed. I'd dismissed the idea of adding Load to the attacker themselves, since the efficiency of borrowed abilities might've not delivered what I'd wanted.

Still rolling away, dust kicking up, I finally came to a stop roughly a few metres from their battle. Jesus Christ, how fast had I been running with Load? Feeling sore in too many different places to count, I coughed, out of breath, but I knew I couldn't rest on my laurels. I darted my gaze around, trying to spy any incoming fireballs. None were spawning just yet. Back at the shrine, Jye and Tam were anxiously watching.

I heard a *tsss* and pushed myself to stand and run again, even as my body groaned in disagreement. The heat of a fireball blasting into the ground behind me gave me a surge of energy. This asshole would be next. Keeping on my feet, and ensuring I made more distance between their battle, I watched Axel's fight in the corner of my eye.

As I'd anticipated, the effect of Load on the glaive had completely thrown the attacker off-kilter. They were still readjusting to it, and now they were closer in reach, Axel was able to get a few hits in, blood splattering from their wounds. My forced range recalibration had paid off almost instantly.

The assailant's next attack went too wide, and Axel dodged it, sliding under. It was the opening he needed. He ducked in, swiping his blade at the attacker's Achilles tendon. Without any armour defending it, his sword sliced straight through flesh. The top half of the assailant's split tendon snapped back up high into their thigh, like an elastic band released from tension, as blood gushed from the wound. The glaive-wielder let out a coarse, guttural scream that pierced the very air and staggered forward, taking their weight on their other leg. Seeing his chance to end the battle, Axel dived in, animosity etched into his face.

I scanned the area, frantically. They had to be here somewhere… The ignition of a fireball snagged on the edge of my vision, a crisp glowing red spot. Bull's-eye.

"There you are, fucker," I muttered.

As the fireball started to streak forward to intervene, defending the injured fighter, I used the last of my stamina to summon [Shield Wall] directly in the location that the fireball had originated from, forming it horizontally.

In that moment, several things happened in quick succession. My [Shield Wall] appeared. A pained grunt sounded. Out of nowhere, the magic caster became visible, falling to their ass, stunned, having been propelled by my shield. The already released fireball singed past Axel's head, forcing him away from his easy victory. He slapped at his smoking crown, swearing under his breath.

Feet pounding dirt, I marvelled that my plan had actually worked.

It was only something I'd just realised; that the shield took up real space and matter when formed. It had been the arrowhead that had landed at my feet after my first [Shield Wall] that had given me the idea. The shield had been summoned into the same spot that the arrow was descending through, breaking the projectile in half. The ranged spellcaster, made out of thicker stuff than an arrow, had simply been ejected by the shield now occupying the same space. The theory that it'd break invisibility was based purely on *Dungeons and Dragons* and holding concentration.

Jye correctly understood this as their cue, launching a certified assault of knives in the magic user's prone direction. Hiss after hiss sounded as they hit their climax, plummeting through the air and then sinking at a dangerously quick speed toward the body of the magic user.

Thunk, thunk, thunk, thunk, thunk.

Each sound a blade eating into their flesh. The magic caster writhed around a moment, sputtering in pain, then with one final twitch they stilled. I didn't have time to reflect on that. Gigi was suffering another influx of arrows. Xe had been under constant assault the entire time. During my attack, all of xir other [Shield Walls] had burst into light, having taken the maximum damage they could. Beneath the one above xem, Gigi had already summoned another. Xe cast a pleading look our way.

I nodded.

I did not like that I was trusting Tam to keep Gigi alive, but with her improved senses as a cat, she had to be able to track the archer down. It was the only hope we had in that regard.

Axel, rage in his eyes, stepped toward the heavily bleeding attacker, their glaive held limply in their hand. He swung his sword at it, and it clanked to the floor, disarming them.

Holding his blade to their neck, Axel stepped in behind them. Even from here, the groaning, the pleading, made its way to me clearly. It was over for them. Axel had won.

With the hope that we could avoid the worst and that the other player was lower level, I borrowed [Intimidation] from Axel. It was a vile feeling. Like dragging my mind through a vat of crude oil. The ability was meant to be able to manipulate emotions. I tried projecting fear and announced, "Stop attacking and reveal yourself, or we kill your last teammate."

The archer was in between one of their volleys, possibly on cooldown. We waited to see what they'd do.

Silence reigned.

Gigi seemed to take this lengthened quiet as the archer's surrender, releasing a sigh of relief, xir small shoulders imperceptibly loosening.

And then as clear as day, the same timbre slap of bowstrings echoed out. Before their resulting projectiles could pelt into Gigi's shield, Axel made true on our threat.

There was no hesitation.

No pause.

He slit the injured person's neck in twain without so much of a blink.

There was a gurgle, and then after the body fell limply to the floor, the only sound punctuating the silence was the thunking of arrows into Gigi's [Shield Wall]. Xe'd only last a few more of those attacks before xe'd be at bodily harm. Where the fuck was Tam?

Abruptly, the rain of arrows ended before the full amount had properly descended. From the other side of the wall behind the shrine, just above the top of the crystalline quartz, I saw a wisp of smoke. The same kind I'd seen firsthand when I'd nearly died. A side effect of Tam transforming.

Speak of the devil.

Just Friends eliminated Test Name.

Just Friends earned 1,000 XP.

Just Friends awarded 121 credits.

It took a second for the monumental announcement to properly settle in. I stared at the system updates in disbelief.

We'd won.

We'd *won*.

And one thousand experience points?! Holy shit! That'd shoot me up to next level, maybe even LVL 3? This was our first real battle, and we'd come out of all alive. Not even just alive! The only one of us that had taken that much damage was Axel, bar my minor (read: major) burn. And Wren could rectify that easily. We'd straight up killed this! But the weirder thing was 121 credits. Why such an odd number? I couldn't think of any justification.

The clutching hand of Wren on the hem of my shirt brought my thoughts back to the real world. Her face was pale white, tears on the verge of falling were glinting in her hazel eyes, her lips fighting back their quivering. She was shaking, looking at the fallen forms of the party formerly known as Test Name. Their blood was seeping into the dirt of the shrine biome, staining the floor red.

The spellcaster's body was a pin cushion of knives.

The glaive-user's neck gaped open, fleshy and pink.

Both were completely still.

Oh.

Oh, fuck.

We'd just killed three people.

The vegetable crisps found their way back up my throat and splattered onto the floor.

XVIII

THE CHOICES WE MAKE

WREN, AXEL, AND I FORMED A HEALING TRAIN. While Axel hadn't fallen into critical health, he was still quite low. He had numerous open wounds from the glaive, none of which seemed life-threatening, but if left untreated could prove to be fatal, the bleeding still outpacing natural regen. The scratches I'd taken from my assist were superficial, but the extent of the burn had taken me by surprise, even though it shouldn't have.

It stretched from just below my right armpit to my bottom rib. The burn was angry and red, with whitened blisters and crusted dark-brown areas seared deeper into my flesh. I couldn't look at it without a profound sense of nausea filling me. That this damage was on my body and I couldn't feel it disturbed me. Mostly it just felt tight. Even as Wren's small hands, enmeshed in the glow of [Healing Hand], laid against my skin, I felt nothing.

I focused on the slash across Axel's chest, borrowing Wren's ability. It was probably the best one I'd used from my entire party. The skill gave off a pleasant airiness that bubbled through my veins. When it met the injury it was meant to heal, the bubbling would simmer into a cold boil. It reminded me of liquid oxygen.

"Thanks," Axel said as I began healing him.

I wasn't fully sure how to talk to him, considering how he'd just killed a person. And I'd helped him do it. As a matter of fact, I'd been the lynchpin that had assisted in the murder of three people.

"Yeah," I replied.

That I'd not yet had one of my attacks was honestly shocking. For a variety of reasons. But I guess what tended to trigger them was thoughts of death. Of not being able to do anything to stop it. Rather than letting my mind consider that, I'd simply dived into combat. Maybe that was another strategy I could employ if I ever felt them creep back. Because you didn't just cold turkey stop these attacks. I'd learned that the hard way.

But now my worries rested on the consequences of our actions. Wren's hands trembled as she healed the scratches along my arm. Without talking, the four standing adults in our party had relocated the camp away from the area we'd battled in. She'd calmed down once the bodies were out of sight.

What else could we even do? She was a child, yes, but she was also a valued member of our crew. We couldn't shield her forever. Even if I wanted to protect her. She had to do her part. With her larger mana pool and unique abilities, she'd have to take the brunt of the healing since I could only do so much.

Unsurprisingly, Tam came back without so much as a hair misplaced. With her, she'd brought the corpse of the archer and had remarked: "Look what the cat dragged in." At any other time that quip might've been funny. Unfortunately, it did nothing to raise the mood of those with compromised morals.

I must've been lost in my thoughts because Axel settled a hand on top of my own, his head tilted. "You good?"

Was I good with having killed three people?

No.

I felt guilty that I didn't feel guilty.

The three ambushers had been intent on taking us out. They hadn't tried to talk to us. We'd given them the chance to surrender. Test Name had no issue with killing us. We had defended ourselves.

I felt sick at the senseless loss of life, at having caused it, but I didn't feel guilty about it. I probably should've. These people were human. They all had loved ones, someone to return to, someone they were fighting for. But it was kill or be killed. I had prepared myself for this eventuality since the moment the Gates appeared.

We'd killed, but we had been forced to in order to survive.

The disgust and sickness inside me condensed into hate. Prior to this, I'd been annoyed and alarmed and concerned and aghast by everything happening. I'd said that I'd only started choosing again when the Gates appeared, and that was true. I was thankful for that.

But being forced to kill someone or die wasn't a choice.

There was no choice.

Whoever or whatever was playing with us, putting us through all of this, had pressed this fate on us. And the weight of those lives would sit on our shoulders for the rest of ours. I was sorry that they'd come across us, that we hadn't been able to talk it out. That it had come down to what had happened. That we were all stuck in this same fucking crazy situation and were just trying to come out on top.

Axel's hand tightened around mine. It was strangely reassuring. Grounding.

He said, "You're alive because of this. I'm alive. All of us."

"Not all of us." Unable to stop myself, I glanced in the direction of the three bodies we'd grouped together, hidden by the shrine between us. We still weren't sure what to do with them. "But you're right."

"Always am." The blond smiled, though there was no joy behind it.

I attempted to return the expression. It probably closer resembled a grimace.

"You're done, Lee," Wren said. A yawn promptly followed her words.

Checking my status, I found it was the truth; I was back up at full health. The skin under my arm had returned to a healthier pink but was clearly discoloured. I guess the level of awful I was feeling was all mental and emotional. Despite logically knowing we'd had no choice, it didn't stop me from wondering if there was anything different we could've done. Any other path we could've taken.

"Thanks, kid." With the hand that wasn't currently in use, I dug into my pants pocket and retrieved the Warhead Axel had given me previously. "Here. I've been saving this."

She smiled and took it but paused. Her head tilted. "Are you sure you don't need this still?"

It was a good question. The sour lollies were the quickest ways to end my panic attacks prematurely. They always had been. Until they had eventually faded away over the years, I'd carried at least one on my person at all times.

I shook my head and curled her fingers over it.

"Don't worry about that."

Immediately, she ripped open the small packet and popped it into her mouth. I didn't even get to see the colour at the speed at which she ate it. Her lips puckered and she clenched her eyes closed in reaction to the quick burst of stringent sweetness. When she opened them again, they were watering.

"S'good," she said, voice strained. She yawned again, revealing that her mouth was starting to blacken. "I think I need to have a nap."

With that, she pushed herself up and wandered over to our haphazardly packed bedrolls. We'd moved everything in a flurry of panic, just eager to get Wren and our items far away from where we'd committed three counts of murder. She unrolled one of the sleeping bags, and collapsed onto it, her face still scrunched up from the sour lolly.

Axel chuckled, and I realised I was grinning too. His hand had remained overlapping mine. A moment later, the dull throb of an almost empty mana pool alerted me to the fading power of my [Healing Hand]. I was nearly at my limit, so I deactivated the ability.

Seeing the glow disappear, Axel withdrew his hold.

"Let's see how you're doing."

"Ugh, don't tell me," he replied, turning his head away and closing his eyes.

Just as he was a bit of a germaphobe, he also somehow managed to be the more squeamish out of our party. How he'd sliced someone's neck with this attitude was beyond me.

I pulled back my hand to check his chest wound. It was angry and raised, but it'd scarred over. I worried it would never return back to its original unmarred form. And Axel was a vain creature. A permanent disfigurement could very well be another reason to send him over the deep end.

Though this wasn't the first time he'd been hurt so seriously. Had the wooden stake injury healed properly?

His shirt was already quite tattered and the majority of his torso was visible. But the area he'd been staked in was still covered. Curious, I peeled back the ragged edge of his shirt to compare the two wounds. Beneath was unblemished skin. Unable to believe what I was seeing, I tested it, running the tips of my fingers over the expanse of muscle, feeling for any possible hidden damage.

There was nothing, though the muscles under my ministrations tensed. The last time I'd checked, the wound at my collarbone had left a faint scar, like a ghostly whisper of my near-death experience. But for Axel, it was like he'd never been hurt in the first place.

His stats really must've been OP.

"I don't even have to say anything," Tam said, having appeared, her arms crossed.

Frowning in confusion, I looked to Axel for clarification. His cheeks were slightly red, and he was not meeting my gaze. Ohhh. I removed my hands from his body, recalling just how much Axel wasn't a fan of others touching him unless he instigated it. Now unsure where to put them, I dropped my hands into my lap, letting them sit there uselessly. For once I'd done something worth the unspoken anger the heat in his face indicated.

Feeling defensive, I explained, "I was checking his old wound. You know, the one we got fighting you."

"Riiight." She took a breath. "I guess my query is strangely relevant then. I wanted to ask what's the go on the stiffs."

Ignoring the innuendo, I said, "You can't call them that."

Tam rolled her eyes. "Cadavers, carcasses, carrion, corpses. Call 'em what you want, we gotta deal with them."

In her shadow walked Jye. "I don't exactly like it, but the cat's got a point. Even if we're not sticking around, there's only a day or two before the bodies'll start to smell. Like smell bad, that is. The smell of dead things."

"Why do you know that?" I asked.

Jye shrugged, their large traps bunching up and then loosening. "Yeah, so hardcore survival family camping was not just camping. We also hunted. Feral hogs and stuff like that. One time, we accidentally left a straggler in the back of the spare ute. Forgot about it for just one day. When we got back, the stench was absolutely rancid. Wished I didn't have a nose."

I thought about the carvings we'd done on the crystalline floors the day before. There was no way we'd be able to dig deep enough into them to bury the corpses. But we couldn't just leave them unceremoniously there. We were murderers, not savages.

I tested the ground beneath my feet since we were currently in the shrine biome. It was no prospect either, the dirt so hard-packed that we'd struggle to even get an inch deep.

"Cremation?" I suggested.

"You wanna light dead bodies on fire?" Tam said with the kind of tone that added "you sick fuck" at the end of her words.

"Want is a strong word."

Axel shook his head. "We can't cremate them. The amount of fuel needed for a fire to completely burn three adult bodies to ash is not something we just have on hand."

"Why do *you* know that?" I asked.

"I read."

"Read what?"

"As cute as this is, it doesn't solve our problem," Tam said, interrupting Axel and me.

Jye, ever the concerning one, began their suggestion. "I'm going to throw something out there. You can't judge me for this. But what about, as a warning sign, we hang their bod—"

In the corner of my eye, I noticed Gigi, absent xir unique coat, dragging something along the ground toward us. I'd been wondering where xe was.

"What do you have there?"

The rest of the party swung around at my question, turning to look in the direction I was frowning.

Xe'd stripped off xir coat and had used it to bundle up something and, unable to pick it all up, had resorted to letting it trail on the floor behind xem. Gigi said nothing, but when xe reached us, xe spread the coat open to reveal what was inside.

It looked like gear, supplies, and weapons.

Immediately I recognised one item, its blade tipped with Axel's dried blood, and the realisation of what Gigi had done had hit me.

"You looted their bodies?!"

The small stranger nodded xir head enthusiastically. "Yes. They had a lot of food."

In a game, it was an obvious thing to do. You keep what you kill. Very Furian. I knew it didn't make sense, but taking their stuff felt *worse* than killing them. Like desecrating corpses. It was on par with grave robbery or tomb raiding.

Gigi considered me for a moment. "Should I not have done this?"

One of Axel's hands found itself on my shoulder. "Hey, come on. It's not like they're going to need any of it anymore."

I sighed and rubbed at my face, stretching taut my cheeks.

"No, Gigi. I guess this is just something we do now."

Xe gave me a large thumbs-up and began divvying up the goods between the rest of us. Jye ended up taking the archer's bow and quiver. Whatever food and miscellaneous items were equally shared, and spare clothes went to whoever they'd likely fit. Luckily, the archer had a smaller figure; the one I'd worried was a child. It was almost as bad, but they'd seemed to be a man in their later years, shrunken from age. Much of their clothing had been shared between Gigi and the pile we'd put aside for Wren.

At the end of the loot division, the only thing left was the glaive.

"If no one else is gonna take this…" I said, picking it up. I was the only one who used anything like it, though "use" was a bit of stretch.

The polearm was heavy and cool in my hands, but knowing it'd been held only moments before by a dead person made me feel some sort of way. I immediately stored it in my system inventory, followed by the food I'd received. Jye and Tam looked on in shock. Looks like Mumma hadn't been feeding Tam everything after all.

"Oh, right. I was going to tell you about this and then… Well, and then we killed three people, so forgive me my lapse of memory."

I went over adding non-Dungeon items into our inventories and watched as the rest of the party followed suit. We discussed whether or not we should add our backpacks to the inventory, and eventually agreed not to, since it was possible we might lose access to our inventories and be cut off. In our bags, we kept emergency rations and immediately necessary items.

Even though we'd all separately added quite a lot to our inventories, it looked as though they weren't going to fill up anytime soon. In fact, it didn't seem they had a limit on storage.

An idea occurred to me.

It was a bad one.

I shared it with the others.

They all gave me a look worse than the one Jye'd started receiving before Gigi's interruption.

"You want to what?" Axel queried, eyes wide.

"I knew it. I knew it! You're a whole nother level of messed up, sunshine."

Jye nodded in acceptance. "I think it's smart."

Having the redhead of all people say that didn't fill me with much reassurance, but I didn't let that show on my face.

"I will do it," Gigi said.

Gently rebuffing xem, I replied, "It might be better to share this burden, but thanks for offering to shoulder it all."

I addressed the others. "So Gigi volunteered, and it was my idea, so I'm involved." I held out my hands, palms up, as if waiting for someone to place an object within them. "Hands up who else wants a body in their inventory."

Eventually, I needled Axel into accepting the position. In hindsight, I'd probably guilted him into it. Still, I found myself thinking this was the best option.

Handling dead bodies wasn't the most hygienic thing, but if we cleared the Dungeon and brought them back to the real world, perhaps we could hold a real funeral for them. Or hand them back to people who loved them. We'd deal with the slings and arrows of retribution then too, if that happened.

The idea of being able to put them to rest gave me the strength to commit to this plan, despite how my body was reacting. My skin felt clammy, and my stomach churned.

With solemn expressions, the three of us, Axel, Gigi and I, walked quietly to the location where we'd gathered all three corpses.

Thankfully, Gigi had the decency to leave them the clothes on their backs. From a distance, they looked like they were resting.

I forced myself to look as I crouched next to the spellcaster.

We'd laid the three of them out on their backs, in a neat row. They stared emptily up into the air. Unable to take the weight of their dead gaze, I closed the magic user's eyes. Other than moving them, this hadn't been the first time I'd touched a dead body. I'd kissed Chrissie on the cheek in the funeral home all those years ago. Much like hers, their face was cold.

The spellcaster's muscles were stiff, and their skin tacky with blood. There was no life left here. I swallowed back the sick that wanted to rush up my throat and took a deep breath. That had been the wrong move. The coppery scent of blood filled my nostrils and made the nausea in my stomach clench harder.

Pushing all this down, I imagined the same thing I normally did when adding something to the inventory. The system reacted as expected. One moment the husk of the person I'd helped kill was there, the next I saw its icon in my window.

I exhaled and nodded to the others.

Grimly, they began the same process.

Once all bodies had been stored, we returned to the Jye and Tam. Both of them were watching over Wren. If I didn't know better, I might've thought the expression on Tam's face depicted affection. As soon as she noticed us, her smile flipped into a frown. That was more like the Tam I'd begun to know.

I let out a short sigh. "Once everyone's at full mana and stamina, we need to move on. We can't risk something like this happening again."

"I'm almost back to full," Jye said.

Axel, Tam, and Gigi shared their statuses; a mix of half restored and half not. Both my metres were quite low.

I looked down at the sleeping form of Wren, and my determination wavered. Some black drool was leaking out of her snoring mouth.

She really was being a trooper. And maybe we were asking too much of a ten-year-old girl. However, it was better for her to be with us than not be with us right now. Perhaps once we got out of here, I'd try to get answers about her family, and we'd reunite them. Actually, yeah. I'd make it a priority.

For now, though, we could indulge in letting her nap a little more.

DUNGEON
HUNTER

XIX

EXPECTATIONS

SET UP ON THE GRASS OUTSIDE, there are five rows of pews between Axel and me. Probably to stop us from getting into it again. It's a closed casket service, out of respect. It's like I can almost see through the oak, to Chrissie's resting face, the skin so cold when I'd kissed her for the last time. The coffin is small, the same height as me. It would've dwarfed her. I hope she's comfortable in there with the extra headroom and foot space.

The cushioning looked soft.

They lower her into the ground, and I'm encouraged by my parents to say something. Getting the words out is hard. My nose is running, and I can barely see the words on my paper as I speak. I can't feel my heart in my chest because it hurts so much.

"I love Chrissie. She'll always be my little sister. She shouldn't be dead. It's not fair. I will miss her all my life."

I finish, hands shaking, world blurry, and my parents both say their farewells through tears as well, and then the ceremony is over. People, faceless strangers to me, mill about us, offering empty condolences.

We add her favourite toys onto her casket before they begin to cover her up. I also give Chrissie my favourite book since I'll never be able to read it to her. The dirt thudding against the casket lid is the only sound for a long time.

When Axel approaches the grave, at first anger hits me. I'm rushing up to confront him, fury cutting through the sadness, ready to throw down again. But he's speaking, very softly, down to Chrissie. He sniffs as he talks, and it causes me to hesitate. My steps slow, but I inch closer to listen in. I only manage to catch the end of it.

"...my sister, but you were the closest I had. This was for you, like always, like I promised."

After taking a moment, Axel releases something into the grave and then walks away to his parents who are also distraught, almost as much as my own. I creep hesitantly to the edge of the hole. Down there, amidst the growing mound of dirt, on top of the book I'd given Chrissie, is a crisp blue raspberry Warhead.

Just like me she loved sour things. I even remember the expression on her chubby baby face the first time she'd tried a lemon. Though for the past year or so, because of several cavities, she'd been banned from eating lollies. She'd taken the ruling with a peculiar grace, never throwing a tantrum or even asking for any. Mum and dad had been proud.

Had Axel been sneaking her these the entire time?

"HEY, LEE, EVERYONE'S BACK UP."
I blinked back the dream, or the memory, or the dream of a memory. As the world rushed back into focus, I became aware that the rest of the party were in various stances in a semicircle around me. They were waiting on me. I must've dozed off while we were letting Wren rest.

I stared for a moment at Axel. It still felt unreal that he was calling me by my name. He was squatting down beside me, the hand that'd shaken me awake midretraction. There were bags under his eyes. If I thought about it, those had appeared, and had never truly faded, after that day.

I'd forgotten that he'd loved Chrissie too. Axel and my sister never got along like me and her, but that didn't mean he hadn't cared about her.

After the funeral, prompted by Axel's actions, I'd dug up the remaining pack of Warheads I had.

A few weeks before everything, my parents had brought me that party packet as a reward for getting good grades. They made me promise not to give any to Chrissie, and so I'd hid them under my bed and had been snacking on them in secret.

I told myself I would eat the rest for her.

Opening the remaining individual packets, one by one in preparation as if in ritual, I'd eventually broken down, sobbing that I was sorry for never sharing them. Thinking about Chrissie, tied to how helpless I felt and how useless what I was doing was, triggered my first ever panic attack.

Scared that I was dying, as punishment for hiding the lollies from my sister, for letting her die, the even more irrational part of my brain thought I could take the lollies with me to her. Through my tears and crushing heart and lungs, I'd shovelled a handful of the Warheads into my mouth.

That the sour flavour of them had shocked me out of the attack was pure happenstance.

I'd never told Axel about that. I don't know how he knew. Yes, they helped me with the attacks. But beyond that, I'd always had them because they reminded me of Chrissie, of the future she'd lost, that we never got to share.

Maybe Axel had kept them for the same reason.

Realising myself, I nodded to his prior words, and I quickly checked my own stats to ensure I was good to go as well. Both my stamina and mana were back to around two thirds. Not a lot of time had passed while

I'd slept, but if everyone else was ready, I wasn't going to hold us back. I think I'd done enough of that.

Standing, I asked Wren, "How was your nap?"

"I feel a lot better." She smiled. "Actually, I had a really good dream. Did you dream?"

"Oh, uh. I dreamt about…" I paused, trying to figure out how to explain it without making it sound bleak. No matter how I cut it, it was going to be a mood killer. Even though the dream hadn't made me sad.

The cutthroat of our party rolled her eyes. "No one actually cares, babes."

"Oi, speak for yourself, I love hearing about dreams," said Jye. "They reflect a person's mental state."

I blanched. "I hope that's not true."

Gigi crossed xir arms, shaking xir head. "I disagree. Dreams mean nothing."

Nodding sagely, Axel seemed to agree with xem. No wonder. With no prompting, once when drunk he'd told me about a dream where he was struck by the realisation he could transform into a car and then proceeded to drive away as a Mazda. If Jye was right, I couldn't even hazard a guess about Axel's mentality at that point.

Wren said, "Well, I dreamt that I lived in a tower in the clouds. And that I could fly!" She spread her arms out and closed her eyes, as if summoning the memory of soaring through the skies. It was a pity there was no wind in this biome. A soft billowing in her pixie cut hair would've sold the image.

I remarked, "You never know, with all these skills, maybe one day you actually can."

This seemed to settle strangely over the others, as if reminding them that nothing was normal and perhaps never would be again. Okay then. I'd wanted to avoid bringing down the party, but it looks like I'd failed that. At the very least I wouldn't have to mention that I'd dreamt about my sister's funeral. Crisis averted…?

"We might as well get going, then."

I turned to face the entrance to the shrine. After the battle, the oddness of it paled in comparison to what we'd done. Though the blue-flamed candles still flickered unendingly, and the light fogginess still hovered in the air, the eeriness had been flattened, desaturated in eminence.

Axel scoffed. "'We might as well get going then'? That's really gonna be the line you use to introduce us to the Dungeon boss? Can't you think of something more grandiose?"

Scowling, I replied, "You don't know it's a boss. Like Tam, or rather Mumma said, it could be a riddle."

"It could be another maze," suggested Jye.

In concert, an upset groan erupted from everyone else.

Wren whined, "Please, no more labyrinths."

As a group we walked up the aged stone steps to the shrine's entry. Either due to its design or the limitations of creativity behind whatever made it, you couldn't see anything inside. The interior was just pitch black as we approached. The closer we grew, the stronger the musty smell of mildew became. All along I'd thought that the biome just gave off that scent, but maybe it originated from the temple itself. Were we walking into an inside swamp?

"I believe it is a challenge."

Frowning, I echoed Gigi, "A challenge?"

"Yes. [REDACTED]."

I repressed the frustration at the censorship. A challenge, huh? I examined Tam's expression to see if any information could be discerned. Perhaps Mumma had told her something. Unfortunately, she looked just as sceptical at Gigi's words. I sighed internally.

If we combined the idea of a challenge with the riddle concept, maybe it would be something like the infamous two-guard problem; the one who always lies and the one who always tells the truth. Or maybe we'd face a sphinx?

We'd reached the shrine's entrance.

I took a deep breath and glanced around at the others. Everyone had a slightly different look of anticipation on their faces: Gigi's was a steeled optimism set in flatly pressed lips. Jye's, a resigned but balanced curiosity in their widened green eyes. Tam's, unshakable confidence only belied by a clenched jaw, revealing the smallest of doubts. And on Wren, concerned apprehension was furrowing her brow.

Axel's features were unreadable. That figured. His gaze met mine and he titled his head, as if to say, *Caught you.* Somehow that small exchange lifted a bit of the worry I felt.

"See you guys on the other side."

Then I stepped through into the building, the blackness swallowing me whole.

The inkiness cleared, revealing a rather standard looking stone interior. It reminded me of one of the dungeons from the Zelda games, but I couldn't pick which one. Jesus, would we have to do all those time-based puzzles? That was not my idea of a good time. Whatever had been causing the dewy swamp scent was gone. Instead, the air was stale and stagnant. But it was, just as we'd lamented, and Jye suggested, a further labyrinth, this time topped with a roof. No more "semicheating," I guess.

What was the point of the mysterious black entrance then?

"That was stupid," I said.

Silence greeted me.

Heart in my throat, I spun around, frantically praying that the others were just taking their time. But there was no entrance behind me. Black or otherwise. The only thing now before me was a cold stone wall.

Fuck.

They'd split us up.

Fear grabbed hold of me. It writhed its way through my limbs and locked me to the spot. The cold sweat breaking out on my brow trickled down into my left eye. If I couldn't borrow my party members' skills when I wasn't near them, I was a dead man walking. But nothing about the ability said it had to be used in proximity to its origin member. I took a deep, stilling breath, forcing myself to stop making logic leaps that flung my mental state into the abyss of defeat.

Tentatively, I tried activating [Thick Hide].

The thin layer spread around me, the unusual second skin suddenly a comforting hug rather than the foreign feeling I'd long associated with it.

At least there was that. However, my nerves were still frazzled and fraught. I hadn't been genuinely alone since… before the Gates. Even when I'd been in Twilight, hell, even when I'd been basically dead, there'd been someone nearby, someone I could rely on. Thinking back on it, before all this had started, Axel had been there, somewhere. I don't think I ever really acknowledged just how much that meant to me, deep down. Without me knowing it, having him in my life was a constant that I'd relied on, like trusting the sun would rise and fall. And I'd wanted to run away from that when I'd wanted to move out?

Well, congrats to me.

Now I was truly alone.

It was cold.

Hoping against hopes, I cupped my hands around my mouth and called out, praying someone in the party would be able to hear me.

"Guys! Are you there?"

Fingers crossed that this was just another stupid scheme to make this more entertaining and that we were in the same instance of the Dungeon and not truly separated.

"Lee?" came an echo from the distance. "Is that actually you?"

A chorus of other voices replied, and the relief that flooded me was tangible.

"What does everyone see?" I asked, trying to identify where each member might be.

"Walls," came one bland reply.

"Real helpful, Axel."

Though I couldn't really talk. It was the only notable thing near me as well.

"Damn, walls is all I see too," Jye said, from the completely opposite direction, and I could visualise them throwing their hands up in frustration.

"It's stone walls 'til the cows come home, sunshine."

"Wren, Gigi?"

"It's dark where I am…" Wren said, dread making her voice tremble.

My fury at whoever or whatever had orchestrated this rose. One day, I don't know how, I'd have a long conversation with the creator of this Dungeon. This conversation would also involve me throttling them to an inch of their life, if they were living. If they weren't… well, I guess I could get creative.

"I would advise no one stays where they are," came Gigi's voice, though it sounded like xe was moving. Was xe… running?

"Why?" I asked, confused. If we wanted to find each other, having us all wandering around was literally the *opposite* way to do that, especially if this maze was as big as the one outside. We were liable to walk past or just miss each other. Besides, it wasn't like there was a time limit on this shrine. I'd been about to suggest we find members one at a time, with Axel starting the search because of his [Swift Footed] trait. I might've considered asking Tam, but knowing her, it would've been a lost cause.

An inhuman roar that thundered the walls around me answered for xem.

"I am being pursued," Gigi said, more calmly than I would've in xir place.

"Oh, fuck this shit. It's dog eat dog right now."

"Tam, don't be selfish," I shouted, now beginning to start walking. I wanted to get away from the dead-end to my back. It would be stupid to remain somewhere I could be cornered. I eventually came to a T and turned left.

"Me? Selfish? Wouldn't think of it."

After that, she said nothing more, even as I called for her.

"What's chasing you, Gigi?" Jye asked. Their shorter breath meant they were on the move too.

"I do not know what to call it."

Gigi must've been nearby, because xir voice was clear. The ground under me rumbled. Continuously checking behind me to ensure I wasn't going to be taken off guard, I picked up speed, shifting to a light jog. Running would just exhaust me and, baby, I was not a runner and track star. A controlled faster-than-walking pace was much more suited to my level of fitness.

Feet slapping on hard ground sounded to my left followed by heavy pounding. Then a booming *THUMP*. It echoed into the floor and walls, vibrating all surfaces, disturbing dust and shaking small stones loose.

Something very large had crashed. If Gigi was trying to stop it from following xem, perhaps xe'd used [Shield Wall] to halt it? But why hadn't I heard the goddamn static hiss? Was it glitching out again?

At the next intersection, I turned toward the direction of the sounds. Perhaps with two of us to chase, whatever it was would get confused and lose track of both Gigi and me. If worst came to worst and it came after me, I could hide behind [Shield Wall] and protect myself, like xe had.

"Gigi, buy some time! I'm coming to help," I announced.

"No, you are most definitely not."

Alarmed, I glanced around to see Axel barrelling toward me.

"What are you—" and then his arms were around me, sweeping me off my feet, the action knocking the breath out of my diaphragm. I boggled up at him, unable to comprehend what he'd just done.

Axel had picked me up.

He was carrying me as we sped along, farther and farther away from where Gigi was, darting about each corner with a single light, precisely measured step. I couldn't believe what was happening. No. This *couldn't* be happening.

Finally mentally caught up, I struggled against him. "What the fuck?"

"Gigi's shields are stronger. You know that."

Furious, I yelled while batting at his hands, "It doesn't mean I can't help!"

"You heard the size of whatever it is. Think your shields would last even *one* hit?"

I didn't parse what he was saying nor did I care. My mana and stamina were mostly regenned, apart from the cap of [Thick Hide]. If I wanted to, I could *make* him stop, but that'd be a waste of precious resources we needed to conserve. Instead, I lifted a hand, threaded it through his hair and gripped, yanking down on it so his gaze met mine.

"Axel, I swear to God, if you don't put me down right now, I'll never forgive you."

He skidded to an immediate stop, kicking up dust. In his eyes, he had that same damn stupid, lunatic sadness. Axel laughed.

"You never change."

With that, he unceremoniously deposited me onto the ground and disappeared around a corner. I scrambled up, swearing. By the time I found my feet and pursued him, I'd completely lost him and the direction he'd gone. The rumbling of whatever situation Gigi was in could barely be heard from where I was.

FUCKING AXEL.

After letting out a frustrated grunt, I shifted gears. I'd wanted to get Gigi away from the attacker because we needed xir defensive abilities if we were to mount a full-group attack. Having xem spending all xir mana and stamina now would bite us in the ass later.

I let out a long sigh.

We still needed the full party for that assault, anyway.

One step at a time.

"Jye, Wren, Tam! Where are you?"

"You know all you gotta do is speak of the devil and you will receive."

The built cutthroat stepped out from my right at one of the pathway offshoots. Meeting her like this was the most insane coincidence. If I hadn't known any better, I would've thought that Axel had tracked her down and placed me here with her. But given her relative radio silence that was impossible. What crazy good fortune.

"You must've saved someone important in a previous life, Tam."

She grinned. "What can I say? Lady Luck has a crush on me."

The way she said it felt like she was implying something more, but I didn't have the time to break her words down.

"Can you find the others?"

"You asking me to go cat?"

I nodded.

"And what's in it for little old me?"

"Not dying to the thing crumbling this maze."

She made a noncommittal noise of consideration and then said, "You better put your running shoes on, babes."

In a puff of smoke, Tam disappeared. Without giving time for the haze to clear, the bob-tailed cat streaked off, forming speed lines of smoke behind her.

Still no ability sound. I couldn't rely on it anymore.

I pounded after her, listening intently for any signs that would reveal how Gigi, and maybe Axel, were holding up against the... *monster*? Was it a monster? No human would sound like it had as chasing down intruders, lumbering through the labyrinth.

Oh. The labyrinth.

Of course, it was a monster.

It had to be the Minotaur.

Real fucking original.

DUNGEON
HUNTER

XX

PROGRESS

A S I RAN AFTER TAM, her little paws pattering across stone floors, I reflected on what precisely I could do to help the party and what might be our best bet in defeating our large opponent. I still hadn't spent the rewards for us "eliminating" the party Test Name.

Before falling asleep waiting on Wren, I'd spent some time combing through the system looking at what I could spend the credits on. Following the same pathway through my stats, I'd selected the **Upgrade** menu, and this time none of my attributes had been grayed out or locked. In fact, it had very excitedly flashed the number of in-system currency I had available in the corner of my screen.

1 21 CREDITS.

Still, I wasn't sure why we'd been awarded them this time and in such an unusual sum. Did we need to kill people to get credits? If that were the case, spending what we had would have to be carefully considered before purchase because I'd strongly prefer to not become a mass murderer. I didn't know about the others, but I could firmly say at least Wren would also like to avoid that fate.

Leaning up against the back of the shrine, the coolness of the stone seeping into my body, I perused what I could actually use the credits for.

Much like in RPGs, it looked like I could put some points directly into my attributes themselves. That, at least, made sense. If I was right about how each of these worked, then this was when I needed to start thinking about how I was going to be building my char— myself up to survive. My class *was* [All-Rounder].

I'd initially thought it to be quite a weak start and branching equally into all areas to be a poor idea, but in the past few situations, nothing except my concern about how limited I was by my low stats had hurt my chances. Should I strive to level up as balanced as I could and not specialise in anything? In any other situation, the thought would be idiotic…

I let my focus wander over the attributes, wondering if I could garner any more factual information on how each one affected us overall. If Gigi's [Shield Walls] were stronger than my own despite them taking the same amount of required stamina, and Axel healed faster and more efficiently than me even though we'd received similarly life-threatening wounds, then the attributes had to impact us on a deeper level. I lingered on the first attribute, CON, trying to work things out and it highlighted itself. A notification box popped up.

Upgrade CON for 5 credits? Accept | Reject

I rejected it, unsure about what that'd actually get me.

And, Jesus, 5 credits? That didn't seem like a fair exchange. Still, that meant 24 attribute value points I could increase, which would massively help me survive. I rechecked our party screen to see everyone's levels, wondering how we were averaging after that XP explosion.

Just Friends Party | LVL 23

Lee | LVL 3 | All-Rounder (Party Leader)

Axel | LVL 3 | Combatant

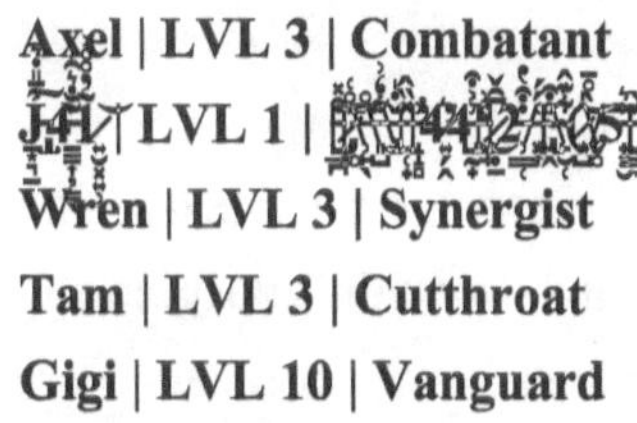

Wren | LVL 3 | Synergist

Tam | LVL 3 | Cutthroat

Gigi | LVL 10 | Vanguard

Oh, God, Jye still hadn't levelled up. That meant they were stuck on that level. I wondered about what kind of repercussions that'd have. As far as I could tell, levels were empty numbers, and credits were what really progressed our stats. The attribute points were paywalled, and that could only be bought out with the system-specific currency.

Well, maybe we could get more credits by selling stuff to Xanthe? That had been the whole point of my exclusive contract with them in the first place. Flicking through my inventory, I selected several nonessential items and thought about selling them. A new screen appeared. Wasn't that always the case?

It was the same colour as the window that'd appeared in Twilight.

Transfer items to exclusive vendor for sale? Accept | Reject

After accepting, I wondered how long it would take for the products to sell. Well, Xanthe was a particularly persuasive merchant. They'd managed to get me on their side. Tam would have you think that wasn't a particularly difficult thing to do, though. We'd just have to wait and see.

While I was in the window, I realised there was a little search bar in the bottom corner. Maybe this was where I could browse items currently on the marketplace? Selecting the button in my mind, the window extended out to display an array of items from what looked like olden day hair pins to devices that could've been some sort of futuristic weapon. Most of them were boasting costs in the millions as starting bids with some on sale at a set "buy now" price.

I filtered from lowest to highest and saw that even the cheapest auction items were well above what my wallet could afford. The very lowest price belonged to an [Ancient Message] that was penned by

[REDACTED] and was 200 credits. It had zero bids. Who had that kind of money to throw away on a random letter?

As I continued to browse the auction house, I came to realise that the entire catalogue was rife with products that I couldn't imagine anyone having any use for. This included things like [Legendary Fork of REDACTED], which appeared to simply be a bronze kitchen utensil, and [Vase of Invisibility], which was a picture of nothing. Both of them had several bids and were valued in the thousands. I couldn't fathom *who* was trying to buy these things. Or where they'd come from.

Scrolling, I eventually came to a familiar item. [KMART 20cm Triple Rivet Chef's Knife] for 2,111 credits. There were dozens of bids, and it looked like there was still a few days left before final sale. What the fuck? It was just… just a knife. We'd murdered three people and only been given 121 credits. Were their lives worth less than 4 percent of a shitty knife that was produced en masse? It didn't make any sense. The only stuff that cost this much and really had no practicality was art.

Wait.

If this was all some sort of fucked up show, were items from our world something like collectibles? And if that were true, where had all these other things come from? A lot of them were simply unrecognisable to me.

Xanthe had said I was early to Twilight. And there'd been hundreds of people there when I'd visited the marketplace. I'd never thought about who those people could all be or where they came from. But Xanthe was a real person, I was sure. Not human but real. Ergo, every other merchant and customer was also real.

There was a thriving and long-established economy behind this fucked up situation.

That could only mean one thing. This had to have happened to other people before. Had to have been repeatedly happening.

I reflected on Xanthe's words, hoping to glean even a nugget of context.

"My [REDACTED] didn't so I've a soft spot for [REDACTED], but many of the others did."

Were they referring to their own people? Xanthe's species didn't manage to do something, but some of the other races of merchants had? What was it? If it was connected to the same thing we were currently going through… Maybe their people hadn't ended up winning whatever game we were being forced to play?

God, this was a lot to parse. The more I thought about it, the more I realised I needed to share it with the party. I needed someone to bounce ideas off on this, to make sure I wasn't going crazy or making up meaning where there wasn't any.

But this didn't seem like a good time. Everyone was taking a moment to themselves, and they deserved it. After we cleared the Dungeon, I told myself I'd voice all this to them. As I made up my mind, I closed the marketplace window. You couldn't make bids or purchases from it, anyway; just view the current stock on sale. Any other player would have to make the dangerous trip to the time-dilating realm of Twilight. But Xanthe had said I only had to put in a request with them.

Returning my attention to the attributes I could upgrade, below them was my singular ability.

When I focused on it, it expanded to describe its use and further information.

[Channel | Unique Ability]

Use a consenting party member's skills. Failure to use ability once activated will result in repercussions. Costs are equal to original party member's.

Huh. That explained the time in the gym when I hadn't used Jye's Load because I never got their consent. It'd sapped me of mana. I didn't like how vague "repercussions" sounded, though. It could mean very well anything. And who decided what counted as a "repercussion"? Trying to push past how ominous the description was, I focused on the words "Unique Ability."

Did it mean I was the only person with this power?

I guess that made me feel a little bit better about starting off with such shit stats. But it was odd that this ability was in the Upgrade section of the menu and I couldn't interact with it. Was I lacking something else that I needed to level it up? How would you even upgrade such an ability?

I wanted to ask the others, but everyone looked like they would prefer to be left alone. After everything we'd just done and been through, I wasn't about to intrude. Still… Casting a hopeful glance to the last person I could rely on, it seemed even Axel was mired in his own thoughts.

With a sigh, I began weighing up the pros and cons of each attribute.

As I ran through the three-lettered items again and again, the world faded away.

⊐⊏

TAM STOPPED ABRUPTLY, and I nearly tripped over her. Regaining my balance, I noticed that her little bobtail was standing on end, her hackles up. She let out an angry growl, her haunches lowered to the ground, as though ready to pounce.

"What is it?" I whispered, trying to steady my breathing.

Being a cat, obviously she didn't answer me.

"Oh, thank fuck. It's you two!" came Jye's voice from around the corner.

A relieved smile on their face, the redhead entered our view, walking at a fast pace toward us. I frowned, gaze flicking down to the still very aggressive feline at my feet. While she'd never shown great affection for Jye, I didn't think the giant generally elicited such intense hostility. Something was wrong. But what?

Not wanting to take my chances, I held out a hand. "Can you stop there?"

Jye's head cocked to the side, confusion etched over their strong brows, but they continued to approach.

"What's wrong?"

"I said stop, dude."

"Why?" they replied, walking ever forward.

Tam hissed and swatted at my shoe, claws bared. *Do something*, she seemed to say.

As far as I could tell, the Jye rushing toward us was the same one I'd seen less than half an hour ago. But they weren't listening to me. And despite everything the redhead said, they seemed to follow my orders. Even when they were questionable. The situation with Wren hadn't changed that.

I tried once more. "Don't come any closer."

They didn't stop.

Fuck.

I borrowed one of Axel's abilities, the vile tar flowing through me, and then, summoning as much fear as I could, I shouted, "Stop or else!"

Their eyes widened, and they flinched, coming to a halt a few steps away.

From how close Jye had come, I could see exactly what Tam had been warning me of. Everything about them was slightly off in colour.

The inside of the maze wasn't lit, not in any classical sense, but a kind of a fog of war existed. You could only see so far ahead and behind. Something within close proximity was evenly lit, as though you were casting a light yourself, but the farther away something was, the darker it appeared.

As close as Jye was, they should've been lit up, saturated like Tam.

Instead, there was a murkiness to their colour, a contrast and hue that hadn't corrected upon their approach. It was uncannily wrong.

This wasn't Jye.

It was some sort of mimicry of our party member.

Just as I was about to start interrogating them, the Fake-Jye turned tail and skittered back the way they'd come. I made a movement to pursue them, but Tam shot off the opposite direction. Shit, she was still after someone from our party. And I couldn't lose her and the chance to find someone else.

Swearing under my breath, I changed course and followed Tam.

We'd deal with whoever Fake-Jye was later. They'd reacted to [Intimidation]. It meant that they had to be another player. Using that ability out of everything had been a risky call to make, but I was trusting the story of the labyrinth and the minotaur and the past events that we'd gone through.

As far as I could tell, this Dungeon had no other difficulties except those tied directly to mazes and traps. We were only meant to work our way through the challenges or around them. Everything else we came up against was not part of the Dungeon. So Fake-Jye had to have been a player, or it was Jye under some sort of weird mind control. Both of which would be affected by [Intimidation].

Lungs beginning to burn, I yelled out, "Everyone, we're not alone!"

A bellow echoed in from incredibly far away; the monster.

The snarky voice that came after said: "No shit, Sherlock."

I was too out of breath to sigh and managed to get out, "Doppelgänger about. They're the wrong colour!"

This earned me silence in reply.

Yeah, I'd like to see Axel come up with some sort of sassy response to that.

"That's racist, Lee!"

I repressed my groan, still sprinting after Tam as she darted around corners.

"What's a doppelgänger?" the giant called out.

Was that actually Jye?

Wren, from wherever she was, said, "It's like a copy of you."

She sounded close. I should've known Tam would hunt her down first. The cutthroat didn't like to show it, but she cared about the young girl. I was actually glad that Tam had picked her. I was worried.

The way she'd described her surroundings as "dark" had made me extra concerned. She *should've* been seeing walls, just like us. It meant something was different with her or where she was.

Well, that was if the person speaking had been Wren this time, if the player hadn't shifted into her.

I had to admit it was a good thing the mimic ability had such an obvious flaw. Based on the colouration issue, it seemed the copied appearance relied on what the user could see. False-Jye must've spied the real Jye from down a hallway or something, leading to the incorrect hues and saturation.

The disguise obviously wouldn't have tricked Jye, since they would know it wasn't themselves, so I'd hoped the mimic had left Jye alone to try it on us instead and hadn't harmed them. The appearance wouldn't punk any of us now, since I'd warned everyone. And even if it found anyone else to copy, so long as they remained a fair distance—

Shit.

They'd come right up to me and Tam.

The mimic might be able to become my perfect copy.

God, this was going to be annoying.

DUNGEON
HUNTER

XXI

FOUND

"HOW DO I KNOW YOU'RE REALLY LEE?" asked Jye from the spot they were sitting, idly trailing their finger through the dirt on the ground.

While it wasn't a bad question, it still pissed me off. I really shouldn't have expected anything different, especially considering that I was the one who'd warned everyone about the mimic running about the shrine labyrinth. However, that didn't mean I hadn't low-key expected the others to discern me from a fake upon first glance. I guess I'd been fooled at a distance too.

"Tam is with me," I said, gesturing to the cat who'd now paused and was licking at a paw.

"You could be summoning her, like an illusion or something."

"Okay, ask me a question."

They ran their hand over an imaginary beard.

"How many siblings do I have?"

I froze. Oh, fuck. How many did they have? It'd been like four days since we'd discussed this in the cabin, and a lot had happened between now and then. I racked my brain, trying to recall the number. They were all younger than Jye, that I remembered. Basically each of them were a year apart. Shit.

"Come on, it's not that hard to re—"

"Five!" I said, the memory suddenly becoming clear, the look in Jye's eyes at the time unfocused and concerned. "You have five siblings. Three brothers and two sisters."

The giant nodded solemnly and stood. "All right, off to find Wren, then?"

Letting out a sigh, I shook my head.

"We already know where she is. We just can't get her out."

Jye tilted their head, much akin to a dog hearing someone saying "vet."

I explained to them that Tam and I'd tracked the young girl down first but that she'd been locked behind a solid wall on all sides. She was inaccessible. That was probably why she could only see darkness. Wren had been locked in an area that we couldn't reach.

I'd been afraid of using [Ground Smash] because the girl explained that her room was really small and she couldn't back up out of range. Her health was similar to mine, and based on what had occurred even just *once* in the cabin, the shrapnel the attack created could have fatal consequences if luck wasn't on our side. Even thinking about what I'd done to Axel made my stomach churn. I also couldn't conjure any way to use Jye or Gigi's abilities to get through.

As always, thinking far beyond her age would have you guess, Wren had come to the same conclusion.

"Come get me soon, okay?" she'd said.

I'd promised her we would.

We were forced to leave her in the dark room all by herself.

It took everything inside me to do that. The idea of it made my stomach churn. Because I knew Chrissie had probably gone through something similar.

"So, she's safe?" asked Jye, wiping at the dust on their pants.

After my warning to the others about the mimic, we'd agreed to keep our shouts to a minimum, to avoid giving them any further information to trick us. The team had since been radio silent. Jye had only known about everyone's status up until then.

"Safer than us. And the copycat can't imitate her either. Probably. But we're down a party member for the fight."

Somewhat less concerned now, Jye folded their large arms over their chest. "What's the plan, boss?"

I considered our options. Without Wren, we could take much fewer risks since I could do only so much healing. "You practised with the bow yet?"

"Got in a few shots while you and Wren were napping before," Jye admitted. Their shifty expression led me to believe that hadn't been enough of a chance to become familiar with the weapon. Okay, so rule that out. I hadn't had time to get used to my glaive either, but swinging around a broomstick seemed ill-advised with the size our opponent sounded. At least Jye still had a bunch of knives left.

After a moment, I shrugged. "Can't go wrong with the classics. Gigi tanks. The beast sounds much bigger and a more visible target than the baller from before, so you should be able to get some range projectile shots in. Since Wren's out for the count, I can play support, buffing everyone and doing emergency healing. Assisting where I can. Axel'll go in for frontal attacks. And, Tam, can we count on you to assist in the front line too?"

She glanced up from her grooming and gave me a look.

"That a yes?"

Tam performed the equivalent of a human shrug, her small cat haunches rising and falling.

Why wasn't I surprised?

"Can you at least take us to the others?"

After a languorous stretch, she set off. I jutted my head at Jye to follow, and we were on our way. As we jogged after the feline, I borrowed [Whetstone] from Wren. The ability tasted like I'd been sucking on coins, a metallic coating over the back of my tongue. After swallowing it back, keeping an eye on my stamina and mana, I buffed Jye.

They flinched and swung their gaze over to me, accusation heavy in their eyes. I smiled apologetically, thinking they'd long since gotten used to the glitch sounds of notifications. Clearly not. Perhaps the [REDACTED] audio was different than the system's. In the corner of my peripheral, I saw 10 of my mana and 2 of my stamina drop away from the usage.

Yikes. That was half my mana. If I did it once more for Axel, I'd be flat out. And my mana regen was *slow*. I'd been timing it with my watch and found that every hour or so, it pipped up around 4 points. I only had my stats to blame for that.

Literally tailing Tam, the sounds of the fight Axel and Gigi were engaged with grew louder and louder, the ground under our feet vibrating from the combat and the knocking into walls. They'd been dealing with it for the past half an hour or so. I had no doubt our help was sorely needed.

A crash exploded from up ahead, and Tam skated to a stop, almost as if to say, "This is as far as I go."

I stared at her, knowing my ability to goad her into helping us had been spent on our last battle. Working her up over her wife wouldn't work again. While she was hotheaded, she wasn't stupid. Tam had to have known what I'd done after the fact.

Instead, I simply said, "If you see an opportunity to go for the kill, do it. Otherwise, stay out of the party's way."

In her green gaze, I saw the acknowledgement before she dipped away.

We turned the last corner to see down the hall exactly what was making the racket. It took a moment to understand what was happening and what precisely we were witnessing. Several [Shield Walls] were dotted around in the air, surrounding the mammoth of a creature. It stood two and a half men tall, its large furry body rippling with corded muscle. While we could only currently see its back, the two points of the beast's horns were still visible poking up from the crown of its head.

It really was a Minotaur.

Fuck.

Axel was jumping between [Shield Walls] to dodge its swinging attacks, a great axe held in its clawed fists, and striking when he could. Judging from the thin cuts on the Minotaur's hide, he wasn't doing much damage. From under a [Shield Wall] closer toward us, Gigi was watching anxiously. A few wounds were scattered over xir body, blood weeping freely down xir limbs. Xir had probably attempted to assist but hadn't been able to do so effectively.

Closing the distance in silence, we watched as Axel narrowly escaped one of the Minotaur's sweeping attacks. Had Axel remained where he'd been, his legs would've been cut out from under him. In raw frustration, the Minotaur swung wildly after Axel, cleaving a [Shield Wall] in two; the ability dissipated in a flutter of orbs.

My chest tightened in concern. He definitely couldn't hold out on his own for much longer. I could see how the fight had sapped him of energy and health already. It was like his battle with the glaive-user all over again. Why did he always throw himself into these fights like this? Was he that confident Wren could heal him back up?

"Gigi, report."

Finally noticing us, our newest member shook xir head.

"We are not doing enough damage. It is a slow beast, both in mind and body. But it is strong. I believe Axel has only cut at a tenth of its life."

I blinked. Maybe a classic approach wouldn't work.

"You have any shields to tank?" I asked.

Gigi frowned. "I am afraid even with one, getting hit with an attack straight on from our opponent would cripple me. My [Shield Walls] barely last one direct assault."

Yeah, okay, classic was completely out the window.

Right now, the monster was focused on Axel, and I doubted it had the mental faculties to strategize beyond what was directly in front of it. So long as the blond was keeping it preoccupied, we could practically do anything else.

However, we just couldn't attack without logic. None of us were equipped with exceptionally damaging moves, so it would be a long, drawn-out battle. We needed to limit the risk dealt to ourselves during the slog we'd have to go through to finally end the Minotaur.

I swung around to Jye.

"You said you had nothing to live for once, didn't you?"

"Right, he remembers my offhand nihilistic comments, but struggles with how many siblings I have."

I raised an eyebrow, and then the redhead let out a huff.

"I'm just joking, dude. What suicidal attempt you got in mind?"

Once I'd explained the plan to them and Gigi, Jye made a face. "You're a little unhinged, you know?"

"Whatever works."

Gigi nodded enthusiastically. "I can do this."

"On go," I said.

"Whatever you're doing, can you guys hurry the fuck up?" Axel shouted, clearing an attack from the great axe by a millimetre, the blade slicing through the strands of blond hair that hadn't made the dodge. They wafted away on the wind created by the Minotaur's weapon as it continued forward.

The combatant took the opportunity for a free swing, his sword eating into the furred flesh of the creature's rib cage. The blade slid along its thick skin, just barely cutting, leaving a beading line of blood in its wake. Still, the monster howled in pain and rage, its black eyes bulging from its semihuman face.

I announced, "Go."

In tandem, Jye and I made a mad dash for two of the [Shield Walls] currently in place. Some of the Minotaur's attacks had already destroyed a few while we'd been talking, and Gigi had mentioned that xe'd regenned enough to form a few more. I'd tried not to show my jealousy on my face. Much like my mana, my stamina only seemed to come back up at around 4 an hour. It sounded like Gigi's entire bar would refill in the same amount of time. I guess that was a perk of being LVL 10.

With our running start, we split to opposite sides of the stone maze hallway, Jye going left and me going right. Taking a deep breath, I sprung from the floor at the same time as Jye. I summoned a [Shield Wall] beneath me to make a platform, as I'd never have been able to jump high enough to get the closest one I was aiming for. Landing on the low friction system-blue floor, my foot slipped, throwing me slightly off-balance. Across from me, Jye practically torpedoed up, their thick leg muscles apparently not just for show. The giant alighted onto their targeted [Shield Wall], continuing their momentum, gaze locked onto their target.

Startled by our appearance, the Minotaur's attention flicked between Jye and I. Not good. Not good at fucking all.

Vaulting to one [Shield Wall] directly in front of the beast, Axel shouted, "Hey, fuckface, eyes on me!"

The Minotaur bellowed, incensed by Axel's cocky defiance, as I was sure it didn't understand his words. I regained my balance, and I echoed Jye's movements as the creature's two-handed axe flung upward to prepare for what would be a devastating attack. It began swinging its weapon, the blade hurtling through the air.

Axel remained in place.

Despite the sweat sheening on him, the blood trickling from attacks he hadn't dodged fully, the tiredness pulling down at him, his gaze met mine, a teasing smile there that said, *Took your time.*

How did he know? How did he always know what I was planning?

The great axe descended, bearing down on him, and just as it was about to land, three [Shield Walls] formed in the scant distance between

Axel and the Minotaur's weapon. The burst of the hiss of abilities was almost reassuring. I took a deep breath and hoped this would work.

The attack completely obliterated the first shield, glimmers of blue and white exploding. The sharpened head of the blade carried into the second shield, splitting it neatly in two. Another shower of blue orbs skittered away as the [Shield Wall] failed.

The Minotaur's great axe chewed into the third shield, the digital material creaking and groaning, cracks forming. But it withstood the hit.

The weapon was firmly lodged into the half-damaged [Shield Wall].

It was stuck.

Axel flipped the bird at the creature from behind his coverage, sticking out a tongue for good measure. An outraged howl burst from the Minotaur's chest, as it began to struggle to pull its axe from its unintentional sheath.

I let out my held breath and gathered my thoughts. Time to fucking go. This was my plan after all. Jye was already jumping down and, as I joined them in the act, I considered activating [Thick Hide], just in case, but decided against it. I'd need all the mana I could for this.

Hopefully, I'd aimed properly.

Falling, I flung out my arms, and Jye and I grabbed onto our separate targets.

The Minotaur's arms.

The air in my lungs oofed out of me on impact, and as gravity dragged at me, I clambered for purchase, fingers gripping onto whatever fur and muscle I could grab a hold of, the trunk of its arm thicker than my body.

On contact, I borrowed Jye's Load and applied as many as my mana bar would allow. I think it was around three times. That would be enough, wouldn't it? I couldn't tell if the Minotaur had a dominant arm, but if it did, please let it be Jye's. Their ability hissed in tangent with mine.

The effect was instantaneous.

The Minotaur's arms shotputted to its sides, Jye and I plunging with them, the floor like a super magnet attracting them.

Unable to control the trajectory of its suction down, the Minotaur's head slammed into the hilt of its own great axe, one of its horns snapping against the metal, spinning away into the distance. Releasing a bellow of surprise, the beast tried to resist the pull, its muscles bulging as it strained but to no avail.

The Minotaur had sunk to its knees, its arms now weights shackling it to the stone floor.

Even like that it still was taller than Jye.

Getting my wind back, I quickly released the creature's arm and stepped away to take stock of the situation. My heart hammered in my chest, blood pumping through my ears.

"Well. That went better than I thought."

DUNGEON
HUNTER

XXII

DEATH BLOW

THERE WAS NO ANNOUNCEMENT, which meant just bringing the Minotaur to its knees didn't mean the system considered this the end of the battle. It was clear what we had to do. The idea left a bad taste in my mouth.

Before us, the half-human beast was howling at its restraint, still tugging at its locked arms. I requested Jye to dart in and add a few Loads to its legs when they could to ensure our approach to put the Minotaur out of its misery would pose no further risk. The giant had yet to complete the action when I heard the hiss of an ability being activated and turned to look at the others.

Frowning, I only found Axel grinning triumphantly down at the Minotaur, perhaps considering ways in which he could deliver the final blow. Obviously, he hadn't heard the sound. This was just another thing I would talk to the others about when we were finally all back together. The list was growing long now. And I really was getting ahead of myself by thinking we would all survive. But there was a weird sort of confidence growing inside me. Perhaps we were really doing it.

Still, the source of the ability being activated worried me. Was it Wren healing herself? Tam fighting the mimic? I hadn't considered what the range of the warning was, so I couldn't be sure. Either way, the both of them would have to face whatever they were doing alone.

"So, what's the go?" I asked, knowing none of us could deal sufficient damage to end the Minotaur right now, especially because all of us had to be low on stamina and mana. With Gigi regenerating half xir stamina in the same amount of time it took for me to restore 4 points, it meant that Jye and Axel would probably get theirs back quicker as well. Lucky them.

If possible, I'd also prefer to not stand around and whittle away at something that cried out in pain. It felt inhumane.

"Target practice?" Jye suggested, stepping behind the creature carefully to do as I'd previously asked. They did not need to bend down to lay nervous hands on the Minotaur's hooves.

I really had to stop extending brainstorming to the redhead.

Pinching at the bridge of my nose, I said, "No, Jye. We're not using a living creature as target practice."

"It should have a weak spot," Gigi supplied.

I glanced over to xem, my brows furrowing in thought. Xir words hadn't been censored which meant what xe was saying had to be common knowledge. I mean, yes, in games, bosses tended to have weaknesses that glowed red for players to attack. There was nothing so obvious about the Minotaur.

The familiar hiss sounded as Jye applied a Load each onto the beast's hoofed feet. It wasn't as much as I'd like, but it was better than nothing. I'd stay clear of the Minotaur's legs, just in case. In reaction, the creature let out a bestial growl, tossing its head about in protest. It looked like little had changed, but it did seem more panicked. The fear on its semibull face did make me feel a little nauseous. If we were going by mythology, the Minotaur was half-human. What we were doing would be akin to an execution or at least 50 percent of one.

"How do we find it?" Axel asked.

He had begun circling the beast, taking a wide berth, his blue eyes narrowed in scrutiny.

"Wish Tam would lend us a hand," I muttered under my breath.

She'd been the one to see the gem in the crystal wall that had triggered the trap. If there was anyone on our team capable of spotting any type of weakness, red glow or not, it would've been her. Too bad she was such a poor sportsman. She was probably skulking about somewhere nearby waiting for a chance to kill-steal. Typical Tam. So we had to pin all our hopes on Axel.

Why were the rest of us so goddamn blind?

"Huh," came Jye's voice as they stepped back from the legs of the Minotaur.

"What is it?"

"On the back of this dude's neck. There's like… I don't know how to describe it."

Curious, the three of us made our way to check it out.

Sure enough, on the back of the Minotaur's neck was a singular discoloration. It could've just been a pigmentation issue with the creature's skin, but the shape was perfectly circular. The marker rested directly above the third protruding notch of the creature's spine. Smaller than a fingernail, on the Minotaur that was taller than when Axel had stood on Jye's shoulders, it was practically the scale of a stray freckle.

"How'd you see that?"

Smiling with embarrassment, Jye said, "I was admiring its delts and traps."

I didn't say anything, though my gaze did slide over the creature's muscles. It *was* well-built.

"Monsterfucker," Axel said, and not in a way that sounded like an insult. Like a casual remark. One might be able to say, "redhead," in the same way, and it'd be a simple fact about Jye.

"That looks like the weak spot," Gigi commented, nodding sagely, completely ignoring Axel for the better.

Following suit, I replied, "I mean, yeah. The spine of any vertebrate is a weakness. We got all our nerves in there. Angel pasta and all that."

This earned me a confused look from the rest of the party. *Lost* wasn't as popular, I guess. The doctor's line about his botched surgery had sat with me since I'd heard it. The imagery was genuinely horrific and visceral. Nerves spilling out of a spine like angel pasta.

Suppressing a shudder, I said, "You might as well say the head is a weak spot. That's just how bodies work."

"We can test it," Axel said, drawing his sword.

"Wait a sec."

The blond paused and raised an eyebrow at me. I was trying to imagine the rewards of this fight. Axel and Gigi had performed well initially, followed by Jye and me, but killing the Minotaur like this wasn't entertaining. It was kind of... boring.

It could affect the experience and credits we might receive after we finished the job. (Thinking of killing the Minotaur as a task we had to complete was the only way I was able to struggle through this.) It was still safer to strike down the creature like this, even if it didn't reward us well. That was a price I was willing to pay. The others may not be so forgiving once I told them, though.

Oh well.

I shook my head, giving Axel permission to continue.

The three of us watched as Axel hopped up onto the Minotaur's calf to get some more height. His blade rose in the air, and he took a moment to line up his swing, practising the movement. Beneath him, the creature squirmed, body writhing, almost like it was attempting to buck Axel off.

It roared in anger, its voice echoing about the hall. All this made the blond's job that much more difficult. Finally, satisfied with the alignment, Axel brought his sword down, so quickly that I wasn't sure I hadn't blinked.

The resulting screech of pain stemming from the Minotaur was answer enough, its limbs attempting to flail, but since they were locked, its body was racked with tremors.

Unlike the rest of Axel's cuts, which had barely gotten through the creature's skin, the one near the "weak spot" had scored directly through, revealing pink flesh and bone, blood pooling out from the injury. Axel hadn't managed to hit it directly in the centre, instead cutting through the bottom edge of the circle. It was a small target and the Minotaur had been thrashing around, so the slight miscalculation was understandable.

"You suck," Jye said and meant it.

Gigi's almost invisible silver brows met at the centre of xir temple.

"It has lost much of its health. Perhaps a third?"

I felt my mouth drop open. "In one hit?"

"This is based on my experience, but, yes."

Storing Gigi's words in the back of my head for the future, as what exactly had xe fought before that could be compared to the Minotaur, I signalled for Axel to give it another try. Fuck whatever rewards we'd get. We were so close to clearing the Dungeon.

Once again, the blond struggled to line up another hit, planting his feet into the calf muscle of the Minotaur for a steadier stance. He waited a bit, lifted his blade, and then swung down.

Another earsplitting shriek cut through the air.

"Only a third or so remaining," Gigi commented.

The Minotaur's body slumped forward. Only the bending of its frame seemed to be keeping it up. That was… good? I was torn on whether to feel bad about this or not. Unlike the people we'd killed, the Minotaur was almost definitely a construct of the Dungeon. But that didn't mean it wasn't real to an extent. It didn't know that it was some sort of programmed NPC. That it was created to be murdered.

Rather I felt more pity than guilt.

"Can you surrender?" I asked the creature, peering into its semihuman face.

Its black eyes fluttered open, staring directly back at me. There was some intelligence there. Maybe something closer to the intellectual level of an elephant or octopus. Perhaps I could get through.

"Surrender," I suggested. "Give up. We don't have to kill you."

Its mouth opened, and it mangled out the words: "Can... not."

"You can't surrender?" I queried, their meaning striking a previously unthought-of horror into me. It wasn't the right time to consider the theory, but that didn't mean it sat well within me.

Weakly, it shook its head. Its black eyes watered, tears beading.

"Kill... me," it pleaded. Its voice was croaky, probably from never being used for anything but screaming, but I could hear the desperation.

We were practically torturing it, killing it like this. This was the best we could do though. And we could grant it release, if that's what it truly wanted.

"We will," I promised, nodding to Axel for the final blow.

He raised his sword up.

Met my gaze.

And swung down.

Third time was the charm. The blade cleaved through the Minotaur's spine, splitting the two sections of vertebrae completely apart. Threads of its spinal cord dangled outside, thin and white. Axel jumped back as the creature's body fell forward completely, all tension and muscle control now outside of its ability, its arms and legs still locked to the floor.

"Now we can get Wren," Jye said, excitedly.

But no notification had sounded.

Grimly, Gigi said, "It's still alive. Barely."

Axel made a move to finalise his kill, but I held up a hand. Swallowing back the bile creeping up my throat, I inched forward, wondering if I should be the one to deliver the last blow. Axel and Jye had already claimed a life in their pursuit of clearing the Dungeon. This one should be on me. As I stepped in to perform the coup de grâce, boots on the ground approaching echoed down the hall.

It was Tam, in her human form. Of course she would turn up at the end of the battle.

"If I saw the kill, I should go for it, right?"

I sighed. Well, maybe I didn't need this on my conscience, after all.

"Sure," I said, retreating, strangely relieved. The Minotaur's expression as it'd pleaded to be killed was heavy in my mind.

Pulling a blade from her inventory, Tam took a similar stance before the Minotaur's downed form and brought her knife up. She held it there, towering over the barely alive creature, aiming. The ability activation I'd heard before must've been Tam returning to human form. That had to have meant she'd dealt with the mimic. But… if she had, regardless on if she'd killed them, we would've—

"Idiots," she said as her blade plunged into the neck of the Minotaur, intentionally missing the weak spot.

Oh, fuck.

~Dungeon Challenge Boss defeated. Dungeon Clear Available~

I finally understood the difference between the notifications and announcements. Announcements were for everyone relevant to hear. Notifications were specifically for yourself. Which meant everyone else in Just Friends had to have heard it.

That we'd been kill-stealed.

The body of the Minotaur evaporated, leaving a single shimmering object in its wake. Not-Tam bent to pick it up. A satisfied grin grew over her face. I didn't have a chance to note what it was before she popped it into her inventory.

"My gosh, that's a lot of credits," she said, the manner of speech so foreign out of her mouth that it gave me chills.

Axel immediately rushed forward, sword drawn, having figured out exactly how we'd been played. She laughed at him, plucked something from her pocket in the time he closed the distance, and pelted it at the floor. It exploded in a puff of smoke, clouding us in darkness. A smoke-fucking-bomb? How in the hell had she—

Jye shouted, "I can't see!"

"I have no mana or stamina to defend," Gigi informed us.

Other than pure melee, our team had expended all our skills.

Through our voices, we found each other in the smokiness, our backs pressed against each other. The only one unaccounted for was Axel since he'd been the closest to Not-Tam before our vision had been compromised. I heard the activation of an ability, the hiss slicing through the panicked tension between the three of us. Who knew what else the mimic had in both their metaphorical and literal pocket?

A hand reached into view, grabbing my arm, causing me to start.

"It's just me," said Axel.

I stared at him for a moment, taking in his expression, his appearance, and his stature. By all accounts it was him.

Another hand grabbed onto my left arm.

"That's not me."

There were two Axels standing to either side of me, shrouded in the smoke.

Behind me, Gigi and Jye tensed; poised, waiting for my reaction. They obviously didn't know one Axel from another. Just like them, anyone else might have been momentarily blindsided. Perhaps if they'd had the chance for any exchange, they might've been able to discern which was real, but given the close proximity of both Axels, any communication would elicit the attack to end either my or Axel's life.

But our opponent had picked the worst person to imitate the appearance of, especially for me. I'd known Axel better than myself once, and while I was still trying to get that back, this wasn't even a question, it wasn't even the inflection to imply confusion.

In both the Axels' free hands, they held swords pointed to the ground. The real Axel would be able to react in time. He always knew what I was thinking. And I knew which Axel was mine.

Barely a second had passed.

In a move that was faster than I thought I was capable of, I snaked my arms around the left imposter, grappling him, pinning his arms to his sides with my own, locking all movement. In that same moment, I heard the clatter of him being disarmed by Gigi and Jye, as Right-Axel brought his blade up to Left-Axel's neck, nicking into his skin.

"Who's the idiot now?" Right-Axel said.

"Still you guys," came a high voice from in front of me, the cloud of smoke beginning to dissipate.

The physical flesh under my hold disintegrated, my arms falling into empty space as Left-Axel disappeared entirely. Standing directly behind the real Axel was someone I didn't recognise at all. They were petite and small framed, blonde, and probably in their late teens. It was their expression that sent shivers up my spine; pure malice. I could tell that the blade in their hand would be used to kill without a second's thought or guilt.

I saw their weapon shift. No one else would have time to react. Especially since Axel's back was to the real mimic and not whatever shadow clone they'd summoned.

With the fake gone, now it was just Axel and I standing face-to-face, the gap of a person still between us. It was kind of apt that was the case. Somehow literally and metaphorically that made perfect sense.

Axel was hurt, had been hurt since his battle with the Minotaur. He was probably sitting just above quarter health. And who knew what abilities or traits this new attacker had. With my warning sounds being unreliable, it was possible they'd even used one to kill the Minotaur.

If Axel took a hit from them, he'd die.

I met my friend's gaze and smiled. His blue eyes widened, as if understanding what I was planning.

Somehow, he always knew.

As the mimic began their attack, hoping to get a strike on Axel's vulnerable back, I repeated almost the same action as I had with Left-Axel. I flung my arms round him, clamping, but this time I spun, taking Axel's place, and hoping I'd been right about something I'd long since theorised about.

The sword ate through my spine, with a force so violent and sudden that the pain that followed was not a surprise. In the corner of my mind, I saw my health plummet. It was my entire health bar. A part of me was satisfied that I'd been right. Axel would've died.

But instead, I guess I had.

XXIII

ONE POINT TO LEE

MY KILLER SNATCHED THEIR BLADE immediately from my back. If I were being honest, it hurt more going out. Imagine for a moment, if you will, the feeling of millions of claws tearing the fibres of your flesh apart. Then add accompanying nausea and a white-out of sight, and you're about halfway there. My back felt wet with eerily warm blood.

I was surprised I hadn't blacked out from the whole ordeal. I guess I was just lucky that way.

"Stupid," the teen said, jumping back, revilement curling their top lip. They blended into the fading smoke, their silhouette eventually disappearing, their abilities possibly on cooldown.

Me? Stupid? I wanted to argue, but they had a point.

I was dead.

Or I should've been.

Thankfully, the idea I'd been mulling over since the Gates appeared had borne fruit. For the longest time I'd been wondering about the wording of the singular ability I'd been granted by this fucked up apocalypse. While the rest of my team had been given at least two abilities (I was making assumptions about Tam here), I'd gotten one, and it would've been absolutely useless had I been alone. However, it used a word that stuck out to me and had been hovering in the back of my mind.

[Channel] Use a consenting party member's skills.

There were no "skills" in the system. There were, however, traits and abilities.

Like the frost melting into dew on a cool morning in spring, using [Channel] to borrow Gigi's [Stubborn] trait, my body felt as though it froze and then thawed. Just like xir trait description said, the blow that should've killed me had left my health remaining at 1 HP. What it didn't say was that, as my knees buckled, my vision beginning to fade, you'd *remain* at 1 HP until health regen kicked in (or someone intervened to either heal or kill you.)

I was two seconds away from being dead, and with my stats, I'd stay like that for a while. At least that answered my question about how [Stubborn] worked with bleeding out.

It was good that Axel was there to catch me before I hit the ground, his arms wrapping around the deadweight of my body. I'd like to see anyone judging me stay on their feet after literally being stabbed in the back. Axel's eyes were wide, panicked, and the fear in them almost made me laugh.

Damn, it was hysterical. Axel, being scared? In what world?

Gigi and Jye quickly stepped forward to defend Axel and I, their eyes darting about, alert for our assailant. Who knew what they would do?

Still, I was supremely disappointed by our party's performance. We'd allowed a single Gen Zer to steal the boss loot, almost kill me, escape, *and* put us on edge. It was a little pathetic considering it was a four (maybe five if Tam was about) vs. one (maybe two if we included whatever that shadow clone had been).

We fucking sucked.

But only because we never knew what was happening. In this new world, where abilities were literally apparently limitless, how could we ever know what people could do? We'd done our best based on what we knew. That the teenager's skills involved conjuring a clone of someone and not turning into them was something none of us could have ever imagined. Who would've?!

Well, these last couple of battles had made one thing clear. We needed someone in our party with the sort of skill that gleaned critical information from opponents. Otherwise, we'd just keep blindly throwing ourselves into situations we might not come out of. We'd been lucky so far, really lucky. And Axel's luck had almost run out this time.

But once again I was thinking about a future that wasn't guaranteed… First, we needed to deal with this goddamned teenager.

I felt surprisingly lucid for someone at 1 HP. Maybe [Stubborn] did something to my emotions. Last time I'd nearly died (wow, that's not something I'd ever thought I'd say), hitting 1 HP had me virtually slipping out of the realm of consciousness. But even bleeding as I was, there was some sort of mental block between the pain and my receptors. When I'd felt frozen and thawed, perhaps something had changed in my body. This was a trait, and not an ability, after all. Maybe they did different things?

That said, I literally couldn't move. The teen *had* pierced my spine. I really hadn't taken that into consideration. I guess I was paralysed. More than [Stubborn] intrinsically rewriting my DNA, full-body paralysis would explain my lack of pain more. It was just much, much, much more bleak of a thought.

I had no control over my limbs, and I wasn't even sure I could blink. I might as well be a useless lump weighing down my entire party. Though that was par for the course for me. I wanted to protect, to help everyone. And yet, again and again I relied on them to shield me instead. Fucking hell. Maybe one day I'd be enough to save them all.

Well, since I was still alive, I had the rest of my life to keep trying. However long that would be.

At least this time I'd saved Axel. I could take some solace and satisfaction in that. Axel who was staring down at me, cradling my limp form, tears beginning to dot along his thick lower lashes. He had that look in his eyes that unsettled me. The expression that spoke of an incoming breakdown, mixed with genuine horror. Oh, this wasn't funny anymore.

I hadn't wanted him to cry.

Speak! I yelled at myself. I tried to say something. Anything. But my mouth wouldn't open. I guess that I hadn't yet swallowed my own tongue was some sort of miracle.

One of his shaking hands reached to my neck, his finger and forefinger testing my pulse. I wanted to cover his hand with mine, to reassure him I was fine. That he didn't need to be scared. As I stared, my body refusing any instruction, the only pain I felt now was a hurt in my chest.

I'm not sure what I would've said. "Sorry?" "I'm sorry I would've died for you?"

Axel pulled me tighter to him, laying his ear against my chest. Huh. His hair smelled like citrus. He did like buying fancy shampoo.

When he pulled back his tears had disappeared, and he exchanged a few words with Gigi and Jye. They were speaking about what to do. Something about finding a defensive position while I healed up. (It was both good and bad that I couldn't tell them my health would take *a long time* to come back.) It was fortunate that when I went down, I had someone capable to take over the helm. However, it did worry me that while Axel sounded calm, there was a flatness in his tone that I'd never heard before.

Was this… better than him breaking down? I didn't know.

It was hard to judge Gigi and Jye's expression from where I was since Axel almost fully encompassed all I could see. There were worse views. But I hoped the two of them weren't as affected as Axel. Neither of them had known me as long, but I knew Jye was pretty in touch with their emotions. And they kind of liked me like a friend? They had to be a little bit worried.

Axel's arms shifted around me, beginning to pull me up, and a flush of embarrassment went through me, thinking back to how he'd snatched me up and carried me away from the battle not half an hour ago.

It smarted that technically back then he'd been right.

I had basically died.

He appeared to be struggling with the burden of my limp body. Just as he managed to heave me up, an ability hissed in my mind, followed by a scream bursting through the clearing smoke.

Everyone's gaze whipped over to the direction it'd come from. The voice the shriek belonged to was familiar since it was the same one that'd been peppering us with insults lately. And that also belonged to the person who'd paralysed me, which was the more serious of the two offences. Probably.

Since I couldn't move my head, my sight was limited to where Axel currently pointed me. Which meant, where I was resting in his hold, I could barely just see the edge of two figures in the distance, obscured by the remnants of smoke. It looked like someone standing over another on their knees.

"Please, don't, please, I beg you, I'll let you clear the—"

Just Friends eliminated Anna Dainsworth.

Just Friends earned 500 XP.

Just Friends awarded 332 credits.

"And Tam comes in with the clutch again. You're all welcome," came the cutthroat's words as she approached us, dragging the corpse of one Anna Dainsworth behind her.

With her free hand, she waved the vestiges of smoke out of her face as she walked. Once she stopped in front of us, she let the dead body go slack upon the floor. It fell with a wet thud. My stomach curled in disgust.

Twice now Tam had killed someone. But neither time had I been able to see her abilities. She really was a conniving little thing. And she'd not given an inch on who Mumma was, not since the cabin. It would've been impressive if it didn't actively thwart me. I wanted to take a deep breath to calm my frustration but couldn't, my body loose and unresponsive.

Tam raised her slit brow, definitely not out of concern, probably out of idle curiosity. She grinned at me.

"Don't say I ain't ever not true to my word, sunshine. I saw the chance to go for the kill and I took it, just like you told me."

This was met by silence. Because I couldn't reply.

"Lee's paralysed," Axel said, tone still flat.

She propped her hands on her hips and shook her head. "I do not envy you."

"Will he ever… be able to move again?" Jye asked.

The giant came into view, and I saw the genuine concern shining in their eyes. A little bit of guilt built inside me. I should spend more time hanging out with them. They were a nice person. Jye deserved more from me than just trying to think of a way to help them. The redhead deserved me to actually be their friend for real. Sigh. I really just needed to be better all around, huh.

"Once his health regenerates, he should be able to," Gigi answered.

"Dibs on Anna's loot, bee tee dubs."

The party, me included, stared in horror at Tam but said nothing in response. I guess to the spoils go the victor. Finding no disagreement, the cutthroat turned to the corpse and started pilfering Anna's pockets and bag. Gigi briefly explained how to access the dead person's inventory, which had never occurred to me, and she shooed xem away, saying she already knew all that. I wanted to get xem to elaborate, but again I couldn't say anything.

Helplessness bubbled up inside me.

Jye, Axel, and Gigi discussed what the next move was. They eventually settled on remaining where we were and letting me heal back up. We really should've been closing the distance between us and Wren, since we had no idea what was happening with her, or if she was even okay, but this was the next best thing, I suppose.

Who would've guessed half the end of the world would involve waiting around?

***

THE OTHERS TOOK THE TIME to take shifts of watch and rest, eating some of the food we'd recovered from Test Name. They'd set up one of the bedrolls and had lain me down on it on my stomach. It was discussed whether they should try to treat my wounds with the first aid kit we'd brought along from the gym, but they decided against it. Something about being worried about causing more harm than good. It was true none of them were qualified.

My health slowly ticked up and so did my mana and stamina. Slowly being the imperative word.

As feeling reawakened in my body, my nerves reconnecting, I realised just how much we'd taken Wren and [Healing Hand] for granted. Her ability must've had an anaesthetic side effect. It had never really hurt regenning health with the skill helping us.

The pain that shook me as my spine healed was indescribable.

Sweat coursed over my body, and my muscles twitched on their own, spasming, clenching outside of my control, as stabs of agony struck different parts of me repeatedly. It hurt more than the strike that should've killed me. More than anything else I'd felt my entire life.

I wanted to scream, the torment lacerating my body, but I could barely breathe.

When blackness finally took me, I thanked a god I didn't believe in.

***

Still, I didn't regret it.

***

I CAME TO, an unfamiliar warmth threaded between my fingers. It was a relief to be able to feel that. Every single one of my muscles ached, but it was barely a tickle compared to the excruciating misery I'd been in before I'd blacked out.

A sigh of released tension eased from me. I hadn't wanted to think about it before, but Jye's words about never being able to move again had spun on a loop in my head. It was nice to know Gigi had been right.

Focusing on what I was holding, I realised it was someone's hand.

I frowned, and with a groan of exertion, I turned to follow the arm to the body it belonged to, sitting up even though each part of me felt heavily bruised. Axel was resting by my side, cross legged, bags dark under his eyes. When he saw me move, he perked up, eyes sparking. With that, I couldn't say. At least it wasn't that sadness I couldn't handle.

"Fuck, man," Axel said under his breath.

That was probably his way of saying thank you.

There was something else he wanted to express, though. I could tell he was holding back. It was in the crinkled edges of his flattened lips. He was probably angry. Anna hadn't been wrong. What I'd done was stupid. If my theory about "skills" had been incorrect, I wouldn't be here to be pinned down by Axel's heavy gaze.

I opted to remain silent and wait for the incoming assault.

"I love you, you stupid shithead."

Yeah, that sounded—

Wait.

What.

Axel inhaled, squared his shoulders, and said, "I've had a crush on you since we were kids, and I've wanted to tell you every day since. Lee, I'll love you every life I live, and no matter what I do, I can't stop. It's like a fucking sickness."

My brain had blue screened.

I had no response.

No words.

Axel's jaw clenched. "And it sucks that I know you don't feel the same way. That you'll never love me back, can't love me back, whatever. But that doesn't stop these shitty feelings I have for you. So, just don't ever fucking do that again. If you ever try to die for me, I'll kill you."

It was like being hit with a ghost freight train. His words thundered through my body, leaving me stricken with a bizarre floatiness. My hand reached out on its own volition, to steady myself, because the world felt loosely tethered to reality. I only dully realised that I'd taken hold of one of his arms, using it to ground myself.

All his words were definitely English. But that didn't stop me from having a hard time making cohesive sense of them. He looked scared; I could feel him trembling. After all we'd been through, this was only the second time I'd seen fear on his face. His panic at my sacrifice suddenly made more sense.

"What?" is all I managed to say.

Axel lifted my hand from his arm and cradled it in between his, now no longer able to meet my gaze.

His touch was soft.

"Come on. Don't make me say it again. Makes me sound like a goddamn simp."

Though I was still reeling, unable to believe he felt this way, his words reverberated in my head, echoing around, and replaying over and over. *You can't love me back.* The way his voice had broken during that sentence. Why had he said that? Did he think being ace meant…

Laughter erupted from me uncontrollably, but the shock on his face shut me up in an instant.

Clearing my throat, I shook my hand loose from his and then, ignoring the pain, leant forward and pulled him into a comforting hug. "And you had the audacity to call me stupid."

He tried to break away, but my face felt hot, and I locked my arms around him. I decided he wasn't allowed to see my expression. Mostly because I wasn't even sure what I looked like at that moment. Maybe we shared the same face.

Axel for sure had enough strength to free himself if he wanted.

I explained, "I'm ace, not aro, man."

His body went stiff against me, and it was his turn to say: "What?"

"Twenty-eight years we've known each other, and not one time did you ever bother googling it or asking me." I shook my head in mock disappointment. "I just don't get sexually attracted to people. I can, however, fall in love."

"But you've never dated anyone!" he sputtered loudly into my ear, almost deafening me.

I leaned back to show him my blank face. "Gee, I wonder whose fault that is."

He blanched. It had been family members' and family friends' running joke that the reason we were both terminally single was because everyone thought we were a couple.

Axel didn't do long-term relationships. He just swept through men. And I was not open with others to discussion on the topic. So, obviously, I'd let the joke run its course because it'd kept my parents off my back. But I'd thought Axel had loathed it because the idea of dating me was abhorrent to him. However… if what he was saying was true, and he'd liked me since we were kids, I guess maybe he'd actually hated those jokes because they made him angry it wasn't real?

My brain could only handle so many revelations.

"Actually, though, it's tough out there finding someone who doesn't expect an, uh, intimate relationship." I cleared my throat. "And, fuck you, I have dated people for your information." There was one date that came to mind that had completely checked me out over a romantic relationship. "But they all kind of fizzled out."

"Then all this time that I've been pining—" He shut his mouth, his cheeks now beet red. "—I mean, all this time we could've…?"

The words hung in the air.

"I mean, you've been a bit of a dick to me since Chrissie died. So no."

Axel laughed, and again it was bitter. I never understood him. Not before, not now. Probably never would in the future either. But now I think I was getting closer. I knew what he was asking. What I'd never thought he'd ask.

In his downcast eyes, I knew he was asking: *Could we be anything?*

Though part of me was still hesitant to accept what he'd said, I replied to his unspoken question. "Well, since the Gates, you've been… different." I didn't want to cause him to breakdown, so I tried to put it into words without triggering him, dancing around the subject by talking about it. "Like, you're you, but also more you. The best parts of you that were my best friend became who you are again, but also… in a worryingly unhinged way."

What was *I* saying now? I think Axel's confession had turned my brain into soup.

But I owed him something of a response, even if whatever had traumatised him was what had caused him to share this. After all, he'd poured his soul out. And it was the soul I'd known when we were kids. The one I'd adored. The one I'd—

Swallowing back my own emotions, I took a breath. "This Axel, the current Axel, you, the one I'd put my life on the line for, *might* be someone I could, you know, maybe…"

"Love?" he offered, so tentatively, so hopefully that I couldn't even mock him like I wanted to. It would've been like kicking a kitten.

"That's just maybe." I didn't want to string him along either. Considering I was still struggling to come to terms with his feelings for me, I wasn't sure how I felt.

It was like being given a pair of glasses and realising you were shortsighted all along, and now everything you didn't know was blurry was in crisp 8K resolution. It was hard to comprehend. My brain was still buffering.

Though, at gunpoint, I would never admit to it, but Axel had been my first crush. One of those puppy crushes you get when you're still a kid. I had been eleven when I realised. We'd still lived in a time where calling people gay was an insult, so I'd repressed it, only thinking about it in moments where it was only Axel and me. It's weird thinking about it now, but spending time with him had been some of the best parts of my childhood.

But then Chrissie had passed, and he'd cast me aside.

Not only had that thoroughly shattered any illusion of affection I had toward him, I think it also fundamentally impacted my self-confidence. If my best friend couldn't love me, who could? It was the domino that teetered my social skills off the edge. That shut me down permanently.

Not that I blamed Axel. Death is never easy. We'd both been affected, just in different ways. Axel chose to leave it behind. And I guess I chose to never leave it.

The memories edged away as his confession replayed in my mind, and a large grin grew across my face. Even if this was Axel's panicked, knee-jerk reaction to me nearly dying, I'd still milk it for what it was worth.

"To clarify, I can't give you answer anytime soon, all right? Because, I'll have you know, it's a lot of pressure knowing that you love me so much that, what did you say, what was it? How did you phrase it… That you'll love me in every life?"

Axel let out a pained groan. "God, that was so cringe."

The anguish on his face truly fulfilled some deep twisted desire in my heart. I couldn't stop myself from ribbing him further. "Blinded by your love for me, obviously. Say, would you agree with Eminem that you love me so much you can barely breathe when you're with me?"

"Sometimes."

My response died on my lips, and the tips of my ears burned. He sounded so genuine that my disbelief was starting to feel like a misreaction. In that same moment, I realised we'd been wrapped in each other's arms for the whole conversation. Suddenly feeling very claustrophobic, I released my hold and tried to lean away.

Axel didn't budge. He could basically lock me in place, given I was still feeling weak as shit.

"I'm not afraid to Ground Smash us both," I said.

He didn't reply, and instead bent his neck to rest his forehead on my shoulder. It wasn't unpleasant being held like this, though I felt overly warm where we were in contact and growing warmer still. I was sure Axel would hear my heart beating loudly in my chest, and that was embarrassing, so maybe I could wiggle out—

"I just… Can I have this for a second?

There was something in his voice that made me stop trying to escape. It was the same emotion I'd heard when he'd first asked to call me Lee. Grief. I guess he could be mourning the world we knew, or even the relationship we might've once had. But, somehow, I knew it wasn't that. It was something else.

Axel was grieving something, someone.

I think all along that brokenness was this same grief. For who? I couldn't say. But it mattered to him. It mattered quite a lot. So, I could stay like this for him. I owed it to him. I could be here for him. The same way I guess he'd always been there for me. Albeit, maybe he had ulterior motives. And also, despite its warmth, this hug wasn't that bad.

Lightly, I leaned my head down and rested my chin on his hair. It was softer than I thought it would be.

I'm not sure how long we stayed like that.

Definitely longer than his requested second.

DUNGEON
HUNTER

XXIV

THE THREAD

WE DIDN'T SAY ANYTHING about it when Jye noticed us, and we broke apart, with cheeks perhaps a little redder, but that was just the blood flow regulating to my body, obviously. The rest of the time was uneventful as my mana came back up enough to start using [Healing Hand] to boost the speed at which my health regenerated. Thankfully, Tam hadn't been paying attention, too distracted by cataloguing everything she'd looted from Anna's body. I didn't want to have to suffer whatever she'd make of what happened.

I wasn't even sure what I made of it all, so I definitely didn't need the cutthroat's commentary and opinion on my previous conversation with Axel and his confession, and that apparently, he'd liked me when I'd liked him, but he'd never stopped. Which was insane. If it was true, how had I never noticed? It was a little tragic. I almost felt sorry for him. Almost.

To be honest, I still wasn't sure how I felt.

Axel liking me couldn't be real.

I mean, if I examined my own emotions, I couldn't imagine a life without Axel. He'd always been there, somewhere. Without him, I don't think I'd have much left. So, yes, I'd been ready to die in his place only hours ago, but it was a different emotion that inspired the action compared to the crush I'd had on him when I was just a kid. Compared to what he said he felt toward me.

Since Chrissie's passing, I'd struggled with understanding and forging attachments to people, both romantic and platonic. I'd known I'd liked Axel when I was a kid because each morning I'd woken up excited to see him. Once he'd deserted me and my crush had evaporated into thin air, growing up being asexual made differentiating my feelings toward others even more difficult.

All I knew was I wanted Axel to be safe. And reflecting on his expression as he'd cried over my nearly dead self, maybe even deeper than that, I think I never wanted him to look like that again. I wanted to take away that sadness that came over him, even if I was the one who caused it.

Maybe that was that how Axel felt about me too.

Having someone admit their love for me was not something I'd ever expected. Hell, it wasn't even on my bucket list. The very concept of it was like one of the stupid icebreakers when starting a new job, and they ask you what you'd do if you won a million dollars. It was a hypothetical "Ah, wouldn't that be nice?" kind of thing that I only ever thought about when I couldn't sleep, and the clock was drawing nearer and nearer to my morning alarm.

I'd never really thought about the kind of future I genuinely wanted. So much of my life was that autopilot "do this and then this" that what I desired never really came into view, always existing either in my periphery or not even allocated any space in my mind. Last time I'd nearly died (again, such a fucking wild sentence to think), I'd realised I'd wanted to protect the people in my party. That it was something I sincerely felt was a purpose to my life. It'd given me motivation to continue existing.

My near-death experience hadn't clarified anything this time. If anything, I'd come out of it more confused. At the very least, I just knew that Axel had needed my support for that moment. And maybe I'd needed to be genuinely relied upon too. For that short time, we were able to take strength in each other. Whether or not I reciprocated his feelings, what had happened had been more like a pro quid pro thing than anything… *more*.

That wasn't to say I completely doubted Axel's words.

He definitely thought he was in love with me. But he wasn't fully in his right mind either.

The weirdest thing was how, other than the words being spoken, nothing had changed between us.

"I'm gonna pretend I didn't see nothing," Jye said, apparently to no one, as they helped me pack up the bedroll before we all set off to finally retrieve Wren.

About time. I was still a little worried about what might be lurking within the walls of this inner labyrinth, so I requested that we all retain the same no-shouting rule we'd instituted when Anna had been running around unchecked. Thus, we'd all been walking without conversation, though "in silence" would've been a stretch.

At my insistence, Tam had deposited Anna's corpse into her inventory, muttering under her breath the entire time very unsavoury things. We'd since begun the walk to the room Wren was locked in with Tam grumbling all the while.

"See what?" I responded to Jye.

The giant's red brows furrowed in confusion. "How you and Axel were, like, all over—" Their eyes widened, and then they grinned. They brought a finger to the side of their nose to tap it a few times. "Oh, I see what you're doing. Got it. See what?"

"Why would you pretend not to see Lee and Axel embracing?" Gigi asked from my left. Fuck, Gigi must've seen us too. Xe didn't talk much unless addressed and I must've completely ignored xir presence. Thinking back on it, yeah, xe had been right next to Jye at the time.

Like an owl, Tam's head swivelled almost 180 degrees to lock wide eyes on me.

"They were what now?"

"Hugging," Axel supplied nonchalantly. I opened my mouth to defend us from whatever Tam's mind was cooking up, but he continued, "The dude almost died. Can't a man hug his friend without suffering accusations?" His blue eyes narrowed. "Or do you not want to break the cycle of toxic masculinity?"

Tam scoffed and turned away, clearly not keen to get baited into an argument. I had no doubt she'd had this particular conversation more than once in her life. Curious, I let my gaze slip from Tam's back to Axel, who was walking on the other side of Jye.

The blond had handled the situation pretty well, all things considered. Though I guess all that socialising he'd done had to have granted him some catalogue of skills to draw upon when called.

I don't know why he'd decided to keep the lid on our… conversation. He wasn't exactly the private kind of person. Did he still not fully trust the others? With his words, he'd pretty much gaslit Jye, Gigi, and Tam into thinking the moment of comfort he'd sought, the emotions he'd confessed, had been nothing but his platonic concern for me. I struggled to read his expression.

He looked tired, the bags under his eyes more pronounced than ever. Had he… had he been watching over me the entire time I'd been out?

Huh.

As if sensing my gaze, Axel's eyes met mine. He waggled his eyebrows at me, grinning widely.

"Admit it, you're impressed."

I snorted. "You wish."

"Yeah, nah. There's only one thing I wish for and, that isn't it."

"What is it then? Bottomless beer bar? A better anime adaptation of *Berserk*? A world where we actually got to watch *The Bastard Son and the Devil Himself*?" I asked, smiling. There were more things I could think of on Axel's wish list but figured I could probably drone on all day if I didn't stop there. "What is it you wish for?"

Instead of responding, he tilted his head, still maintaining eye contact with me.

Oh.

But it just didn't make any sense.

I'd never done anything worthy of these feelings.

Jye made a face, their gaze flicking back and forth between me and Axel. They said, "I'm getting the vibe that I'm cockblocking something here. I can swap places, if you want, guys."

"No, no, no, that's okay," I began, not allowing Axel to get a reply in edgewise, my own words pelting out of my mouth like machine-gun fire. "Besides, we're nearly there, aren't we, Tam?"

"Yep," she said, popping the "P." "Just around this turn and we'll be at one of the walls."

Even though I'd had time to reflect on Axel's confession, it hadn't really fully sunk in.

We turned down the last left corridor and found ourselves at a dead-end.

"Lamb chop, you still in there?" Tam asked, raising her voice.

Wren's tone was panicked. "Tam! Is everyone okay? I got the notification that Lee was at critical health!"

The brunette cast a cursory glance over Gigi, Axel, and I, all sporting healing injuries and then said, "Yeah, everyone's entirely spick and span."

"We're fine," I said as reassurance.

"I didn't even get a scratch on me!" Jye remarked.

"I'm so happy to hear your voices."

Guilt roiled inside me, but I quickly repressed it. We couldn't have done anything before. Swallowing back the emotion, I pushed positivity into my tone when I asked, "You ready for your taste of freedom?"

The young girl was silent for a moment. "I don't know about that. When I got the notification that the challenge was finished and the

Dungeon was available for clearing, the lights came on in here. It revealed a… kind of lock on the ground I didn't see before. I think… I think this is the exit room."

So, if we somehow figured out a way to destroy the wall without hurting Wren, there was the risk of damaging the lock that cleared the Dungeon. Man, fuck whoever designed this. All the traps and puzzles were so stupid. And why had Wren been teleported *into* the final room? Pinching at the bridge of my nose, I asked, "Can you describe what you're looking at?"

"There's a divot under an old carving. I think something is supposed to be put into it."

She went on to explain that the carving looked like a woman sitting behind a contraption. When prompted to further describe the device, Wren was unable to name it. She was a ten-year-old, after all. She tried to give us the general shape, but it was like playing blind charades.

A woman behind a contraption. Connected to the labyrinth. The final room after the Minotaur was defeated. While I was thinking, Jye, Axel, Gigi, and Tam were offering suggestions of what the device could be. They went through dozens of things, from a log splitter to an old camera. None of them really made sense. Half of what Gigi said was censored.

Contraption. Minotaur. Labyrinth.

Of course!

"Wren. Have you seen *Sleeping Beauty*?"

"Yeah, I love Disney movies."

"The contraption. Does it look like the thing the princess pricks her finger on?"

"Kind of… It looks different, but if I squint, all the right shapes are there."

The others looked to me.

"It's a spindle. The carving is a woman spinning thread."

Gigi frowned. "How does this help us?"

Sighing, I said, "I don't know."

"Nice work," Axel added, sarcastically. For someone who said they loved me, he was awfully fucking mean to me sometimes.

"You thinking Ariadne's string?"

I nodded at Jye, surprised they knew the name.

"Don't look so shocked, man. Mythology's cool. And with the whole Minotaur thing, it makes sense."

"String, you say."

Tam had been quiet the entire time, so this comment was unusual from her. Perhaps feeling the weight of the party's gaze, she said, "Don't kill a cat for being curious."

"They literally made a saying about that," Axel replied, crossing his arms over his chest.

I added, "You're never curious about anything except when it involves mocking us."

"Hey now, sunshine, that ain't true. I'm plenty curious, I just don't speak, is all."

Even with the four of us staring her down, Tam didn't seem like she'd break.

"What's curious about it?" Wren asked, her voice muffled by the wall between us.

Tam's shoulders slumped, and she let out a defeated sigh.

With an annoyed expression, she lifted a hand and plucked an item from thin air. She'd retrieved something from her inventory. It hovered above her palm for a moment before it settled onto her skin. The item was barely larger than a fist.

"Anna had this on her. Didn't think it would help. Still don't think that."

In Tam's hand, she held a skein of golden thread. No, rather it wasn't golden but *gold* thread. The sheen of it was unmistakably metallic, and it sat heavy in her hand. The party stared in silence for a moment. Jye whistled. I recognised the glint. It was the loot that dropped when the Minotaur had been slain.

"You were gonna share this with us when?" I asked.

"Never, if I had my way, babes."

Rolling my eyes, I held out my hand. "Give it here."

"Don't wanna."

Stepping in quicker than sight, Axel closed the distance and snatched it from her before depositing it into my hold. All things said and done, Tam probably could've put up more of a fight. She'd let Axel take it. Her concern for Wren was obviously winning out, but not enough to stop whatever farcical show she was putting on.

"You're welcome," Axel said, his pinkie lightly brushing against my hand as he released the thread, his skin warm. I glanced up, and I realised I couldn't tell if the touch had been intentional or not. There was a very cocky expression on his face, in the bend of his brow. For once I found myself not hating it. In fact, as I tried to focus on the matter at hand, I recognised instead that it had just been comforting.

No time to unpack that.

I examined the skein, bringing it closer to my face, taking in the unusual material. It was cool to the touch and heavier than it looked, surprisingly hefty for such a relatively small item.

As a hobby, my mother bought secondhand jewellery and then sold them again. She'd needed a model for the marketing photos, and so I'd handled my fair share of gold and silver.

Testing the pliability of the skein, I came to the realisation that the thread was likely entirely gold. Not like it'd be valuable anymore when we got back to the real world.

"I never got into most mythology. Too much incest for my taste," Tam said. "What's the thread got to do with anything?"

"The hero, Theseus, uses it to trace his steps back to the start of the labyrinth," Jye answered. "Though he does dump Ariadne later on an island. Dick move, really."

"Thissy-who?"

Gigi's brows were furrowed. "I thought these names would be moderated."

"Shut your mouth, you alien," Tam hissed.

Annoyed, I growled, "What are you two talking about?"

"[REDACTED]," Gigi said, then frowned. "I see. It is censored when I speak about them."

Jye's brow furrowed but they didn't say anything, probably stifling their reaction to the glitched noise.

"That's right, and keep it that way. Mumma says we can't tell them anyway."

I sighed, accepting that I should've known this conversation wouldn't go anywhere.

"This ball of yarn isn't gonna be a lick of help, besides. Obviously, we're supposed to use it *inside* the end room."

"It could be magic!" Wren's excited voice said from the other side of the wall.

There were weirder things that had happened. The kid could be right. Maybe the gold thread did hold some sort of magical power. But what could it possibly do to get us to the final room? And how did I make it *do* something?

Looking back down at the skein, experimentally, I said, "Activate."

Nothing happened.

Axel smirked, and I wanted to smack him.

"If you're so smart, you try getting it to do something!" I shouted, embarrassment heating the tips of my ears.

Frustrated, I lobbed the skein at him. He ducked under it, the thread unravelling as it sailed through the air. It plunked to the ground, continuing to roll toward the dead-end wall.

"You were meant to catch that," I said, trying to repress the irritation.

"And you were meant to reject me. The future is full of surprises, isn't it?"

I blinked, my anger deflated by his unprovoked admission. Axel had thought that… I'd just shut him down? That I'd immediately reject him?

"Why would you—"

"Not to interrupt your little loving tiff," Tam began and I opened my mouth to disagree and realised I couldn't find the words to defend myself since technically she was right. She continued, "but…" She gestured forward to where the skein had stopped rolling.

The four of us who'd not been paying attention boggled.

A trail of thread had released, leaving a line of gold string along the ground to the dead-end wall… and partially through it. The skein had rolled halfway into the stone wall. Without questioning it, I stepped forward and kicked the item further. It disappeared completely, leaving only the single thread behind.

On the other side of the wall, Wren let out a little yelp of surprise.

"How did you…?" she began and then didn't say anything else. We watched the thread on the floor shift as Wren apparently picked the skein up.

"Should I put it in the divot?" she asked.

I glanced at the party and silently got their agreement.

"Do it, Wren."

Taking a deep breath, our eyes glued to the thread, we watched as it minutely shook with Wren's hidden movements.

"I'm placing it."

The thread stilled.

XXV

ACTUAL ANSWERS

~DUNGEON 16 CLEARED for the first time by Just Friends~

Fuck.

We'd done it. Granted, we'd killed four people to do it. Five people, if you counted the Minotaur.

I was still debating that. I'd assumed the beast had been generated by the Dungeon. Though… Xanthe was a lizard person who'd clearly had sentience and intelligence, and all the other creatures in Twilight had also been a type of being.

What if the Minotaur was just another race that hadn't accomplished the same thing Xanthe's people hadn't? When it had spoken, it had said it couldn't surrender. So, if the Minotaur had been real, and not an NPC, we had killed what was essentially a slave, unable to escape the invisible constraints placed upon them, put up to the firing squad. If the "first time" in the Dungeon announcement meant what it said, would the Minotaur be destined to die again and again and never be able to break free?

If that was the case, I wasn't even sure about how I'd feel. It was a far crueller fate than anything else I could really imagine.

I wanted to feel elation that we'd cleared the Dungeon, but I couldn't summon the emotion. Just a weird sense of resignation.

We'd been dealt such random shit since we'd entered the Gate that when the world fell away into infinite empty white after the clear announcement, it was actually kind of anticlimactic. Part of me had been expecting another series of challenges or some impossible to understand puzzle to follow.

Ending it here was… bad writing. No two ways about it.

This simply reinforced my opinion that this entire thing sucked, not just as a Dungeon, but as entertainment. Really now. What was engaging about watching a handful of people standing around hemming and hawing over what to do with a ball of yarn? Add to that, making the labyrinth so large that even had there been other players in the Dungeon, which was likely considering the time that had passed, that we'd run into only four meant that it was highly probable most of the other people who'd entered would end up dying of malnutrition. That was akin to watching grass grow, if by grow you meant "die from not being watered."

It paled in comparison to the CBD Dungeon Wren had described. An arctic winter biome and monsters in snow ambushing you when you least expected it? Now that was entertainment. Well, at least when it was happening to someone else and they weren't real people. On a TV show or in a book, I'd have eaten that right up. But this Dungeon was…

What wasted potential. Everything really just felt like whoever had developed this had read the CliffsNotes about Theseus and dragged and dropped random shit onto their canvas.

Wren appeared before me as the wall popped out of existence like the snap of the fingers. A piece of weight fell from my shoulders upon seeing her. I hoped the time alone in the room hadn't been too hard on her.

She looked stunned, her hazel eyes wide in awe, though I noted those same eyes were a little reddened. Had she been crying? My heart hurt. I told myself we'd make finding her family a top priority.

As she gaped at our white void surroundings, I was glad she was still capable of childlike wonder. We hadn't robbed her of that with all the awful things she'd been complicit in as a member of our party. Speaking of our crimes, I still didn't know exactly what we'd do with the corpses we'd stored in our inventories. Bury them somewhere in Brisbane? Dump them in front of a funeral home and hope for the best? We'd definitely not be tossing them into the Brisbane River as per Jye's suggestion.

Nexus available.

Huh. That was completely new. I'd long since stopped being surprised by sudden reveals like this. However, that it was a notification, not an announcement, piqued my interest. It had to be for our eyes only. For those who had cleared Dungeons. I didn't want to jump the gun but a Nexus sounded very much like a fast travel hub. Should I be concerned that I didn't think waypoints seemed beyond the pale these days?

Everyone in the party had been transported along with me to the white space. Or maybe they simply remained where they'd been previously standing as the world changed. I really couldn't tell. One moment we'd been facing a stonewall dead-end and the next nothing but white emptiness. Here we cast no shadows, everyone instead impossibly lit evenly from each and every direction. It was difficult to tell if we were standing on floor or floating as whatever horizon line should've existed simply didn't. From the weight of my feet, I figured we were likely applying pressure to them, so the former was probably the truth.

There was barely a moment to take it all in when an unfamiliar voice, timid and shaking, spoke from behind us.

"Uh, don't hold back… What did you think?"

Why the hell did they have a British accent?

On edge, the six of us span on our heels to face them, attempting to summon any weapon we could. Rather than succeeding in arming ourselves, the buzz of rejection sounded. Okay. Very cool. So, we were defenceless in this new zone. It was just one thing after another, wasn't it? No rest for the… Were we wicked? There wasn't enough mental space to consider that train of thought as I focused on the person standing before us.

They were shorter than average with a brown bushy beard and, contrarily, sparse hair upon their head. Other than their general comportment of standing hunched over, as if ready to fold into themselves at the slightest provocation, they were the exact image someone might conjure when you were asked to imagine what "uncle" meant. They fiddled with the hem of their polo shirt, eyes nervously darting everywhere but to us.

What the fuck.

"What the fuck?" I said, more annoyed than alarmed, though I tried to activate [Channel] to borrow [Thick Hide] anyway as a precaution. Hearing the hiss of an ability shortly follow my own, it sounded like Axel had done the same. At the very least, we could use skills here. That was some solace. It gave me a modicum of relief, the second defensive skin pooling over me.

"My Dungeon… Please… You can be brutally honest. I'm ready to hear it." They paused, their brow crinkling. Their face fell as they threw up their hands. "It was awful, wasn't it? I knew it, oh my heavens… I'm a sham. I'll never [REDACTED]."

I blinked. There was a lot to process.

"Your Dungeon?"

Their eyes, an unnatural shade of gold, flashed open and their cheeks reddened.

"My deepest apologies! I didn't introduce myself. Heavens, I'm such an idiot. I'm, uh, well, maybe you've heard of me? I'm Nabu." Their head tilted at our lack of response, then they let out a defeated sigh. "God of wisdom, schooling, and the arts… No? Not ringing any bells? I knew this would happen, I knew it…"

I looked him up and down, taking in the khaki shorts, and thongs that revealed hairy toes.

"You? A god?"

"Well, uh, no offence intended, but as far as you humans are concerned, yes, that's right. But! That doesn't mean I'm not open to criticism. Er… Constructive criticism, that is. As the first to clear my Dungeon, I'd dearly… love to hear your feedback." As he spoke, it sounded very much like he was dreading any and all critique, his hands wringing with anxiety, his voice trembling.

So… this was who we could blame for the entire thing?

He stood there, nervously twiddling his thumbs, a shaky, uncertain smile all but hidden by his impressive beard.

What were we meant to say?

What were we meant to do?

I'd been fantasising about confronting this person since we'd entered, but now we'd come face to face, he looked and acted like an amateur writer after submitting their first manuscript. I was torn between sheer outrage and wanting to let him down gently. Like I wanted to pummel him to the floor and also deliver a compliment critique sandwich as he lay there recovering.

It was a baffling combination of emotions.

"An honest review is all I ask," Nabu said, his voice cracking.

This man, this "god," had put us in life-and-death situations, and I knew I should be angry, but when I reached for the feeling deep down in my gut, I came up empty. More than anything else, I felt that this Deity or whatever was just… pathetic. Not worth my anger. Saving a dying worm would inspire more emotion in me. It didn't stop me from imagining him exploding into pieces. There was some catharsis to be had from that.

As if everyone felt similarly, the rest of the party started answering his plea.

"Zero out of ten. Don't quit your day job," Axel said, his voice flat.

"I got a few notes for improvements, but it wasn't bad. It just wasn't good," Jye added as they folded their arms across their chest.

"Respectfully, I could pull something better out of a unicorn's ass," Tam remarked with a scowl.

"It seemed a little silly," came Wren's considerate response. "Though it did get very scary."

"I do not think the other Deities would've enjoyed it." Gigi accompanied this statement with a shake of xir head.

My own head nearly exploded from the overstimulation all this information was providing. We'd been in a god's Dungeon and there'd been Deities watching us and Gigi had known and Tam had to have known too. Was that who the sponsors were as well? Other Deities? What did Deities even mean in this context? I'd never heard of Nabu, but my familiarity with mythology only extended to the more common Greek, Roman, and Egyptian pantheons.

Or was he another world's god?

I cast my mind back to Tam's first description of the Dungeon from Mumma (Who I now realised had to be a goddess? What the fuck). "[REDACTED] is a wily one."

Wily in what way? The way he was snivelling? He had all the gravitas of a senior chihuahua.

In fact, Nabu looked close to tears, his bottom lip quivering.

"R-Really? It was that awful?"

Gripping onto my flying thoughts, I took a deep breath.

"Before I give you my honest opinion, I've got to ask," I began, "why?"

He cocked his head to the side; the incoming sobbing on hold. He blinked back the tears. "Why what?"

"Why everything?"

"Oh, dear heavens, yes, I suppose half the fun is you not knowing. But as I'm, uh, duty bound to sponsor one of you, I suppose it'd be in my best interest to inform you." His golden gaze skittishly roamed over our party as he spoke. Uncharacteristically, there was something of dismissal when he got to Gigi, and his eyes didn't linger over Tam for long at all. Was that fear? "Of course, you two are spoken for, but I'll annul everyone's limitations insofar as I can."

What? Gigi was spoken for? Xe had a sponsor too? I hadn't seen it on xir player data. Maybe xe'd chosen not to show it? Had that too been moderated, just more efficiently? And what did Nabu mean, "annul everyone's limitations"? God, fuck everything.

With a wave of his hand, the whiteness shifted immediately into a generic lecture hall. Nabu gestured to the auditorium desks as he took to the teacher's podium at the front.

Whatever.

I took a seat at the closest chair and the others followed suit, filing into one row.

Nabu cleared his throat, and began explaining, running his hands over his beard as he spoke. It should've been distracting, but I don't think anything would've torn our focus from the words that began coming out of his mouth. Especially now that it seemed whatever censorship had been put in place had been lifted, at least to a certain extent. Ah. "Annul limitations."

"Hmm, uh, well, I've never done this before… But to put it plainly… Humanity has been graced with the honour of entertaining us Deities. Of course, again no offence, as you all were, you would hardly be anything worth watching, as flimsy as you were. So, we granted you the players, or rather the agents or actors in this, ahem, grand performance, enhanced skills and abilities. You're expected to put on a show."

I'd been right.

Nabu had beaten me to sharing this with the others, though maybe it was for the better. However, being validated like this was like… congealing concrete in my guts.

I felt sick. I didn't know it until now, but I hadn't wanted to be right. I didn't want how messed up my theory had been to truly be our reality. Even as event after event had provided more than enough evidence to prove me correct, I still wanted to be wrong.

People dying, killing each other, for the sake of entertaining others? The concept was so inhumane, so alien, that the only thing that could've ever made sense was that the ones putting humanity through this were Deities. Only someone so far removed from mortality could think taking someone's life, their suffering, was fun to watch.

"But this is only the beginning," Gigi said, interrupting Nabu. "What comes next is…" Xe grimaced, the expression entirely unfamiliar on xir face.

Jye nodded. "Yeah, like Gigi said, xir whole planet was wiped out, and all xe had left was xir coat." They pounded their chest again with a closed fist and jutted their chin in Gigi's direction. Grimly, Gigi nodded back, appreciative of the support.

I swivelled my head to stare at the redheaded giant who had sat to my left.

"What?" I said. "When the hell did Gigi say any of that?"

Jye's thick brows furrowed. "Like, before xe joined the party. You gotta clean out your ears, dude. It was xir answer when I asked if I could have xir coat."

I replayed the interaction in my mind, and then I reflected on every exchange Gigi and Jye had had where Gigi's words had been moderated. The giant had never seemed confused. All along, I'd believed Jye had just gotten used to the glitch noise since they hadn't reacted. But… I guess whatever was wrong with Jye's system meant Gigi had never been censored. Come to think of it, not once had Jye mentioned a word about any redactions. All along… we could've gotten answers.

I wanted to scream.

I wanted to strangle Jye.

Instead, I just sighed.

"Okay, so how does it get worse then? My imagination's a little shot right now, so just give it to me straight."

"Well, the Dungeons are what you may know as a kind of matinee. A warm-up."

"Is it kind of like a tutorial?" Wren supplied as she readjusted herself in her seat to lean on her knees. Before, she'd been half-sunk under the room-length desk.

With a click on his fingers, Nabu nodded. "Yes. Similar to a tutorial."

"Then when do we get to the real game?" I asked, dreading the answer.

"Ah, well, yes, um, you may have noticed your levels have no real impact on your skills." The others blinked blankly and so I waved him on. "They're actually more for us, really. To keep track of how everyone's... fairing. Once the majority of parties reach an average level of 10, they will take centre stage." He flourished shaking hands, spreading them wide.

I swallowed back my growing fear. "And what about the rest? The parties that don't hit that average?"

"Culled, of course. So we only have the cream of the crop in the spotlight."

The party said nothing.

If it was the majority of parties, that was over 50 percent of humanity. So... four billion people would be executed eventually, if they weren't already dead. I didn't even question it. After all, you just had to look at what the Deities had done so far. They'd messed around with our minds with the Dungeon compulsion, they'd janked up the very physics and matter of our world with the systems they'd granted us, they were capable of forming pocket dimensions. Killing so many humans might be as easy as Nabu creating this lecture hall. A singular gesture.

My mouth went dry, my mind reeling.

Was there no way of stopping this? The scale of death and loss would be unimaginable. But it seemed unavoidable. Like Nabu had been through this exact same thing again and again. That this doom was inevitable.

My head span. Underneath the detached disgust and horror for the rest of humanity, there was something closer. It was personal bias, I knew. I prayed my parents would be okay. And beyond that, I recognised that they didn't have more significance than the rest of the human race, but still… they mattered to me. There were such a small handful of people who did.

I forced myself not to glance at Jye, the implications of Nabu's words reverberating about in my skull endlessly.

Jye couldn't level up. It meant everyone else in our party had to reach even higher levels faster than everyone else in the world if we wanted to survive the culling. Of course, the other option was something I would never consider.

But was that even possible? Based on the experience bar, each level required double the previous one. If I was doing the maths right, which had never been my strong point, to just reach LVL 10, we'd need over 120,000 XP. And then to just get from 10 to 11, we'd need that all again. The most XP we'd been awarded was when we'd eliminated Test Name; 1,000 XP. How the fuck were we meant to get 240,000 XP?

Was it even possible to save Jye, for us to make the cut before the culling?

The familiar thread of panic began to wind through me, my chest beginning to tighten.

Fuck, not now! I had so many other questions. I needed answers.

But my body wouldn't listen. My muscles seized, almost outside of my control.

Of course. It figured. I knew it. I knew I wasn't fixed. That I couldn't just be normal.

I gasped for air, reaching for my throat, choking, choking, choking. I tried to breathe, to remember the pattern. It had been so long since I'd needed it, I had almost forgotten.

Breathe in for six, hold for four, out for six. Your happy place.

Struggling to inflate my lungs, I counted to six. My vision began to swim, the lecture hall flashing between existence and a kaleidoscope.

I clenched my eyes closed to limit the sensory overload.

Hold.

Jye would be fine.

Hold.

We'd be fine.

Hold.

We could save them.

Hold.

We could survive, all of us.

I exhaled to six.

My happy—

To my right, warm fingers slipped between my own.

My heartbeat ticked to a slower pitter patter, and my breathing began to even. The world stilled. Slowly as I continued the pattern, the awareness of control tendrilled back through me. That said, the energy required to regain myself, to settle, had completely spent me. I don't know how much time had passed.

It suddenly occurred to me why my near-death experiences hadn't had such a big impact on me. Each of these attacks… they were basically the same as dying. I guess I'd been trained to die.

Axel's furrowed brow was the first thing I saw when I finally opened my eyes. I must've looked like a mess because the concerned gazes of the rest of the party, and Nabu's too, were drilling holes into my skin. I felt like shit, and my hand was clammy and sweaty in Axel's. As I stared, I noticed I'd clamped onto him so tightly my nails had dug crescents into his skin, pinpricking it red.

Guilty, I snatched back my hand almost instinctively.

A beat passed as I realised what I'd done. He'd tried to comfort me when I was having a panic attack and I'd reacted like that? Jesus Christ. Even without the pressure of knowing his feelings for me, just as a friend that was a shitty thing to do. Why when it came to Axel, did I always mess up like this?

He stared at me.

I dreaded whatever would follow that look, my panic swallowed by regret.

"That was kinda homophobic, man," he finally said, a shit-eating grin splitting across his face.

A croaky, surprised chuckle escaped me. It was good he wasn't hurt by my reaction. Well, emotionally hurt at least. My grip had to have done some damage.

"As much as I love this, can I ask, you two done?" Tam asked, her slit-brow raised in whatever the opposite of amusement was.

"Sorry to inconvenience you with my crumbling mental health, Tam."

Wren echoed her in a much nicer tone, "Are you okay now, Lee?"

Letting my saltiness drop, I nodded. "Yes, thank you for asking."

Nabu cleared his throat. "So, um, I believe it's standard to allow you questions, queries, and comments."

I'd talk to Jye later about this. About keeping them alive with us. Yeah. Time to store these stupid fucking fears in the back of my mind until some future period. I'm sure that'd be absolutely fine and would have no lasting repercussions. It was probably bad being sarcastic in your own mind.

Wren, who excluding Tam and Axel, seemed to be taking this news the most calmly, leaned forward, apparently happy the floor was open to the myriad of questions her inquisitive mind sought to answer. "What happens to the parties who make the spotlight?"

"Um, well, they act in several arcs until there's but one final party left standing."

Just Friends fell silent. One party. Out of eight billion people.

I didn't know if parties had a maximum capacity but even without one, there would be a certain amount of people entirely unwilling to join others. Tam, for example. Speaking of, the cutthroat appeared to be cleaning dirt from her nails.

"And then after that?" Wren prompted, curious, still strangely even.

The god smiled, clearly happy with a student like Wren. He truly was the god of schooling. "The party wins a prize."

"Oh! What's the prize?" she replied, swept along with his enthusiasm.

Nabu clapped his hands together in delight.

"Anything you wish! Well, to be more precise, the Deities will grant the party a wish."

"A wish?" I echoed, my voice sounding foreign in my own ears.

"Any wish! You can wish for anything at all!"

His response settled in silence around us.

Oh.

The solution was so obvious.

It came to me faster than I thought my neurons could even fire.

"I could… wish for everyone who died to come back?"

"You certainly can! Heavens, I know it sounds too good to be true. Uh, granting wishes doesn't seem possible. But, well, you can just ask Gigi. After all, xe got xir wish granted."

If it were possible, the newest member of our party shrunk to an even smaller size under the weight of our collective gaze.

DUNGEON
HUNTER

XXVI

GG

NODDING, GIGI SAID, "I did receive my wish."

The rest of us exchanged a look.

"You can't just say that and nothing else," I replied. "What was your wish— No, wait, even before that. Who *are* you? *What* are you?"

I'd long known Gigi couldn't be normal. Had recognised for quite a while that the things xe knew and said, even with the moderation, were so alien that xe wasn't your average party member, per se, but this was far beyond anything I could've ever imagined. I guess it didn't help that I'd never tried to close the gap between us. The most I could tell you about Gigi was xir player stats and that xir coat was inexplicably the coolest thing I'd ever laid eyes on. Given the technology of it, I probably should've suspected something was off.

Well, more off.

It did make me second-guess what I actually knew about everyone in Just Friends. Of course, I knew Axel... mostly, but the extent of what I knew about Jye was pretty limited. I knew less about Wren. Could count the number of facts I knew about Tam on one hand. Then there was Gigi who I hadn't even investigated beyond their class. Mostly I was familiar with everyone's character over their background.

It was weird that I knew them all so little but felt protective about them, and that even somehow included Tam though I knew she didn't hold me in the highest esteem. Maybe that was what happened when you put your life on the line together. Still, I needed to put in the effort to get to know everyone better. Always adding things on to my to-do list, wasn't I? And if I wanted to survive this with everyone, getting to know them all better wasn't a bad thing.

Gigi scratched at xir chin, as if finding the words to explain xemself.

"I am Linnikian. This form I have taken is not how I originally appeared. My people come from—" Xe frowned. "That is not right. The Linnikians are no more. I hail from a now dead world far from Earth."

Nabu let out a sliver of nervous laughter. "Uh, well, that was your choice, though."

Everyone was still staring at xem.

Gigi breathed out. "It is true. I was selfish. My wish only served myself."

Wren's brow was crinkled. "What did you wish for?"

Gigi looked away, eyes now downcast through xir silver lashes. "I am too ashamed to say. But Nabu tells the truth. My wish was granted."

"You've been keeping the lid on this jar the whole time. Why should we trust either of you?" Axel demanded, his voice writhing with disgust.

Xir expression was strained. "I withheld nothing. Jye can attest to that." Gigi's shoulders squared, and xe lifted xir head to meet Axel's gaze. "My sole purpose is to offer assistance. Should you not want me to travel with you farther, I will leave the party."

"Then fuck off," the blond said.

I held up a hand. "Wait, hold on there. Let's not be too hasty."

Gigi had done nothing duplicitous in the time we'd known xem. Xe'd worked with us well and contributed to the party in a way none of us could. Not to mention that xem being LVL 10 was something we couldn't ignore with the culling. Having such a monumental leapfrog in our party average may very well be what would toe us pass the line. It didn't matter that Gigi was… a genuine alien. That was the least of our concerns.

Rather, there was something else gnawing at the edge of my mind. Something that didn't make sense, now that I knew about the wish and Gigi's background.

"Look, we're gonna talk about your past in more depth at a later time, okay, Gigi? But you better believe you're not off the hook. We deserve answers."

The small Linnikian nodded solemnly. I guess this not being their original form explained xir weird accent and appearance. What had they based it all upon? I'd definitely be asking that in the future. The silver *really* was a choice. Actually, the whole look was something else entirely.

I flicked my gaze back to Nabu, focusing on the inconsistency I'd noticed with his explanations. "I met a merchant in Twilight, the marketplace. Xanthe. They said their people didn't succeed. How's that possible? You make it sound like the winners receiving a wish at the end is what always happens."

The god's head tilted to the side, confused. Then his eyes widened in realisation.

"Oh! Occasionally the matinee is, uh, not enough to entertain us. A bit of a flop, er, if you will. As divine punishment for failure, said population is… hmm, well, eliminated. There aren't meant to be survivors. Though, uh, they do slip through the cracks." He ran a hand over his beard, consideration on his plain face. "This merchant you speak of must be quite lucky. Perhaps they had an, uh, overly indulgent sponsor during their event. Some do get too attached, I'm afraid."

"Wait, wait, wait." I pinched at the bridge of my nose. "So, you're saying we might not even *get* to the average culling?" I said, wondering how much worse things could get.

Nabu looked embarrassed. "Well, it doesn't happen often. Maybe, hmmm, one out of ten times?"

How many races had they put through this? How many worlds had been destroyed, people killed? It was mind boggling. Why did they think they were allowed to just… fuck around with people like this?

My thoughts returned to the details of Nabu's answer; a 10 percent chance humanity wouldn't make it out of the tutorial. At this point, I was simply exhausted with the emotional weight this had placed on my shoulders. It was like taking a billion psychic damage every time Nabu spoke. I slumped back into my chair, letting this new information soak into me. We were doomed.

Wren raised her hand.

"Yes, young lady?" the god responded.

"I've been wondering. What's a sponsor do?"

Nabu's face lit up.

"Oh, I'm so glad you asked! Well, essentially… we support you in your performance, and, ah, gain acclaim as you succeed." He waggled a finger. "Um, but don't go thinking you can just load up on sponsors, see. A player can only ever have one sponsor, and, well, their sponsorship is binding until the end of the event."

It made sense; that's what sponsors were, really. I'd watched my fair share of Twitch streams. The sponsor's little logo popping up in the lower third constantly burned the brand into your head. The more popular the stream, the more exposure the sponsor got.

I frowned. But this was different. It wasn't like the gods would send us merch or something. "What does this 'support' entail?"

"Uh, you saw it during your fight with Tam… Didn't you? Her sponsor intervened. Of course, well, such interventions are dependent on the managing Deities, but they're much, um, cheaper than anonymous spectator interactions. In fact, Tam's sponsor—"

Tam cut him off. "Mumma doesn't want her identity revealed yet."

"My apologies!" Nabu bowed low, glancing around as if expecting to be struck down. He stood slowly, testingly, then continued, "Tam's sponsor would've had to, uh, sacrifice a bit of belief to assist her. But, of course, Tam's performance would've earned her a lot back."

My brain had stopped trying to make sense of things. It was like joining the final lecture for a subject you'd never even heard of.

"What."

"Oh dear, I appear to be getting everything all mixed up, heavens." Flustered, Nabu cleared his throat. "A Deity's strength… directly correlates to the amount of belief they've gathered." He hmm'd for a moment before adding, "Ah, to put it simply, uh, we sponsor players to gain belief."

"Like… a religion? You want more followers?"

"No, no, no, silly. You could say we're well past that now. It is more similar to… uh, tangible respect or reputation in energy form. Many Deities do not participate in this event. Most are, uh, content to watch. The better a player performs, well, the more belief a Deity sponsoring them garners from those spectating. As belief is the only thing that matters to us, uh, it is both our lifeforce and currency. Tam's sponsor would've paid belief to intervene, see."

Under Wren's breath, I heard the muttering of: "So belief is kinda like the kids' screams in *Monsters Inc*?"

Though I was still struggling to properly interpret Nabu's explanation, Wren's analogy didn't sound wrong. Belief was what gave Deities' power. If a sponsor's player performed well and impressed other Deities, the sponsors gained belief. It was really going to be hard not to imagine the entirety of humankind as that one kid Randall kidnapped and soulsucked. In fact, the only real difference between this whole "event" that Nabu was describing and *Monsters Inc.* was that sponsors required an additional, unreliable middleman: other Deities.

This time Jye's hand shot into the air as they raised their voice. "Wait a momento. Who's the dudes getting the dough?" At Nabu's lack of comprehension, they elaborated, "You know, the peeps running the show. The head honchos."

"That's such a good question! Uh, well, the ringmasters, as it were, are The Divinities and their underlings. The strongest of us." Nabu pursed his lips in thought. "To add to that, each Dungeon and arc are assigned managing Deities. For… lesser Dungeons, they're usually volunteer managers, but for players and sponsors with more belief behind them, uh, you might be lucky enough to be moderated by someone with true clout!"

"Is this… a lesser Dungeon?" I asked, knowing the answer.

Meekly, Nabu nodded. "Uh, it's my first time participating. I wanted to try my hand, um, maybe gain a bit of belief. Test the waters, as it were. Hence my desire for honest feedback."

It felt like one blow after another. We were less like a show they were watching and more like… dogs they were racing and betting on, being trained to run at their whistle, the rabbit we chased a singular ever-moving goalpost of a wish. How fucking demeaning. But what could we do? It seemed like it was genuinely do or die. And if we won, we could save everyone.

If we won.

The odds didn't seem in our favour. Six people out of nearly eight billion.

When this had all started, I'd called it the end of the world as we knew it. But when this was over… it would really just be the end of the world, especially if a party won the prize who weren't so altruistic as us. So, we had to try. Right?

The god gave a shaky smile. "All right then. Um, if that's all the questions you had, who wants to be sponsored by me?"

Collectively almost everyone in the party made the same face.

"Yeah, no. Hard pass," Axel said.

"I'm sorry, dude, but I don't think I'm ready for that type of commitment yet," Jye replied.

"Let me get back to you." I felt kind of bad, but the best I could do was a soft no. Nabu would not be a good sponsor, based on everything he'd said.

"Oh, me!" Wren sprung up, standing on the room-length desk, scrambling forward. "Sponsor me!"

Aghast, our mouths opened to object, but before any of us could intervene, Nabu appeared alongside her in a flash, a hand offered out. "Oh, a pleasure to be working with you, Wren, uh, Makris."

Huh. So, her last name was Makris. That thought played dully in my mind as we all dived forward to stop her.

She took his hand, ignoring the exclamations of protestations exploding from our party.

We'd reacted a breath too late.

A burst of air shot out from their shaking hands, and above them a sigil of a classic stylus, glowing gold, twinkled into existence before evaporating into motes.

Apparently satisfied, Nabu teleported back to the front of the lecture hall. He started humming contentedly. I stared, slack jawed, glancing between the god and Wren.

I couldn't believe what had just happened. Wren had been sponsored by what basically was a minor god. What support could he possibly provide her? If belief was their currency, this Deity was a beggar. And a rank amateur at that!

And, to top it all off, it was irreversible and permanent.

Fuck.

Suddenly those leashes parents sometimes put on children made a lot of sense.

Nabu plucked a pocket watch from his khakis. "Well, um, I have a Dungeon to take notes on, but I promise I will be keeping an eye on you, my dear. Ah, but before I send you all on your way." He turned to me. "You there. I'm still, uh, waiting on your feedback."

I fell under the weight of his full golden gaze, seeing in it the power he held. It pinned me to the spot. It was the first time I'd looked him straight in the eye, and in them I saw the immensity of what Nabu truly was. It was like staring into the abyss and knowing you were nothing but a speck.

Words froze in my mouth.

I knew instinctively he could smite me where I stood. My life was nothing to him. Less than a single flap of a butterfly's wing in the whole of the universe. A cold sweat broke out across my brow. The beating of my heart slowed in my chest, the feeling so akin to dying, of being crushed and immobilised by an invisible weight, that, for a second, I wondered if he'd already killed me and my brain had lagged before catching up.

Nabu broke eye contact, offering an encouraging gesture, and the feeling was gone.

Trying not to show the effect he'd had on me, intentionally controlling my breathing, I hesitantly gathered my thoughts. There was a lot I wanted to say. But given what I'd just sensed and how he was Wren's sponsor, I knew I should hold my tongue. I carefully figured out how to phrase what I wanted, what I'd felt going through his Dungeon.

"The overall concept can be entertaining, but right now it's all bogged down by a large disconnect between sparsely plotted events and unrelated environments. You need to tighten up the scale, make challenges more streamlined, and…" I paused, wondering if I should even mention it. "And give the Minotaur free will."

Nabu gave one slow nod. Then a smile crept over his face. "I knew I'd saved the best for last, and, well, that's a rather interesting idea with the Minotaur. Would certainly throw an element of randomness into it. Oho, I like it!" He had a little giggle to himself. "Thank you, Lee. How quaint. Thanking mortals, huh. The Divinities would laugh." Nabu gave us a tiny wave. "I wish you all a good show, and I look forward to Just Friends's progress."

I blinked.

We were outside the Gate, asses hitting the road, back in Brisbane. I barely parsed the change in our location and the smarting ache on my bottom. Though I should've been relieved we were home despite the unwelcome pain, my focus went immediately to the ten-year-old.

Deity Commentary available.

Ignoring the most recent notification, I exclaimed, "Wren!"

My first thought was to immediately admonish her for her hasty actions as I grumbled to a stand. Stuff like this got others killed. Not checking in with other people was part of why Chrissie had died. I'd thought Wren had a solid head on her shoulders, but maybe I was giving her too much credit.

Getting to her feet too, she turned to me with a frown. "What?"

"You can't just do stuff like that."

"I just thought that the earlier we get sponsors, the better," she said. "Also, I was a bit worried about what might happen if we all rejected him."

The golden force of his gaze filled my mind. Because of his timid personality, I'd easily forgotten Nabu was one of the Deities playing with us. Even though he included himself in all the explanations, his appearance and demeanour had lulled me into a false sense of security. That last moment however… What *would* have the god done?

It was my turn to frown. "You might have a point about Nabu. Still, what made you think an earlier sponsor would be better?"

Wren explained, "Nabu said Deities get belief based on how their players perform. More belief is more support. So long as we stay alive, the earlier we get sponsors, the more belief they get, the more help we get. So, any sponsor early is better than none."

It was a logical train of thought, rather advanced for her age, but I was beginning to accept that she was just like that. I mulled over her words and realised she hadn't taken into consideration one thing. Something huge.

"What if the sponsor just claims all the belief for themselves and doesn't help their player?"

"Doesn't seem like a strat that would pay off," Jye remarked as they chose to recline on the bitumen instead.

I kicked at a rock on the floor, channelling all my frustration into launching it clear across the road. "It's safer. Think about it. A passive sponsor garners belief and puts no investment in. Sure, they might not receive much belief, but they'd lose nothing either. It's like a fucking idle game for them where they never have to click a single cookie."

Axel breathed out from between clenched teeth, correcting himself to a squat. "C'est la vie. Nothing to be done now. Did you at least get anything from it, Wren? A stats boost or something?"

Wren shook her head.

"Stingy motherfucker," Tam commented from behind crossed arms; she'd been the only one of us quick enough to catch herself before falling to her ass when the chairs beneath us disappeared.

She looked surprised by her own words. Perhaps that she'd let her true thoughts slip.

Gigi had crossed xir legs and was sitting with perfect posture, hands resting on xir knees. Xe let out a disappointed sigh. "That is unfortunate. A sponsor should grant their player a unique title as their first supporting act. Though it does cost belief. Perhaps Nabu did not have enough."

God, I knew he was a shit option. The rest of us had been right to reject his sponsorship. All we could do now was hope he'd come through for Wren when we needed him too.

Mentally, I also made a note to stop using "God" as a curse or exclamation. It was weird to use when Deities genuinely existed. Like I was somehow directing my thoughts toward them. And that made me feel dirty.

Tam gave Wren the side-eye. "You jumped the gun, gumdrop. I only accepted Mumma's sponsorship because of her power. Nabu ain't nothing but a garnish when you coulda had a feast, if you'd put that impatience on ice."

Wren said, as quiet as a whisper, "Those aren't the only reasons I did it. Also… I just… I…"

The party turned to her, concern etched into the furrows of our brows. There was something vulnerable in the way she'd said those few words, shaky even.

"Use your words," Axel urged.

In unison, Tam, Jye, and I smacked him along the backside of his head in response, and he hissed in pain, properly chastised. How Jye closed the distance made me marvel. Truly, exasperation made one capable of great things.

But Axel's words had steeled Wren's resolve. She exhaled a sharp breath of air from her nose. "I took Nabu's sponsorship because I didn't want to be so helpless like I was in the labyrinth, because even if he's weak, he's stronger than me!"

Her fists were balled tight, hands white from the force, her cheeks flushed, and she was trembling slightly. It was determination fighting against fear. I'd been completely wrong about her being mostly okay in that dark room. I'd been an idiot. I could remember being ten. Being locked in a small pitch-black room by myself would've had me screaming.

Feeling like the worst person in the world, because surely I was to have dismissed Wren's bravery as I had, I approached her and took one of her small quivering hands in mine. She met my gaze, biting her bottom lip to keep from crying, though the tears looked to be beading along her bottom lashes.

I knew she expected me to continue my original admonishment.

I'd dropped out of soccer after Chrissie had died. I hadn't told my parents until they'd asked why I hadn't been going to practise on Thursday afternoons. The sport hadn't felt fun anymore. Because whenever I'd pass the ball, every recipient had been Chrissie as I helped her perfect passes on the expanse of drought-dead grass in our enclosed yard back home. I'd only joined because she'd wanted to play, and our parents hadn't allowed her to go to the field alone, even if they thought the town was a safe place.

Understandably, when they'd found out I'd quit, they'd gotten angry at me, outraged. They'd urged me to rejoin. Told me I'd regret it. Said I'd be missing out on something special and quitting was letting the negative emotions win.

My parents hadn't been wrong; I could see that as an adult. Everything they'd said had come to pass, and those upset attempts of coaxing me were done out of concern for my overall well-being. But in that moment, all those years ago, their words wouldn't have changed anything, wouldn't have changed my mind. What I'd really needed to hear was something else entirely.

I kneeled down beside Wren; her hand still in mine.

"I'm sorry things felt out of your control." I don't know if I was talking to her or my past self. "Big decisions like this… they're yours to make, it's true. But they affect all of us because you're one of us. Just next time you feel like making an important choice like this, can you please talk to us first?"

Her eyes widened. I'd hoped I'd said the right thing.

"Can you promise us that?" I continued.

She wiped away the beginnings of her tears with the back of her hand and nodded. Through a few sniffles, she said, "I promise I'll try."

Feeling relieved by her reaction, I let her hand go and affectionately ruffled her hair. "By the way, congrats on your sponsorship. Nabu's going to drown in the belief you'll attract for him."

She smiled weakly. "Thanks, Lee."

"Hey, it's the truth. With or without his help, you're gonna grow even stronger, I can tell."

Tam agreed. "He won't know what socked him with you, sugar."

"He's about to get jacked with belief."

"I believe he has underestimated you, and all of us," Gigi added.

Axel, never the type for heart-to-hearts, began, "Look, I'm having the time of my life standing out here ala the *Eva* finale, but, here's a fun idea: we take this party somewhere else we're not vulnerable to—"

"Put your hands up!"

One of us needed to get some sort of proximity detector. This was getting ridiculous. We'd been ambushed again and again. Alongside some sort of stat checking ability, enemy locating should be on our list. The next time we got a breather, I'd take a magnifying glass to the Upgrade window and figure out what was what. There had to be some way to Upgrade our abilities. I'd brute force it, if that's what it took.

"For real-real, where did you get a shotgun in Australia?" Jye asked, more intrigued than scared.

I stared down the barrel of the weapon to the person who held it as I raised my hands into the air.

"Where's my daughter? She went in a few days ago! What did you do with her?"

The person speaking appeared to be middle aged, petite, and with blonde hair that was beginning to gray at the temple held back in a severe ponytail. The expression on their face was a steeled resolve. A finger curled over the trigger, unwavering. It was clear our assailant meant business. There would be no hesitation. But this... was all too eerily familiar.

My heart fell.

"Mrs. Dainsworth?" I asked, feeling weak.

DUNGEON
HUNTER

XXVII

BY ANY OTHER NAME

S HE SCOWLED, her grip on the gun tensing.

"We never married. It's Carrie. Just Carrie."

"Carrie," I began and then froze.

What was I supposed to say? "Sorry, we killed your daughter"? "Anna literally stabbed me in the back, and if I hadn't taken a huge gamble, she would've taken my or Axel's life"? "Oh, my bad, Tam took everything Anna owned when she looted her corpse, hope there was nothing sentimental on it"?

"The longer you hesitate, the more suspicious you become," Carrie said, the furrow in her brow deepening, her finger curling a hair's width tighter around the trigger.

This hadn't been on my bingo card. Running into the mother of someone we'd killed wasn't even on my radar of things to consider. I had barely come to terms with the fact that our party would likely not survive and that we were essentially fighting a losing battle. Not that I was ready to admit defeat, but it was a dire situation that seemed practically hopeless.

It very much felt like we'd never win, but we'd die trying.

So, it was understandable that my mind was reeling as I wondered how to explain *anything*.

"You been in a Dungeon yet?" Axel asked, putting himself between me and the gun.

He was buying me time to think. I could kiss him.

The older woman cocked an eyebrow up. "I have. I walked in and out of the CBD one. Anna was supposed to do the same in this one. To stop the itch."

"Why didn't she go into the CBD one, like you?" Wren asked, her voice curious but quiet.

Carrie shook her head, expression subtlety softening at the girl. "Group of upstarts surrounded it, demanding payment from anyone wanting to be let in. I was lucky to slip in and out before they set up their barricades. Only reason they've not put up one here is because of me."

Standing there with her weapon, I had to acknowledge she *was* a formidable opponent.

Her gaze swept over the group. "I'd hazard a guess that you're Just Friends?"

We nodded.

"I'll ask again now that we've been properly introduced. Where's my daughter, and what did you do to her?"

The truth would kill us.

That was an undeniable fact.

I didn't want to take the risk of someone in our group taking a full load of buckshot to the face.

Like some sort of *Sherlock* scene, the events seemed to play out before me. If either Gigi or I used [Focus], we could tank the hit and rely on [Stubborn] to survive it, I guess. Wait, no. That only worked in Dungeons. And add to that, if both of us activated [Focus] at the same time, we'd fuck things up, and without us having a suspicious exchange there was no way of relaying that information and selecting only one of us.

Sure, Axel might be able to dodge with [Swift Footed], and, if she reacted in time, Tam might be able to transform and avoid the attack in her smaller form. But Wren and Jye were sitting ducks.

A single [Shield Wall] protecting them probably wouldn't be enough at this range either—and with the potential spread of buckshot, Gigi and I would have to instantly set up a wide array of the shields with at least two rows to eliminate all possible hits for them and us. And, again, there was no time or way to communicate *any* of this to xem without us immediately getting shot up as a result. I still had [Thick Hide] up from the Dungeon clear, so my mana was currently capped too.

Axel could maybe disarm her, quick as he was, or Gigi and I could summon a [Shield Wall] near her hands, but I didn't like the odds of Carrie not being able to fire off one shot reflexively before either of those plans could be completed.

If the entire party just straight up went full frontal assault, maybe we'd be able to come out of this alive. In fact, it would've been the perfect time for Nabu's first show of aid. But since we weren't in the Dungeons... Did that mean he didn't care? There were no managing Deities attached to Earth, or at least Nabu had said only the Dungeons and arcs got them.

Outside of Dungeons... were we on our own?

Fan-fucking-tastic.

I repressed the depressive sigh that threatened to overcome me.

It wasn't like anything had really changed after clearing the Dungeon and Wren getting a sponsorship. We were almost exactly where we'd been before we'd stepped into the Dungeon's shrine. We'd be alone all along, really.

The six of us against the world, the gods, the universe itself, even.

The six of us facing off against a woman no taller than 1.5 meters wielding a shotgun.

Though, as she regarded us with a steely glare, all I saw were my own mother and father looking back.

I made my decision.

Took a breath.

Then lied through my teeth.

"We stumbled into her in a fight with three other people," I said. "She was holding up really well, but we lost sight of everyone in a smoke bomb she threw. Not knowing what was happening, we hid, and by the time the air was clear… I'm sorry, Carrie."

Her jaw clenched. I hoped the rest of my party wouldn't correct the inaccuracies of my story.

"Tell me how you know her last name, then."

I didn't have to pretend to feel awful about what I was saying or about what I was doing. Carrie had only stepped in and out of the CBD Dungeon. She had no idea what happened inside them and had gathered no XP either. So, this was my answer. My stomach churned.

I didn't want to see more death if I could avoid it.

Using [Channel], I borrowed [Intimidation] and felt sick as I conjured more lies. The ability choked me with its tar. It felt deserved.

"From where we were hiding, we heard them… This is going to be hard to hear… They… they bragged about killing her and they…" I swallowed. "They looted her body. But we ended up fighting them and got everything back. Didn't we, Tam?"

The cutthroat's eyebrows shot up, but as Carrie's barrel swung in her direction, she began pulling all of Anna's belongings from her inventory, placing each item slowly onto the ground.

Carrie was eyeing the growing pile, her expression gradually but surely cracking. It had to be a lot to take in. But she had to have assumed the worst already, right? Anna not returning immediately meant something had gone wrong. In the back of her mind, Carrie had to have expected this fate for her daughter.

When Tam laid a single silver necklace down, the older woman shook her head.

"Enough." Her voice cracked. "I've seen enough!" Swallowing her emotion, Carrie directed the shotgun back toward Axel and me.

She stared at us for a long time.

I hoped [Intimidation] to impress trustworthiness had worked.

Her upper lip twitched as she jutted her chin at us. "So, you got them, right? The ones who… You made sure they can't do that to anyone else?"

I nodded, feeling ill.

"We didn't know what to do, but…" Trusting that the older woman was beginning to believe my lies, that the [Intimidation] had set, I turned my back on Carrie and strode over to Tam. The mother's eyes and weapon remained trained on me, following my movement. I whispered my instructions to the cutthroat.

Making a very unpleasant expression, Tam followed my requests. First, she placed the inventory-retrieved sheet, looted from Test Name, into my arms, and then kneeled to summon what I'd asked for.

The surprisingly fresh-looking corpse of the teenager appeared the next moment, laid out along the road, parallel to me so that she fell into my shadow.

I made sure to block Carrie's view, angling myself over Anna, knowing full well how it felt to see a loved one's face after their murder.

Gingerly, I spread the sheet over the teen, taking in for the first and last time just how young she had truly been. Probably would've freshly graduated high school. She would've been starting university next year. And we'd stolen her future.

No, I told myself.

It hadn't been us.

It was the Deities.

Had life continued as it was, as it should've, I doubted Anna Dainsworth's and my paths would've crossed. The fact that Tam had taken Anna's life, that Anna had made an attempt on almost every member in Just Friends…. None of the blame should rest on us players.

These thoughts did nothing to stop the guilt.

In the end, we'd still killed her.

"What's that? More of her things?"

Tucking the sheet tighter to her body, I then stood, lifting her up, cradling her to my chest. She was cool, even through the cloth, and though she was light, I felt as if I was carrying an impossible weight.

I turned to face Anna's mother.

"We brought her home."

Carrie stared for a moment, as if parsing my words, trying to find meaning in them. Step by step, I approached, the cloaked figure in my arms becoming more distinct in form to her watchful scrutiny. I worried for a moment that Carrie wouldn't believe the covered body to be Anna's. But, as I came closer, Carrie's gaze shook, and almost against her own control, her gun lowered. Tears began to water in her gray eyes. The same colour as eyes that would never open again.

"Oh, baby girl…"

I guess a mother always knows.

Carrie's weapon fell from her grip, clacking to the ground, and she rushed to meet me, grabbing at Anna's body, desperate to make contact, to hold her. She pressed her face to Anna's veiled one, hands scrabbling to take her daughter back. I let Anna go, feeling the weight shift over. But most stayed.

The older woman's knees buckled beneath her, causing them both to fall to the floor. Though I stepped forward to help, I froze as the air from their sudden movement fluttered the sheet up at Anna's head to reveal her face. The material settled down around her shoulders. I was for once thankful that Tam's death blows had always been so precise and discreet.

Had Anna's chest been rising and falling and her skin not as pale as the sheet she was wrapped in, one might believe the girl to simply be asleep.

Carrie stared at her for a long moment. I knew she was trying to deny this was her daughter.

The older woman began to sob. It started as a single choked breath.

Softly, ever so softly, as if she were afraid the girl would break, she lifted a shaking hand to Anna's face, hovering just over her cheek.

"You shouldn't have gone in by yourself. I told you. We were supposed to go in together! Why do you never listen to me?"

My own throat was dry, and I realised I was crying as well. Suddenly I was thirteen again, my pillow drenched in tears, as I asked Chrissie similar questions. Why didn't you stay inside the school gates? Why didn't you tell me? I told you to always go to class as soon as the bell rings!

I took in a shaky breath, obliterated by a realisation.

I don't know when it had happened.

But I'd become the same monster who'd taken Chrissie.

No matter how I had been justifying it to myself. No matter the words I'd been using. We'd taken Anna's life. We'd killed her and hadn't thought twice about it.

This wasn't a game.

This wasn't a show.

This wasn't a race.

"Why... why, baby girl? Why'd you go in without me?" Carrie asked between gasps of breath, her face creased into anguish.

This was wrong.

I struggled to tear my gaze from them, blurry as it was, knowing that some part of me needed to commit this to memory, to never forget this sharp, stabbing, sickly pain, and so I was only able to check on how the others were fairing in my periphery, my concern for them winning out over my own emotional turmoil.

Wren had sought solace in Jye's arms as the giant gently ran a hand over her hair, their hand large enough that it encompassed her full head. Gigi solemnly held xemself, arms wrapped tight around xir chest, and Tam had the decency to be looking away, her brown eyes downcast. What about...

Axel, who'd been shadowing me this whole time, nudged me with his shoulder. His head tilted, as if to ask, *You good?*

Did he feel no guilt? No remorse?

It was hard to tell with him. There was an unreadable expression on his face. Surely, he felt something about this? I didn't have the emotional bandwidth to handle taking on Axel's repressed feelings right now and so pushed those questions to the back of my mind.

Shaking my head slightly in response, I said, "I'm sorry, Carrie. This is the best we were able to do."

She didn't acknowledge my words, simply continued to cry, holding her daughter's body close, rocking slightly. It was probably for the better. I don't know if even I'd have believed what I said then.

Was it the best we were capable of?

Despite nearly losing our own lives, and taking others, I think somewhere deep inside I'd been trying to ignore the severity of it all. I hadn't wanted to take accountability and responsibility.

I'd refused to accept what our killing meant.

It meant someone was gone forever. Someone who might be loved. Someone who might be hated.

It was someone, and then it wasn't anymore. Just as Chrissie had been.

A whole person erased from existence permanently.

No.

Not permanently.

I wiped at my tears.

The wish.

Though it had been the first thing that had occurred to me when it had been mentioned, the power of it, the potential of it, suddenly shifted in my mind, spurred on by the scene unfolding in front of us. This was how we'd take responsibility for the suffering we'd inflicted, the pain we'd be putting others through.

Before, the idea of wishing everyone back to life had been just that, wishful thinking. It was unlikely Just Friends would ever be strong enough, good enough, to be that party that won. Hell, we'd try as hard as we could, but I think underneath it all, I had accepted we wouldn't win. That us receiving the wish was a pipe dream.

But looking down at Carrie and Anna, the guilt and injustice morphed into concrete resolve. An unshatterable determination.

We would win.

We'd take responsibility.

And we'd bring everyone back.

Everyone.

We remained in vigil long enough for the sun to sink into the horizon of the city, staining the sky hues of red.

EVENTUALLY, CARRIE'S TEARS DRIED, and she gathered herself.

Voice hoarse, she asked, "How do I…"

"You just think it, while in contact," I hastened to answer, desperate to help.

She nodded. The older woman pressed her lips to Anna's forehead, and then her daughter's body was gone; stored in Carrie's own inventory. At least she didn't have to carry it home in her arms. It was a small consolation.

While we had waited, Wren and Gigi had collected Anna's items and put them into one of the bags we'd looted from Test Name. They'd placed it by Carrie.

Wiping herself off, she plucked the shotgun from the ground, slung the bag over her shoulder, and stood. Though she was small framed, as she brushed away the remnants of her tears, she looked every inch one of the strongest people I'd ever seen. Carrie breathed in deep and then exhaled. I remembered the same expression on my parents' faces.

It was the resigned look that said the world kept turning, even in the throes of tragedy.

Carrie's gray gaze met mine.

"I suppose I should thank you." I opened my mouth to reject whatever thanks she would give, but she continued with, "But words mean nothing. Come. I'll bring you back to meet the rest of the squad. There was talk of a barbie when I left for this watch."

It would be wholly immoral for us to accept any gratitude for what we'd actually done. I never wanted to lie to, manipulate, or take advantage of this grieving woman ever again. Unfortunately, I wasn't quick enough to protest as Axel slid in before I could say anything.

"We'd really appreciate that. Haven't had cooked food since we entered the Dungeon."

"A barbie *would* hit the spot," Tam said, running a hand over her chin.

"You guys got lamb?" Jye asked.

Reluctantly, Carrie admitted, "Mostly roo."

Jye shrugged, patting their abs concernedly. "Protein's protein."

"It might be nice," Wren added, looking over at me sheepishly.

Gigi's almost nonexistent brows furrowed. "I do not think my understanding of Barbie is correct in this context."

Controlling my expression, wondering how the others felt okay with this turn of events, I let out a sigh. They'd all rolled with my story, none of them disagreeing. Presumably, they'd thought it was the best course of action. I didn't know about that. Surely if it'd been the right thing, I wouldn't feel as nauseous as I did.

Worse yet, I was unable to think of a reason for refusing that didn't make us sound guilty or suspicious. And the fewer lies I told, the easier it would be to maintain them.

I nodded.

"Lead the way."

AFTER QUICKLY DISCUSSING a walking order, with Axel and Tam at the back, Tam to keep watch on any small details, and Axel to run forward and warn us if anything approached from behind, we followed Carrie several blocks.

The walk gave me some much-needed time to let my emotions settle. I knew I should've spent the time looking over the newly introduced Nexus or the Deity Commentary, but I was barely able to focus on anything other than working through my thoughts about Anna and Carrie and the nameless members of Test Name who we also owed accountability.

Eventually, we arrived out front of a Tentworld with a guard standing alert, well, at least metaphorically. As far as bases went, one could do worse than a camping supplies store. In fact, other than a hardware store like Bunnings, Tentworld might very well be one of the better options; everything you'd need to survive off the grid, all in one handy location.

I was kicking myself, not having thought of it. Given that I hadn't, that meant the average layman wouldn't either, protecting Carrie's crew from any errant would-be looters.

I took back my initial judgement.

Tentworld might very well be the best emergency apocalypse base.

Upon sighting us, the watchman out the front of the store perked up, sitting ramrod straight in their camo camping chair, hand held to a small object at their chest. Their gaze was pinned to us as we came closer and closer. Carrie waved, but it did nothing to relax them.

They appeared to be in their late twenties. With dark eyes, a slightly crooked nose that spoke of at least one break, and a short black mullet, I wondered why something about them seemed familiar. Nothing was coming to mind, but aesthetically, I guess they were the type of person some would consider runway attractive; tall, lean, and with striking features. Maybe I'd seen them in a local advertisement or something.

Pursing brown lips, the lookout whistled when we were finally in speaking distance. "If my eyes don't deceive me, Ms. Underwood, none of the six people you've brought back are your daughter."

Carrie's left eye twitched. "We'll talk about that later, Galbraith. For now, these guys are my guests."

At that, the lookout arched a perfect brow but lowered their hand. Their movement revealed that pinned to the fishing vest they wore was an electronic rape whistle. That for certain would alert anyone within the vicinity; a decent alarm system when there wasn't any electricity to run a standard security set up. The more I saw, the more impressed I was with Carrie's base and planning.

They said, "Bit out of character for you, but I can live with a little improv now and then." They paused, brow crinkling, and then asked, "If I were to say one, two, buckle my shoe, you'd reply?"

"Red fish, blue fish." She scowled. "And I'd also say that I thought I told you to stop pretending you know me, boy."

I forced myself not to frown. It was obvious the bizarre call and response was to check something. Was it to find out if she was being forced to bring us in? It was a crazily thorough system they'd developed. I don't even know if I'd would've considered half of what they had. Though I had the excuse of nearly dying twice.

Their conversation did give me pause. Galbraith was around the same age as Axel and I, give or take a few years. We were closer to twice her daughter's age than not. That Carrie called him "boy" felt a little ridiculous, bordering on insulting. And taking in consideration she'd asked us to call her Carrie also cast their back-and-forth in a different light.

I honestly couldn't tell if they were friends or if they hated each other and what that meant for us in the long run.

But none of that stifled the respect I had for both Galbraith and Carrie's squad and their planning. It was remarkably meticulous, and I wistfully wished my own party would work together so well despite our own twisted webs. In the back of my mind, I also started considering how we might invite them to Just Friends or if we even could, though I was beginning to have hesitations about adding more people, considering the new average we'd have to meet.

That said, based on everything I'd seen, they'd be fantastic additions. But the weight of my lie to Carrie made the idea distasteful. I'd also be liable to slip up eventually. And that wasn't something we could risk outside of the Dungeons, not right now.

So, maybe just Galbraith, then?

We'd only met, but he seemed like a reasonable dude, and, honestly, out of the current people I was travelling with, he would probably be a welcome respite of normality. It'd depend on his class and abilities if I extended an invite. (And if we could even expand our party anyway.)

But those decisions and ideas would have to be considered much later. Fuelled by how organised the Tentworld situation had been, I was making plans that I couldn't cash or even think about cashing anytime soon. I pushed them to the back burner in my head.

Galbraith grinned in response to Carrie's words. "There's the Ms. Underwood I know and love." His gaze wandered over our party, following the file we'd walked in, and then his mouth fell open so wide I was surprised his jaw didn't hit the floor.

"No fucking way. Zeke? Is that really you?"

The mulleted man stood from his chair, surprised delight clearly written on all over his face, warming his eyes. Stunned, we all stiffly turned, not too dissimilar to the mechanical rotating heads of arcade-game clowns, to stare at the person he was addressing.

"Not dead yet, Killian?" Axel smiled, stepping forward to fall in line with me and Carrie at the front of our party.

"They'd have to take me kicking and screaming. You know me, baby."

Glancing between Axel and him, I decided I wouldn't be inviting

Killian Galbraith to our party.

XXVIII

MEAT CUTE

"FANCY DIGS YOU GUYS GOT," Jye noted, staring at the tents as we walked through the store or rather their base. The redhead was being completely genuine, but to any other person it probably would've come off as sarcasm.

I went to elaborate, but Killian let out a little chuckle. "Aren't they just? I bagsed the biggest and best one." He pointed to a ridiculously large tent that stretched the size of a master bedroom. "It's a Zempire Delta Force V2."

Jye's green eyes lit up.

"Oh, dude, my family always used to dream about buying the V1!"

Killian nodded enthusiastically. "They had good taste. But the V2 is a slam dunk on improvement, if you ask me."

Even though no one was asking him, the mulleted man went on to explain all the updates they'd made on the design to an enrapt Jye as we exited through to the employee parking out back. The mouthwatering aroma of grilled meat all but swept me off my feet. It was crazy to think but it was as if I'd forgotten how freshly cooked food even smelled.

The person manning the barbecue, tongs in hand, and an apron saying "Kiss the Chef," turned to us. Their reaction was a stretch to call a greeting.

They blinked defeatedly at us. "Six more mouths to feed, huh?"

Seemingly about my height, the chef in question looked to be no older than sixteen. They still had the chubby cheeks of a child though their face was dotted with the telltale signs of puberty; a fresh reddening of acne and a wispy scattering of facial hair.

Almost cartoonlike, the six of us hovered closer to the barbecue area, leering at the sizzling steaks with salacious gazes.

"I'm guessing you're hungry?" the teen asked, voice completely void of any emotion.

Killian introduced her as Phoenix before listing off all our names. How he'd remembered them in such a short time, I didn't know. It made me wary of him. What else about us was he committing to memory? It was suspicious. Not to mention, he'd gotten along with everyone in the party so well. Too well.

He'd had Wren *and* Gigi smiling within moments of talking to us and had even managed to finagle Tam into something resembling a conversation. Well, the fact that he and Jye got along didn't mean that much. Jye's hyperfixations of anime and K-pop, and tents apparently, were easy ways of winning them over. It was like feeding a stray their favourite treats to lure them in. And then there was Axel, who Killian apparently was on a middle-name basis with.

Thus, I had decided to maintain a neutral distance from him, remaining sceptical of his ulterior motives, wishing I knew more about him and Carrie and Phoenix. That said, part of me was relieved Carrie wasn't with us.

She had replaced Killian on lookout duty so he could take a break for dinner. I doubted she would have any appetite tonight either. I hadn't been able to eat properly for just over forty-eight hours after I learned about Chrissie. It would probably be worse for her, I imagined. Maybe I'd try and bring her something easy to eat if I could find anything still in our stash later tonight.

I told myself that wasn't guilt talking.

"That smells so good," Wren said, rubbing her hands together like a praying mantis before its prey.

"It's just meat," Phoenix said.

Jye exclaimed, "I never understood the phrase 'I could eat a horse,' but I am not playing right now. I *could* eat a horse."

Phoenix replied, "Well, this is cow and kangaroo."

"He was talking about the amount."

Jye smiled. "Quick note, dude, I use they/them."

"Oh," Killian said, glancing up and down Jye. He cleared his throat. "Sorry, I'll keep that in mind."

The redhead shrugged. "No harm no foul."

"I know they were talking about the amount. I was joking," Phoenix continued, still as deadpan as ever.

"Were you, Fifi?" Killian's eyes narrowed.

"Was I, Kilo?"

They stared at each other for a moment, standing off, like they were ready to throw down, but then they both broke into smiles. He patted her on the shoulder and took a seat in one of the numerous camping chairs that they'd set up for dinner. Phoenix returned to cooking, carefully flipping one of the few beef steaks on the grill.

Jesus. They had cute nicknames for each other. Why didn't Just Friends?!

The answer came to me unbidden. I guess even though we'd been in life-or-death situations, we hadn't really… bonded on a level that would develop in-jokes like that. There'd been moments but nothing concrete. Meanwhile, it seemed like these past two weeks since the beginning of the "event" had served to work as a team-building activity for Carrie and the others. Hell, I'd have hesitated to call my party a team at all. We were crudely cut cogs grinding each other into spinning.

"So," I said, sitting across from Killian, "is it just you three?"

He laughed.

"It varies day to day. Six, generally. But people come and go, you know?"

I mostly certainly did not know.

Axel had sat next to Killian. He poked an accusing finger into the man's shoulder and said, "You still love to host, huh?"

Killian swatted away his hand, grinning. "Says the man with the rotating party schedule."

That explained why he'd looked familiar to me. He'd probably been in our apartment at one point. Oh. The memory flashed in my head. No. It had been more than that. I'd seen him coming out of Axel's room in the morning, hair mussed, shirt buttoned all wrong. Huh.

I cleared my throat. "You guys meet in uni then?"

A bark of laughter escaped Killian. "Uni? Me? Please. Academia is my brother's domain. I'm what the officials call a failure."

Concerned I'd poked a wasp's nest, and not knowing how to respond, I sought Axel's gaze, pleading for assistance. He poked his tongue out at me, so quickly that had I blinked I might've missed it. This fucking guy. It was clear where his loyalties lay.

"There ain't any stock standard path for life, Killian. The dice are rolled, and you just gotta hope you can work with whatever they land on," Tam said, joining us.

Bitterly, I realised Tam had never once called me by my name. She'd called me a hundred endearments under the sun, ranging from "darling" to "dandelion," and none of them ever genuine, but not once had she addressed me by name. Scrap nicknames. Our party was barely on a first-name basis.

"My teacher once said that failure doesn't exist as long as you're alive," Wren said.

"That's a nice sentiment," I replied, smiling at her.

Jye shook their head. "Sorry, Wren, but I disagree 100 percent. Failure's everywhere. It's how you learn, man. Without failure, you'd never improve in anything."

The Linnikian who'd been quiet until now, and had chosen to sit cross legged on the floor, said, "I believe both points carry merit. Failure is not an end condition, as Wren's teacher implied, and is rather continuous events one must work through while we continue living, as Jye has stated."

"Holy fuck, you can talk?" Killian said, brows high in surprise.

"And philosophise."

The man groaned, running a hand through his hair. "I tell you that academia is not my forte and you guys open up Aristotle's auditorium in my outdoor dining space."

"You started it with your whole 'woe is me' routine," Axel said, teasingly.

"Hey, I'm allowed to wallow in my flaws. It's called reflecting."

"It's called being a sad sack," Phoenix announced from the barbecue, her voice monotone despite its increased volume.

I was surprised she could hear us so clearly from there. Maybe that was one of her traits?

"I gotta say it's nice to get a chance to talk to you, man," Killian said.

Blinking, I lifted a finger and pointed it to my chest. "Me?"

"Yeah, you always shut yourself in your room whenever I was over. I don't bite, you know."

"Liar," Axel remarked flatly.

He chuckled. "Okay, you got me there. I bite, affectionately."

"You nip."

I stared at them as they continued to joke back and forth. Clearly, Axel was having a good time. I hadn't seen him smile this much since the Gates had appeared. It was like whatever haunted him had been completely forgotten. Which was good, wasn't it? He deserved to be happy, to enjoy himself.

Why, then, did it make me feel unsettled?

No, I knew why.

The chemistry between Axel and Killian was hard to ignore. The two of them clearly got along well. I wondered why they'd stopped seeing each other. Though Axel did tend to go through guys quickly. He was just that kind of person. Killian didn't seem to mind about their short shared past either, entertained as he was by Axel's wheedling. It wasn't the first time I'd seen Axel flirting with other people in front of me.

Though it was for Tam, and, frankly, it was surprising she hadn't commented on it or remarked something snarky to me. She loved to poke fun at us on the daily. The cutthroat in question was idly taking in the outside dining area, her eyes carefully and slowly absorbing all the details. Noticing me staring, she coolly met my gaze.

Ever so minutely I shook my head.

No, Tam, we are not going to be robbing or attacking or making an assault on these nice people who are offering us steak.

She shrugged back, not even slightly perturbed that I'd seen through her plans.

"Putting you on the spot a bit, but you ain't got a cold one lying around, do you?" Tam asked.

Killian shot a finger gun to an esky by the back door. "Help yourself. We're running a little low, but first in, first served."

She got up and, instead of grabbing one drink, plucked the navy 10L esky from the ground and brought it back over, popping open the lid to offer it to us one by one so we could grab something. I'd never been a beer person, but I honestly figured I might need one. The past couple of days had been rough.

When she came by to me, I said, "Didn't think you were the type to share."

"Drinking alone is depressing, babes." There was a slight shift in her expression, minuscule, even. "And I've had my fill of that for today."

Dipping my head in appreciation to Tam, partly out of genuine surprise she'd felt anything about what had occurred today, I pulled a bottle out from beneath the ice and found I'd selected a pear cider instead. Well, that was a nice surprise. They fit my palate a little bit better than the rank bitterness of a beer.

I'd always been more of a cocktail person; a habit that was fuelled by Axel's guests bringing mixer drinks for his "get-togethers" and then never finishing them. The blond, on the other hand, was a beer-only type of guy, so I wasn't surprised when he searched through the remaining ice to track down the second last one.

Briefly, I questioned where they'd gotten ice from but realised they would've had generators in the store and fridges plugged into them. All they'd need was fuel, and if they'd acted fast enough, they could've gotten a lot. I didn't doubt their group was capable of it. They'd managed their food situation markedly well.

When Carrie had subbed in for Killian, they had explained they knew someone who was a butcher. When their power went out, their merchandise had defrosted. They'd put it on ice, but it couldn't be frozen again because of bacteria. It was why the meal tonight was literally a carnivore's dream. All of it was on its last legs.

Tam returned to her seat, her beer in hand, and I twisted the top off mine, then raised my drink into the air.

"To..." I paused, unsure what dedication would be appropriate. "To new friends."

In that I was including everyone I'd met since the Gates appeared. Jye, Wren, Tam, Gigi, Carrie, Killian, Phoenix. It was a reach to call them all friends, but that was something we could work toward. Something I wanted to try, anyway.

The clink of glass bottles sounded against mine as they all completed the toast, echoing, "To new friends!" to varying levels of enthusiasm, followed by everyone downing their first sip of their beverage.

The cider was cool and crisp, and I savoured it, letting out a sigh of enjoyment that fell into sync with the others, as if someone had pressed a button to cue a group satisfactory moan.

As we glanced around at the coincidence, we all shared a laugh.

Wren had joined in with a bottle of coke and was sipping it with relish. We should hit another grocery store and see what we could loot. Maybe there'd be some leftover soft drink we could ration out for her later. Actually, better than that, it might be the right time to try and take her home. Her parents were probably worried to death. Honestly… she might have a better chance with a different party than us. Tomorrow that'd be on the top of the list to talk through with the rest of the party.

"Dinner's up," Phoenix said, and it was all she needed to.

Within seconds, our party was lined up at the fold out white tables, piling meat upon meat onto the plastic picnic plates that had been prepared. It'd felt like forever since I'd been to a barbecue proper. Apartments weren't really the best place to host, and I hadn't exactly been the most social person.

I found myself standing beside Killian, and we reached for one of the serving tongs at the same time.

He pulled his hand back, gesturing for me to take it. "Guests first."

As I debated if I should do the polite thing and play the "no, you" game, Axel slid between us and sniped the last piece of steak on that plate.

"You snooze, you lose, guys," he said with a smirk, then he retreated to a chair.

Shaking his head with an amused smile, Killian commented, "Classic Zeke. Selfish to the bone."

"He's not," I replied instantly without thinking. I wasn't sure why. Axel could be self-serving and almost always put himself first, historically. Killian wasn't wrong, not really, well, regarding the Axel he knew, at least.

But I knew better.

The mulleted man's smile slipped slightly, and then he shook his head. Was he disagreeing? Self-correcting a thought? I couldn't tell since I'd only known him for such a short time. I hoped it was the latter, that he was reconsidering his understanding of Axel. I know I'd had to recently.

Unsure how to continue my exchange with Killian, I decided to pretend it didn't happen.

Taking one more kangaroo steak, I returned to my camping chair. There were no utensils out. It might've been a contingency against water concerns. Washing cutlery was probably a waste of the resource. Using my fingers, I picked up one of the beef steaks—I couldn't tell what cut— and took a bite. It was far overdone and near as salty as the ocean, but as the savoury flavour of it and the char of its bark hit my tongue, I felt my eyes water.

That first steak was gone in a second.

The silence surrounding us as we ate was all anyone would need to know about how much this meal meant.

I let my gaze drift over the content expressions on everyone's face. Tam was chewing aggressively at one particularly sinewy steak, tugging with her hands. Jye's plate was already empty, and they were side-eyeing the remaining vestiges we'd left on the serving platters. Gigi seemed to treat the meal with a scholar's interest, nibbling on the edge of a steak, thinking deeply, and then repeating the action. Wren had retrieved some napkins from her inventory and was using them as a barrier between her hands and the meat, her eyes alight with joy as she took bites. Axel ate his steak absentmindedly, his gaze drifting into the infinities before him.

Phoenix had taken a seat beside Killian, and the two were sitting in companionable silence as they dined.

It was nice, eating like this.

We'd been through so much in the past couple days that this quiet, this pleasant moment, seemed like a different world entirely. For this meal, it was like the world wasn't ending. That humanity wouldn't be eliminated until there was but one party left. That our lives weren't literally on the line, even right now, as other people progressed in levels while we remained stagnant here, eating.

When we finished, a casual conversation began to flow between everyone, prompted by Wren saying she wished she could learn how to cook as easily as it was to use an ability. The discussion naturally moved on to what abilities we wished we'd gotten instead of what we'd been granted.

I listened intently to Phoenix and Killian, trying to glean what kind of skills they had, but the two of them kept dancing around the details. As Jye went into their desire to become 2D, I started to tune out, and instead focused on my menu. It'd been a while since I'd brought it up. In fact, none of us had really discussed our separate screens beyond that first conversation Jye, Axel, and I had had back in the gym.

That seemed like an eternity ago now.

We'd practically been different people.

My Upgrade screen came up from my prompting, and I figured it was as good a time as any to start breaking down the components of our stats. There probably wouldn't be another lull like this again. Not when I knew the breakneck speed Just Friends would have to be earning XP at, if we wanted humanity to even get past this tutorial.

And so, I paid the credits required to increase each attribute one by one while Wren started talking about invisibility, and Gigi nodded sagely, agreeing with the strategic usefulness of such an ability, pointing back to our fight against Test Name.

Glancing between my health, mana, and stamina as I spent the credits, I noticed the following:

1 CON increased HP by 5.

1 INT increased mana by 5.

1 STR looked to increase stamina by 2, but when I got to DEX and added 1 point, my stamina went up 3, which led me to believe it rounded down but both attributes' points were worth a 2.5 stamina increase.

None of these changes really made me feel any different, which sucked. I'd been hoping for their upgrades to make a real difference. I also didn't see a tangible shift when I increased END and WIL, which could mean they were more passive. I'd keep an eye on them when I exerted [Channel] later. Maybe the changes would be more noticeable then.

I'd spent 30 credits out of the 453 we'd gotten, putting the remainder at 423.

If each attribute cost 5 credits each time, that meant I could level up my attributes eighty times and have a few errant credits left. That was… insane. There was no way that'd be right. I couldn't imagine being that strong or having a health pool so wide that my life wouldn't be in danger all the time. There had to be a catch.

Maybe there was something else to spend our credits on. Maybe upgrading abilities? There was also the marketplace, Twilight. The last time I'd checked, all the items on auction had seemed useless, and some were still censored. But with the knowledge I had now… Perhaps I could buy something that might be useful for the future?

What really irked me was that even with the upgrades, my singular ability remained grayed out. Had I still not unlocked it? What prerequisite was needed? Why were the fucking Deities so stingy with information? What was the point in giving us these powers if we didn't even know how to use them properly? What kind of show could we put on as stunted as we were?

Grumbling to myself, I finally noticed an almost invisible arrow beneath [Channel]. It had definitely not been there before. Well, the system updated as I discovered new information. This was possibly an extension of that. As if feeling my gaze fall upon it, the arrow expanded to a dropdown to show two empty slots.

I could get two more abilities?

Clicking into one of the slots resulted in the following information:

Current available abilities:

Test Name: [Volley] [Locate] [Smithing] [Fireball] [Cloak]

Anna Dainsworth: [Mirror Aid] [Track]

Mouth going dry, I stared, letting the full momentum of what this meant hit me. This was all so very *Chronicles of Riddick* that I needed a moment.

I took a breath. We had access to the abilities of the people we killed. All this did was give further impetus for the slaughter that was sure to come. There was no way that literal murderers, who killed for fun, weren't going to become aware of this soon. Maniacs would take advantage of this.

Forget us not making it out of the tutorial.

Humanity could implode upon itself with this knowledge.

Breath held, experimentally, I selected [Mirror Aid] to see what would happen.

Insufficient credit.

Holy shit. How valuable had Anna's ability been? I shifted my focus to [Locate].

Purchase [Locate] for 250 credits? Accept | Reject

I rejected the purchase and then tested the others. I could afford the remaining abilities, but only [Fireball] was cheaper, at 50 credits. So, some abilities started inherently better than others. Or maybe they'd been upgraded already?

Still, without knowing the details of each ability, I was hesitant to spend any of our hard-earned currency on them. I could hazard a guess what each meant based on how our past opponents had used them, but there'd likely be some sort of balancing restriction to each one. And, to be honest, [Fireball] was just kind of shit, in my opinion.

As it was, I still didn't have the mana or stamina pool to really take advantage of anything. Well, not yet. If I spent more points on my attributes, maybe I could—

"Earth to Lee. You catch that?"

I frowned, not expecting to be addressed by Killian. "Huh?"

He rolled his eyes. "I asked what ability you'd want."

Meeting the expectant gazes around the group, I was put on the spot with not a relevant thought in my head except that the more selfish a person was in this fucked situation, the more they'd be rewarded. The more you killed, the more you won.

"Uh."

Axel's blue eyes seemed to rest heavily on me, searing into my own. I truly could never understand him.

I looked away. "I guess mind reading?"

At that, everyone groaned.

Jye said, "That's so cliché. Just say you wanna be Edward and get it over with."

Defensively, I explained, "I just thought that it'd be useful in battles! Being able to know everyone's next action and all that."

"Sure, sure, sure," Jye replied, and a wicked expression formed over their face. They waggled their thick brows. "I know what you'd really use it for."

This elicited a peal of laughter from the others sans Wren. Mortified, my mouth fell open. "Jye! I'd never— I don't even— Why would I— *Who* would I—"

The giant snickered and slapped a hand onto my back, putting a stop to my sputtering objections. "I'm yanking your chain, man. Besides, the only person you'd use it like that on is pretty easy to read anyway."

I didn't parse their words, still shaken by their casual assumption of my relationship with sex and sexuality. And here I'd been thinking Jye had guessed. They were kind of dense, so I don't know why I'd ever thought the redhead would be able to put two and two together regarding this.

Okay, so I had never specifically told Jye I was ace. But that they'd just defaulted into thinking I'd be into stuff like that annoyed me. The expected allosexuality of society sometimes rubbed me the wrong way. But I wasn't about to lecture everyone. I didn't have the energy in me for it.

Besides, it's not like I was disgusted by, hated, or looked down upon people's sexual desires and fantasies. Just that I didn't relate to it in mind or body. I never wanted to peek in someone's dirty thoughts, as Jye had implied, about me or otherwise. All that stuff kind of just existed in a realm that didn't overlap with mine. It wouldn't do anything for me. *And it would be a complete invasion of privacy,* which was my other point of contention.

"That's true enough," Killian said, replying to whatever Jye had said last, and his gaze lingered over Axel for a moment.

He'd been staring at the blond half the night, and Axel had shared glances back, occasionally tucking a loose strand of hair behind his ear. I didn't need to be allosexual to know what that all meant. Yes, Axel had confessed to me, but that didn't mean anything, really. And I wasn't the kind of person that held others back.

Tam let out a chuckle. "You know, I mourned the loss of shitty soap operas when power failed. But fuck *The Bold and the Beautiful*, this is the good drama, right here."

Confused, I raised an eyebrow. "What are you talking about?"

She laughed again and didn't answer.

In the corner of my eye, I saw Wren yawn, covering her mouth politely, and as it so often does, the yawn caught on, infecting Gigi, then Jye, and then finally me. As my jaw stretched open, suddenly I was aware of what toll the day, the discoveries, the emotions, had taken on my energy level, the fatigue sinking deep into my bones.

Cutting my own yawn off, I turned to Killian. "It might be time to head to bed for the night. Could you show us the guest tents?"

Phoenix demanded, without any inflection, to take his place, since as she put it, "I cook therefore I do not clean."

We threw all our trash into the wheelie bin, and I momentarily lamented the number of items we should've recycled. But that was for a world we'd left behind. A world where we didn't kill people for gods.

"I'm kind of in awe that I got to hang out with a party that cleared a Dungeon," Phoenix said, not betraying an iota of emotion, as she led us back inside to where we'd be staying.

Carrie had invited us to stay permanently, but that was a weight too great for me to handle. So I'd accepted lodging for the night for Just Friends and said we'd talk about it in the morning after I figured out a way to politely reject her offer. She'd briefly informed Killian during the lookout handover who we were, and he'd relayed that to Phoenix, obviously.

"Yeah, well, there's nothing special about us, really," I replied.

"I wouldn't say that. Most of the first clears aren't done by the people who enter first," Phoenix replied.

"What do you mean?"

"Oh, well, the announcements we got today, for example. Dungeon 3 was cleared by party XXX. It was first entered by Rohit or something, right?"

Had we stopped receiving Dungeon notifications because we'd cleared one? It wasn't like we could ask Phoenix that. But it made sense. There was no reason to inform us about the Dungeons after we had that conversation with Nabu. Or maybe it was just another way to control us by limiting the information we received.

I simply nodded. "I guess we're just lucky."

"Well, this is you. Sorry, but we're expecting some guests later tonight. We'd usually have enough single tents for all of you, but this is what's open."

We'd arrived at a little grouping of tents. There were two single tents with the zipper doors open, four closed, presumably taken and prepared for their scheduled guests, and two larger ones which looked suitable for two people or so. I would've thought they'd have more available in general, but Killian's words came back to about people coming or going. Perhaps they gave away the tents.

The six of us shared a look.

Phoenix said, "I'll let you all sort it out amongst yourself."

"Mine, mine, mine," Jye declared, sprinting to one of the single tents, giggling uproariously. It was a humorous sight to see such a large buff person dive full-force into an open tent. Where they had hit the back of the material, it formed an indent of their head.

"I am not comfortable sharing an enclosed sleeping location," Gigi said, and as if we agreed, which we hadn't, xe set off to claim the other one.

Tam eyed the rest of us before letting out an exaggerated sigh. "The things I do for my people." Her shoulders slumped. "You ain't a kicker or snorer, are you?"

Wren frowned. "I don't think so."

Defeatedly, Tam trudged toward one of the double tents. "Well, come on. No lollygagging, sugar pea. I want a full undisturbed eight hours for once."

Wren followed her into their tent, quickly wishing us goodnight with a smile. As the brunette zipped the tent up behind them, I heard Wren saying, "Can I plait your hair, Tam?" There might've been a grumbled agreement but I couldn't be sure.

Feeling confident that Tam would protect Wren with her life, I made a move for the remaining two-person tent, as did Axel. This stopped me in my tracks.

"Oh, you're… staying with me?" I asked, confused.

He paused, as if frozen.

"I can't?" His tone was neutral, but just under it I could detect a shakiness.

Immediately worried that this might cause a slip in sanity, I replied, "No, no, it's not that you can't, I just assumed… I mean, you and Killian…"

Axel's blond brows met in consternation. "Killian and I, what?"

I swallowed back the words, and they were sticky in my throat. "It's nothing. Well, you can get settled in first. I wanna check in on Carrie."

Exhausted as I was, I still felt responsible for Carrie sitting out there alone. Axel seemed a little concerned, but he nodded and went to the tent while I fumbled through the remaining food we had looted from Test Name. At the very bottom was something hard and small. It must've gotten lumped in with everything else and lost in the divvying.

It was perfect.

DUNGEON
HUNTER

XXIX

MOMENTS

"THIS GUN'S LOADED. Next time announce yourself, Castillo."

I nodded, heart hammering in my chest, and watched as Carrie's weapon swung away from me. She'd been a breath from shooting me until I'd thrown my hands up in surrender. Carrie was a little scary. I was glad I was on her good side, even if I'd lied to get there.

Dragging the camping chair I'd borrowed from inside, I settled in next to her, scanning the dark streets. Only the moon illuminated the area near us, casting soft shadows that danced with the gentle night breeze.

There was no activity.

She let out a groan. "What do you want, anyway? I'm not in the mood for chitchat."

"Thought you might be hungry," I replied, offering her the small item I'd found in our loot.

She stared, then scoffed.

"I'm old but I'm not a granny, Castillo. You really think I want your pocket-dusted Werther's hard caramel?"

I kept my hand out and sunk deeper into my chair.

"Jesus Christ. You're just like Galbraith. You think you know me? You don't. I don't want your pity in the form of cavities."

I said nothing, leaving my hand where it was, and a moment passed. Her brow crinkled. "You…!"

Irritated, she snatched the plastic wrapped caramel and opened it before popping the sweet into her scowling mouth. I withdrew my hand. From where I was sitting, I heard her stomach gurgle in response to the food.

I hadn't eaten after Chrissie died, but that was because I hadn't been able to keep anything regular down. My parents eventually gave up and let me eat whatever would stay inside me.

Her sullen expression deepened, but I could tell it was embarrassment over this weakness being revealed. It was almost refreshing to see something other than the same resigned emotion on her face.

We sat there for a while. The city was still without traffic, without electricity. You could see the stars dance on the rooftops of buildings without light pollution.

It was quiet.

I wanted to tell her what my plan was. That I was going to bring Anna back, eventually, but it would be too much for a grieving mother. It would be sick and twisted to even mention it. Had someone dangled that in front of my own mother when Chrissie had died, I think I would've seen red.

"You lose someone, then?" she asked, voice soft.

I nodded.

She smiled bleakly. "Figured."

"My sister. A long time ago," I said.

The pain was old but it still hurt, like a healed scar aching in the cold. The police said it was sheer coincidence anyone stumbled across her body that day at all. For a long time, I'd thought them finding her had been the worst part of it. Without it, she would've just been missing.

Why had I needed to know for certain she was gone? It would've been better to think there was a chance she was okay somewhere, somehow. Mrs. Brown had told me it brought closure. It hadn't, not really.

But that was the same reason I'd brought back everyone's bodies.

Carrie's voice croaked as she said, "She used to sit with me like this on our porch, talking shit. Anna was a scheming little bitch sometimes, but I loved her with all my heart. I was proud of her. I never said that to her."

I didn't reply. It was important to simply listen to her now. That's what I needed to do. No. It was the very least I could do. Though sitting there, trying to console her, I felt like an imposter.

But she needed someone. Carrie hadn't told Killian about Anna yet. And I wasn't sure about their relationship so I don't know if she ever would. She needed someone to talk to. If my sessions with Mrs. Brown had taught me anything, it was that. Even if during them I hadn't taken the opportunity.

She continued, "We argued the night before she left. She said she'd be fine to go in alone. In and out. To stop the itch. She told me I shouldn't risk it, since I was good already. But I said no. We'd go together."

Carrie was crying again.

"She did it to save me, and I hate her for it."

I thought for a moment, wondering if I should say anything, or even *what* I could say. I reflected on our fight with Anna and how she'd treated us. Reconciling this mother's recollections of her daughter and the young woman we'd met wasn't that hard. Taking a risk, I remarked, "If it's any consolation, when we saw her fighting, it looked like she was enjoying it."

The older woman let out a startled laugh.

"She would've. Sounds just like her." She paused and wiped at her tears. "Wish I'd been there to see it."

There was a rustle from the left and Carrie's gaze flung to it, eyes seeking, hopeful. Her gun hadn't moved, forgotten in her lap. A possum screeched from the tree it perched in before scurrying away. Carrie's face markedly fell.

"That's actually the worst part," I said.

She turned to me. "What is?"

I smiled sadly. "Every door opening feels like she'll be the one walking through it."

Carrie blanched, then she let out a long, drawn-out breath. When her lungs were finally empty, she slapped her hands onto her thighs decisively. Maybe it was because she was older than my own parents had been or because Anna had been older as well, or maybe it was just because of who Carrie was, but the graying blonde had the kind of levelheadedness in this situation that I simply couldn't fathom.

"Welp. I'm not good for this, not as I am. You wanna take over, or should I call Killian in to cover?"

I considered letting the man suffer, knowing he'd grabbed three alcoholic drinks, but shook my head. My tiredness had faded, replaced with a deep melancholy instead. I wondered if the guilt would ever leave me. Part of me hoped not. Maybe because that'd mean I stopped being human.

Besides, if Carrie trusted me enough to take on lookout, that was something I couldn't betray. Even if most of the belief came from me using [Intimidation].

She nodded. "Here."

I accepted the electronic rape whistle from her. Glancing once more out into the darkness, she sighed, mumbling under her breath. I didn't catch it, but for once I didn't want to try. Whatever she said was between her and her daughter.

"Phoenix will be out in a few hours for her shift. Should be quiet. It is most nights." She gave me a tight smile. "Good luck."

With that and a pat on my shoulder, Carrie was gone.

Time passed.

I let it.

The end of the world was a slow process.

⌐¬

"YOU'RE NOT GOING TO USE that on me, are you?" came a voice I knew all too well. It was welcome in the darkness of the night, a comfort, though a surprise he'd come to seek me out. Checking on Carrie had been my tacit permission for him to do what he wanted without the weight of my presence around.

"It depends," I said, glancing up at him, grinning. "Given your feelings for me, can you control yourself in our tent tonight?"

With a chuckle, Axel dropped into the seat beside me.

"Well, I'm not gonna jump you, if that's what you're asking." He raised an eyebrow, the smile on his face widening. "Unless you want me to."

"I don't," I said. I took a breath. "And I probably never will."

"Ah." He cleared his throat, a sudden stiffness in his posture. "So, that's your answer, is it?"

"It's *an* answer," I replied, not meeting his gaze.

"Lee, I told you I was prepared to be rejected. I kne—know you. But you can't say vague shit like that." He huffed from his nose. "It makes me think we might have a chance, and that's worse."

I thought about the conversations, the barbecue, about what I'd seen. It had been on my mind all night. So much so that in the silence after Carrie had left, I hadn't been able to paw through anything else from the system. I'd sat there thinking about it.

Staring up at the stars, I said, "I can't… give you what Killian can."

"What are you talking about?" Axel frowned.

This wasn't the discussion I wanted to have tonight. Or ever, actually. But it was something we had to talk about. The whole thing made me feel a little nauseous. I'd had similar conversations on dating apps, and they never went well. People never read profiles.

"Look, as much as you know me, I know you, man. I know what sex means to you. You're a whore"—I held up a hand to stop his objections—"and I mean that in a caring non-slut-shaming way. You like to have sex. And I…" I tried to find the words. "I don't think I really want to, ever."

Axel folded his arms across his chest, unimpressed.

"Yeah, well, I'm 100 percent certain I've accidentally walked in on you jerking off before, dude."

I rolled my eyes, irritated that he was hitting below the belt, literally. "First of all, that's because you never knock. Secondly, are you really trying to invalidate my asexuality?" I'd gotten enough of that, even in queer spaces. His words had triggered an anger that had long been dormant. "And three, sex and masturbation are two completely different things. I can get off physically doing things like that, but I'll never get hard thinking about fucking you."

Axel's cheeks flashed crimson.

"Don't say that with such a straight face!"

I sighed. Frankly, figuring out how to deal with horniness when there wasn't ever any reason or mental outlet for it had been the bane of puberty. Getting off was the same thing as a massage or a chocolate. It just felt good. There was nothing underlying the activity other than the physical aspect of it. And doing that with another person wasn't appealing enough for what it gave.

Truth be told, I'd actively sought it out a few times during university, out of curiosity, and hadn't really gotten much out of it. My partners, Tinder matches, seemed to enjoy themselves after a bit of a delayed start. They'd thought my lack of immediate arousal due to nervousness and inexperience. I hadn't corrected them.

The act itself felt systematic. It was easy to judge how to make someone else feel good; touch them there, kiss here, linger a moment longer, compliment them, match their murmurs, let them reciprocate, find completion together. I'd leave in the early mornings after and often receive a text later asking if we could hook up again some time. The few times I'd done it, I'd left them on read.

Because for me… I hadn't hated it and could see why others participated in it, but those people had helped me finally understand, truly and fully, that sex wasn't something I actually wanted. Given my usual inability to know what I wanted, the clarity this had brought me had stayed with me.

Sure, ultimately, it'd been enjoyable, something of contentment to be had out of a job well done, but it felt like an unnecessary difficulty and complexity I was adding to my life for no reason, especially as I wasn't physically drawn to others to do it in the first place. Since then, I'd basically put the whole activity on lock and hadn't really looked back, except when another stranger stepped out of Axel's room in the morning.

Still, based on said blond's reaction, he definitely didn't know any of that. We'd become flatmates after university, so he'd not been privy to my handful of experiments. What kind of image did Axel have of me in his head then that my words had shocked him so? Did he really think me the cliché, virginal, fumbling innocent that media often portrayed asexuals as when we were lucky enough to get representation?

Rubbing at my face, I stretched my cheeks taut before releasing them. "I doubt I'll ever want to have sex, Axel. And I know you like it. It's part of you and important to you in a relationship." Tongue-tied, he sat there silently as I continued, "Look, I feel bad enough that you've liked me for so long, and you thinking I was aromantic is what kept you from saying anything." My stomach churned. "That you'd have to sacrifice something like this is too much."

There was no pause before he replied, and he took my hand in his.

"I'd have you any way I could, Lee."

What now?

In thought, Axel scratched at his cheek, which was still pink. He looked prettier blushing like that as it brought out the blue in his eyes. He really did piss me off in so many different ways. This fucking guy.

Axel continued, "Okay, that line sounded a little desperate, but it's true. Sex or no." His thumb ran softly over the skin of my hand. "It's you I want."

I'd hit my limit. I'd tried to play the considerate card, expressing legitimate concerns, but the tenderness in Axel's voice and touch had pushed me too far.

I tore my hand out of his, throwing mine up in the air. "Why?!"

"'Why?'" he echoed in confusion.

Furious, I stood up, staring down at him. "I'm a terrible friend and have been for over a decade now, I'll never be sexually attracted to you even if I think you're so beautiful it should be illegal, I can't help you with your problems because I'm useless to you, I'm constantly putting you in danger and just magically trust that you'll know what to do somehow, you always mock me at my lowest, and, hell, I'm not even good looking enough to make Jye think twice! You shouldn't even like me, let alone 'love' me! So, why do you?!"

Axel's lips parted in shock.

My face felt hot, and my heart was racing with what had to be rage, and I refused to think about everything I'd just spewed out. Wait. Had I called him beautiful? I'd said that out loud?

"You're asking why I love you?" he said in disbelief, thankfully ignoring the rest.

Phrasing it like that made me sound insane and demanding. But, in for a penny…

"Give me one good reason. Because I just don't understand, Axel. You've never…" I paused to take a breath. "I can't believe you actually like me like that. You say you do. I know you've said it. But it doesn't make sense, it just doesn't…" I let the words trail away, not even sure what I was trying to say.

Axel made a face. "I like you just because."

I waited for him to elaborate.

He scoffed before saying, "Okay then, Mr. Everything Needs A Reason. Tell me. Why does anyone like anything?"

It was my turn to frown. I thought about the question and its answer, perplexed. Why *did* someone like something? It was a surprisingly complex question. But eager to show that there had to be some justifiable explanation, that "because" wasn't a reason, and therefore he didn't actually like me at all, I continued plucking away.

Speaking as I thought, I replied, "People like things because they make them happy or they enjoy them or because the thing makes them feel good."

Axel stared at me, wordlessly. He let my words sink in as he crossed his hands in his lap, looking a little too smug, and the expression wasn't bad on him which was worse.

He waited.

Ah, fuck.

I guess I'd answered my own question.

Mouth going dry, I said, "You're saying I make you happy?"

He nodded.

"You... enjoy being around me?"

Another nod.

"And that it feels good to be with me?"

He smiled sweetly and stood as well, closing the distance between us. I stepped back, suddenly afraid. Of what, I didn't know. I was just scared. No, I knew what it was. But I didn't want to admit it. Because if I said it out loud, I'd have to tell him everything. And we'd never spoken about that.

Axel's gaze was soft as he stared at me.

"You make me a better person, Lee. You always have. Without you..." There was that faraway look in his eyes, the one that sometimes stole him, and for a second, I was afraid he'd break down. But he shook his head, and it was gone. "I like who I am when I'm with you."

"Ah-hah!" I exclaimed, poking a finger into his chest to push him away from me. "Maybe that's all you actually like. Maybe you don't like me at all." I wanted to gain some distance from him. Emotionally. Physically. He was getting too close. And he couldn't.

Axel let out an exasperated sigh. "Of all the— For you not to believe I like you is in-fucking-sane." Yeah, insulting me was definitely the right way to go about this. It actually helped my mind calm a bit.

A moment of silence fell between us, and I thought it was the sweet, sweet end of our conversation. He ran a frantic hand through his hair, his eyes widening manically. "Wait a tick. You said you wanted to see my player stats once, right?"

I nodded slowly, not sure where he was going with this.

"I can't… I can't show you everything." He growled in anger. "But, fuck, you agree that the windows don't lie, right? That what's written is fact, immutable."

I reflected on the system and then agreed. It had never once included nonfactual content. It hid stuff and only revealed it slowly, but I didn't think it was even capable of telling a lie.

"Yeah?"

"Here."

Party member Axel wants to share player data. Accept | Reject

I'd known Axel had been hiding something about his stats since the beginning. That he'd chosen now to share it was baffling. Taking my time, I mentally confirmed acceptance, and the data transferred over onto a new purple-blue window. I started reading.

Traits:

[Swift Footed] Move faster on foot.

"I knew about this," I said, confused.

"Keep reading," he instructed, as though it physically caused him pain, his cheeks impossibly reddening further. It was the most flustered and perturbed I'd ever seen him. Part of me was secretly enjoying it, but as soon as I realised that I killed the thought in its place.

[Devoted] The player you love will receive system warnings as long as they stay within eyesight.

I reread it three more times, not believing the words before my eyes.

"It's been… it's been you, the whole time?"

It was true. The notifications, the warnings, they all stopped when Axel wasn't near. That had been the common denominator. It wasn't that they were unreliable or that they were glitching, or that my own system was broken like Jye's. It was Axel's presence. I hadn't put them together because it simply didn't occur to me; Axel being near me was normal, even when he wasn't close, I knew he was there.

Suddenly my brain was sent flying back to his confession.

He'd meant it.

Every single word.

Axel loved me.

Like the bottom Jenga block pulled, pieces started tumbling, crashing around me. Axel during our childhood, and how he was my best friend until he wasn't, Axel during our teenage years and how he hated me but defended me from bullies, Axel during university and how he remained so aloof but I still saw him every other day, Axel during full-time work and how he asked if I wanted to be his flatmate.

All those small acts.

I had never understood him.

I'd always thought it was his parents, Uncle Seb and Auntie Li, asking him to watch out for me, for their godson. But the entire time it was Axel. Again and again, it was Axel.

Even since the Gates had activated… From him having the Warheads on him to him carrying me away from the Minotaur, from him wanting to call me by my name to what he had implied he wished for. All along… all along, it'd been me, for me?

I just hadn't… I hadn't accepted it was real. I'd thought he was deluded. Or confused. Or broken.

Because it couldn't be real.

Because that would mean confronting something far worse.

Testing the words, I said, "You like me."

"I like you."

"You love me?"

"I love you."

"Huh."

"What?" he asked, head tilted.

I blinked. "I didn't mean to say that out loud."

"You still haven't given me an answer."

It would mean…

Frowning, I said, "I'm not gonna have sex with you."

Laughter exploded from him. "Not that. I don't care about that. Well, I do, it's a bit of an ego death I'll have to go through, but that's neither here nor there."

I swallowed. "I don't not like you."

"Not an answer," he admonished.

It meant that…

"I'm still thinking!"

"What's there to think about?"

"A lot."

"I'd wait an eternity for you, Lee," he said, and I could tell he meant it. "But, come on, that's a little mean, don't you think? Cut a dude some slack." He was pleading, practically begging.

"I don't have an answer yet."

Frustration coloured his next word. "Why?"

"You're asking why?"

"Yeah, that's why I asked why, dumbass."

Back then it meant…

"You really want to know why?"

"I do."

"I'll tell you."

"Then tell me!"

My jaw clenched.

"Because you tore apart my heart, you fucking asshole. You said you'd loved me since we were kids, yeah? But after Chrissie, when I needed support—no, when I needed *you*, you abandoned me. If that's all your love amounts to, then I don't want it!"

The shock that overcame Axel was almost comical. He wobbled where he stood, like a stack of body parts connected loosely with a thread. I hadn't anticipated my words to have had such a large impact on him.

Trying to remain unfazed but failing, I said, "I adored you, Axel. Full on heart eyes, woke up and fell asleep thinking about you type of crush. You were every part of my stupid, little trusting heart. And you shattered it. I never recovered. I still haven't."

I felt like an idiot confessing all this after it had been so long. But it had soured and festered and never healed. I'd never told any living person. We'd never spoken about our fallout, what had caused the monumental shift in our friendship.

"You liked me?" he asked in a voice so quiet it was barely audible.

Steeling myself, I continued, "You think normal kids beg their parents to spend time with a friend 24/7? Newsflash, they don't! That's abnormal! It was almost an obsession."

"*You* liked *me*?" he asked again, even more unsure.

I sighed, the relief I wanted to feel from saying all this not nearly as gratifying as I'd thought it would be. "It doesn't matter now. And you're taking that to your grave, by the way. Our parents can't ever know. They'll never let me live it down."

"Why didn't you say anything?" Axel demanded.

I gave him a pointed look. "We were kids. It was, what, 2005? Boys didn't like boys, or if they did, it wasn't supposed to be said out loud. And guess what? You never said anything either. But whatever. That moment's passed."

"Lee, I never knew. Not once did I… You never told me."

"And I'd planned to die never sharing it. Well, I almost did," I said with a dry laugh.

"I'm sorry."

It was too little too late.

Far too late.

I breathed in to calm myself. "I care about you. I always will, and I always have. Your feelings for me don't change that. But I still can't give you an answer right now unless you want it to be no."

"I'm sorry," he said again, his voice hoarse.

It was like I'd flipped his entire world on its head somehow. My confession of old feelings wasn't such a monumental thing. I'd only kept it secret because it wasn't something that had ever needed to be said. Well… That wasn't true. It was something I'd never shared because I hadn't thought Axel would ever care. Apparently, he did. He cared enough that he looked like a ghost.

Immediately guilt curled my stomach, the desire to comfort him overcoming me. "Hey. We were kids. Kids are unquestionably stupid. We did dumb things."

The man before me looked broken, as if something in him had snapped. I groaned, feeling bad. I hated seeing him like this. It squeezed at my chest. And it wasn't even that unknown thing that had hurt him this time. It was me. I couldn't let this go on.

I gritted my teeth, steeling my resolve, knowing what I was about to say would and could change us. More than his confession had. I shouldn't. I knew I shouldn't. I'd never recover. I was fine being someone to keep him from hurting himself, being someone watching him be happy with another.

To be his friend again, to have that back, would be best.

But those years of automation, those years of "yes, and," those years of choices I'd never made flooded me.

I wanted more than that.

I was just horrified of it.

"Why do you think I keep telling you I can't answer yet?" I asked, my throat closing up as I finished, a nervousness skittering through me.

His eyes met mine, the darkness in them fading, like a drowning man clutching to a life preserver they'd been thrown. He knew exactly what I meant. And I'd known he would.

"You don't want to say no," he said, his voice a whisper.

"Well, I didn't say that, exactly."

He let out an exasperated sigh before shaking his head, a weak smile on his face.

"Jesus Christ, you're the worst. You're lucky I think that's cute."

What now?

My cheeks and the tips of my ears alighted. Oh. No, no, no, no, no. I wasn't blushing because Axel called me cute. That would be fucking embarrassing. That would be humiliating. Not after everything I'd said about me not being able to answer him right now. It would confirm something that wasn't true. He'd get the completely wrong idea.

I prayed it was too dark, that my complexion would hide the pinkness, that—

"Tam was right," Phoenix said from behind us. "This *is* better than *The Bold and the Beautiful*."

DUNGEON
HUNTER

XXX

GOODNIGHT

HE TWO OF US STARTED, my heart in my throat. "Damn it, Phoenix! How long have you been standing there?" I asked, mortified.

"Long enough to hear the juicy bits."

I pinched the bridge of my nose. "Okay. Well. I'm going to bed. I need a break. From all of this."

The teenager nodded, letting us pass. Then she paused before hesitantly asking, "Hey, did you guys run into a girl named Anna in your Dungeon, by the way? She's Carrie's daughter and my... friend. Carrie won't say it, but she's been super worried about her."

I wasn't sure how to reply. The older woman clearly hadn't shared Anna's fate with Phoenix, despite her and Anna's friendship, although her hesitation suggested something else. But it wasn't my business to divulge the news of her passing either. So how did I word this without tangling myself into a different lie completely?

Axel's head tilted. "We did, but we lost her."

Once again, I was left impressed by Axel's ability to manipulate his truth to steer the conversation elsewhere. And with such a fast turnaround. He'd always been a quick thinker.

Phoenix let out a short disappointed huff; the most emotion I'd heard from her all night. "Well, that sucks." Her gaze wandered in the direction of the street of tents the permanent residents stayed in, a glint of concern in her big doe eyes.

"I don't think Carrie's been sleeping. At all."

Axel and I exchanged a look.

I said, "Let's hope she gets some rest tonight, then."

The black-haired teen nodded. "I'll see you all in the morning for breakfast." She leaned forward and whispered, conspiratorially, "Word of warning: Killian always burns the toast. He scrapes the black stuff off, but you can still taste the residue."

After thanking her, and pawning off the whistle, Axel and I returned to the guest tents.

There was an awkward moment as I crawled in and he followed after me while we set up our sleeping situation. For some reason, an air of tension rested between us, something that had never been there before. Was it because everything was out in the open now?

"I can sleep outside the tent, if you want," Axel finally offered, his voice low. The others already seemed to be fully asleep, soft snores and breathing stemming from their respective tents. He continued, "We're all already inside anyway."

Frowning, I replied, "Why would I want you to do that?"

His eyes narrowed. "Look, I know it may come as a surprise to you, but I'm trying to be a gentleman." At my blank expression, the blond elaborated, "I do not control sleeping-Axel. He may spoon you."

"Come on, man, don't be weird about this." I wriggled into my sleeping bag, now overly conscious of the warmth emanating from Axel beside me.

"As the Deities as my witnesses, I've given fair warning. I cannot be tried or blamed for—"

"Just shut up and go to sleep."

With a chortle, he zipped his sleeping bag up around him. Then he lay down, putting our faces only centimetres apart. His breath tickled against my lips, and I could've counted each of his eyelashes. In that single moment, I found my gaze tracing the planes of his face; the highs of his cheeks, the point of his nose, the curve of his jawline, the dip of his cupid's bow. All of it was proportioned to sublime perfection. He really was frustratingly gorgeous.

Axel smiled as I scowled.

"Roll over," I demanded.

"I sleep on my left."

Irritated, I clamped my eyes shut, simmering in the darkness of my clenched eyelids. I could only fall asleep on my right, though I did toss and turn a little in my dreams. With any luck, I'd kick him in the night. It would serve him right, being so obstinate.

Despite how close we were, I was exhausted enough not to mind, my body loosening. As I began to doze off, Axel spoke, his voice a fraction above a whisper.

"Did you really think I'd sleep with Killian tonight?"

My eyes flashed open, meeting Axel's. Yeah. He really did know me too well.

I paused before saying, "It seemed likely."

"Jealous much?" He smirked.

Giving him a death glare, and embarrassingly realising that's exactly how I'd felt and hadn't known it until he'd confronted me with it, I rolled over, not caring that I was unlikely to fall asleep on my left.

Maybe I had been jealous of Killian: at the ease he made friends, at how simple his feelings for others were conveyed, at how much he'd made everyone smile. At the mere fact that he was uncaringly allosexual; a free pass at a normal untroubled life, being able to want and know what it was to be wanted back.

There was silence for a while as I worked my way through these thoughts, stewing in them.

Behind me, his breath hot on my neck, Axel asked, "So, you really don't feel anything from this?"

It was genuine curiosity, I could tell, and it brought me out of my previous downward spiral.

I'd never really discussed what my asexuality meant in terms of physical intimacy, despite Axel's openness regarding sex in general. It wasn't a casual conversation one had with a friend. And, given we weren't even really friends for a long time, it was something I'd never talked to him about.

Not to mention, Axel's breadth of experience shadowed mine, so maybe it was a little bit of an inferiority complex too, which made no sense as I wasn't even particularly interested in the sport. But emotions didn't always make sense.

"Mostly I feel awkward," I answered honestly.

"No desire to like… do anything?"

A spark of annoyance warded off the sleepiness that was beginning to take over, despite how I was lying. "Axel, for the last time, I'm not having—"

"I wasn't asking!" he hissed, and I could imagine his cheeks going pink.

It had amused me and taken me aback earlier how flustered he'd gotten when talking about sex with me. He was usually so cavalier about the topic, especially since he was fairly progressive in that regard. The things I'd heard him talking about with his party friends would've made Dionysus blush.

I felt him shift to his back. He had to be staring up at the tent roof.

When he spoke, his voice faltered. "I just… I don't know. By now you should've given me a straight and unquestionable no, so I'm just trying to understand what I'm supposed to do."

I didn't even try to fight the yawn that hit me. "It's not that deep. Just act normal."

My muscles began to loosen as the world started to fall away. I was so tired that I'd be out like a light in a few more seconds, my sleeping arrangements be damned. I was utterly and completely drained.

"So *you* say. But if you were acting normal, you'd have kicked me out already."

The weight of the day was tugging me into unconsciousness.

"I said mostly awkward."

The fabric of his pillow rustled, and I could tell he had turned his head to face me again. I didn't have to guess what his expression would've been. "And what's the rest then?"

My breathing had slowed, and my senses began to dull. I thought about my response to his question as I fell into nothingness. What else did I feel? That was easy enough to answer. Under everything, it was how I always felt around Axel.

"Safe."

Blackness claimed me. I was sure the muffled crying I heard was from my dreams, and it faded into the kaleidoscope of nonsense that followed.

A SOUND EXPLODED INTO THE QUIET of the night. Both Axel and I bolted up, deer in headlights, panicked, groggy.

During the night, I must've rolled onto my right again, as had Axel, based on the overlapping direction we had sprung awake. The residual warmth lingering around the front of my body began to fade, the numbness of my arms from where they'd found themselves during my sleep tingling to life. Wait. Had I—

"*That* was a gunshot," Axel stated, his eyes red and voice hoarse.

There was the sound of commotion to our far right. As we scrambled to get out of our sleeping bags, and my brain caught up to being conscious, I suddenly and irrevocably knew what had happened.

I fell back to the tent floor, weak limbed and ill, my body losing all control of itself at the realisation.

No.

No, no, no, no, no.

Phoenix's high-pitched scream cut through the open expanse of the warehouse that was Tentworld. Killian's came next, guttural and deep, and pained. He was repeating the same words again and again.

I'd been wrong.

I was always wrong.

⌗

We buried them together at dawn.

⌗

"YOU'RE WELCOME TO JOIN US at another time, but right now…" Killian's words trailed off, his face bleak.

I nodded silently.

We didn't need to say anything else.

In a daze, Just Friends wandered away from Tentworld, leaving Killian to take a seat at the front lookout. One of the expected guests that had the misfortune to arrive during cleanup offered to take over, but the man shook his head. His hands gripped Carrie's shotgun tighter, his fingers whitening.

When Killian had spoken during the funeral, I'd finally understood their relationship. Carrie was… had been a high school teacher. She'd taught him, once. He'd said, fondly, that she was the only teacher he'd ever had that could kick his ass into gear. Phoenix had been too beside herself to speak, but that alone was more than words could ever say. The guests shared their stories too, but their faces and speeches were a blur to me.

Glancing one last time at Killian, the carefree man I'd dined with the night before now completely gone, I believed his words about Carrie setting him right. He looked like he'd aged years in the past few hours. I wasn't sure a smile would find itself home on his face again.

As we walked, my stomach churning, I heard Gigi mutter under xir breath. "I do not understand."

"She was sad," Wren explained, voice as light as air itself.

"Suicide does not change that."

"It stops it."

"Man, I fully get it," Jye said in a way that concerned me.

Gigi shook xir head. "Killing oneself does not stop the sadness. It is simply redistributed to others."

"She made her choice. Not one I agree with, I gotta say, but I ain't her," Tam commented, her eyes betraying only a glimmer of remorse.

I should've told Carrie.

If only I'd told her about the wish.

My feet stopped moving beneath me, too heavy to walk any farther.

"Was I right to lie to her?" I questioned, though it really wasn't what I wanted to ask.

Was it my fault?

Did I kill her?

The others came to a rest next to me.

Axel nodded. "She would've killed someone in our party if you hadn't."

"But she died instead."

"She chose to give up," Tam said.

I shot her a glare. "We killed her daughter."

Gigi's silver eyes blinked slowly, and xir hand reached out to gingerly pat my arm. In xir gaze, I could see a pain I had never noticed before. It was hard when I barely knew Gigi, but it was obvious xe'd have to have gone through something similar if xe'd won xir wish.

The Linnikian shook xir head slowly. "It is the price that must be paid for the prize."

"But we didn't pay it!" Anger fired off easily from me; it had been burning inside my gut for a long time. "Someone else did, and everyone else will have to."

Jye folded their buff arms. "Look at it this way, man. Do you really think other parties are going to use their wish to bring everyone back? I know when Nabu told us, it wasn't my first thought."

Wren spoke up. "I didn't think that first either."

Brow furrowed, I glanced to the rest of the party.

Tam shook her head with a scoff. "Absolutely not."

"It is not how I spent my wish," Gigi said, eyes downcast.

When my gaze fell on Axel, he grinned, and my thoughts were slingshotted back to our conversation about what he wished for. I repressed the memory, squashing any emotional reaction, hoping the flush I felt along my neck wasn't visible.

"So, none of you thought to use it to save humanity?"

The party shrugged.

"I said you were messed up, sunshine," Tam remarked. "Only someone with a complex has that idea come to them at the drop of a hat. You got scars, babes. Ugly, ugly scars."

Ignoring her ability to accurately claw into my psyche, I asked, stunned, "What the hell did you all think first then?"

Jye snorted. "Dude, first of all, to justify this, fuck humanity. We've made a mess of the world. My first thought was like… a reset. Scrub religion and capitalism and everything that puts a divide between us all. Start it all again from the ground up, you know?"

"What about your siblings?" I hissed.

They shrugged, almost apologetically. "I don't know what to tell you, man. I wasn't thinking about anyone else at that moment."

"Tam?" I wasn't sure why I was checking with her. She was the most tight-lipped in our party.

"I'll give this one to you as a freebie, dandelion. I only got a handful of people I care about. That's all that flashed through my mind. Not a lick of a thought was given to those outside that personal circle."

I had no doubt Just Friends was excluded from her tight-knit group.

Sheepishly, Wren said, "I think my first thought was that it would be really cool to live forever and know everything." Her gaze flicked up to meet mine with a smile. "Sorry."

Gigi frowned. "I have not heard tell of any worlds that chose full resurrection. Most parties who win are not so generous." Xir expression told me that xe hadn't been so kind with xir wish either.

I didn't bother to ask Axel, knowing and being mortified by his past words.

So… it had just been me?

"I mean, after you said it, obviously it made sense," Jye said. "It just wasn't at the top of my wants list, you know? Like, people matter. You can't just throw them away." They paused, and I could tell they were thinking of two very specific people. "Well, not all of them, anyway."

The ten-year-old nodded enthusiastically. "Exactly! As soon as you said we'd be able to bring everyone back, I realised that was the right thing to do with the wish."

Tam rolled her eyes. "Bigfoot has a point because I wouldn't bring *everyone* back, but I ain't got much of a say in this. Though I guess I can't have a happy life without a society to operate in."

It was baffling to me how no one else had considered it.

"Why was it *your* first thought?" Axel asked, head tilted in idle curiosity.

"It just seemed like the only thing we should use the wish for," I replied.

"Like the right thing to do?" he offered.

"Yeah, I guess."

Tucking a hand in the bow of my arm, Axel said, "And that's why you didn't tell Carrie what we did, right? Also why you didn't say anything about the wish. You thought it was the right thing to do."

My jaw clenched, thinking about the dark sleeping bags we'd buried hours before. "Yeah."

"There you have it. Your moral compass might be on a high horse, Lee, but out of the six of us, you're the only one whose first thought was to save the entire human race." Axel's smile was surprisingly warm and soft. "You're a better man than you think you are."

"It just feels like Carrie's death could've been avoided," I said, weakly, almost defeated by the tenderness in his gaze.

Tam let out a long sigh. She sounded disappointed. "Babes, if we're really doing this, if your goal is to win this whole thing… No deaths can be avoided. It's all downhill to hell from here."

I shook my head, putting my foot down. "No, we can't think like that."

"I hate to agree with her, but Nine Lives here is not wrong, dude," Jye said. "You're gonna die of guilt if you blame yourself for every death we see."

"We'd be no better than the Deities if we treat every death like a stepping stone."

This sobered the redhead and the cutthroat, and their expressions darkened.

Wren frowned. "So, you're going to keep count of them too, then." She was referring to my previous words about not letting her worry about the lives she saved or didn't, about my tallying them instead. She looked concerned.

And perhaps it was too much to take the weight of every human life on my shoulders.

But someone had to.

Taking a breath, I started walking again, tugging Axel along to his surprise, since his arm had remained entwined with mine. "You're right. All of you. And, on that note, your morality metres are absolutely out of fucking whack. Thankfully I'm here to steer you all in the right direction."

The others jogged to catch up, and I got an earful from Jye, Tam, and Axel, but their exclamations only amused me. Us having this conversation did nothing to quell my guilt about Carrie's suicide, or about Anna and Test Name's deaths, or even the sinking understanding of the many, many, many more deaths to come we'd have a hand in some way or another, but it solidified something of a foundation beneath me.

None of them had questioned our ability to win, to receive the wish.

I don't know why they believed in me or why I believed in us either.

But it felt good knowing that these people were by my side.

It was a thin line we were going to have to walk now, between making sure the Deities didn't get bored and end the tutorial prematurely, and ensuring everyone didn't level up ahead of us. And yet right now it all seemed possible.

We walked along the middle of the road, occasionally stopping to glance into abandoned vehicles, or stepping into the long since looted stores that lined the streets. That wasn't to say there was no activity.

It seemed as though some nature was beginning to return to the city, with kangaroos bounding along sidewalks and birds flocking over the now quiet canopies of trees planted into road verges. We came across several people, but there was something of a sceptical air about most of them, and, with nods, we were simply metaphorical ships passing in the night. Conversation did not appear to be welcome.

I didn't blame them, considering what Carrie had said about the group demanding payment at the CBD Dungeon. In fact, I'd been expecting outright hostility from most.

Despite that, in a park we passed, a family was out having a picnic, and we gave them a wide berth. Who they were, how they'd gotten here, why they'd decided to go for lunch in the park during the death throes of modern life, none of this I knew. But staring at them, and their smiling faces, I made up my mind.

I had two promises to fulfil.

One I'd sworn to Axel when he'd been dying to my hand.

That we'd see the end of this together.

The other, one I'd made to myself, was a little easier, but somehow the idea hurt.

It was time to take Wren home.

DUNGEON HUNTER
ACT II

A nihilistic gym-junkie weeb. A tough-as-nails romantic. A devoted but broken partyer. A mysterious ageless savant. An occasionally sailor-mouthed orphan.

And then there's their party leader, Lee—he forgot how to want. While his team, Just Friends, might be bizarre, it's one he's realised he wants to protect.

In order to stay alive, Just Friends must grind through Dungeons and reach LVL 10 before the Deities orchestrating this system apocalypse grow bored and cull Earth.

As Lee navigates equally challenging problems, from courtship to multiple deaths, one thing has become clear:

Levelling up has never been so important.

Coming soon...

ABOUT THE AUTHOR

Lazarus James is a BIPOC, nonbinary, and ace-spec creative with a love for everything fantasy, most recently manhwa with those blue screens and dungeons. (You might've guessed that based on the book.)

One day, they asked themself, "Why are the main characters always straight men? And why do the two who are obviously in love never end up together?"

The story Laz has written is their own self-indulgent answer to these questions.

They also want you to know that they have two lovely cats affectionately called Lady and Young Man, though their government names are Darjeeling and Earl Grey, respectively.

CONTENT WARNINGS

There are a number of sensitive topics in this story. Below is a detailed list so readers may be informed.

Mentions of abandonment, child abuse, emotional abuse, and racism.

Brief animal cruelty, confinement, LGBTQIA+ discrimination, and suicide.

Graphic cursing, death, grief, emotional trauma, injury, murder, and violence.